THE LONG SHADOW

Liza Marklund

CORGI BOOKS

TRANSWORLD PUBLISHERS
61–63 Uxbridge Road, London W5 5SA
A Random House Group Company
www.transworldbooks.co.uk

THE LONG SHADOW
A CORGI BOOK: 9780552161961 (B format)
9780552169332 (A format)

Originally published by Piratförlarget in Swedish in 2008
as *En plats I solen*
First publication in Great Britain
Corgi edition published 2013

Copyright © Liza Marklund 2008
English translation copyright © Neil Smith 2013

Addresses for Random House Group Ltd companies outside the UK
can be found at: www.randomhouse.co.uk
The Random House Group Ltd Reg. No. 954009

The Random House Group Limited supports the Forest Stewardship
Council® (FSC®), the leading international forest-certification
organisation. Our books carrying the FSC label are printed on
FSC®-certified paper. FSC is the only forest-certification scheme
supported by the leading environmental organisations, including
Greenpeace. Our paper procurement policy can be found at
www.randomhouse.co.uk/environment

Typeset in 11/13pt Sabon by
Kestrel Data, Exeter, Devon.
Printed and bound by
CPI Group (UK) Ltd, Croydon, CR0 4YY.

2 4 6 8 10 9 7 5 3 1

MIX
Paper from
responsible sources
FSC® C016897

THE LONG SHADOW

Part 1
AFTER NEW YEAR

Nueva Andalucía: 03.14

The night was pitch-black. She could just make out the orange trees lining the road as black shadows on the edge of her vision. Three cats' heads stuck up out of a rubbish bin, the headlights catching their eyes.

The rain had stopped but the tarmac was still wet and shiny, reflecting the light from the streetlamps. She had the car window open and was listening to the wet hiss of the tyres on the road, the crickets chirping, the wind rustling the trees. The air was damp and chilly.

It was as peaceful as could be.

She braked and stopped uncertainly at a crossroads. Was this where she was supposed to turn left, or was it the next one? She was clutching the steering-wheel in a cramped ten-to-two grip. All this random building work – no town planning, no regulations and therefore no maps. Not even Google Earth had been able to help with the new districts.

Well, this must be it. She recognized the golden knobs at the top of the gate to her right. Everything looked so different in the dark. She put the indicator on so that the truck behind her could see which way she was heading.

The two vehicles were driving with dipped headlights. Anything else would have been impossible on such terrible roads. And a car with no lights would arouse more suspicion than one with headlights on. She swerved to avoid a large pot-hole in the middle of the road, then checked in the rear-view mirror that the driver following her did the same.

The car's headlights swept across the gateway at the edge of the estate, an overblown affair in black wrought iron with a pair of concrete lions on either side, and her shoulders relaxed. She tapped the code into the pad on the pillar below one of the lions, and the gates slid open. She peered up at the night sky.

The clouds had rolled in from Africa during the afternoon and settled like a thick blanket over the whole coast. Somewhere behind them was a full moon. She noted that the wind was picking up and hoped they'd be finished before the cloud cover started to break.

The roads inside the gates were, in marked contrast to those outside, smooth, with perfectly edged pavements and neatly trimmed hedges. She passed three turnings before she swung to the right and carried on down a slight hill.

The villa was to the left, its terraces and pool facing south.

She drove some ten metres past the house, parked by the pavement in front of a vacant plot and waited patiently as the truck driver pulled up behind her. Then she took her briefcase, locked the car, went to the truck and climbed up into the cab beside the two men.

She pulled on a pair of latex gloves, took out the syringes and attached the first needle. 'Lean forward,' she said to the first man. He groaned quietly and obeyed – there was barely room for his belly under the dashboard. She didn't bother cleaning the area on his buttock, just stabbed the needle into the muscle. 'There you go,' she said. 'Start unloading.'

She moved so that he could get out. Then she sat next to the driver.

'And this is better than gas-masks?' the driver asked, staring in some trepidation at the needle in her hand. He spoke relatively good Spanish but, of course, Romanian was also a Latin language.

'I'll be having one as well,' she said.

He unbuckled his belt, put his hands on the wheel and leaned forward so that she could get at his backside. 'It stings,' he said.

'Don't be such a baby.'

Then she pulled up her skirt and stuck the last syringe into her thigh.

'And you only want the safe?' the man asked, as he opened the door and got out.

She smiled, leaned down over the briefcase and put two litre bottles of San Miguel in the little cubby-hole between the driver's and the passengers' seats.

'Only the safe,' she said. 'The rest is yours. Help yourselves.'

The driver looked at the beer and laughed.

The fat man had got his tools and the tubes out, and had put them beside the gate to the house. 'And you can guarantee that this'll knock them out?' he wondered, regarding the canisters with a degree of suspicion. They didn't look like they usually did. He peered up at the house as the full moon shone from a gap in the clouds. They needed to get going.

She concentrated and tapped in the code to open the gate. The panel on the alarm turned green and the lock clicked. 'Oh, yes,' she said. 'It's guaranteed to knock them out.'

11

URGENT

ATTORNEY GENERAL DEMANDS JUDICIAL REVIEW OF TRIPLE-MURDER CASE

STOCKHOLM (TT) On Monday, Attorney General Lilian Bergqvist will submit a request for the judicial review of the case against the so-called Axe Murderer, financier Filip Andersson, TT has learned.

Filip Andersson was sentenced to life imprisonment for three brutal murders on Södermalm in Stockholm. He has always maintained his innocence.

'In December last year, once the real murderer was killed, Filip Andersson was finally able to tell the truth,' says his lawyer, Sven-Göran Olin. 'Filip's sister, Yvonne Nordin, carried out the murders.'

Almost four years ago Filip Andersson was found guilty in both the City Court and Court of Appeal, and received the maximum sentence available for three counts of murder, blackmail, extortion and desecration of a grave. All three victims, two men and a woman, were mutilated during the attack.

The evidence against Filip Andersson was regarded as weak even during the previous trials. He was convicted on the strength of a DNA trace from one of the victims on his trouser leg, a fingerprint on a door handle and an unpaid debt.

The attorney general's submission to the Court of Appeal will summarize the evidence the prosecutors are planning to present.

(cont.)

The Princess in the Castle
Among the Clouds

The light was utterly white. It drifted through the rooms, like a stream, around chandeliers and curtains and stags' heads. She could hear it whispering and giggling by the beams in the ceiling.

It was so easy to breathe.

In fact the air was so clear and pure that sometimes she became a feather, a silent pale-blue feather that swirled around in the white light on sunbeams and tapestries of hunting scenes.

I said she was silent, didn't I?

Oh, she was silent, so silent, because the Führer mustn't be disturbed.

Everybody spoke quietly and respectfully in the castle among the clouds, and thick rugs on all the floors and stone staircases took away their whispering and hid it in a safe place.

Her favourite place was *die Halle*, the room that was as big as an ocean, with windows looking out onto the clouds and the snow-capped mountain below.

Sometimes she danced in *die Halle*, silently, of course, and lightly on her bare toes, with the sculptures and paintings and the dolls as her appreciative audience. Her dress, all that thin fabric, fluttered around her with a life of its own, and she jumped and twirled until her head was spinning. Yes, she was a princess, the Princess in the castle among the clouds, and she danced for the horses and the dead deer and all the beautiful wooden carvings on the ceiling. Nanna always tried to stop her, of course, but she ignored her. Nanna was just a grubby *Landwirtmädchen* who had no right to tell her what to do, because she was the *Princess in the castle among the clouds*.

13

Once she danced right into the Führer.

Nanna, the stupid woman, had run off crying because she had bitten her arm, and she had been able to dance for ages all on her own in *die Halle*, but the Führer wasn't angry with her, not at all.

He just caught her in his long arms, leaned over and put his hands on her shoulders. He had blue eyes, red-rimmed, but the Princess wasn't looking at his eyes. Instead she was staring in delight at the hairs sticking out of his nose.

She knew she had misbehaved.

Now Mother would be cross!

It was Nanna's fault!

'You're a proper little Aryan, aren't you?' the Führer said, then touched one of her blonde ringlets, and she felt the force flowing out of him, just as Father had explained to Mother.

'Am I blessed now?' she said.

He let go of her and walked away, towards the residential quarters, and Blondi trotted after him, her tail wagging. That was the last time she saw him.

She wasn't always in the castle among the clouds, of course.

When they were in Obersalzburg she, Father and Mother lived in the Hotel Zum Türken with the other officers' families. Mother called it the Turk: 'Why are we stuck in the Turk while the Goebbels family stay up at Berghof?'

Mother often spoke of the apartment, the one on Friedrichstrasse, which had been bombed to ruins by *die verdammten Verbündeten*, the damned Allies. 'It was lucky for us that one of us is still thinking rationally,' she would say, looking sharply at Father, because Father hadn't wanted to evacuate: he had thought it was a betrayal of the Führer, a sign of loss of *faith*, but Mother had insisted. She had emptied the apartment and arranged for all their belongings to be taken by train to the house in Adlerhorst.

14

As the Russians got closer Mother ordered a car from the Party and sent the Princess and Nanna and three trunks with her beautiful dolls and dresses to Harvestehuder Weg.

The Princess didn't wanted to go. She wanted to stay in Adlerhorst; she wanted to go to the castle.

But Mother put a label round her neck and was very abrupt, and her face was red as she gave her an awkward farewell kiss that the Princess wiped away at once. The car door slammed.

They never made it to Harvestehuder Weg.

They were stopped outside a town that she didn't know the name of, and the soldiers took her things and dragged Nanna off with them into the woods, and they shot the chauffeur in the head, getting blood and stuff on the Princess's coat.

All she had left when she got to Gudagården was her coat and dress, and her doll Anna. Onkel Gunnar and Tante Helga's address, *Gudagården in Södermanland, Schweden*, was on the label tied round her neck, and that was where the Princess was sent when there was no one left to look after her.

I don't remember anything myself, but I've been told.

How Onkel Gunnar put the rich kid's clothes and the doll in a pile in the courtyard, poured paraffin over them and lit a fire that would echo through the decades.

'The sinner must burn in Hell,' he was supposed to have said, and that might well be true.

Monday, 3 January

1

Annika Bengtzon poked her head through the editor-
in-chief's half-open door and knocked on the wooden
frame. Anders Schyman was standing with his back
to her, sorting through piles of paper spread across
his desk and all over the floor. He turned, saw the expectant look on her face and gestured towards a chair.
'Close the door and sit down,' he said, sinking onto his
own chair. It creaked ominously.

She glanced suspiciously at the pile of paper by her
feet, noting what appeared to be a plan of the newsroom. 'Don't say we're going to rearrange everything
again,' she said, as she sat down.

'I've got a question for you,' Schyman said. 'How do
you see your future here on the paper?'

Annika met his gaze. 'How do you mean?'

'I'll get straight to the point. Do you want to be lead
editor?'

Her throat tightened. She opened her mouth, closed it
again, then looked down at her hands on her lap.

'You'd be in charge of all news coverage throughout
the day. Five days on, five days off. Co-ordinate sport
and entertainment with the editorials, opinion pieces
and news. Make the final decision about what to put
on the front page. You'd have to sort out the set-up of

19

the various departments with their respective bosses. No web stuff or any of that crap. You'd sit in on management meetings and would be able to influence budgetary decisions and marketing strategies. I'd want you to start as soon as possible.'

Lead editor was a huge deal: she'd be the second most powerful person on the paper, just below the editor-in-chief, and head of all the subsidiary departments. She'd be in charge of the news editors, entertainment editors, the head of sport and all the other little potentates who considered themselves important.

'I have to restructure,' Schyman said, when she didn't respond. 'I need to be able to rely on the people who are directly answerable to me.'

She was still looking down at her hands. His voice was going over her head, bouncing off the wall and hitting the back of her neck.

'Are you interested?'

'No,' Annika said.

'I'll double your salary.'

'I've tried having money,' she said. 'It's nowhere near as much fun as people say.'

The editor-in-chief got up and went over to the window. 'This time last year we were under threat of closure,' he said. 'Did you know that?' He glanced over his shoulder to see her reaction. She continued to play with her grandmother's emerald ring on the forefinger of her left hand.

'We managed to turn the ship round,' Schyman said, facing the newsroom that stretched out in front of him on the other side of the glass. 'I think it's going to work, but I don't know how long I'll be staying.'

He looked at her. She moved her head and let her gaze slip past him, out towards the newsroom. 'I don't want your job,' she said.

'I'm not offering you my job. I'm offering you the position of lead editor.'

'What about Berit? She could do it.'

'What makes you think she'd want it?'

'Jansson, then. Or Spike.'

He sat down on the desk with a sigh. 'There's no shortage of volunteers. But I need someone with decent judgement.'

She laughed in spite of herself. 'And you're asking me? That says a lot about the level of competence in this newsroom.'

'The alternative is for you to be on a rota. You'd sit at a desk, make calls and do whatever the news editor tells you.'

She suddenly realized how uncomfortable the chair was and shifted to ease the strain on her back. 'Doesn't this need union approval?' she asked.

'The union's no problem, believe me,' he said.

'Putting me on a rota would be crazy,' she said. 'You know I get far better stories if I look after myself.'

He leaned towards her and she stared at his knees. 'Annika,' he said, 'the cutbacks we negotiated last autumn have all gone through. We no longer have the resources to support any reporters on special conditions. You'll report to Patrik as your immediate superior.'

She looked up at him. 'You're joking.'

He folded his arms. 'We arranged it between Christmas and New Year. As lead editor you'd be his boss. You could steer him, make sure he stays on the right track. If you start working as a reporter on a rota, you'll have to do whatever he tells you.'

'But I gave him a job,' Annika said. 'I can't have him as my boss. And if you're after someone with judgement, then Patrik's pretty much the last person—'

'We need good judgement further up the organization.

21

At head of news level, I need someone with Patrik's enthusiasm, someone who finds everything interesting.'

Annika stretched her neck and looked towards the decimated crime desk, where Patrik was sitting with his nose pressed against his screen, typing with his elbows in the air. He had managed to get the only comment from the prime minister the day the minister for business had resigned: he'd run after his cavalcade all through central Stockholm and had finally been rewarded with 'Are you crazy, you stupid bastard?' When he'd got back to the newsroom he had described the whole event as a triumph.

'Well,' she said, 'if you're after passion, you should certainly promote Patrik.'

'You'll be on the day shift, Monday to Friday,' Schyman said, standing up. 'No overtime and no antisocial-hours payments. We've been shutting down our local news teams around the country so you could be sent anywhere at a moment's notice, even abroad. You'll have to take over the series of articles about the Costa Cocaine that Patrik was planning, for instance. You can go and sit at the news desk and Patrik will be over to give you the papers.'

'Wasn't that just an excuse for Patrik to fly down, top up his tan and go swimming?'

'You're wrong. The Costa Cocaine is an exclusive series of articles. The initiative came from the paper's editorial management. We've set up a collaboration with the Police Authority and the Justice Department to have access to privileged information. So we're going through with it.'

'What'll happen to the day-shift desk?' she asked, glancing at her workstation, with her computer, jacket, bag and an array of notes.

'That's going to be the features department,' Schyman said, gesturing towards the plan on the floor. 'The crime desk is turning into the discussion and opinion section.'

She got up and left the editor-in-chief's glass box.

She really couldn't care less which chair she sat in or which articles she had to write. Her husband had left her, taking with him half of her time with the children, her house had burned down and the insurance money couldn't be released. She was living in a three-room flat in a building owned by the police association, arranged by her contact in the forces, Detective Inspector Q, under highly dubious circumstances: someone could appear at any moment and turf her out.

She gathered together her things and made her way to one of the cramped spaces around the main news desk. She hardly had space for the computer on the desk in front of her, so she dropped her jacket, bag and notes on the floor beside her chair. She sat down, raised the seat, checked that the computer was connected, and sent an email to Inspector Q: 'I've moved into the flat, but I still haven't seen anything that looks like a contract. And FYI I'm thinking about digging into the extradition of the kitty-cat. A.'

That would give him something to think about.

Then she reached for a telephone and called the Justice Department. She asked to be put through to the minister's press secretary, who sounded very stressed when she answered.

Annika introduced herself and said where she worked. 'I'd like a comment from the minister about the extradition of an American contract-killer who goes by the name of the Kitten,' she said.

'A what?' the press secretary said.

'I know she was handed back to the US in exchange for us getting the cop-killer, Victor Gabrielsson, home from prison in New Jersey. I want to know why, and how it came about.'

'The minister never makes statements on matters concerning national security,' the press secretary said, trying to sound robotic and uninterested.

'Who said anything about national security?' Annika said. 'I just want to know what you did with the Kitten.'

'Can I get back to you?'

Annika gave the woman her mobile and direct line numbers, as if there was any chance of her calling back. Yeah, right! She hung up, then dialled Berit Hamrin's mobile. Her colleague answered at once.

'Have you been demoted as well?' Annika asked.

'With Patrik as boss,' Berit confirmed.

There was the sound of traffic in the background.

'Where are you now?'

'I've just pulled out onto the E18.'

Annika could see Patrik sweeping towards her with a bundle of notes in his right hand, and moved the receiver closer to her lips. 'Here comes the boss,' she said quietly. 'This is going to be interesting.'

As he sat down on her desk, she hung up and moved the computer aside.

'Okay. Things are really going to start moving now,' the newly appointed head of news said, leafing through his notes. 'We've got a fire in a flat out in Hallunda, people gassed to death on the Spanish coast and a bus crash in Denmark. Start with the bus and check if there were any Swedes on board.'

'Lilian Bergqvist is asking for a review of Filip Andersson's case,' she said, switching the computer on next to Patrik's thigh.

'Old news,' Patrik said. 'We all knew she was going to do that as soon as we revealed that his sister was the real killer. Berit can write a note about it.'

24

When *I* revealed who the real killer was, she thought, but said nothing.

'The gassing in Spain sounds pretty grim,' he went on, handing over the notes. 'Looks like an entire family is dead, including the dog. See if you can make anything out of it, ideally a picture of them all, with the name and age of the dog. People are always interested in Spain – it must still be the biggest tourist destination for Swedes.'

'Haven't we got a stringer down there?' Annika asked, remembering a picture byline of a suntanned man with a clenched smile.

'He's back home in Tärnaby for Christmas. The fire in Hallunda feels a bit thin, but maybe they had to evacuate and poor old Hedvig couldn't get down in her wheelchair, or something else that would be good in the mix.'

'Okay,' Annika said. He'd already learned the vocabulary. *Good in the mix.* Bloody hell. 'There's a couple of other things I was going to check out,' she said, making an effort to sound calm and composed. 'I got a tip-off that the government was involved in a peculiar extradition case, and I've got a meeting at two o'clock that might lead to an interview about . . .'

But Patrik had already got up and was on his way over to Features.

Annika stared at him. She decided not to get upset. If he chose not to listen to his . . . subordinates, then that was his problem. She leaned back in the chair. She was pretty much the only person in the newsroom.

She'd been called in by Schyman at eight o'clock that morning, and had assumed he would make another attempt to persuade her to accept one of the senior editorial positions. There were usually a few years between offers, but this time it was different. He'd tried before to push her into accepting head of news and head of supplements, and she had even accepted and become head of crime for a short time, but never before had he offered her lead editor.

She let out a sigh. The way he had described it, five days on, five days off, she would still have been sharing the job with someone, probably Sjölander. She wouldn't just have been held responsible for all the idiotic things that would inevitably have arisen while putting together the news section, but would also have had to sit through interminable meetings about budgets, marketing plans and staffing issues. I'd rather cover fires in blocks of flats in Hallunda, she thought, as she rang the section head of the emergency services control room.

Smoking in bed, the section head told her, one dead, someone who'd taken early retirement. Fire extinguished. Limited smoke damage. No evacuation.

'And who was the person who died?' Annika asked.

He leafed through his papers.

'The flat belonged to a . . . I've got it here somewhere . . . Jonsson . . . Well, no one famous, anyway.'

No one famous = no story.

They hung up.

The bus crash had involved a group of kids, a hockey team on their way to a tournament in Aalborg. The accident had occurred when the bus slid slowly off an icy country road in Jutland, and ended up on its side in a ditch. The children had had to scramble out through the driver's window.

Annika emailed the details to the picture desk and asked them to keep an eye open in case any pictures of terrified children appeared. The story wasn't worth anything except as a caption to a photograph.

The gassings in Spain was trickier to get to grips with. Patrik's note had been a printout of a telegram from the main news agency, consisting of three lines stating that a family with two children and a dog had been found dead after they'd been gassed in connection with a break-in.

She started by going to the website of the only Spanish newspaper whose name she knew, *El País*, and was caught by the main headline: *España es el país europeo con más atropellos mortales de peatones.*

She squinted at the screen. She really should be able to understand it. Two years of Spanish at school wasn't much, but online newspaper language wasn't very demanding. She thought it meant that Spain was the European country with the highest mortality rate for pedestrians – 680 last year.

She closed the article and went on searching for something like *Familia muerto Costa del Sol.*

Nada, niguno, vacío.

But *El País* was a national paper, presumably based in Madrid. Maybe they didn't bother with things that happened down near the edge of Africa. But surely a whole family dying ought to warrant a mention, at least in the online edition.

She stood up and went to fetch a plastic cup of coffee from the machine, returned to her desk, sat down with it and thought. Gassed in connection with a break-in? She'd never heard of that before. She typed the words into Google and got one hit.

Something wrong with the translation?

She blew cautiously on the coffee and took a careful sip. It tasted even worse than yesterday's.

She went back to Google, tried 'gas' and 'break-in', and this time the results were better.

'Driver knocked out with gas during break-in,' was fourth on the list. The article was from Radio Sweden and had been published on 14 December 2004. Several pallets of flat computer screens had been stolen from a lorry at the Shell garage at Västra Jära on highway 40, just west of Jönköping. Neither the driver nor his dog, who had both been asleep in the cab, had noticed the robbery. When he had woken up the driver had had a headache and felt sick. The police suspected he had been knocked out with some sort of gas. They had taken blood samples to see if they could find any trace of it.

Here we go, she thought, and scrolled down the screen.

'Thieves drugged dog with gas – rapid rise in burglaries in Stockholm,' she read. The article was from *Metro*, and was only a week or so old.

She went into the paper's archive and carried on looking.

'Thieves used gas on tourists – Four people knocked out in campervan – Heavy doses of hexane gas can cause serious injury,' and 'Action-film director robbed with gas – *The whole thing was terrible*'.

The article was about a Swedish director whose home on the Spanish coast had been broken into. He and his girlfriend had woken up the next morning to find all the doors wide open and the flat empty.

'So, we're back to being foot-soldiers again,' Berit said, putting her handbag down on the other side of the news desk.

'Happy New Everything,' Annika said.

'How are you?' Berit asked, hanging her coat on the back of her chair.

Annika's hands hovered above the keyboard. 'Pretty good, thanks. This year has to be better than last because anything else just isn't possible.'

Berit put her laptop on the desk. 'Is it just you and me left?' she asked.

Annika looked round.

Patrik was talking animatedly into his mobile over

by the sports desk, there were a few people from the online edition in what had once been Entertainment but which now produced copy for cyberspace, and one of the Sunday-supplement editors was hanging around the picture desk. Tore, the caretaker, was laboriously fixing that day's flysheets – the newspaper's yellow posters – to the notice-board.

'Newspaper wars are just like any other,' Annika said. 'The ground troops are cut and everything gets spent on technology and smart bombs. When did Schyman talk to you?'

Berit Hamrin pointed at Annika's coffee. 'On Friday. Is that drinkable?'

'Negative. He called me this morning. Did he want you to join the management team?'

'Head of news,' Berit replied. 'I said thanks but no thanks.'

Annika glanced at her computer screen. Schyman had offered her the more senior position. 'I'm looking into a fatal gassing in Spain,' she said. 'A whole family was killed in a break-in on the Costa del Sol.'

Berit switched on her computer and went to the coffee machine. 'Give Rickard Marmén a call,' she said, over her shoulder. 'I don't know his number, but if there's anything going on in Spain that's worth knowing, he'll know about it.'

Annika picked up the phone and dialled Directory Enquiries.

Engaged.

She went back into Google, thought for a moment, then typed *buscar numero telefono españa*. Was that the right spelling? Search telephone numbers Spain?

The first result was for something called *Paginas Blancas*.

Bingo!

She narrowed the search to Málaga and typed in 'Rickard Marmén', then pressed *encontrar*.

Who'd have thought it?

He lived on the Avenida Ricardo Soriano in Marbella; his landline and mobile numbers were listed.

Berit sat down with her coffee.

'So who's Rickard, then?' Annika said, with the receiver in her hand.

'An old friend of my brother-in-law. He's lived down there for twenty years now, has tried his hand at pretty much everything you can think of and failed at all of it. He's rented out sunbeds and bred stud horses and run a guesthouse, and once he had a share in a company selling log cabins.'

'On the Costa del Sol?' Annika said dubiously.

'As I said, he always fails.'

'What's the dialling code for Spain?'

'Thirty-four.' Berit pulled a face as she tasted the coffee.

Annika tried the landline first. After five rings an electronic voice said something unintelligible in Spanish and she hung up. She tried the mobile number, and two seconds later a male voice said loudly: '*Sí, dígame!*'

'Rickard Marmén?'

'*Hablando!*'

'Er, my name's Annika Bengtzon, I'm calling from the *Evening Post* in Stockholm. You do speak Swedish, don't you?'

'Course I do. What can I do for you?'

He had a strong Gothenburg accent.

'I'm calling because I've been told you know about everything that happens on the Costa del Sol,' she said, glancing at Berit. 'I was wondering if you knew anything about gas being used in a break-in somewhere down there?'

'Gas? In *a* break-in? Listen, love, we don't have any other sort of break-in here these days. Every break-in uses gas. Gas-detectors are more common than fire-alarms in the villas of Nueva Andalucía. Anything else you want to know?'

There was a lot of noise in the background. It sounded like he was standing beside a motorway.

'Er, okay,' Annika said. 'So, what exactly is a break-in involving gas?'

'The thieves pump some sort of knock-out gas through the windows or air-conditioning. Then, while the occupants are asleep, they can go through the whole house. They usually take their time, have something to eat in the kitchen, open a bottle of wine.'

'And this is the most common type of break-in, you say?' Annika asked.

'It's an epidemic. It started five, six years ago, although gas was sometimes used before that.'

'Why is it so common down there?'

'There's a lot of money here, darling. Thick bundles of cash under mattresses all round Puerto Banús. And there's a significant criminal element, of course, and plenty of poor bastards who'll do anything for a bit of cash. They caught a gang of Romanians last autumn. They'd cleaned out more than a hundred villas right along the coast, from Gibraltar up to Nerja.'

'The news agency's just let us know that a whole family's been killed by gas in a break-in,' Annika said. 'You don't happen to know anything about that?'

'When? Last night? Where?'

'Don't know,' Annika said. 'Just that everyone died, including two kids and a dog.'

Rickard Marmén didn't answer. If it hadn't been for the traffic in the background she would have thought she'd been cut off.

'Does he know anything?' Berit asked.

Annika shook her head.

'Killed by gas in a break-in?' he said, and the traffic noise behind him changed. 'Can I call you back?'

Annika gave him her numbers. 'What do you make of it?' she said, once she'd hung up.

Berit bit into an apple. She seemed to have given up on the coffee. 'Crime on the Costa del Sol or this latest reorganization?'

'The reorganization.'

Berit put on her reading glasses and leaned towards the computer screen. 'You just have to make the best of things,' she said. 'If someone else is responsible for my work, I get more time for the stuff I really want to do.'

'Such as? Your own articles? Gardening? Deep-sea diving?'

'I write songs,' Berit said, and concentrated on the screen.

Annika stared at her. 'What sort of songs? Pop songs?'

'Sometimes. Once we sent in an entry to the Eurovision Song Contest.'

'You're kidding. You made it to the *green room*? What was it like?'

'The song didn't get very far. The last I heard, it had been picked up by a local group in Kramfors who play it at gigs around south-east Ångermanland. Have you read Lilian Bergqvist's report to the Court of Appeal?'

'I haven't had time. What's it called?'

'"Application for Judicial Review in the Case—"'

'The song.'

Berit took off her glasses. '"Absolutely Me",' she said. 'One of the lines is the ground-breakingly innovative "To be or not to be". Now, I've spent thirty-two years working on this paper, and if I'm lucky it'll stay afloat for another ten. By then I'll be sixty-five, and ready to retire. I like finding things out, writing articles, but I don't really care who gives me the jobs or which desk I sit at.' She looked at Annika intently. 'Does that make me sound bitter?'

Annika took a deep breath. 'Not at all,' she said. 'I feel exactly the same. Not that I can retire any time soon, but we've changed direction so many times that I don't even feel travel-sick any more. "To be or not to be". What about the rest?'

'"No more crying, no self-denying",' Berit said, putting her glasses back on and turning to the computer again. 'What do you make of Filip Andersson's chance of a pardon?'

'The fact that it's the attorney general herself requesting the judicial review adds weight to it,' Annika said. She went onto the attorney general's website and clicked through to the request.

'You met him in Kumla Prison a few months ago, didn't you?' Berit said. 'Do you think he's innocent?'

Annika glanced through the report. Reading about these murders always unsettled her. She had been in the patrol car that had been first on the scene that evening, and had wandered blithely among the victims. Then, last autumn she had come across Filip Andersson's name several times when she'd been digging into the case of the murdered celebrity police officer, David Lindholm. Filip Andersson had been a reasonably successful financier, famous for his appearances in gossip magazines until he became known throughout Sweden as 'the Södermalm Axe Murderer'. He had been a close friend of David Lindholm.

'Those people were killed by Filip's lunatic sister,' Annika said. She shut the website. 'How well do you know Rickard Marmén?'

'I wouldn't say I know him well,' Berit said. 'My

brother-in-law, Harald – Thord goes fishing with him sometimes – has had a flat in Fuengirola since the late seventies. When the children were small we used to borrow it for a week every summer. Rickard's the sort of guy you bump into sooner or later if you spend any time down there. I'm not so sure that Filip Andersson *is* innocent.'

'He's a fairly unpleasant character,' Annika said, typing *Swedes Spain Costa del Sol* into Google. She clicked a link and found herself at www.costadelsol. nu. A moment later she read that the Costa del Sol had a Swedish-language commercial radio station, broadcasting twenty-four hours a day. There was a monthly Swedish magazine, a Swedish newspaper, Swedish estate agents, Swedish golf-courses, Swedish restaurants, Swedish food shops, Swedish dentists, vets, banks, construction firms and television engineers. She found a diary that informed her, among other things, that the Swedish Church was planning to celebrate 'cinnamon-bun day'. Even the mayor of Marbella turned out to be a Swede or, at least, was married to one. Her name was Angela Muñoz, but she was evidently known as Titti.

'Bloody hell,' she said. 'Marbella looks as Swedish as a rainy Midsummer Eve.'

'But with a rather better chance of sun,' Berit said.

'How many Swedes live there?'

'About forty thousand,' Berit said.

Annika raised her eyebrows. 'That's more than there are in Katrineholm,' she said.

'And that's just the permanent residents,' Berit said. 'There are plenty more who only live there for part of the year.'

'And a whole family has been murdered,' Annika said, 'in the midst of this Swedish idyll.'

'Good angle,' Berit said, picking up the phone to call the attorney general's office.

Annika clicked and read 'Latest news from Spain'. The Spanish police had seized a large shipment of narcotics in La Campana, 700 kilos of cocaine hidden in a container-load of fruit. Three leaders of the controversial Basque party ANV had been arrested. There were fears of drought again this year; a whale had beached outside San Pedro; and Antonio Banderas's father was going to be buried in Marbella.

She closed Google and went into the paper's own archive. Loads of Swedish celebrities seemed to have houses or apartments down there, actors and artists, sports stars and businessmen.

She picked up the phone and dialled International Directory Enquiries, and had better luck this time. She asked for the numbers of La Garrapata restaurant, the *Swedish Magazine*, the *South Coast* newspaper and the Wasa estate agency, all of them in the district of Málaga.

Then she started ringing round.

None of the Swedes who answered on their crackly Spanish telephones knew anything about anyone being gassed to death in connection with a robbery, but they all had juicy stories about other break-ins, the history and development of the area, the weather, the people and the traffic.

Annika found out that there were more than a million people living in the province, half a million in Málaga and a couple of hundred thousand in Marbella. The average temperature was seventeen degrees in winter and twenty-seven in summer, and there were 320 days of sunshine each year. Marbella had been founded by the Romans in 1600 BCE, when it was known as Salduba. In 711 the city had been conquered by the

35

Arabs, who renamed it Marbi-la. The oldest part was built on Roman remains.

'We were still in animal skins when people down there had running water and air-conditioning,' Annika said, after she'd hung up.

'Do you want to go and get some lunch?' Berit asked.

They logged off their computers so that no one could send fake emails from their accounts. Annika was digging out a lunch coupon from the bottom of her bag when the phone on her desk rang. The number on the little screen was eleven digits long, and started with 34.

'Annika Bengtzon? Rickard Marmén here. Okay, I've looked into that break-in. It seems to be true.'

He must have moved from the motorway because now there was silence in the background.

'I see,' Annika said, losing hope of finding a lunch coupon, then discovered a crumpled one in the side-pocket.

'Did you know it was Sebastian Söderström's family?'

She was about to say, 'Who?' but gasped instead. 'The ice-hockey player?' She let the coupon fall to the desk.

'Well, it must be ten years since he last played in the NHL. He's been living down here for a while, runs a tennis club. As far as I've been able to find out, his whole family was wiped out, including his mother-in-law.'

'Sebastian Söderström is dead?' Annika said, waving at Berit to stop her heading off to the canteen.

'He had a wife and two fairly young kids.'

'What did you say about Sebastian Söderström?' Patrik asked, suddenly materializing beside her.

Annika turned her back on him and stuck a finger in her free ear. 'How reliable is this information?' she asked.

'Hundred per cent.'

'Who can confirm it?'

'No idea, darling. But now you know.' He hung up without waiting for a reply.

'What was all that about?' Patrik asked.

Berit came back to the desk and put her bag down again.

'Check out Sebastian Söderström on paginasblancas. es,' Annika said, and Berit logged back in, typed in the details and read: 'Las Estrellas de Marbella, Nueva Andalucía.' The number had nine digits, and began with 952.

'What's going on?' Patrik asked.

'Just need to check something,' Annika said, dialling the number of the villa in Las Estrellas de Marbella. After five rings an electronic female voice said '*Ha llamado a nuevo cinco dos . . .*' She hung up and dialled the press office at the Foreign Ministry.

'Don't get your hopes up,' Berit said, who could see what number she was dialling. 'They're usually the last to know anything.'

After the Asian tsunami the Foreign Ministry had got its act together and had been almost helpful for a while, but now they were back to normal.

'My name's Annika Bengtzon and I'm calling from the *Evening Post*,' she said, when the call was finally answered. 'I'd like confirmation that the family gassed to death in a break-in at Las Estrellas de Marbella in the south of Spain last night were Swedish citizens.'

'We haven't received any information to that effect,' the woman at the Foreign Ministry said abruptly.

'Perhaps you'd like to check,' Annika said, and hung up.

'My Spanish isn't good enough for the Spanish police,' Berit said.

'Neither's mine,' Annika said.

'Interpol,' Berit said.

37

'Europol,' Annika said. 'They're more active.'

'WHAT?' Patrik shouted.

Annika jumped. 'I have a source who says that the family gassed on the Costa del Sol was Sebastian Söderström's. He was with his wife, children and mother-in-law.'

Patrik turned on his heel and yelled, '*Sport!*'

Annika took three long strides and put her hand on his shoulder. 'Calm down,' she said, as he spun round to her. 'I need to get confirmation. You can't get Sport to start writing his obituary until we know it's true.'

'They need to start making calls,' Patrik said.

'And say what? That we *think* he's dead? And even if it's true, we don't know that his family has been informed.'

'You said they all died.'

Annika groaned. 'Maybe he's got parents, brothers and sisters.' She took another step forward, stopping right in front of him. 'A bit of advice, Head of News. Try to curb your enthusiasm. You'll end up in the ditch if you carry on like this.'

Patrik paled. 'Just because you didn't get promoted,' he said, and stalked off towards the sports desk.

'We'll have to try to get confirmation,' Berit said, picking up the phone.

After several phone calls the Spanish police had confirmed that five people had been killed the previous night just outside Marbella in what looked like a gas attack in connection with a burglary. There would be no comment on the identity and nationality of the victims until tomorrow lunchtime at the earliest.

They took a break and hurried down to the canteen.

'Sport isn't exactly my strong subject,' Berit said, once they were sitting at a window table with plates of beef stew in front of them.

Annika broke off a piece of crispbread and looked out at the greyness beyond the window. 'He played professionally in the NHL for several seasons,' she said, 'first with the Anaheim Ducks, then Colorado Avalanche. He was in defence. In the early nineties he was selected to play for the Three Crowns national team several years running. I think he was in the team that won gold in the World Championships in Finland in 'ninety-one, and Czechoslovakia in 'ninety-two . . .'

Berit put down her fork.

'How do you know all this?'

Annika took a sip of mineral water. 'He was my ex-boyfriend's idol,' she said, and Berit let the matter drop.

'There's something about fading sports stars,' she said. 'They seem to attract misery.'

Large raindrops were striking the window.

'Imagine hitting the top when you're twenty-four,' Annika said. 'You'd spend the rest of your life as a has-been.'

They skipped coffee and went back up to the newsroom.

Patrik was practically jumping up and down beside Annika's chair. 'I've got something for you,' he said. 'As of this afternoon Kicki Pop is going to be presenting the radio programme that goes out before P1's in-depth news programme. I want you to call Erik Ponti at Radio News and find out what he thinks about that.'

Annika stared at the . . . head of news, and waited for the laugh that would tell her it was a joke. It didn't come. 'Are you kidding?' she said. 'I'm busy with the murders in Marbella. That's a huge story. There are loads of Swedes down there who—'

'Berit can deal with that. I want you to do this now.'

She couldn't believe her ears. 'You're telling me to call Erik Ponti and try to get him to bad-mouth a female colleague? One who just happens to be young and blonde?'

'He's famous for saying that bimbos are the lowest of the low.'

Annika sat down, her back ramrod straight. 'Ponti may be pompous and self-important,' she said, 'but he's not stupid. He criticized a blonde female colleague once when he had every reason to do so. But considering the amount of shit he caught, do you really think he'd do it again?'

Patrik leaned over her. 'Make the call,' he said.

Annika picked up the phone and dialled Radio News.

Erik Ponti didn't feel like making any unpleasant comments, not about Kicki Pop personally and not about her programme.

'What a surprise,' Annika said, pulling her jacket on and heading towards the caretaker's desk.

'Where are you going?' Patrik called after her.

'I've got a meeting at two o'clock,' she said, over her shoulder.

'Who with?'

She turned round and looked him in the eye. 'There's such a thing as confidentiality of sources,' she said. 'Ever heard of it?'

'Not where your superiors are concerned,' he said, and his ear-lobes were dark red.

'Not where the legally responsible publisher is concerned,' she corrected.

Then she went to the caretaker's desk and booked out a car from Tore.

2

The rain was heavy now, so she had to keep the windscreen wipers on. It was only half past one but darkness was edging in, creeping up on frozen pedestrians, filthy streetlamps and lorries with flickering headlights.

She was heading west, towards Enköping, past Rissne, Rinkeby and Tensta. She passed blocks of flats, terraced houses, empty schools and an abandoned football pitch. The traffic on the motorway ground to a complete halt outside the railway station in Barkarby and Annika peered through the windscreen of the car in front to see if there had been an accident she could phone in to the paper. It didn't look like it. Maybe a pedestrian had been knocked down. Or someone had jumped in front of a train. That was fairly common.

Soon the traffic was moving again, if slowly. The residential buildings thinned out, pine forest and industrial units taking over. The road surface was terrible, with brownish-grey sludge thrown up at the windscreen. She switched the radio on, but it was in the middle of a segment of adverts so she turned it off again.

The scenery outside became increasingly monotonous. The industrial units vanished, leaving just the pines. Their branches reached out towards the car, the

41

same dirty Volvo she had driven out to Garphyttan on the December day when she had found Alexander.

At Brunna she turned right, towards Roligheten. All of a sudden the rain stopped. Annika had a terrible sense of direction and compensated for it by scrutinizing maps and writing detailed directions for herself. Left at Lerberga, then left again after 800 metres, past Fornsta. Through an army training area, then right.

She was heading for Lejongården, a rehabilitation home for families, situated by the water of Lejondals-sjön, where Julia Lindholm had been staying with her son since he had been found.

Annika had promised to visit them, but had kept putting it off. She didn't know what to expect. She and Julia had met only twice before, both times under difficult circumstances. The first time, they had stumbled upon the gruesome murder scene on Sankt Paulsgatan on Södermalm. Annika had been shadowing Julia and her colleague Nina Hoffman on their shift in patrol car 1617 that evening. The call hadn't sounded terribly serious, a domestic dispute, so Annika had been allowed to go with them as long as she agreed to stay in the background. Nina had ushered her away as soon as they had found the bodies.

The second time they had met, Julia had been under arrest on suspicion of murdering her husband, police officer David Lindholm, and her son Alexander. She had been sentenced to life imprisonment by the City Court. No one seemed to care that she had always maintained her innocence, and claimed that another woman she had never seen before had shot her husband and abducted her son.

Annika had only met Alexander once, on the night she had rescued him from Yvonne Nordin's cottage outside Garphyttan. He had been missing for seven months.

The headlights lit up a rough-hewn red wooden façade, the sort of red that reflected, which meant that it wasn't proper old-fashioned paint but a modern oil-based version. This was the place she was looking for. She pulled up in front of the house, engaged the handbrake, switched off the headlights, but remained seated in the darkness with the engine idling.

Lejongården was a dark, squat, single-storey building located on the shore of Lejondalssjön. It looked like a day-centre, or perhaps an old people's home. A little playground was visible in the light from the porch. The water lay still and grey in the background.

'I really do want to thank you,' Julia had said on the phone.

She adjusted her hair, switched off the engine and stepped out onto the gravel drive. At the porch she stopped to look out across the lake. A few naked birches shivered hesitantly along the shore, their branches as grey as the water. There was a wooded island a hundred metres or so out in the lake. In the distance she could just make out the faint rumble of the motorway.

The door opened and a woman in a Norwegian-patterned cardigan and sheepskin slippers leaned out into the porch. 'Annika Bengtzon? Hello, I'm Henrietta.'

They shook hands. Henrietta? Should she know the woman?

'Julia and Alexander are expecting you.'

She stepped inside. There was a vague smell of damp. Pale linoleum floors, pink fibre-glass wallpaper, plastic skirting-boards. Straight ahead, behind a half-closed door, there was what looked like a meeting room. She could make out some brown plastic chairs around a veneered table, and heard someone laughing.

'I'd like you to behave perfectly normally,' Henrietta said, and Annika instantly felt herself tense. 'This way.'

Henrietta led her down a narrow corridor with a row of doors to the right and windows facing the car park on the left.

'This reminds me of the only time I ever went Inter-Railing,' Annika said, hoping she sounded normal.

Henrietta pretended not to hear her. She stopped at a door halfway along and knocked.

There were no locks or room numbers, Annika noted. She had read on the home's website that they tried to maintain 'a cosy atmosphere to make people feel cared for and safe'.

The door opened. A triangle of yellow light stretched out across the floor of the corridor. Henrietta took a step back. 'Alexander's baked a cake,' she said, ushering Annika in. 'Just let me know if you'd like me to take him out to play for a bit.' She addressed this last remark inside the room.

Annika paused in the doorway. The room was much bigger than she had expected, rectangular, with a large picture window at the far end, and a door leading out to a terrace. A double-bed and a small child's bed stood next to each other just inside the door, and further in there was a sofa, a television and a table with four chairs.

Julia Lindholm was sitting at the table, in a sweater whose sleeves were too long, her hair in a ponytail. Her son had his back to the door, and his arms were moving as though he was drawing frantically.

Julia got up, ran over and hugged her hard. 'I'm so glad you could come,' she said, still holding Annika tightly.

Annika, who had been holding out her hand, hugged her back awkwardly. The door closed behind her. 'I wanted to see you.'

'Not many people have been allowed to visit yet,' Julia said, finally letting go and walking over to the sofa. 'My parents were here for Christmas, and Nina's visited us a few times, but I've said no to David's silly mother. I don't want her here. Have you ever met her?'

'No.' Annika let her bag and padded coat fall to the floor beside the sofa. She looked at the boy, could see his fragile profile behind his hair. He was drawing with thick crayons, firmly and intently. She moved closer, sank down beside him and tried to catch his gaze.

'Hello, Alexander,' she said. 'My name's Annika. What are you drawing?'

The boy clenched his jaw and went on drawing with even greater concentration. The lines were thick and black.

'David's mother's so confused,' Julia said, 'and it would be worse for her if we met at such a strange place as this. We'll wait and see Grandma when we get home, won't we, darling?'

The boy didn't react. The sheet of paper was covered with black stripes. Annika sat down next to Julia.

'He's not talking much yet,' Julia said quietly. 'They say it's not serious, it'll just take time.'

'Does he say anything at all?' Annika asked.

Julia's smile vanished. She shook her head.

He spoke to me, Annika thought. That night. He said several things. *Are there any more sweets? She's horrid. She's really horrid. I like the green ones.*

Julia went over to the window and stopped with her back to the room, Annika could see from her reflection that she was biting a fingernail. Suddenly she rushed to the phone on the wall next to the terrace door.

'Henrietta, can you look after Alexander for a bit? . . . Right away. Thanks so much.'

The silence when she hung up was electric. Annika's mouth felt dry, and her fingers itched. She squeezed her hands in her lap and looked down at her grandmother's emerald ring. A long minute passed before the carer, or whatever she was, came into the room, took Alexander by the hand and said, 'Shall we go and watch a film, you and me? *Finding Nemo*?' She turned to Annika. 'It's about a little-boy fish who gets lost when he's with his dad but then finds his way home.'

'Yes,' Annika said. 'I know.'

The silence lingered once she and Julia were alone.

'Well, as you know, I work for the *Evening Post*,' Annika said, to break the silence. 'Do you want me to write about you in the paper? About you and Alexander? About how things are for you here?'

Julia bit her thumbnail. 'Not yet,' she said. 'Later, maybe. Yes, later. I want to explain, but right now my head's in too much of a mess.'

Annika waited quietly. She hadn't been expecting Julia to want to talk about what had happened since her release, at least not this afternoon, but she had been hoping that she might want to at some point. For the media, crime stories always ended when the case was solved and the perpetrator convicted. Few people wrote about the consequences of crime, the victims' long and difficult path back to a relatively normal life.

'I'm so angry,' Julia said, quietly, almost with surprise. 'I'm absolutely furious with the whole world.' Slowly she walked over to the table and sat down on Alexander's chair. She was so slight that she almost vanished inside the big sweater. 'And they tell me that's normal as well. Everything's so fucking normal!' She threw out her arms in frustration.

'Have you been here since you were released?' Annika asked.

Julia nodded. 'It was the middle of the night. They took me down to the duty court and held the custody hearing at half past one in the morning, then drove me out here. Alexander was waiting for me.' She looked out of the window. It was dark outside now. 'I wasn't well in prison,' she said. 'I wasn't well here either to start with. Alexander wouldn't have anything to do with me. He wanted to be with Henrietta.'

'And that's perfectly normal as well?' Annika said, and Julia actually laughed.

'You've got it,' she said. 'But they're very professional here. Nina says so – she's checked them out. This is the Rolls-Royce of family rehab centres, according to Nina, and it's only reasonable that society should have to compensate us for the injustice we suffered . . .'

Annika could hear Nina Hoffman's voice behind Julia's words. Julia's best friend, the police officer with whom she had shared her training and patrol car, had been one of Annika's sources in her investigation into David Lindholm. Annika could see Nina now, her tight ponytail, firm gaze, determined expression.

Julia stood up again. 'Do you want coffee, by the way? There's some in the flask. And Alexander didn't make the cake, Henrietta did, while Alexander sat beside her scribbling birds' nests.' She picked up the drawing at the top of the pile and held it up to Annika. A chaos of heavy black lines covered almost every millimetre of the large sheet. 'That's normal too,' she said, putting it down again.

'Maybe some coffee,' Annika said. 'The stuff we have in the newsroom is undrinkable. We reckon someone poured cats' pee into the water tank.'

Julia gestured towards the flask but made no effort to stand up. 'We'll be here for at least three months,' she said. 'It's for Alexander's sake, they say. He's the one being taken care of. Right now, we're an emergency case, still under investigation.' Her voice cracked on the last word. 'It takes the doctors eight weeks to evaluate

47

how disturbed we are. Then we get treatment for anything between two and six months. After that we get to live on our own, but fairly close to the home. The emphasis at this place is on relationships between parents and children. I'll be getting support and advice on my parenting. Afterwards I can have follow-up support at home . . .' Her head dropped into her hands and she started to cry.

Annika, who had been pouring a cup of coffee from the flask, screwed the lid on and put it back on the table as quietly as she could. 'It's only natural for you to be angry,' she said. 'Alexander too. I'm not particularly fond of shrinks, but I dare say they're right. It's probably normal for the two of you to be utterly furious.'

Julia took a napkin from the pile beside the cake and blew her nose. 'They say that six months is like a lifetime to a small child. Alex spent seven months up in the woods with that madwoman, so of course he's angry. He probably didn't get any answers to his questions about where David and I were so, as far as he was concerned, we might as well have been dead. And the doctors say that he was aware his life was in danger. He had a lot of bruises and cuts on his body, so she evidently didn't hold back on hitting him.'

'How is he now?'

'He'll come to me, but he doesn't want to look at me. He sleeps badly at night, keeps waking up and crying. We've had to start putting him in nappies overnight again, even though he'd been dry for almost two years.'

'How do you spend your days?' Annika asked, sipping the coffee, which was very good.

'I have individual counselling sessions, and soon I'll be able to join in with group therapy and talk to some other mothers. That's supposed to be very helpful. Alexander messes about in the sandpit, draws and plays with balls. When we're discharged from here, the childhood psychiatry unit will take over his case.' She let out a laugh, suddenly nervous. 'Oh, listen to me, going on,' she said. 'I really just wanted to thank you for everything you've done for us. I mean, you were the one who . . .'

Annika was clutching her cup. 'That's okay,' she said. 'I'm just glad I could be useful.'

Silence descended again.

'So,' Julia said, 'did you have a good Christmas?'

Annika put her cup on the saucer. Should she tell the truth? That she and the children had spent Christmas Eve surrounded by boxes in Gamla stan, eating ready-sliced ham from the Co-op and watching Donald Duck on the laptop? That she had handed her children to their father for New Year and Twelfth Night, and that they were much happier with him?

'Oh, yes,' she said. 'Now I've got a lot on at work. Today I've been researching a really gruesome murder down on the Costa del Sol.'

Julia stood up. 'The Costa del Sol's a terrible place,' she said, 'especially Estepona.'

Annika looked down at her hands. Why had she chosen that subject for small-talk? She knew that Julia had had a terrible time down there with her husband. 'Sorry,' she said. 'I didn't mean to—'

'We spent six months there,' Julia said, 'and David was off travelling almost the whole time. I was pregnant and didn't have a car, and it was several kilometres to the nearest shop. I had to drag those bags of groceries home in thirty-degree heat.'

'It must have been awful,' Annika said.

Julia shrugged. 'He was working deep under cover. Sometimes he'd be gone for weeks at a time without getting in touch. It went on for years, the duration of that bloody operation. Years!' She spun round. 'And I never did find out what it was all about. Drugs or money-laundering or something like that.' She moved towards Annika. 'And do you know what the worst part was? I was so terrified that he was going to get hurt. That something would happen, something dangerous. And what did happen?' She laughed. 'He fucked a crazy bitch once too often so she shot his head and his cock off, and they locked me up, and Alexander . . .' She was close to Annika now, staring into her eyes. 'They say Alexander's going to carry the scars of this for the rest of his life. And no one believed me.' She slammed her hand so hard on the table that the porcelain jumped. '*No one believed me!*'

Suddenly Annika realized that visiting time was over. She pushed the coffee-cup aside and stood up.

Julia slumped into her chair and stared vacantly ahead. 'Who'd have thought it would be Yvonne Nordin, of all people?' she said.

Annika stiffened. 'What? Did you know her?'

Julia shook her head. 'No, I never actually met her, or Filip Andersson.'

Annika went to pick up her coat. 'Speaking of Filip Andersson,' she said, 'the attorney general has applied to have his case reviewed.'

'Nina will be pleased,' Julia said tonelessly.

Annika stopped, coat in hand. 'Nina Hoffman? Why would she be pleased about that?'

Julia scratched the back of her left hand. 'Of course she'll be pleased. Filip's her brother.'

3

Annika tore out her mobile before she had even opened the car door, then sat in the driver's seat and dialled Nina Hoffman's number from memory. Why the hell hadn't she mentioned that she was the sister of Filip Andersson and Yvonne Nordin? It took ages for the call to connect. Annika stared out at the dark windows of the rehabilitation home as the phone rang.

How many times had she and Nina discussed the Södermalm murders, and whether Filip Andersson was innocent or guilty? And Filip's contacts with the underworld, and with David Lindholm? After she had visited Andersson in prison last autumn she had gone to see Nina afterwards to tell her about it . . .

There was now an engaged tone, as if the call had been rejected.

Throughout their conversations Nina had had a hidden agenda. Maybe she had been lying the whole time. Maybe she had talked to Annika only to find out what she knew, and try to direct what she wrote.

Annika dialled the number again, as she watched the lights go on in the corridor inside the building. Henrietta was walking along it with Alexander. He was so small that Annika could see only the curls on the top of his head.

There was a click on the line and the message service clicked in. Annika hurriedly ended the call, as if she'd been caught doing something she shouldn't.

She'd trusted Nina, but Nina hadn't been honest with her. Annika had asked her to dig out Yvonne's passport picture, and Nina hadn't said they were sisters.

Annika dialled the mobile a third time. Voicemail again. She cleared her throat. 'Er, hello, this is Annika Bengtzon,' she said. 'Happy New Year. Listen, can you call me when you get this? Okay? 'Bye for now.'

She called Reception at Police Headquarters and asked to be put through to the duty desk of the station on Torkel Knutssonsgatan. The man who answered gave his name as Sisulu. 'Nina Hoffman's on leave,' he said. 'She'll be back on Sunday.'

Annika thanked him and put the mobile on the passenger seat, started the car and pulled out onto the road, heading back towards the office.

When she reached Kallhäll she remembered she had no reason to hurry anywhere. She didn't want to get back to Patrik and his little notes, and she was in no rush to return to the as yet unfurnished flat on Agnegatan.

When the mobile rang on the seat beside her and she saw her ex-husband's number on the screen, she felt strangely elated.

'Hello, Thomas here.'

She took a deep breath. 'Hi,' she said, rather too brightly.

'What are you doing? Are you driving?'

She laughed, feeling the warmth spread. 'I've just been out on a job and I'm on my way back. No problem.'

'Listen, we're planning Easter, and we were wondering how you're fixed that week?'

The happiness was wrenched from her body with a force that felt quite physical. 'Are you using the royal *we*?' she asked, trying to sound light-hearted. It didn't work.

'Easter's late this year – Maundy Thursday's the twenty-first of April – and it's the following week that's a bit tight. I'm away at a conference, but that's my week for the kids, so I was wondering if we could maybe swap . . .'

'I can't answer that,' Annika said. 'I got a new job at the paper today, and it's going to mean a few changes.'

'Don't you think you should have discussed it with me first?' he said curtly.

Raw anger flared. She clenched her teeth and swallowed. 'It won't affect my weeks with the children, so I couldn't see any reason to mention it to you.'

'Okay,' he said crossly. 'Sophia wants to talk to you.'

He passed the phone to his new partner.

'Hi, Annika.'

'Hello,' Annika said.

'We've been having a discussion, my girlfriends and I, and we've got a little invitation for you.'

Annika took a deep breath and forced herself to stay calm.

'You work with the written word so we wondered if you'd like to join our reading group?'

Reading group? Jesus Christ. 'Erm . . .' Annika braked at the traffic lights at the Rissne junction.

'This week we're reading a wonderful book by Marie Hermanson, *The Mushroom King's Son*. It's about working out what really matters, finding your place in the world. The son grows up in the forest but he really belongs on the coast. Do you like Marie Hermanson?'

Annika had read *Clam Beach*, and had started a book about a man who lived under some stairs, but she hadn't finished that one. 'I don't know,' she said. 'Things are a bit tricky right now, I started a new job at the paper today, so everything will be a bit up in the air for a while.'

'A new job?' Sophia said. 'But how's that going to affect our weeks with the children?'

There, right there, was the limit of how much crap Annika felt she had to put up with.

'Listen,' she said, 'there's a slim chance that I might discuss a serious change in my work with the father of my children, but I will never discuss my career with you. Have I made myself clear enough?'

Sophia Fucking Bitch Grenborg sounded rather put out. 'Why are you so aggressive? I only want what's best for your children.'

Annika let out an evil laugh. 'You're such a fucking hypocrite,' she said, far too loudly. 'If you wanted what's best for my children, you wouldn't have torn our family apart, you fucking . . .' She had been on the point of saying 'bitch on heat' but felt that it wasn't quite adequate. 'I haven't got time for you and your book group,' she said instead. 'There isn't a chance in hell that I will ever be friends with you, so just drop it, okay?'

She clicked to end the call without waiting for an answer.

For the first time she didn't feel remotely ashamed of shredding Sophia's absurdly expensive bra at a petrol station outside Kungsör. And she felt less guilty now for having sent a tip-off to the paper from a fake email address that had made sure Thomas's investigation at the Ministry of Justice was closed down suddenly. He didn't seem to be suffering. He was now organizing new legislation in the area of international financial crime, and he certainly hadn't seen fit to discuss *that* with her.

Considering that it was rush-hour, the traffic was sur-prisingly light, but it was a short week after a public holiday, and a lot of people were still away, like Nina Hoffman.

She got back to the paper in time to pack up her laptop and go home.

'Oy!' Patrik yelled, the moment he caught sight of her. 'You're flying to Málaga first thing tomorrow morning.'

Annika dropped her things back on the desk. 'What are you talking about?' she said.

'You're booked on a flight that leaves at six thirty a.m.,' Patrik said.

'For fuck's sake,' she said. 'I can't go anywhere. I've just moved – I haven't even had time to unpack.'

'You can't have that many things, can you?' Patrik said. 'Your house burned down, didn't it? Clobbe from Sport is on holiday in Marbella. He's not going to win any prizes, but he can do the main piece for tomorrow. You can have a handover meeting with him when you get there. Then you need to concentrate on getting confirmation of the victims' identity, and if it *is* Sebastian Söderström, you'll probably be there the rest of the week.'

Annika stared down into her bag. Erik Ponti's arrogant lies about how much he valued Kicki Pop and had nothing whatsoever against P1 being invaded by noisy talk-shows were still ringing in her ears.

But, of course, she was working to a rota now.

'The tickets, then,' Annika said. 'Where are they? Or have I just got a booking number? Where am I staying? Do you want me to hire a car? Have we got an interpreter? Have we established contact with the local police? And who's going to be taking the pictures?'

Patrik stared at her briefly, then puffed out his chest. 'You can sort all that out once you're there,' he said. 'There must be freelance photographers in Spain. And take the chance to do a bit of research on the Costa

Cocaine as well. You'll be doing a series of articles on drugs and money-laundering, the ones I'd have written if I hadn't been promoted.'

He hurried off to the entertainment desk.

Annika turned to Berit. 'Unbelievable!' she said. 'He thinks being head of news means running around and giving people advice about things that are bloody obvious.'

'The booking number of your flight to Málaga's in your email,' Berit said, without looking up. 'A couple of Scandinavian police officers are stationed in Andalucía. You've got their names and numbers in another email. Start by calling them – they're bound to know a local interpreter. Take your own pictures. I managed to book out a completely automatic camera. You just point and click. Call as soon as you know anything.'

She pointed at a little camera case on the desk beside Annika. 'Fly carefully,' she said, 'and good luck.'

Annika groaned. 'Why didn't you take the job, Berit?'

There was an echo as she closed the door of the flat. She stopped in the hall for a minute or so, as she usually did, listening to the sounds from the street and feeling the draught trying to get into the stairwell.

This flat was much darker than any she had lived in before. It was higher off the ground, on the fourth floor. The trees obscured the light from the streetlamps. Outside her bedroom window she had nothing but a starless sky.

From the hall she looked through the living room into the darkness that would be Ellen's room. The kitchen was immediately to the left, a modern, minimalist affair that she instinctively disliked.

She turned on the lights, took off her padded jacket and let it fall in a heap on the floor. She went quickly past the kitchen and into her room, where she curled up on the bed.

There wasn't much wrong with the flat itself. It was actually quite nice. It had three rooms, apart from the kitchen and the bathroom, and it was fairly spacious, with a large hall that could be used as a living room, which meant that she and the children could each have their own bedroom. The keys had been delivered by courier to her temporary home in Gamla stan the day before New Year's Eve. She had spent New Year's Eve hiring a car and moving the few possessions she had managed to acquire since the fire.

She looked up at the smooth ceiling. There must have been some heavy plaster detail up there at some point, but the building had been renovated at the end of the 1930s and all its ornamentation had been stripped out.

She had found out that the building, known as No. 1 Walnut Block for bureaucratic purposes, was a co-operative apartment block, where each occupant owned a share of the building. This flat was owned by the National Property Board. She had no idea how Q had got hold of it or how long she would be able to live there.

She turned on one of the bedside lamps and plumped up the pillows behind her back, turned her head a little to the right and looked out at the sky. She could see the bedroom in the villa on Vinterviksvägen. She had felt so abandoned and alone there. She closed her eyes and remembered the fire, the smoke, the panic.

Thomas hadn't been at home. That evening he had left his family and gone off to Sophia Grenborg. Annika had had to save herself and the children. She had lowered Kalle and Ellen out of the bedroom window on the first floor using sheets, then jumped out and landed on the terrace table.

She had been suspected of arson.

After several months of forensic investigation, they had found a fingerprint on a Molotov cocktail in the remains of the house that could be linked to the real culprit: an American contract-killer known as the Kitten.

Which made little difference to Annika.

The Kitten would never be held responsible for the fire.

Instead of arresting her, Inspector Q had used her to negotiate a prisoner exchange with the American authorities: the FBI got the Kitten, and the American justice system sent home a Swedish citizen from a prison in New Jersey.

'You sold out my home, *my children's home*, just to get a bit of credit with the CIA and bring home a cop-killer,' she had said to Inspector Q.

That was when he had joked about organizing a new home for her, and now here she was, in number 28 Agnegatan, in the same block as the flat she had lived in when she'd first arrived as a summer temp on the *Evening Post* ten years before. She had no windows facing in that direction, or she could probably have looked into the little house in the courtyard where she had spent that hot summer when everything had begun, before the children, before Thomas, when Sven was still alive . . .

The phone rang somewhere in the flat, the landline. She flew up, unable to remember where she had plugged it in.

After the fourth ring she found it on the floor of Kalle's room.

'Annika Bengtzon? Jimmy Halenius.'

The under-secretary of state at the Ministry of Justice, the minister's right-hand man.

Thomas's boss.

She cleared her throat audibly. 'Thomas has moved

out,' she said. 'I told you.'

'I want to talk to you, not him.'

She moved the receiver to her other ear. 'Oh,' she said. 'Really?'

'I heard from Britta that you wanted a comment about the extradition of an American citizen towards the end of last year. As you know, the minister isn't in a position to comment on individual cases, but I could outline some of the issues involved in a more informal way.'

'Britta?' she said.

'I'll be at Järnet on Österlånggatan from seven p.m. Come if you're interested.'

'On the record?' she asked.

'Absolutely not,' he said. 'But I'll pay for dinner.'

'I don't have dinner with politicians,' she said.

'As you like. Well, thanks, and goodbye,' he said, and hung up.

She replaced the receiver and lowered the phone to the floor. There were no lights in Kalle's room yet, so she was standing in the dark by the window, gazing down on the naked treetops.

Really she ought to unpack.

She looked at the time.

She didn't have to do that this evening. She had never expected to hear back from anyone in the department. Shouldn't she go and listen to what he had to say? Besides, she'd met Halenius before when Thomas had had some colleagues round for dinner.

Her eyes fell on the boxes.

It's a tough decision, she thought. Dinner at a fancy restaurant with a highly placed source or an evening with Kalle's Brio train-set?

Järnet turned out to be one of the restaurants in Gamla stan that Annika had walked past many times and peered into, as if the people inside lived in a different, much more beautiful, world from her own. It always looked so cosy, with candles, gleaming cutlery and glasses filled with wine. Outside in the street there was always a bitterly cold wind blowing.

A simple sign with the name of the restaurant was swinging and creaking above the entrance. She pushed open one of the grey-green double-doors and found herself in a lobby. At once a waiter appeared out of nowhere. He took her padded jacket without giving her a numbered ticket or asking for fifteen kronor as a wardrobe fee.

It was ten past seven. She had chosen the time carefully, didn't want to seem too keen but didn't want to leave him waiting on his own for too long either.

The dining room was small, only ten or so tables. Jimmy Halenius was sitting in a far corner, immersed in one of the evening papers with a glass of beer in front of him. Not the *Evening Post*, she noted, but its main competitor. 'Hello,' she said. 'You're reading the wrong paper.'

His brown hair was sticking up in all directions, as if he'd got into the habit of rubbing it in frustration. He stood up and held out his right hand. 'Hi,' he said. 'Have a seat. I've already read the right paper. Memorized it, in fact. Do you want a drink?'

'Mineral water,' she said, hooking her bag over the back of the chair.

'Throw caution to the winds and have a Coke. My treat.'

She sat down. 'Not the benevolent state's, then?'

He folded his arms and raised his shoulders slightly with a smile. 'Unlike yours, my expenses are in the public domain,' he said. 'I think we'll keep this in the family.'

Annika unfolded her napkin, glancing at him surreptitiously, his demeanour and the way he was dressed. He didn't exactly exude power. He was wearing a blue-striped shirt under a fairly crumpled jacket. No tie. Jeans.

'So, am I to understand that the Kitten's extradition is something else we're going to keep in the family?' she said, looking him in the eye. 'Why are you being so secretive about it?'

Jimmy Halenius folded the paper and put it into a shabby briefcase. 'I need to know that this will stay between the two of us,' he said.

Annika didn't answer.

'I can tell you some of what you want to know,' he went on, 'but you can't publish it.'

'Why should I listen to you if I can't write about it?' she asked.

He smiled and shrugged. 'The food here is good,' he said.

She looked at her watch.

He leaned back in his chair.

'The Kitten was responsible for the murders at the Nobel banquet just over a year ago,' Annika said.

'Correct,' Jimmy Halenius said.

'And she murdered that young scientist out at the Karolinska Institute.'

'In all probability.'

'And she burned down my house by throwing fire-bombs into the children's bedrooms.'

'We're assuming that's what happened.'

Annika rubbed her forehead. 'This is completely incomprehensible to me,' she said. 'How can you refrain from prosecuting one of the most ruthless criminals ever to have been caught by the Swedish police?'

'Obviously this is about what we got in exchange,' the under-secretary of state said.

'And that's what you were thinking of telling me?'

He laughed. 'What would you like to eat?' he said. 'At least the menu's comprehensible, for the most part.'

Annika picked it up. 'This can't just be about some shabby little cop-killer in New Jersey,' she said. She could identify a lot of the dishes on offer, fried herring with dill butter and puréed potatoes, for instance. But things like the 'gremolata emolution with potato confit' were rather more difficult.

Jimmy Halenius chose the carpaccio of venison with black chanterelle mushrooms and Västerbotten cheese as a starter, then grilled steak with shallot purée, roast Hamburg parsley and Västerbotten croquettes.

She ordered vendace caviar and reindeer casserole.

'Looks like you're very fond of Västerbotten cheese,' she commented, as the waiter glided off to fetch their wine, a South African Shiraz.

'Well, you're sticking to Norrbotten,' he said. 'Reindeer and vendace.'

'Even though I'm from Södermanland,' she said, raising her glass of water.

'I know,' he said.

She opened her mouth to ask how he knew, then remembered their last meeting at the villa in Djursholm.

'You used to have an old Volvo, didn't you?' he had asked back then. 'A 144, dark-blue, lots of rust?'

Annika could still feel how the blood had coursed through her body, turning her face dark red. She put down the mineral water. 'How did you know I'd sold Sven's car?' she asked.

'It was my cousin who bought it,' he said, and drank some beer.

She stared at him. 'Roland Larsson?' she said. 'He's your cousin?'

'Of course. We were best friends growing up.'

'He was in my class at the Works School in Hälleforsnäs!' she said.

Jimmy Halenius laughed. 'And he had a huge crush on you.'

Annika started to laugh as well. 'God, he did, didn't he?' she said. 'I almost felt sorry for him.'

'We used to lie in the hayloft at Grandma's on summer evenings, down in Vingåker, and Roland would spend hours talking about you. He had an old photograph he'd cut out of the paper, of you and a few other people, but he'd folded it so only you showed. He kept it in his wallet.'

The waiter came over with their starters and poured their wine. They ate, silent.

Annika pushed her empty plate away and studied the man opposite her. 'How old are you really?' she asked.

'Two years older than Roland,' he said.

'Who was one year older than me, because he had to repeat a year.'

'Education wasn't exactly a priority in the Halenius family. I was the first to make it to university.'

'Are you from Södermanland as well?'

He took a sip of wine and shook his head. 'Östergötland, Norrköping. I grew up on the third floor of a block of flats on Himmelstalundsvägen.'

'So are you Social Democrat royalty, then? You know, Mum a local councillor, Dad a union boss?'

'God, no,' he said. 'Dad was a Communist. I was in the Red Youth to start with, but the Social Democrat youth movement had better parties. And much prettier girls. I got Roland to join as well. He's still on the town council for the Social Democrats down in Flen.'

She visualized Roland Larsson, his rather squat frame and long arms. He and Jimmy Halenius were actually fairly similar. She didn't know he had gone into local politics. 'What else is Roland up to, these days?'

'He usually works in the ice-cream factory each summer, but he's signing on at the moment.'

'Does he still live in Hälleforsnäs?'

'Last autumn he took the leap and went all the way to Mellösa. He moved in with a divorcee with three kids who has a place just behind the local shop, the one on the road out to Harpsund.'

'Not Sylvia Hagtorn?'

'Yes, that's her name! Do you know her?'

'She was in the class above us. Three kids? I wonder who with.'

The waiter removed their plates and brought the main course. He refilled Jimmy Halenius's glass.

'Are you married?' Annika asked, glancing at the ring finger of his left hand.

'Divorced,' he said, as he attacked his steak.

'Children?' she asked, picking at the reindeer stew.

'Two,' he said. 'Twins. One of each. They're six now.'

'And you have them every other week?'

'Since they were eighteen months.'

'How do you think it works?'

He drank some wine. 'Oh, you know,' he said. 'How do you think it works?'

She swirled her wine in the glass. She didn't usually like red wine and this was particularly heavy. 'I hate being divorced,' she said, meeting his gaze. 'I miss my children so much I feel like dying when they're not with me. And I . . . Well, I have a few problems with Thomas's new . . . partner.' She had almost said, 'I hate Thomas's new fuck.'

'Really, why?' He sounded almost amused.

'She's a walking cliché. I don't understand what Thomas sees in her.'

'So you don't think she tore your family apart?'

Annika gripped her cutlery tightly. 'Well, of course she did. If it hadn't been for her, I'd have my children with me all the time.'

Jimmy Halenius scooped some potato on to his fork. 'Do you really believe that?' he said. 'Didn't you and Thomas do a pretty good job of tearing your family apart without anyone else's help?'

She was so taken aback that she dropped her knife. 'What the hell would you know about that?' she said.

He gave a short laugh. 'Oh,' he said, 'I don't know anything about the two of you. I just know what mistakes I made. I was awful to live with. I didn't communicate. I could start a world war about the tiniest things, but when it came to the really big issues I just expected her to know what I wanted. And now I've started four sentences with "I". I'm fairly self-absorbed as well. Did I mention that?'

She burst out laughing. 'That could have been me you were describing,' she said, astonished. 'I was a terrible person to be married to.' And the moment she'd said the words, she knew they were true. 'I never even told him that I knew he'd been unfaithful. I just took my revenge, over several months, without explaining why. He didn't realize a thing, obviously.'

The waiter asked if they'd like anything else, and Jimmy Halenius consulted his watch. 'Shall we move on somewhere else and have a few drinks?' he asked.

Suddenly Annika remembered the flight to Málaga the next morning. 'Shit!' she exclaimed, glancing at her own watch. 'I haven't even packed yet!'

'Are you going somewhere?'

'I have to be at Arlanda at half past four.'

'Then there's no point even thinking about going to bed,' he said cheerily.

'I disagree,' she said, and fumbled for her bag.

Halenius called for the bill and paid in cash. He asked the waiter to summon a taxi, then helped her on with her jacket.

Outside it had started to snow, hard little flakes of ice swirling through the air and hitting her face like needles. The sign over the door creaked in the wind. A group of young men, with slicked-back hair, wearing English oilskin coats were marching down the middle of the street, waving wine bottles and mobile phones.

A taxi glided towards her. Jimmy Halenius stepped out into the road and the restaurant door closed behind him. He wasn't particularly tall, maybe ten centimetres taller than her. 'Where are you flying to?' he asked.

'Málaga,' she said, as the taxi got closer.

'Ah, España,' he said. '*Entonces, vamos a salutar como los españoles!*' He took hold of her shoulders, pulled her towards him, air-kissed her left cheek, then the right. 'The Spaniards kiss twice,' he said, his lips close to her ear. 'It's worth remembering when you're there.' He let go of her and smiled, his eyes narrowed to slits.

A taxi pulled up alongside them and stopped. 'I'll be in touch,' he said, and opened the door for her.

Annika got in without thinking and let him close it behind her. She saw him turn away and walk off towards Järntorget, turn up his collar against the wind and disappear round the corner.

'Where to?' the driver asked.

And only then did she realize that she knew no more about the Kitten than she had when she'd arrived.

Tuesday, 4 January

4

The light was so bright that she had to close her eyes. She stood there swaying on the steps of the plane for several seconds before she could open them enough to make her way to the ground. Her knees and back ached. The low-cost airlines weren't joking when they said you got what you'd paid for. The local buses in Stockholm were a Utopia of personal space compared to the sardine tin that had flown her to Málaga.

It was warm, almost twenty degrees. A smell of aviation fuel and burned rubber hovered over the cement apron. She was shepherded onto a huge bus that swallowed all the passengers, and realized it had been a mistake to wear her padded jacket. She tried to wriggle out of it. Impossible. Instead she sweated and suffered as the bus jolted its way along the endless terminal building towards the entrance.

The entire airport seemed to be a huge building site.

The deafening sound of cement-mixers and earth-movers reached all the way into the baggage hall. There were lots of different conveyor-belts, close together, and they rattled and creaked as they transported suitcases and sports equipment in an endless torrent.

'Do you know where I can hire a car?' she asked an elderly man. He had a large stomach and a vast golf-bag.

He gestured towards Customs, then to the right.

She squashed her jacket into her bag and went with the flow.

On the floor below the baggage hall, another equally large hall stretched out, full of car-hire companies. She walked hesitantly along the counters. All the usual names were there, Hertz and Avis, as well as some cheaper options with enormous queues. At the far end there were a few local firms. Tucked away in a corner she found a shabby desk with a girl who was sitting half asleep under a sign that read 'Helle Hollis'.

What the hell? Annika thought, and hired a Ford Escort.

It took her a quarter of an hour to find the car in the huge garage. It was small, blue and anonymous. She threw her case into the boot and put her bag, notepad, mobile, camera, the guidebook she'd bought from the bookshop at Arlanda and the map from the hire company on the passenger seat, then squeezed behind the wheel and switched on her mobile.

She had read Clobbe's worthless article online at Arlanda. The headline was 'Death in Paradise'. The short text was piled high with clichés: 'The sun is shining in the sky, but there is a chill in people's hearts. They wanted nothing more than to live a peaceful life, but instead they got a brutal, early death.'

She had decided there and then not to bother Clobbe with any sort of handover.

'You have four new messages,' her electronic voice-mail told her.

The first was from Patrik, telling her to call the newsroom as soon as she landed.

The second was from Patrik, wondering if she was there yet.

The third was from Patrik, shouting excitedly that

70

the Spanish police had confirmed that Sebastian Söder-ström and his family had died of gas poisoning, and how come she hadn't managed to find that out, seeing as she was there on the scene?

The fourth was from Berit. 'We've divided it up like this,' her message ran. Annika could hear her leafing through some notes. 'I'll put together Sebastian Söder-ström's life-story from old cuttings. Sport will take care of his ice-hockey friends in the NHL and get comments from them. You can have three articles: "All about the gas murders", "The life of the family on the Costa del Sol", and that old classic, "Idyll in crisis". Let's catch up this evening. Good luck!'

A man came over waving both arms, shouting something at Annika inside the car. She presumed he wanted her space. She locked the door and picked up her notepad and mobile.

The man banged on her windscreen.

She wound down the window a centimetre. 'What?' she said.

He was waving his arms and shouting and she pretended not to understand.

'Sorry,' she said. '*No comprendo.*'

The man started threatening to call the police.

'Go ahead,' Annika said, closing the window again. 'Good idea!'

She dialled the number of the first of the two Scandinavian police officers whose names Berit had given her, a Knut Garen, who turned out to be Norwegian.

'My name's Annika Bengtzon, I'm a reporter on the *Evening Post* newspaper. I was given your number by—'

'I know, I spoke to Berit Hamrin yesterday,' the policeman said. 'She said you'd be in touch. Are you in Marbella now?'

'I'm on my way.'

'Let's meet at La Cañada at two o'clock.'

'Lackanyarda?' Annika said.

'Outside H&M,' the policeman said, and ended the call.

Lackanyarda, she wrote on her pad, started the engine and came close to running down the gesticulating man as she wove her way through the garage towards the exit.

The traffic was terrible. She understood perfectly why the Spaniards were European champions at knocking over pedestrians on road crossings. Car horns blared and drivers shook their fists.

'Calm down before you have a heart attack,' she muttered, trying to make sense of the road signs. She failed.

The reconstruction of Málaga Airport was a massive project. Immense concrete skeletons stuck up into the sky in every direction, and there were great piles of reinforced steel along the side of the road. Lorries, forklift trucks and diggers fought for space with cars, mopeds and the courtesy buses that carried people into the terminals from the long-stay car parks. All of the roads were provisional, painted with a mess of lanes and arrows.

There was no logic about the places she was supposed to aim for either – the girl at the Helle Hollis desk had warned her about that. In order to get to Marbella, she should aim for Cádiz or Algeciras, and take the toll motorway to start with, but then she had to head for San Pedro de Alcántara. That was important because otherwise she'd end up in Estepona.

'And that's a terrible place. I've heard about it,' Annika had said, thinking of Julia.

The girl gave her a blank look. 'I live there,' she said.

Annika passed Torremolinos far below on her left, an endless grotesque chaos of shabby white buildings strung out along the Mediterranean coast. She overtook several VW camper-vans with French plates that seemed to have all their occupants' belongings strapped to the roof, and was herself overtaken by a German-registered Mercedes. A Spanish BMW was weaving between the lanes and came close to hitting a Seat. She clung to the wheel and wondered what *lackanyarda* was.

When she reached the toll-paying section of the motorway, the traffic decreased radically. She could relax a bit and admire the dramatic scenery.

Thousand-metre-high mountains stretched all the way to the sea. The four-lane motorway, broad and smooth, clung to the mountainsides and leaped across valleys. Large advertising hoardings for nightclubs and estate agents lined the road, sometimes beside the abandoned ruins of old farm buildings. Newly built residential areas with boldly coloured villas started to pop up as soon as she passed the toll-booth. She had to dig her sunglasses out of her bag, the colours so bright they hurt her eyes: the clear blue sky, the green of the valleys, the pastels of the houses, and the sea glittering like a shattered mirror.

Just outside Marbella, next to a shopping centre that reminded her of the one at Kungens Kurva outside Stockholm, the motorways merged once more, and the traffic was as crazy as before. She kept to the right and managed to be in the correct lane when they split again. She didn't want to end up in Estepona.

By the slip-road to Istán the motorway made a broad sweep towards the sea. There were more houses. She thought she should probably turn off soon and try to find a hotel. At the next moment she saw one to her left. 'HOTELPYR.com,' she read on the sign that stood out against the sky. She turned off towards a bullfighting arena.

The Pyr was in the middle of Puerto Banús. She got a corner room on the third floor with a glorious view of the motorway.

'Do you know something called *lackanyarda*?' she asked the receptionist.

'La Cañada? It's a shopping centre. It's huge, on the way to Málaga. You can't miss it. Turn off towards Ojén.'

Ah, she thought. The thing that looked like Kungens Kurva. It was half past one. She went back out to the car.

Naturally, she missed the turning. She saw the development flash past on her left just as she realized she'd gone too far. After a moment of panic she managed to avoid ending up back on the toll motorway. She searched the jungle of incomprehensible Spanish advertising slogans, road signs and electronic messages for a slip-road that would let her turn round and head back the way she had come. She found one just after the Costa del Sol hospital.

It was only as she was pulling into the jam-packed car park at the shopping centre that she noticed her shoulders were hunched somewhere near her ears. She forced them down into their normal position, squeezed the car past a British-registered Jaguar and parked beside the exit.

Inside, the mall was thick with people. On the flight, she had read in the guidebook that the days before *el día de Reyes*, Epiphany, were among the busiest shopping days of the year. Most Spanish children didn't get their Christmas presents until Twelfth Night, and it looked like every single last-minute gift in southern Spain had to be bought here.

The temperature was the same inside as out, she

74

noted, as she headed across the polished granite floor. The sun was shining through the glass ceiling several floors above, reinforcing her impression that she was still outdoors. She was forced forward by the flow of people, past exactly the same shops as there were in the shopping centres back home: Mango, Zara, Lacoste and Swatch. She found a floor-plan and realized she was standing by the entrance to H&M. She couldn't see anyone who looked like a policeman in the mass of people, so she stood with her back to the plate-glass window to avoid being trampled.

In front of her a huge Christmas tree reached up towards the roof, its bright green giving away that it was plastic. Christmas baubles, two metres across, hung from the beams in the roof, and a few palms leaned against a concrete pillar. They were so ugly that she presumed they must be real.

'Annika Bengtzon?'

There were two of them, and their appearance screamed plain-clothes Scandinavian police. One was very fair, the other ash-blond; they were both wearing jeans and comfortable shoes, and were very fit, exuding the confidence that only men in positions of unquestionable authority possessed.

She shook their hands with a smile.

'We're in a bit of a hurry,' Knut Garen said, 'but there's a tapas bar upstairs with an excellent view of the car park.'

His colleague introduced himself as Niklas Linde, sounding as if he was from northernmost Norrland.

They took the escalator up and pushed their way to a window table where, as promised, they were treated to a magnificent view of ten thousand cars.

'Thanks for taking the time to see me,' Annika said, putting her pen and notepad on the table.

'Well,' Knut Garen said, 'this is the way it works. All contact between the Spanish police and the Swedish authorities has to go through us. We co-ordinate communication.'

'To begin with, I was wondering if you know of a good interpreter,' Annika said. 'Preferably Swedish to Spanish, but someone who can translate from English would be fine.'

'You don't speak Spanish?' Garen said.

'*No mucho*,' Annika said. '*Comprendo un poquito.*'

'Carita,' Niklas Linde said. 'She's Swedish, lives with her family down here, works with translations and stuff when she's not interpreting. I'll give you her number.'

Garen took out his mobile. 'This whole business with the Söderströms is just tragic,' he said, as he looked up the interpreter's number in his phonebook. 'Break-ins involving gas have been getting more and more common, but we've never seen one go so badly wrong before. Here you are, Carita Halling Gonzales.'

She jotted down the woman's landline and mobile numbers. 'Will you be working on the case?' she asked.

'The Spanish police will be in charge of the investigation,' Linde said. 'We're not actually operational here.'

'We're working on a different case at the moment,' Garen said. 'You might have reason to write something about that in the future. Greco and Udyco seized seven hundred kilos of cocaine from a warehouse in La Campana last week, and we think there's a Swedish connection.'

'Greco?' Annika said.

'The specialist Spanish unit that deals with narcotics and organized crime. We work with them a lot.' He glanced at his watch.

'I've got a few general questions about crime down here,' Annika said. 'I've read that the Costa del Sol is

76

also known as the Costa del Crime. Is that an exaggeration?'

'Depends how you look at it,' Garen said. 'There are four hundred and twenty criminal organizations here, involved in everything from growing hash and smuggling cocaine to car theft, people-trafficking and illegal gambling. It's estimated that there are about thirty contract killings in Málaga alone each year. The sex industry is huge, employing more than forty thousand people. There are at least a hundred known brothels.'

'How common is the use of gas in break-ins?'

'Extremely,' Linde said. 'The victims are often foreigners, as well as rich Spaniards, of course. It's believed that the gangs identify their victims at the airport, follow them to their villas or apartments, then knock them out with gas when they're asleep. There've been cases of people waking up to find their homes stripped bare, including the rings from their fingers. It often leaves them in a very bad way, and I don't just mean the effects of the gas.'

'Can I quote you on that?'

'Of course,' he said, 'but not by name. I'm fairly incognito here.'

She let her gaze linger on him: what exactly was his role? 'And I understand that Swedes have been the victims of gassings before this,' she said.

'We have a hundred or so Swedish cases each year,' Garen said, waving over another dish of *jamón serrano*.

'What do you think about this particular break-in?' she asked.

The police officers looked at each other.

'I mean,' Annika said, 'didn't they have a gas detector? I've heard that everyone in Nueva Andalucía has one, these days.'

'There are indications that this wasn't an ordinary gas attack,' Linde said.

'I don't know if we should . . .' Garen said.

Linde leaned across the table and lowered his voice. 'The victims weren't in bed when they were discovered,' he said. 'The woman was lying dead behind a door, and the man was found across a desk. The gas detector had been set off, and that probably woke them up. Someone switched it off.'

'And the children?' Annika said.

'They were on the landing outside their parents' bedroom. Their grandmother, a pensioner, was the only one found in bed. Maybe she couldn't move too well, we don't know.'

Annika was thinking hard. She didn't bother asking about details like the victims' names and ages – the news agencies would have that sort of thing. 'How did the gas get inside the house?'

'Through the ventilation unit at the back of the building. The thermostats in the house were set at twenty degrees and it was cold last night, no more than eight, nine degrees. When the temperature outside fell, the heating came on and the whole house was gassed at the same time.'

Annika looked down at her notes. 'This might sound like a strange question,' she said, 'but what was the man doing on the desk?' She couldn't bring herself to say his name.

'The desk was right under the air-vent,' Linde said. 'When he was found, there was a duvet beside him. It looks like he noticed the gas pouring into the house and tried to stop it with the bedclothes, which makes this case even more unusual.'

He fell silent, and the two policemen looked at each other.

'What?' Annika said. 'Why?'

'Normal knock-out gases, like hexane, isopropanol and carbon dioxide, are invisible,' Linde said. 'If any of those had been used, he wouldn't have been able to see it.'

She made a note of the gases, guessing at their spelling. 'So this time something else was used? What?'

Linde shook his head. 'It must have been stronger than normal, seeing as it killed them when they were awake and trying to escape, and it was probably visible. Like mist or smoke.'

Annika shuddered. 'So they died pretty quickly?'

'Well, they were paralysed more or less instantaneously.'

'The children too?'

The policemen didn't answer, and Annika could feel nausea rising in her throat. Was there anything else she needed to know? 'Who found them?' she asked, shuffling through her notes as she tried to suppress the urge to throw up.

'The cleaner. She worked there five days a week and had her own key.'

'And she definitely wasn't the one who gassed them?'

'If she'd wanted to rob them, she could have done it last week when the family was away in Florida for Christmas.'

'So things were stolen as well?'

'Everything of value. The safe's missing. The thieves, or killers, rather, smashed down the wall that the safe was cemented into and took it with them, presumably unopened. All the artwork's missing, along with computers, televisions and other electronic equipment, as well as any jewellery and cash. It looks like they took their time.'

'What does "took their time" mean?' Annika asked.

'At least twenty minutes for the safe, and the same again for the rest of the job.'

'Any idea what time of night it happened?'

'The killers got into the house at three thirty-four.'

Annika's eyes widened. 'How do you know?'

'That's when the alarm on the gate was disconnected.'

'"Disconnected"?' Annika said. 'Did they cut the power? Pull out the cables?'

Garen looked at his watch again. 'The only explanation I can come up with is that the killers knew the code,' he said, standing up.

5

Annika remained sitting at the table after the police officers had left and took her phone out of her bag. She began with Carita Halling Gonzales's home number.

No answer.

She dialled the mobile number, and a woman's voice answered: '*Sí, díga?*'

'Carita Halling Gonzales?' She could hear children shouting in the background.

'*Soy yo.*'

'My name's Annika Bengtzon. I was given your name by Knut Garen. I'm a reporter on the Swedish *Evening Post*, and I could do with an interpreter for a few days. Is it right that you interpret from Swedish to Spanish?'

'Will you please be quiet?' she said, away from the phone, and the children's laughter died down. 'Yes, I'm an interpreter, but things are a bit crazy today. I mean, it's Twelfth Night tomorrow . . . No! Listen to me!'

Annika pressed the bridge of her nose between her thumb and forefinger and tried to summon some patience. She ought to have asked for some other names.

'What sort of job is it?' Carita Halling Gonzales asked.

'*Está libre?*'

Annika looked up and saw three fat women pointing hopefully at the empty chairs round her table.

'*No*,' Annika said, lowering the phone. '*No libre.*'

The women started to sit down regardless.

'*No libre!*' Annika roared, waving her hands. The women glared at her indignantly and made their way towards the other end of the bar.

When in Spain, speak as the Spaniards do, she thought, and raised her phone again.

'I'm here looking into a number of deaths,' she said. 'A Swedish family, a Sebastian Söderström, his wife and children. Maybe you've heard about it.'

'Goodness, yes,' Carita said. 'I only found out this morning. It's awful. We've been expecting something like this to happen – there've been so many break-ins using knock-out gas down here.'

Annika was making notes to help her remember the quote. 'Did you know the family?'

'The Söderströms? No, I can't say I did, really. I'd met them, of course. Our children go to the same school.'

'Which one?'

'Marbella International College. What would the job entail?'

Annika scratched her head. She didn't like travelling, and had always avoided it as far as she could. She'd never worked with an interpreter before. 'My Spanish is too poor for me to make myself understood,' she said, 'and I've never been here before. I need help with the most basic things, talking to people and finding my way to where I want to go.'

'I'll check with Nacho,' she said, 'if I can get hold of him. He's probably got patients now, of course.'

'Nacho?' Annika said.

'My husband. He's a paediatrician. Can I call you back?'

Annika leaned back in her chair and put her mobile on the table. She ought to ring Patrik, even though there was no point. She closed her eyes and leaned her head against the wall. She really was horribly tired. When the alarm-clock had gone off at three fifteen that morning she had almost thrown up. Now she felt her neck relax as her head lolled to one side and her chin dropped. Her entire body was heavy with sleep and she sat up with a start, blinked several times, then picked up her mobile again.

Patrik answered at once, of course.

'I'm doing a couple of pieces,' she said. 'I'm writing the details of the gassing – I've got quite a lot of new information. I've spoken to a mother who's got kids in the same school, and I'm going to do a piece about the family and their lives here as well.'

She held her breath in the hope of avoiding the clichéd 'Idyll in crisis' piece.

'What about the "Idyll in crisis", then?' Patrik asked. 'That's what you're there for, to describe the panic in the Swedish colony.'

Is it? Annika thought.

'Idyll-in-crisis is my middle name,' she said. 'Every word will be dripping with horror. *No te preocupes.*'

'Hmm,' Patrik said, not sounding convinced.

Two bleeps on the line told her she had a call waiting. 'I have to go,' she said, and took the other call.

It was Carita Halling Gonzales. 'Hi,' she said, 'it's all okay. I can take the job. I charge forty euros an hour, plus expenses.'

'Er, okay,' Annika said, presuming that was the usual rate for interpreters. 'What does "expenses" mean?'

'If I'm going to be driving you around, I'll charge for petrol, that sort of thing.'

'I've got a car,' Annika said. 'Well, it's only a Ford. Can you start straight away?'

'Oh, hang on, a police car . . .'

There was a crackle on the line followed by a long silence.

'Carita?' Annika said tentatively.

'Sorry, they've gone now. You're not allowed to use your mobile when you're driving. Nacho got a sixty-euro fine last week. Where are you now?'

'Lackanyarda,' Annika said.

'Poor you, on a day like today. Do you want to meet there or somewhere else?'

'I'm staying in a hotel called the Pyr. It's—'

'Let's meet up there in fifteen minutes or so. See you soon!'

'Wait!' Annika cried. 'Can you bring the latest school yearbook?'

Carita Halling Gonzales looked exactly like the women shopping in La Cañada: thin, blonde and sun-tanned, slightly older than Annika. Gold ear-rings and rattling bracelets. A tight low-cut top and a leopard-print bag.

'Nice to meet you,' the interpreter said, shaking her hand warmly as she dropped a gold-cased lipstick into her bag. 'What do you want to do first?'

'Head out to the villa where they lived. Do you know where it is?'

Carita Halling Gonzales raised her eyebrows. 'Somewhere in Nueva Andalucía,' she said. 'You haven't got a more specific address, or a *supermanzana*?'

Annika stared at her: a what? A super apple?

'Block, district,' the interpreter said.

'Oh,' Annika said, pulling out her notepad. She leafed through it until she found the details Berit had got from *Paginas Blancas*. 'Las Estrellas de Marbella,' she read out.

'The Stars of Marbella,' Carita said, shaking her head. 'No idea. We'll have to call Rickard.'

'Marmén?' Annika said.

'Do you know him?' Carita Halling Gonzales said in surprise.

'Doesn't everyone know Rickard?' Annika said, digging out the number from her notes.

Oh, yes, Rickard knew where Las Estrellas de Marbella was, all right. He'd run a decorating business in the not-too-distant past and managed to make a few deliveries there before the company had gone bust.

Carita wrote the directions on Annika's pad. 'Thanks, big kiss,' she said, then handed the phone back to Annika.

'Do you want to drive or shall I?' Annika asked.

'You drive. I'll have my hands full trying to make sense of these directions.'

They got into the car and passed beneath the motorway.

'Go past the bullfighting arena,' the interpreter said, pointing a varnished fingernail. 'What sort of articles are you going to write?'

'I've already met a couple of police officers who told me some of the detail about the actual murders,' Annika said. 'Now I want to have a look at the house, so I can describe the area it's in, maybe talk to some neighbours. Then I was thinking of trying to meet up with some of the Swedes living here, see if they can tell me how this sort of event will affect their lives, if at all.'

'Murders?' Carita said.

Annika glanced at the woman beside her, who was looking in a compact mirror and picking something off her teeth. 'The police don't think this is an ordinary break-in. The thieves used some strange kind of gas that killed the family almost instantly.' She thought for a moment. 'They didn't actually call them thieves, but murderers.'

'How awful,' Carita said. 'Left at the roundabout.'

The road meandered between high concrete walls, dense cypress hedges and thickets of hibiscus and bougainvillea. Behind the walls and vegetation they could make out roofs of terracotta tiles, paved gardens and close-cut lawns.

'What huge houses,' Annika said.

'Expensive too,' Carita said. 'That one up ahead, for instance, is on the market for nine and a half million.'

Annika peered at the black wrought-iron gates as they drove past. 'That's a lot, of course,' she said, 'but it's what villas out in Djursholm cost.'

'Not kronor, euros,' Carita said, looking at the directions. 'Right here, I think.'

They drove on for another kilometre or so. The interpreter was looking around, very alert.

'That part up there must have only just been finished,' she said, pointing up to the left. 'I don't think I've seen it before. Watch out for that pothole!'

Annika had to swerve sharply to avoid it. 'Bloody hell,' she said. 'How can the developers leave the roads in this state?'

Carita sighed. 'A few years ago the whole of Marbella Council was arrested. That hole has probably been dealt with and paid for several times over, but the work probably took the form of renovations on the home of the head of the highways department . . . Ah, here it is.'

A grand gateway that looked like something from an old Western appeared as they drove alongside a tall hedge. *Las Estrellas de Marbella*, it said, in curling gold lettering. An angel with marble wings was playing a harp right at the top. Two pink stone lions roared silently.

'That's the most tasteless thing I've ever seen,' Annika observed.

'It'll pass,' Carita said. 'After a couple of years down here you're pretty much inured to it.' She opened the passenger door and got out of the car. 'I wonder how you get in.'

There was a post containing a keypad in front of one of the stone lions. Annika pointed at it. Carita skipped over and tapped in a few numbers at random. Nothing happened. 'We'll have to wait for someone to go in or out,' she said.

Annika switched off the engine, grabbed the camera and went out into the afternoon sun. 'What weather,' she said. 'Is it always like this?'

'From November to March,' the interpreter said. 'Then it gets warmer again.'

Annika took a few shots of the gateway. 'Have you lived here long?'

Carita frowned and counted on her fingers. 'Almost seven years now,' she said. 'My husband's Colombian, and we couldn't live there for a number of reasons, so we moved to Sweden first, but that didn't work. Do you know what happens in Sweden?'

Annika shook her head and listened to the wind. She could hear a car approaching.

'Nacho, who's a qualified paediatrician, couldn't even get a job delivering papers. The government employment agency wanted to send him on a course so he could work as a hospital cleaner. Have you ever heard anything so ridiculous?'

A silver Jaguar cabriolet swung in towards the gate and a man pressed a remote control. The gates glided open. Annika and Carita jumped back into the car. Carita waved cheerily at the man in the Jaguar as they drove in.

'So we moved here instead,' she said. 'Nacho got a job at the hospital straight away. We're very happy. It's a bit like south California.' She looked at the directions again. 'Down here,' she said. 'It's supposed to be on the left-hand side of the road, a little way down the hill.'

The house loomed above them, heavy and solid. It stood on its own in a cul-de-sac, facing south towards the sea, with a mountain to the west. The drive was blocked, partly by a large gate and partly by a police cordon.

Annika parked next to the pavement further down, beside an overgrown plot with some abandoned foundations in the middle. They got out, and she took the camera from the back seat. They walked rather solemnly towards the house.

The drive continued to climb behind the gate and swung off left towards a carport. Two cars were parked there, an urban jeep and a smaller soft-topped vehicle. Annika raised her camera and took a few pictures.

The house stretched up towards the sky, a mixture of two and three floors, in an irregular and elaborate design. It was all terraces and balconies, bay windows, pillars and various types of arch, curved balcony rails and ornate iron balustrades. At the top there was a tower with arched windows. The garden was full of fruit trees and large palms. In front of the house was a paved pool area.

The whole plot was in shadow. Annika suddenly became aware that there was a cool breeze from the mountain. She fired off a series of shots of the house against the sun in the evening light. 'Have you any idea how long the family lived here?' she asked, folding her arms to keep warm.

Carita looked up at the house. 'It can't have been long,' she said. 'The estate's so new.'

'But the trees?' Annika said. 'They look very mature.'

'Down here you buy palms when they're ten metres tall. They deliver them on lorries with articulated digger attachments. Do you think this is a bell?' She pressed something that looked like a switch on one of the gate-posts.

A few seconds later the terrace door opened and a uniformed police officer came out onto the sun deck. Carita waved frantically. Annika hid the camera behind her back. The man came towards the gate and stopped a reasonable distance away.

Carita rattled off something in Spanish and the policeman sounded irritated when he answered. Carita pointed at Annika and said *Suecia* and *amiga* in a pleading tone, as well as a lot more that Annika didn't understand. The policeman looked friendlier now, but shook his head sadly, *hoy no, imposible, mañana si.*

'You can get inside the house early tomorrow morning,' Carita said, taking her sympathetically under the arm and giving her a consoling pat on the shoulder with her other hand. 'I told him you were a friend from Sweden, that you're devastated by the tragedy and that you'd like to go in and say a last farewell to your friends here, in their home.'

'I don't usually lie about what I'm doing or who I am,' Annika said, ill at ease.

'I don't think the constable reads the *Evening Post*,' Carita said, heading back towards the car.

Annika had put the camera into its case and was about to get into the driver's seat when her mobile rang. She looked at the display. Bosse calling.

Bosse?

'Hello?' she said hesitantly.

'Annika? This is Bosse. Bosse Svensson.'

Of course. The reporter for the other evening paper –

she'd done some serious flirting with him. She still had his number in her phone. She turned away from the car and took a few steps into the abandoned plot. 'What do you want?' she asked quietly.

'Okay,' he said, 'it's about work. I'm holding a picture that I was wondering if you'd like to comment on.'

Silence.

'What sort of picture? What are you talking about?'

'I've got a picture of you outside a restaurant and you're cuddling the under-secretary of state at the Department of Justice.'

Annika stood perfectly still and let the words sink in. '"Cuddling"?' she said.

'Well, snogging, then.'

Annika's jaw dropped as she stared at the derelict foundations. 'Snogging? With Halenius?'

'And I'm giving you the chance to comment.'

She shut her eyes and put a hand to her forehead. The Spanish air-kisses just before she'd got into the taxi. The group of noisy rich kids with their mobile phones in their hands.

She let out a deep sigh. 'And you're thinking of publishing the picture? In the paper?'

'That's the idea.'

'And you're wondering if I'd like to comment?'

'Of course you have to be given the chance to explain yourself.'

She snorted. 'Okay,' she said. 'This is my comment. I'm so relieved I never fucked you, Bosse. I've heard you're completely useless in bed. Otherwise I have to refer to source confidentiality. Who I talk to, what we talk about, and how we do it, all of that is protected by the constitution. I have no intention of breaking the rules simply because you can't handle rejection, Bosse.'

There was a long silence. Annika could hear the

sounds of the newsroom at the other end of the line. She knew Bosse was recording what she said. She wasn't about to say anything in such a way that he could edit her words and replay them online or to his bosses.

'I've been told that you drank a great deal of wine. Is that true?'

'I didn't want to drink wine with you, did I, Bosse? Has that left you feeling insulted?'

'So you don't want to comment?'

'You're married, aren't you?' Annika said. 'A wife and three kids in Mälarhöjden?'

Another silence.

'Annika,' he said. 'I'm serious. We're going to write about this. We've got information that Halenius was on duty that evening, but instead of doing his job he was out at a restaurant, drinking and flirting. And you always make such a big deal of your high moral standards and journalistic integrity. Can't you see what this will do to your credibility?'

'Did you volunteer to make this call, Bosse, or were you ordered to do it?'

He sighed and Annika heard a click. Presumably he was switching off the recorder.

'You realize that we'll ask his department to show us the receipt?' he said. 'Credit-card receipt, taxi receipts . . . It'll all come out.'

'If it was your idea to call, that means you still haven't got over me and you want revenge. If you were ordered to do it, you have remarkably little backbone, seeing as you didn't refuse. Are we done?'

'You're not going to get away with this,' Bosse said.

She cut him off.

'Problems?' Carita said.

'Not really,' Annika said, unable to stop herself imagining Thomas's face when he opened the other evening paper the next day. 'Shall we try knocking on the neighbours' doors?'

Hardly anyone answered.

No one had seen anything.

No one wanted to say anything.

6

'Where are we going now?' Carita asked, as they reached the first roundabout on the way back to the motorway.

'Somewhere there are plenty of Swedes who'd be happy to talk to a reporter from one of the Stockholm evening papers,' Annika said.

'La Garrapata restaurant or the Los Naranjos club-house,' Carita declared. 'Left here, then.'

Annika pulled out but the interpreter put a warning hand on her arm. 'Watch out,' she said, pointing at a red Land Rover approaching from the right. 'That looks like a Brit and they're lethal. They always look the wrong way at roundabouts. They're used to driving on the left.'

Sure enough, the driver pulled out in front of Annika without looking in her direction. Annika braked hard and blew the horn, and the driver of the other vehicle gave her the finger.

'Their driving doesn't get any better when they've been drinking wine all day long,' Carita said. 'Turn right here. The golf club or the restaurant?'

'Preferably not the golf club,' Annika said.

She recalled Sven's description of golf: 'The easiest sport in the world, hitting a ball that isn't moving.'

The interpreter guided her through winding roads past

several golf courses, massive villas and huge apartment complexes. In one way or another they all bore similarities to the Söderström family home. Nothing understated or tasteful. Annika stared in fascination at a four-storey building in gold and white that looked like a birthday cake – there was an entrance from a road above it, which meant you could park in the attic. Next door there was a pistachio-green house with a pink roof and five gold onion domes.

'Is this what south California looks like?' Annika asked.

'The flashier parts of Los Angeles,' Carita said. 'I grew up in Beverly Hills. This is the closest we get to the USA in Europe. Did the police say anything else about the break-in? Have they got any leads?'

Annika realized that she hadn't actually asked them, which was ridiculously sloppy. 'Nothing they wanted to tell me about,' she said. 'What sort of people are we likely to see at the restaurant?'

Carita thought for a moment. 'Ordinary,' she said. 'Some who got fed up with the Swedish climate, a few who moved here for their children's sake, and others who've sold their businesses and spend their time drinking wine or playing golf. What's the ground clearance on this car, by the way? Oh, well, it's probably okay. Head down to the riverbed.'

Annika stopped the car. 'What?'

'Down into the river. There's cement at the bottom. That way we won't have to fight our way up to the N340. There are terrible hold-ups at this time of day because of the roadworks.' She saw the sceptical look on Annika's face. 'It's not deep.'

Annika drove cautiously over the edge, through a clump of reeds and down onto the riverbed. Sure enough, the water was only a few centimetres deep. She followed the river for a few dozen metres and emerged on the other side of the motorway.

'You do seem to be building an awful lot of new roads,' Annika said, looking at the dormant roadworks in the rear-view mirror.

'The N340? New? It was built by the Romans and has hardly had any work done on it ever since. Okay, here we are. You can park.'

'On the pedestrian crossing?' Annika asked, but Carita was already out of the car.

They were in an older residential area with chalk-white terraced houses. Annika picked up the camera and flash and followed her towards the restaurant.

'La Garrapata,' Annika read, from the sign above the entrance, where the menu was given in three languages: Swedish, English and Finnish. 'Does the name mean anything special?'

Carita was adjusting her hair. '"Tick". Why anyone would want to name a restaurant after a blood-sucking insect is beyond me, but they did.'

La Garrapata was a modest establishment. The glass door facing the street had an aluminium frame that rattled when you opened it. There was condensation on the inside of the windows. Carita stepped in and let out a little squeal. She set about air-kissing all sorts of people, first the right cheek, then the left, just as Jimmy Halenius had demonstrated.

The pictures couldn't be that bad, Annika thought. It had been dark, she hadn't noticed any flash and there certainly hadn't been tongues.

They were in a room with about thirty tables and a bar with space for maybe twenty guests. A large screen on the wall was showing Swedish television.

'This is Annika Bengtzon,' Carita said. 'She's been sent by the *Evening Post* to write about the poor

Söderström family, and she was wondering if any of you would like to talk to her about them . . . Lasse, you knew Sebastian! Tell us!'

There was deathly silence. Annika felt herself blushing. This wasn't how she usually worked. She took pride in the way she approached her interviewees, slowly but unambiguously. She always made sure to explain the purpose of the interview clearly, so that no one could feel they had been tricked into anything. They usually did anyway, because they didn't think Annika had portrayed them generously enough.

But Lasse cleared his throat, came over to them and started to talk about his friend Sebastian, loudly and with feeling, in front of the whole restaurant.

All very un-Swedish, Annika thought, writing so fast that her arm ached.

'Sebbe could have picked any sport,' Lasse said. 'He was just as good at all of them. The fact that he ended up in ice-hockey was mainly chance – he was almost as good at golf and tennis. He knew he had a gift and wanted to give something back to the world.'

Lasse sniffed, and several of the guests nodded and dabbed their eyes with napkins.

'He wanted to do something worthwhile with his money and time,' Lasse went on, 'not just sit at home polishing his trophies. That's why he got all those talented poor kids into the tennis club and why he employed Francis to train them. He'd been given the chance to develop his talent when he was young, and he wanted to give other kids the same opportunity.'

He started to cry. 'I remember the last time we were there with Leo and My – it must have been just before Christmas. Sebbe had organized a club tournament where the winner got not only a cup and a new tracksuit but also a place at Marbella International College until they took their International Baccalaureate exams at eighteen.'

There was a murmur among the guests and Lasse nodded. 'Yes,' he said, 'a place at MIC. The girl who won was ten years old. That prize cost Sebbe a cool half-million, but he was overjoyed. "She's great," he said. "She'll go far. Imagine being able to follow her progress over the years, watching how she develops, being there when she graduates . . ."'

Several of the women were crying too.

Annika wondered about taking out her camera, but decided to wait until the tears had dried. Who were My and Leo? The dead children?

She glanced at the time. This mustn't take too long. She was going to have to call Niklas Linde again to ask if they had any leads on the murderers, and she had three articles to write. She also had to make sure she got to bed at a sensible hour: tomorrow was bound to be tough as well. She said, in a loud, clear voice: 'Sebastian's wife, did anyone know her?'

A woman with a blonde pageboy haircut and designer jeans stood up. 'Vivve was a Swea,' she said, 'so we all knew her.'

Almost all the women nodded.

'Vivve was a *svea*': what the hell did that mean? Annika make a note in her pad and kept her eyes down to mask her confusion, waiting for the woman to go on.

'Even though she was so busy with the children, the school and Sebastian, Vivve always made time for her committee work, and we should remember that she looked after her mother and Suzette as well whenever she was down here.'

'Did she have a job?' Annika asked.

The woman pursed her lips. 'Yes, she did, but having

a job isn't as important down here as it is up in Sweden,' she said, then sat down.

Oops, Annika thought. I just trod on someone's toes.

'I appreciate that the Söderström family were well known and very popular in the Swedish colony on the coast,' she went on, hoping that she'd expressed herself correctly. Evidently she had, because everyone murmured their agreement.

'Veronica – Vivve – had been here ever since she was a little girl,' said an older woman, who was sitting alone at the table closest to the kitchen, with an almost empty wine bottle in front of her.

Annika had to crane her neck to see her. 'Did she grow up in Spain?' she asked.

The woman fingered her glass, and her eyelids fluttered. 'I came here at the same time as Astrid, her mother. Astrid made everyone feel happy. And Veronica was the most beautiful child you ever saw. She went on to become a model, of course . . .' She seemed to lose herself in her memories.

Astrid had to be the dead mother-in-law. 'How long had you known Astrid?' Annika asked.

The woman refilled her glass. 'Almost forty years. She was my bridesmaid when I married Edgar, and she sat next to me when I buried him last year. Here's to you, Astrid!' The woman drained her glass and Annika felt her throat tighten. She had to cough to clear it. She stood up, went over to the woman and sat down beside her. The guests took this to mean that the group interview was over and started to talk among themselves at their tables.

Annika asked the woman's name, how old she was, and whether she could take her picture. Her name was Maj-Lis, she was sixty-nine, and happy to have her picture taken, if it was really necessary. Annika took several using the flash, from the front, no artistic flourishes. Then she put a consoling hand on the woman's arm before moving on to Lasse and repeating the process.

He had known Sebastian for five years. They had met when Lasse started playing tennis at Sebastian's club, a fairly small set-up, just five courts but with a fantastic view, up in El Madroñal. Lasse's own children were the same age as My and Leo, eight and five, but Lasse was divorced, these days, and his ex-wife had moved back to Sweden, so he only had the kids occasionally during the holidays.

The blonde woman, who was a *svea*, like Veronica, whatever it meant, didn't seem to know the dead woman terribly well. Neither did any of the others.

Annika took pictures of some of the *sveas*, then gathered the guests together for a sad group picture. With that, she was almost done. 'Will this tragedy affect your lives down here?' she asked.

A large, blond man who hadn't said anything before stepped forward. 'I think it just emphasizes the importance of fitting a gas detector,' he said. 'As you all know, I sell top-class alarms in my ironmonger's down in San Pedro, so I'd advise anyone who hasn't already got one to fit one now. We're open till two p.m. tomorrow.'

All of a sudden Annika felt she couldn't take any more of this. She went to Carita, who was deep in conversation with two men in light knee-length shorts, and tapped her on the shoulder. 'I'm done,' she said, and the interpreter stood up at once.

They thanked everyone, waved and left the restaurant.

'That seemed to go well,' Carita said, when they were back in the car. 'Where are we going next?'

'I need to write this up,' Annika said, starting the engine. 'Shall I drive you home?'

'It's kind of you to offer, but you'd never find your way back to the hotel. Straight ahead, the Hotel Pyr is just round the corner. Anyway, my car's in the Corte Inglés car park. Here's the school yearbook, by the way. Just drop me off outside. I'll invoice for the cost of the car park, if that's okay?'

'Sure,' Annika said. She took the neatly bound book printed on glossy paper.

'Oh, Veronica was a *svea*. What does it mean?'

'She was a member of the Swedish Women's Educational Association, Swea. They're all over the place. One of my mum's friends started it in Los Angeles in the late 1970s.'

'Are you a member?'

'I don't have time. Turn off here.'

A minute later Annika pulled up in front of the hotel. 'Just one more thing,' she said. 'Do you think the death of the Söderström family will have any effect on the lives of Swedes on the Costa del Sol?'

'Definitely,' Carita said. 'Everyone will be a lot more careful after this. See you tomorrow!'

She slammed the car door and tottered off along the pavement in her high-heeled boots.

Annika let out a deep breath. 'Everyone will be a lot more careful after this.'

There was the last quote of the day.

Darkness fell quickly. There was a faint rumble from the motorway. The bright yellow lamps lining the roadworks cast harsh shadows across the room.

Annika put her bag, the camera and the plastic bag with all her books and maps on the bed and went to close the curtains. She paused at the window to look out at the cluttered view. There was a solitary tennis court below her window. Two of the floodlights were broken,

100

leaving the far end in darkness. On the other side of the motorway, buildings clambered up the valley towards a massive cliff-face. Light from windows, neon signs and streetlamps glowed and shimmered in the darkness. Then the mountains took over. The Sierra Nevada lay in the distance, with twenty peaks of more than three thousand metres, and she could see the foothills standing out like black giants against the starry sky.

She opened the window. The evening was still mild.

The children would have eaten by now. They had probably sat down to watch their favourite television programme, but it would be over. Ellen had probably been on the point of falling asleep, and if she had dropped off it would be difficult to get her to sleep again in bed. Then she'd be impossible in the morning.

She closed the window, took out her phone and dialled Thomas's number. He answered, sounding abrupt.

'Are you in the middle of eating?' she asked apologetically.

'Sophia and I are having a glass of wine,' he said. 'The children are watching kids' programmes. Did you want anything in particular?'

She sat on the bed and pulled her knees up under her chin. 'I'd like to talk to them,' she said.

He sighed theatrically, then shouted, 'Kalle, Mum's on the phone,' and Annika heard her son call back, 'But the sport's on.'

'You've got stiff competition,' Thomas said.

A moment later she heard running footsteps. 'Hello, Mummy,' Ellen said.

Annika's shoulders relaxed and a smile rose up from her heart. 'Hello, darling, were you asleep on the sofa?'

A hesitant pause. 'Maybe,' Ellen said. 'Can we have a dog?'

'A dog? We live in a small flat – we can't have a dog there.'

'Anna's got a dog, a brown one, and it's not big.'

Annika stifled a sigh. This debate arose every time any of the children at nursery school got a new pet. 'It's lovely that you like animals – I do too – but we have to think about what's best for them. You can play with Zico when we go to see Grandma and Granddad in Vaxholm.'

'Zico's nice.'

'He's lovely. What did you do at nursery today?' The little girl, who had evidently been fast asleep in front of the television, sounded full of energy as she related everything she had done that day. Eventually Kalle came over and joined in with the conversation. No disasters, no crises, no nasty little horrors taking out their own low self-esteem on her kids today.

She said goodbye with lots of kisses and goodnight hugs, then sat for a minute or two with a warm, sad lump in her chest.

It was now completely dark outside. An ambulance drove past on the motorway, its siren blaring. She got up and closed the curtains, then turned on the main light and the lamp on the desk and got out her laptop. She felt utterly exhausted.

How many times had she plugged in this computer? Every time she arrived at work, and every time she got home.

The base of her spine ached when she sat down. The chair creaked. She logged into the hotel's network; fifteen euros a day. She leaned her forehead in her hands for a minute or so, then got going. She took out her mobile and called Patrik Nilsson. 'Annika!' he cried. 'Where have you been all day?'

'Oh, just sitting around drinking coffee,' she said.

'I'm going to send you three articles: the fatal gassing and break-in, the family, and idyll-in-crisis. There are pictures for everything. How much do you want me to write?'

'I don't know what you've got,' Patrik said.

'How much space have you kept?'

'Three double-page spreads and the centrefold, although Berit's doing that with sport.'

'I'll send things through as I finish them so you can start work on them,' Annika said. 'You'll have the first in an hour or so.'

They hung up and Annika rang Niklas Linde.

He answered on the fourth ring, and she could hear club music in the background.

'A quick question,' she said. 'Have the Spanish police got any leads on the perpetrators?'

Thud, thud, thud.

'Now I'm disappointed,' he said, and Annika bit her cheek. What had she done wrong?

A woman was laughing so hard somewhere in the bar that she was practically howling.

'There was me hoping you were after my body,' Linde said, 'but you only want me for my brains.'

Okay. He was one of those.

'I wonder if Constable Linde might have had a few glasses of *vino tinto* since we last met?' Annika said, looking at the time: half past eight. At that moment she remembered she hadn't eaten since the awful sandwich she'd had on the plane that morning.

'And a few *cava*s,' he added. 'Do you want to come down and have a glass or two?'

Thud, thud, thud.

'Not tonight,' Annika said. 'I've got articles to write. That's part of the deal.'

'Some other night, maybe.'

Thud, thud, thud.

'Maybe. Who knows? Any leads in the case?'

'Just a moment,' he said, suddenly sounding completely sober.

There was a bang and crash on the line and she had to take her earpiece out.

'Hello?' he said. The thudding was gone. Now the sound of traffic was in the background.

'I was asking about leads,' Annika said.

'They've got quite a lot to go on,' Niklas Linde said. 'Tyre-tracks from two different vehicles, both types identified. Footprints from three suspected perpetrators, shoe sizes confirmed. There's also other evidence that I can't divulge at the moment.'

'So the police are fairly confident of solving this crime?'

'It's just a matter of time,' Linde said. 'Have you eaten?'

'Er,' Annika said, 'no, but . . .'

'Where are you staying?'

'In a hotel called Pyr. It's—'

'Fancy that! I'm at the Sinatra Bar down by the harbour – it's only three hundred metres away. Do you want me to bring you an emergency sandwich?'

She couldn't help laughing. 'Ha, not a chance!' she said. 'Sleep well.' She clicked to end the call, picked up the hotel phone and called Reception. The hotel didn't offer room service.

The minibar was full of ridiculously expensive miniatures of spirits, but at the back she found two bars of chocolate and a dusty tub of roasted almonds. She ate the lot as she wrote the article about the murders. She referred to anonymous sources inside the police investigation, and described how the thieves, three people in two vehicles, had opened the gate to the road leading

104

to the Söderström family home at three thirty-four in the morning, made their way round to the ventilation unit at the back of the building and released an as yet unidentified gas into the system. She outlined the police theory about the family's panic-stricken actions when they realized they were being gassed: how the gas detector had woken them, how the father had tried to stop it using the duvet, while the mother rushed to open the door for the children, then their instantaneous paralysis and death. Then how the thieves, or murderers, had stripped the house of valuables, and driven off.

She described the positions of the bodies when they were found by the cleaner, the police leads on the perpetrators, and how it was 'just a matter of time' before the culprits were caught.

She added some facts about gases used in break-ins. Hexane: a common industrial solvent, and a constituent of petrol and oil; it smells; large quantities required to knock someone out. Isopropanol: a solvent used in sprays such as de-icers, windscreen-washer fluid and detergents; has a characteristically strong smell; takes several hundred grams to knock someone out. Carbon dioxide: a natural constituent of air, forming about 0.03 per cent by volume; several kilograms needed to render someone unconscious, which would cause a fair amount of noise if it was pumped into a room quickly. Narcotic gases: used as medical anaesthetics, such as enflurane and isoflurane; fast-acting and capable of knocking someone out in very low percentages. More than two per cent by volume can be fatal. Laughing gas: used for medical purposes and as an oxidizer in finely tuned engines; a relatively high percentage, 65–70 per cent by volume, needed to send someone to sleep.

She wondered how the thieves had avoided dying from the gas. They must have worn masks.

Then she wondered what the other evening paper was doing, as her article vanished. She ought to have bumped into one of their reporters somewhere along the way. That she hadn't suggested one of two things: either she was a long way ahead and had found better material, or she was on the wrong track entirely and had missed the real story.

Time will tell, she thought grimly, loading the photographs from the camera onto the computer.

Her mobile rang. It was Anders Schyman. 'I've just had a strange phone-call from a reporter on the other paper,' he said. 'Have you been snogging some bigwig from the Ministry of Justice outside a restaurant?'

'No,' Annika said. 'We had dinner. He gave me some information about something, then air-kissed me when we left. Are you worried?'

'Not at all. Is everything going okay?'

'Fine, although I've a lot to do.'

'I won't disturb you any longer.'

The pictures of the house were good. It looked as it was, big and flash, with long shadows over the garden.

She even offered a suggested headline: 'KILLERS KNEW THE CODE'.

Then she set to work on 'Idyll in crisis'. She described the residential area, how scared the neighbours were, the air of sadness in the Swedes' regular bar, and then Carita's quotes, albeit anonymous: 'We've been expecting something like this to happen. There have been so many break-ins using knock-out gas down here', and 'Everyone will be a lot more careful after this'.

She attached a picture of the grand gateway to the residential area, then the photographs of the Swedes, with their names and ages.

That left the hardest piece: the article about the family.

She went into the *Evening Post* website. The main article was about an argument between a television presenter and a politician, followed by an item about a reality television star being insulted in a live broadcast. The rest of the news followed, in order of importance. The fatal gas attack was in seventh place.

There were pictures of the five victims: Sebastian Söderström, 42, Veronica Söderström, 35, My Söderström, eight, Leo Söderström, five, and Astrid Paulson, 68. The photographs were of variable quality, and none seemed recent.

She started by going through the school yearbook – or, rather, annual report – that Carita had lent her. The Marbella International College yearbook beat most Swedish coffee-table books in terms of size and quality. It included a presentation of the school, a run-through of all the subjects, facilities and premises, then photographs of all the classes, neatly lined up in their pale-blue uniforms.

After a few minutes she found Leo and My's pictures.

Leo was much older than he had been in the picture on the paper's website, with unkempt blond hair and a gap between his front teeth. He'd looked as if he might turn out to be a troublemaker. My was wearing a pale-blue dress and her hair in plaits. Annika swallowed hard and called Reception to ask them to scan the pictures and send them to her computer. A weary young man with acne collected the book and promised to do as she had asked.

It certainly looked as though the Söderström family had had an idyllic life. But was it really? Wasn't it a bit rigid and confined? Veronica had been active in a women's association and Sebastian had been involved with kids who were good at sport. Leo looked a bit of a

107

troublemaker and My was sweet. The stench of stereo-typical gender roles was so strong it was all she could do not to hold her nose.

She put her hands over her eyes, so tired that the room was spinning.

Then she started writing. She wrote about Sebastian and his desire to give something back in return for having been given so much, about the tennis tournaments in the sun where poor kids won the chance for a better life, about how involved Veronica had been with her friends and family, about how cheerful and supportive the grandmother had been, in good times and bad.

When she had finished, she was in tears.

She emailed the final article and the scanned photographs, then went to bed without even brushing her teeth. The last thing she thought about was Jimmy Halenius and the picture to be published tomorrow in the other evening paper. She tried to work out if it bothered her but fell asleep before she had come to any conclusion.

Wednesday, 5 January

7

It was raining. Annika was standing at the gate to the Söderström family's villa. She could hardly see the house through the sheets of rain sweeping over the garden, dense as waterfalls.

'Costa del Downpour,' Carita Halling Gonzales said, coming up to her under a huge golf umbrella. 'It doesn't sound quite as catchy, does it?' She flicked the switch that acted as a doorbell and peered up at the house.

'Do you really think it'll be the same policeman as yesterday?' Annika asked. 'And that he's really going to let us in?'

Carita took a firmer grasp of her handbag, a checked one today. 'Oh, yes,' she said. 'He's here, you can be sure of that. You can't take that big camera in. He'll know straight away that something's not right.'

The terrace door of the house opened. Annika ran back to the car and tossed the camera onto the back seat. 'Can I leave everything here?' she called. 'Or do you think it'll get stolen?'

'I should think this road has had its share of crime for this year,' Carita said, waving at the policeman.

Annika watched as he approached the gate, blurred through the rain. She checked her mobile was in her bag. She'd taken pictures with it before. Pretty poor, admittedly, but publishable.

'Are you coming, Annika?' Carita called.

She jogged back towards the interpreter as the policeman pushed the heavy gates open. 'I'm sorry,' he said, in rough English, and shook Annika's hand formally.

She nodded and wiped the rain from her face.

The pool in front of the house was huge. The dark-wooden loungers looked black in the rain. She couldn't get any sense of the view, everything beyond the garden hidden by curtains of rain.

'This is how they got in,' the policeman said, showing them the broken terrace door.

'Do you want me to translate?' Carita asked.

'I'm fine with English,' Annika said.

They stepped inside the house and the policeman closed the door behind them. The silence surrounding them was as dense as the rain. Suddenly Annika felt she couldn't breathe.

'The gas?' she said, turning towards the policeman. 'Is it gone?'

'Long gone,' he replied.

They were standing in a large hall that stretched up to the roof on the second floor, at least six metres, maybe more. Two staircases, one on either side of the hall, led upstairs. From the centre of the ceiling hung a huge wrought-iron chandelier. The floor, creamy-white marble, was shiny and ice-cold. Alcoves in the walls contained replicas of classical statues.

She couldn't shake the feeling that it was hard to breathe. The air seemed damp and stale.

'Where do you want to start?' the policeman asked, and Annika jumped.

She felt in the bottom of her bag and pulled out one of Ellen's stuffed toys that had ended up there by accident.

It was a little yellow dog that her daughter had won on a stall promising prizes for everyone at the funfair in Stockholm. 'My daughter,' she said. 'She wanted me to give this to My.'

'You have a daughter?' the policeman said.

'The same age as Leo,' she said, as the policeman led the way up the marble staircase.

Annika followed the policeman as softly as she could, with Carita a few steps behind her. A cold draught was blowing through the house – a window was open somewhere. She didn't want to ask again but couldn't help wondering if all the gas had really disappeared.

Upstairs, a corridor led off in each direction. The rain clattered against the tiles. The policeman turned left. The sound of their footsteps echoed on the stone floor. There were two doors on each side of the corridor, and an ornate double-door at the end.

The policeman pointed at it. 'That's where the children were found,' he said.

Annika's throat tightened. The parents' bedroom, she thought, trying to force herself to think clearly and sensibly.

'And this was the little girl's room, but of course you know that,' he said, opening the door to the first room on the left.

The pink and gold room was fairly small and french windows led out onto a large terrace with a view of the pool. She could just make out the golf course through the rain. In one corner stood a pink desk with a leather top, covered with paints, brushes and paper. There was a glass of dirty water that My had dipped her brush into when she changed colours. The bed in the other corner was unmade, left as it had been when the child had got up, woken by the gas alarm.

Annika coughed, walked into the room and went

113

over to the bed. At its foot sat a doll with curly brown hair. She picked it up.

'*Creo que la señora quiere estar sola,*' Carita said to the policeman, and Annika got the drift: I think the lady would like to be alone.

The policeman closed the door behind her. There was a deathly hush in the room. The rain was still drumming on the marble terrace outside.

She clenched her teeth and got out her mobile. She aimed it at the bed and clicked. Then she went to the picture on the desk. It was of a girl riding a brown horse. The sun was shining and the grass was green. The girl was laughing. Tears welled in Annika's eyes and she had to bite her cheek. Then she held out her phone and took several shots. She put it back into her bag, glanced at the door, then picked up the painting, rolled it up and put it into her bag. She left the little yellow dog on the pillow, then went back out into the corridor. She closed the door carefully, but a little sign on it, saying, 'My's Room', rattled.

Carita and the policeman had gone into the parents' bedroom – she could hear them talking quietly. One of the double-doors was ajar, and the grey daylight was illuminating the far end of the passageway.

Annika took out her mobile. Her hand was trembling as she took a picture of the door behind which the mother and children had been found dead.

She walked slowly along the corridor, putting her mobile away again. The next door bore a sign that read, 'Leo's Room'. She felt in the bottom of her bag again and found one of Kalle's broken toy cars. She opened the door and went into the boy's bedroom.

The room was in chaos. The bed was unmade – she could almost smell the lingering warmth from the sleeping child. On the floor, clothes, cars and toy dinosaurs were all mixed up. There was a large bookcase full of sports equipment, tennis racquets, golf balls and baseball gloves.

On the desk, which was green, there was a plate with a half-eaten sandwich and a glass of chocolate milk. The edges of the cheese were hard and yellow. There was a skin on the milk. She pulled out her mobile and took several pictures: the bed, the chocolate milk, a teddybear on the floor.

'Señora?'

The policeman was standing in the doorway. Annika spun round. She still held her mobile and Kalle's car. She gulped. 'For Leo,' she said, putting the car on the pillow. Then she went out, turned left and walked straight into the parents' bedroom without a backward glance.

This room was several times the size of the children's. A heavy desk dominated the right-hand wall. Her eyes were automatically drawn upwards to the air-vent.

'Señora, I must ask you to hurry. The detectives are on their way. Do you want to leave anything for the eldest girl as well before you leave?'

The eldest girl?

She turned to the policeman and nodded.

The man gestured for her to leave the room first.

'Just one moment,' Annika said, putting a hand to her forehead.

'Of course, naturally,' the policeman said, and stepped into the corridor.

The bed was big, with a two-metre-high headboard made of dark wood. The covers with which the father had tried to stop the gas were no longer on the floor. The police had bundled them into a heap in the middle of the bed.

That's where they spent the last night of their lives,

115

where they woke up to the howl of the gas detector,
where they died, unable to get to their children . . .

She took a picture of the bed. Then she aimed the mobile at the desk and the air-vent and took a couple more.

She hurried out into the corridor. The constable made sure the door was closed properly behind her. They went back down the stairs together. Carita was waiting by the terrace door.

'Just one more,' the policeman said, turning left through the hall.

They passed the kitchen, a rustic affair with a heavy wooden table in the middle and dark shelves along the walls, covered with painted ceramics.

He stopped outside a door beside the kitchen. A sign hung on it: 'Suzette's Room'.

Who's Suzette? Annika thought, but obviously she couldn't ask.

'Where is Suzette?' she said instead. 'She wasn't here when it happened, was she?'

The policeman opened the door. Annika looked in at a tidy teenage bedroom. The bed was made, the bedspread arranged neatly. A laptop like hers was on the desk, but switched off. Beside the door a sun-bleached poster of Britney Spears was pinned to the wall.

The policeman consulted his watch. 'Señora,' he said, 'I must ask you to leave now.'

Annika nodded. 'Thank you for being so kind,' she said, and walked back quickly towards the kitchen.

When she got back to the hallway she glanced at the other rooms. She could see a large living room, with dark-brown leather furniture, and a library, with built-in bookcases.

'*Muchas gracias*,' Annika said, then she and Carita stepped out onto the terrace again.

The downpour had stopped, leaving the ground steaming, water trickling off the stonework.

They walked slowly back towards the road and the policeman opened the gate for them.

'Did you get what you wanted?' Carita asked.

Annika leaned against the car and closed her eyes. 'Your powers of persuasion are astonishing,' she said. 'How did you do it?'

'I was thinking of invoicing for it under "sundry expenses". You don't imagine he let us inside the house just because we were nice and he was kind?'

I really am incredibly naïve, Annika thought.

'A hundred euros was enough,' Carita said. 'After all, you were only a grieving friend. He'd never have let a reporter in, but no one's ever going to know the difference. The evening papers might be available down here, but their sales are hardly impressive. Where are we going now?'

'Do you know anything about a Suzette?' Annika asked.

The interpreter shook her head. 'Who is she?'

'There was another child's room, a teenager's, next to the kitchen. It said "Suzette's Room" on the door . . . Hang on, didn't someone mention a Suzette yesterday? That woman who was a Swea with Veronica?'

'Another child?' Carita had paled.

'I need to check this out,' Annika said, opening the car door. 'How do we get back to the hotel?'

She dropped the umbrella on the floor, tossed her bag onto the bed, her jacket onto the floor, and leaped at her laptop. Fingers trembling, she opened the other evening paper's website.

Before she had set off they hadn't managed to post anything about either the gassings or her and Halenius,

117

but now both stories were there. The gassings were at the top, but she felt obliged to start with herself and the under-secretary of state.

The picture taken outside the Järnet restaurant looked worse than she had imagined. It wasn't very clear, thanks to the darkness and low resolution of the camera, but you could definitely see it was her in the light from the restaurant windows. Her hair was blowing in the wind, cascading behind her. Halenius seemed to be hugging her, his lips close to her ear. He was either kissing her cheek or whispering.

'Star reporter and hotshot politician's big night out!' the headline shrieked.

At least she was a star reporter. She settled down and read the start of the article:

Schyman: 'I have complete confidence in her.'
Evening Post crime reporter Annika Bengtzon spent last night partying with the justice minister's right-hand man.
'They were drinking wine and kissing in public,' a source told us.

She straightened her back, affronted. What was this rubbish?

Beside the bed her mobile started to ring. Should she carry on reading, or answer it?

In the end she pulled her phone out of her bag and checked the screen. 'Hello?' she said, and noticed that her voice sounded very high.

'I've seen the picture,' Thomas said.

'Er, okay?' Annika said.

'Did you do it just to embarrass me?'

Her eyes widened in surprise. 'Oh, Thomas,' she said, 'you're not jealous?'

'For fuck's sake, Halenius is one of my bosses. Can't

you see what an awkward position you're putting me in? Can't you see what people are going to say?'

'*You*'re lecturing *me* about putting people in an awkward position?'

Thomas snorted. 'Don't you ever think about anyone but yourself?'

She was so angry she had trouble saying anything. 'You hypocrite! You left me and the kids in a burning house and ran off to your little fuck-buddy. I've been homeless for six months, falsely accused of arson, at risk of losing my children because *you're* trying to take them from me, and now you're the one who feels all upset. You make me feel sick!'

She was about to end the call, the way she usually did, but changed her mind.

Instead she waited, taking quick, shallow breaths.

'Annika?' he said.

She coughed. 'I'm here,' she said.

'How can you say I left you in a burning house?'

'You did.'

'You're being very unfair. I went round to Sophia's because you and I had a row, and when I came back to talk to you the house was in ruins. How do you think that felt? I didn't know if you were okay, if the children were still alive—'

'It's always about you!' she said. 'Poor Thomas!'

He sighed deeply. 'You always manage to make everything my fault . . .'

'You were unfaithful to me,' Annika said. 'I saw you together outside NK. You were holding her and kissing her, laughing with her.'

Now it was Thomas's turn to be silent. 'When?' he finally asked.

'The autumn before last,' she said. 'I was on the other side of the road with the children. We'd just bought

119

Kalle some wellingtons, we were on our way home, and—' The tears welled up and she couldn't stop them trickling between her fingers and onto the phone, like a burst dam. She cried for a long while, messily and uncontrollably.

'Sorry,' she said, when the sobs subsided.

'Why didn't you say anything?' he asked quietly.

'I don't know,' she whispered. 'I was probably scared you'd leave me.'

The silence that followed echoed with surprise.

'But,' he said, 'you drove me away. You stopped talking to me, you wouldn't let me touch you . . .'

'I know,' she said. 'I'm sorry.'

They were silent for a long while.

'So now you tell me,' he said.

She laughed and wiped away the last of her tears. 'I know,' she said.

'The children say you've got a new flat,' he said. 'Have you bought it?'

She blew her nose on a tissue she found in her bag. 'I'm renting,' she said. 'I got the place through contacts.'

'Your new friend Halenius, or someone else?'

Defiance bubbled up again, but she swallowed it. 'No,' she said. 'Not through him. And that picture in the paper is utterly misleading. We had dinner and he gave me information about something I'm working on. When we said goodbye he kissed me on both cheeks because I was flying to Spain early the next morning. I didn't drink any wine – I don't like red, you know that . . .'

'God, the things you journalists do,' he said.

She wiped the mascara from under her eyes on the tissue. 'Mainly it just seems ridiculous,' she said. 'But it's probably worse for Halenius.'

'The article says he was on duty that evening.'

'I haven't had time to read it,' Annika said. 'And if Jimmy Halenius has committed some kind of work-related offence, that's really not my problem. More like yours, actually.'

They both laughed, with a warmth that surprised Annika.

Then Thomas sighed. 'God, I'll get some stick on Monday,' he said.

'You won't be the only one,' Annika said.

They laughed again, then fell silent.

'Can I come round with the children on Sunday evening? Then I could have a look at the new flat.'

He'd never made that sort of offer before. He had never once visited the office in Gamla stan where she had lived for six months. 'There's not much to see yet,' Annika said. 'I haven't even had time to unpack.'

'Where is it?'

'Agnegatan 28.'

'But that's—'

'Our old block.'

They were silent again for a few moments.

'How are the children?' Annika asked.

'Good. We're in the park. They're chasing each other. Do you want to talk to them?'

She shut her eyes for a few seconds. 'No,' she said finally. 'Let them play.'

'So, shall I come round at about six o'clock on Sunday?'

They ended the call and Annika was left standing with the phone in her hand. Then she slumped onto the bed and crept under the bedspread. The sharp-edged brick that she had got so used to carrying around in her chest was suddenly less noticeable. It felt smaller, lighter, and the edges weren't quite as sharp. Just a little while, just a few minutes, just long enough for her to enjoy . . .

She was on the point of falling asleep when she sat up with a jolt. She had to read the article about her.

She straightened her back and cleared her throat, as if she were about to give a speech.

'By Bo Svensson,' she read. Bloody gorilla, she thought.

Annika Bengtzon's day-job is to keep watch on those in power in Sweden. Today we can reveal that she goes much further than that. The night before last she was seen in the Järnet restaurant in Stockholm with the justice minister's right-hand man, under-secretary of state Jimmy Halenius, a Social Democrat.

The picture shows the couple enjoying their night out together, kissing and cuddling.

A statement from the *Evening Post* says that her employers have full confidence in their reporter. 'I have every faith in her judgement,' says editor-in-chief Anders Schyman.

Does this damage Annika Bengtzon's credibility?

'Absolutely not.'

But other commentators don't agree.

'Annika Bengtzon crossed the line when she kissed her source,' says political journalist Arne Påhlson.

How will this affect Annika Bengtzon's credibility as someone who reports on those in power?

'Clearly, that's going to look a bit threadbare now . . .'

She had to get up and take a walk around the room.

Who the hell was Arne Påhlson to sit in judgement on her? An overhyped dime-a-dozen reporter, who was being wheeled out as some sort of expert on ethics and morals.

She returned to the laptop.

At the Ministry of Justice, where Jimmy Halenius is one of the most senior officials, the significance of the pictures is being downplayed.

'The fact that politicians and journalists are in contact with each other is hardly news,' the justice minister's press secretary said.

The department is reluctant to confirm whether or not Jimmy Halenius was on duty on the evening in question.

Annika Bengtzon herself has referred to the confidentiality of sources and has declined to comment.

She pushed the computer aside and stood up. Her heart was pounding. It was incredibly unpleasant to read about herself in the third person. As a human being she had no value: she was merely a symbol, a punch-bag; she had been set up in a version of reality that was untrue.

She realized how impotent she was in the face of the paper's sweeping generalizations. It didn't matter that what they had written was either wrong or irrelevant. The only thing that mattered was the media's judgement, the newspaper's world-view, its redacted truth.

She picked up the laptop, but resisted the urge to throw it at the wall.

She sat down, took three deep breaths and rubbed her eyes.

Then she read the article again.

It wasn't well written. Admittedly, every article like this followed a ridiculously formulaic template, but this one was particularly clichéd. Bosse had clearly had trouble expressing himself.

She felt rather embarrassed at her first reaction: to feel sorry for herself.

Was this what she did? Did she ride roughshod over other people in her articles?

Of course. Probably every day.

What was the alternative? Should she stop looking for headlines and pictures, just report, never reflect?

She walked around the room, then thrust the thought aside. She sat down again and scrolled through the rest of the other paper's website to see what they had written about the gassings. The reporter was their Madrid correspondent, a stylish woman in her fifties who presumably spoke fluent Spanish. They had a picture of the house from the road as well, but with the shadows at a different angle. The photographer had his own byline, a Spanish name. So, they were a team and must have been there earlier in the day.

The article contained the facts Annika had got from Niklas Linde, but here they were attributed to sources within the Spanish police. The reporters had evidently gone to the Los Naranjos golf club to speak to grieving Swedes there. They had ended up with the same sort of quotes that Annika had taken from La Garrapata.

In other words, a dead heat between her and the Madrid stringer.

It was always a relief not to have been outdone . . .

Her mobile rang again, and sounded somehow angrier this time. She let it ring twice before reaching out for it. She sighed. 'Hi, Patrik,' she said.

'The golf club in mourning!' Patrik shouted. 'The tennis club in mourning! See if you can't get together a group of old ice-hockey stars for a minute's silence in memory of Sebastian Söderström on a green somewhere. Why limit it to old players? Get any sports stars you can find!'

'I've got a number of other angles,' Annika said. 'Pictures from inside the house, from the scene where they died. There might be another child in the family, a girl who survived. I need to look into that a bit more.'

'The sports stars is a much better story. Make sure they all look fucking miserable.'

Annika closed her eyes. 'I don't have a photographer with me,' she said.

'You've got a camera, haven't you? Call once you've sent the picture. By the way, what sort of behaviour do you call hanging out with the under-secretary of state and snogging his face off in public?' Then he was gone.

Annika let her mobile fall to the floor. This was crazy.

She got up and walked to the window. It was a long time since she had been in this situation. During her years as an independent reporter she had been excused jobs designed to reflect the world-view of the head of news. Instead she had reported what she had thought proper and important. There was a difference between creating reality and reporting it.

If a gang of former sports stars took it upon themselves to mourn their colleague with a minute's silence, she wouldn't have any problem reporting on the event, but staging the image was something completely different.

She went back to the computer, opened the website of Spanish Directory Enquiries, and looked up the numbers for Sebastian Söderström's tennis club and the Los Naranjos golf club. She rang both.

The tennis club was closed, a man said, in English with a Spanish accent. No, nothing was planned to commemorate the deceased owner. Yes, he'd call her if they changed their minds. Neither had the Los Naranjos golf club planned any sort of ceremony to mark Sebastian Söderström's death, but he had been a member so perhaps that wasn't a bad idea. In fact, it was an extremely good idea. They'd been thinking of something along those lines that morning. Round about four o'clock that afternoon . . .

She bit her lip as she hung up. She had adapted reality to make it fit her five-column tabloid format.

She went back to the window.

The clouds were so low that they had surrounded the large mountain in front of her with thick grey cotton-wool. The traffic was moving sluggishly along the old Roman road.

Who could she call to find out more about Suzette?

She went over to the minibar and found that the cleaner had restocked the chocolate. She helped herself to a Snickers bar and threw herself on the bed with her mobile.

Knut Garen answered at once. He seemed to be standing close to running water.

'I'm in Granada,' he said. 'You'll have to call Niklas Linde about that. He's still down on the coast.'

She swallowed her question about what he was doing in Granada and dialled Linde's number. He answered after four rings. 'Now isn't a good time,' he said in a low voice.

'Quick question,' Annika said. 'Do you know anything about a girl called Suzette who lived in Sebastian Söderström's villa?'

'Negative. I've got to go.'

Annika ended the call. She felt oddly indignant.

Did they really have that much to do, or did the two police officers simply not want to talk to her?

She ate the chocolate and tossed the wrapper into the wastepaper basket, then sat down at the computer. The Spanish Directory Enquiries website was still on the screen.

She typed in the name of the Swea woman, whose name was Margit. She wasn't listed in the *Paginas Blancas*, so she couldn't call her.

Maj-Lis, the older woman, was there, however. She

126

lived in an *urbanización* called Los Cuervos in Estepona.

'What's this about?' she croaked when she answered, then cleared her throat loudly. 'Why are you asking about Suzette?'

'She's got a room in the Söderström family home,' Annika said. 'Who is she?'

'Can you hold on just one moment?' The woman put the phone down without waiting for an answer. Annika heard her shuffling off somewhere, then coughing and hacking and spitting. A toilet flushed. She came back to the phone. 'Oh, Suzette,' the woman said, with a sigh. 'She's Sebastian's daughter from his first marriage. A proper little storm-cloud. What do you want to know?'

'What was she like? How old is she?'

The woman coughed. 'Fifteen, sixteen, I should think.'

'She wasn't in the house during the break-in. Do you know where she might be?'

'Well, I suppose she's with her mum in Sweden.'

'So she doesn't live here?'

'Just sometimes during the holidays, if that. Suzette isn't very easy to deal with.'

Annika was clicking her ballpoint in frustration. If there was one thing she was allergic to, it was generalizations about teenage girls 'not being easy to deal with'. That was how they had described her at school in Hälleforsnäs. 'In that case, why did she have her own room?'

'Oh, Astrid probably insisted. Astrid always stuck up for the girl. Sometimes I thought she was the only person who liked her. Suzette used to call her Grandma.'

'Even though she wasn't her grandmother?'

Maj-Lis fell silent, then sniffed. When she spoke again her voice was weak and broken. 'It's so hard to accept that she's gone. How can people just disappear? Where do they go? God, I wish I were Christian.' She blew her nose loudly. 'Of course it's terrible about Veronica, Sebastian and the children, but I was so close to Astrid. I can still feel her here, right next to me, a sort of warmth, a vibration in the air. Hold on . . .'

Annika heard the sucking sound of a cork being pulled from a bottle.

'Cheers, Astrid.' Maj-Lis took an audible gulp of wine.

'So Suzette lives with her mother,' Annika said. 'Do you know where? You don't happen to know her mother's name?'

'Sebastian's first wife was a mistake, according to him. I can't remember her name, but it's something pretty plain – it reminded me of an actress in a seventies porn film. She was his childhood sweetheart from somewhere out in the suburbs, if I'm not mistaken. I never met her.' She took another audible gulp of wine.

'And they were married? Do you know if she's still called Söderström?'

'Oh, yes, they were certainly married,' Maj-Lis said. 'It was a really messy divorce. She demanded half of all Sebastian's earnings from his time in the NHL, but he was about to use that money to buy the tennis club.'

'And Suzette, is her name Söderström?'

'Veronica took his name at once, didn't hesitate. She wanted a large family, lots of children, and she wanted them all to have the same surname.'

Dear old Maj-Lis was starting to get a bit drunk.

'Well, thanks very much indeed for your time. Would you mind me calling again if . . .'

'Veronica never forgave her. Never!'

'Thanks, goodbye,' Annika said, and clicked to end the call.

She hesitated for a moment, then dialled Berit's mobile.

Her colleague was at home, not in the newsroom. 'I'm on a rota, these days, you know. I get evenings, weekends and public holidays off from now on unless I'm told otherwise at least two weeks in advance,' Berit said.

'Oh,' Annika said. 'In that case I'm not supposed to be working either.'

'Not according to the locally negotiated agreement,' Berit said. 'Congratulations!'

Annika heard a tap being turned on, then running water. 'I could have spent today unpacking the children's toys.'

'Wouldn't it be better to do that with them?' Berit said. 'Or they might get the feeling that they live in a hotel.'

Annika sat up straight. 'Of course,' she said. 'Why didn't I think of that?'

'Let's try to learn from each other's mistakes,' Berit said. 'How are you getting on?'

'Have you got a few minutes to go through a couple of things with me?'

The running water stopped. 'Of course,' Berit said. Annika heard her pull out a chair and sit down.

'I got inside the family's house this morning and took some pictures on my mobile,' Annika said. 'I'm about to load them into the laptop and see how they turned out. And I've uncovered another child, a teenage girl who evidently survived the gas attack.'

'What?' Berit said. 'How?'

'She wasn't there,' Annika said, 'so it's not quite as dramatic as it sounds. But someone should still try to talk to her. She lives with her mother somewhere in Sweden.'

'That's brilliant. Who's dealing with that in the newsroom?'

'No one,' Annika said. 'Patrik just shrugged it off. He wants grieving sports stars.'

'That's a bad call,' Berit said calmly. 'Of course he can have his grieving sports stars, but a child who survived mass-murder is considerably more important.'

Annika breathed out. Of course she knew that, but it was still a relief to hear someone else say it.

'Have you got the passwords for the national ID database with you?' Berit asked.

'Of course. I'll have a look from here.'

'If that doesn't work, I'll be back on duty on Friday,' Berit said. 'What sort of weather are you having?'

'Very grey,' Annika said. 'One more thing.'

'Halenius,' Berit said.

'Hmm,' Annika said.

'Were you really kissing? It looks like it in the picture.'

'Actually we weren't,' Annika said. 'Does it matter?'

Berit thought for a moment. 'From now on it'll be difficult for you to look into anything that Jimmy Halenius does,' she said. 'But there are other people who can do that.'

'So you don't think I've blown my credibility?'

'A bit, maybe, but it'll pass.'

'Thanks,' Annika said quietly.

'Remember to make a note of the overtime,' Berit said. 'You won't get paid, but you take it as time owing.'

They hung up.

Annika's chest felt warmer and lighter. She opened the national ID register, logged in and waited while the site loaded.

Investigative journalism had largely stopped being a competitive sport the moment the database had gone online. Subscriptions were expensive but, thanks to the funds they generated, Annika now had access to all the details of every Swedish citizen, their name, age,

ID number, current and previous addresses, taxable income, directorships, the colour of their car, details of any property, their credit rating, and any debts they might have. It also included all the details of every business, organization and official authority in Sweden and fourteen other European countries: their annual accounts, financial state and creditworthiness.

She clicked to get into individual records. A form appeared on the screen. She could search either by name or ID number, so she moved the cursor to name: Söderström, Suzette. Gender: female.

She left the rest blank.

The results came up. There was just one person with that name in Sweden. A Jannike Diana SUZETTE, born sixteen years ago, a resident of 77 Långskeppsgatan, Bromma, in the region covered by Stockholm Council.

So what might her mother be called? The facility that enabled you to search for relatives in the database had been removed after 11 September 2001, so now it was considerably harder to find that information.

Annika clicked to see local registration details, which gave her the postcode of Långskeppsgatan. Then she did a new search of individual records, with slightly different information. She filled in three boxes: gender, the postcode for Långskeppsgatan, and the surname Söderström.

The computer searched to find any woman called Söderström within the same postcode. If Suzette was registered at the same address as her mother, and her mother's name was Söderström, she ought to show up, unless she was one of the nine thousand or so Swedes whose records had been protected and concealed by the authorities.

Direct hit!

Söderström, LENITA Marike, aged forty-two, and

registered as living at number 77 Långskeppsgatan. She had four bad debts, according to Svensk Handelstidning Justitia, and a current debt outstanding with the national enforcement service for 42,392 kronor. She wasn't active in any businesses, wasn't self-employed and wasn't registered as owning a motor vehicle. The debts consisted of unpaid television licences, outstanding tax and a payment plan with Ikea that had fallen into arrears.

She switched to a free website that listed every phone number openly registered in Sweden, along with a map identifying where the number was located, even including pictures of the buildings in question.

Annika filled in Lenita Söderström's name and address, but there were no results. Suzette Söderström's mother had either an ex-directory number or a pay-as-you-go mobile. She removed the name and searched for the address alone; 77 Långskeppsgatan turned out to be between Blackeberg and Råcksta in the west of Stockholm. She clicked to look at a satellite image of the area, and saw that the postcode covered several blocks of flats at the end of a street containing several different types of building. The old asylum, Beckomberga, was just round the corner, she noted, although these days all the nutters had been discharged and rehabilitated to lives they were in no fit state to handle.

She went to the minibar and took out a small Toblerone.

How was she going to get hold of Suzette's mother, Lenita Söderström? Maybe she was active in some association, listed as a contact person. She went back to the laptop and Googled her.

The list of results was short but categorical.

Lenita Söderström, Facebook.

Annika clicked and opened a Spanish page with a

picture of a blonde woman on the screen. With the help of the flag in the top right corner she switched language and the page appeared in English. *Sign up to Facebook to connect with Lenita. Already a member? Login!*

She clicked on a sentence at the right-hand side: *Send a message.*

A page containing a long form appeared. To contact Lenita Söderström, she would have to register on the site. Okay, she'd heard of Facebook – several people at work seemed to spend all day on their Facebook pages. They appeared to compete about how many 'friends' they had, and got terribly excited if anyone 'poked' them. The sort of thing she had grown out of when she was eight.

What the hell?, she thought, and filled in the form. She typed her name, said she worked for a company, date of birth, email address, then thought up a password. Finally she ticked the box saying she had read the *Terms of Use and Privacy Policy*, which she obviously hadn't, then clicked *Sign up*.

Well, that all seemed fairly painless.

Confirm your email address.

Oh, so it wasn't done yet?

She clicked on *Go to hotmail now.*

There was a message in the inbox of her hotmail account, containing a link for her to click on. A new message appeared on the screen. *Welcome Annika! Your account has been created.* She clicked on *Search for friends*, typed in Lenita Söderström and found herself on a page where she could send a direct message to Suzette's mother. She explained who she was and what she wanted, said she wanted to contact both Lenita and Suzette, that it was urgent. She ended the message with her mobile number.

What a ridiculously elaborate way of getting hold of

133

someone, she thought, irritated, as she was obliged to fill in a *security check* before the message could be sent.

She looked at the time. She had to hurry if she was to eat anything before the golf club got started with its act of remembrance.

8

'Here it is,' Carita Halling Gonzales said.

Annika braked in the middle of a roundabout and pulled in next to several recycling tanks for glass and plastic. The clouds had broken up and a hesitant sun was casting wary shadows. She locked the car. Four flags were flying on tall poles next to the golf-club car park: Spanish, Andalucían, Swedish, and one with a yellow, red and green emblem on a white background.

'What's the Gais flag doing here?' Annika asked.

Carita Halling Gonzales squinted up at the sky, then switched her attention to the little pocket mirror she had in her hand. 'The what flag?' she said, taking her lipstick out of its gold case.

Annika pointed. 'That last one. Is the owner a mackerel?'

The interpreter looked thoroughly confused.

'Gais is a football club in Gothenburg,' Annika said. 'Their supporters are called mackerels.'

'Percy Svensson's just sold the club to four Swedes. One of them might be one of those fish. The entrance is over there.' Carita put her lipstick back in her bag, a silver one this time.

A brick staircase led up to an over-elaborate gateway surrounded by huge orange trees. Annika pushed the door open and gasped. 'So this is how the other half lives,' she said. 'Talk about an escape from reality!'

White marble terraces stretched out in front of her. Some ducks were swimming on an artificial lake. Bright green lawns rolled towards the horizon, smooth as women's legs in adverts for razors. Little golf buggies were driving about on dusky pink cement paths. Men with neat haircuts and dark-blue sweaters draped over the shoulders of their white polo-shirts were relaxing at round tables.

'Is that someone you know?' Carita pointed at a middle-aged woman and a very young man who were waving in their direction.

The other evening paper's Madrid correspondent and her toy-boy photographer. 'I know who they are,' Annika said, 'and they must have recognized me.' From today's paper, she thought, but didn't say so. Carita probably didn't keep up to date with the Swedish media. There was no reason to tell her about that picture.

The door behind them flew open and a crowd filled the marble terraces in just a few moments. They were so different in their dress and behaviour from the other guests that everything stopped.

'And are these colleagues of yours as well?'

'The Swedish broadcast media,' Annika said, in a low voice, as the men began noisily setting up cameras and tripods, then laying out long cables and microphones.

The rumour about the minute's silence had obviously taken flight.

The guests who had been eating and drinking in the club's restaurant streamed out among the tables on the terrace, enticed by the cameras and the concentration on the television crew's faces. As soon as a film crew showed up anywhere, everyone's attention immediately focused on it.

'Can you see any sports stars here?' Annika whispered to Carita, as she made sure that her camera had enough charge.

'They would probably be your mackerel, I suppose,' she said, pointing at several bald, overweight men in dark-green blazers with the yellow, green and red emblem on the lapels.

People were still pouring out of the restaurant. Soon the staircase was crowded with them.

'What's this circus about?' a man in a pale-blue polo-shirt asked just behind Annika.

'A minute's silence for Sebastian Söderström,' Annika said, trying to work out if he was an old celebrity.

The man stiffened and adjusted his sunglasses. 'Really?' he said. 'That'll be pretty gloomy.'

Annika pulled her pen and notepad out of her bag. 'You think it'll be a moving act of remembrance?' she asked politely.

The man laughed. 'They'll be mourning all the money they're never going to get back. Half the people standing here have invested in Sebastian Söderström's crazy fantasy projects.'

Annika's pen stopped. 'How . . . What do you mean?' she asked.

The man tucked his shirt neatly into his golf trousers. 'Söderström was a persuasive bastard. His few seasons in the NHL meant people thought he was capable of shitting gold. The most tragic thing of all is that he believed it too.' He stopped another man in a polo-shirt, pale green this time, who was on his way down towards the golf course. 'Sverre, have you heard? They're having a little memorial for Söderström. We're supposed to stand for a minute to mourn him in silence.'

Sverre's face turned red. 'That bastard,' he said, turned on his heel and went back inside the restaurant.

Annika watched him go. 'What sort of fantasy projects?' she asked.

The man smiled. 'The introduction of the new global sport of stickball, for instance. You've never heard of it? Funny, that. Or the racetrack that was going to be built in the Sierra Nevada, but which turned out to be in the middle of a national park. And then there was that tennis club . . .'

'I got the impression that Sebastian Söderström was pretty well off,' Annika said, noting that several other guests were leaving the terrace.

'It wasn't his own money he lost but everyone else's. Otherwise he wouldn't have been able to carry on for as long as he did. And that tennis club was a financial disaster. I mean, giving away millions in prize money just for club tournaments— Sonja!'

The man in the pale-blue polo-shirt hurried down the terrace steps to a woman in a pink cap. Annika watched as they exchanged a few words, and saw the woman get annoyed. She turned on her heel and walked back towards Reception.

'Excuse me,' Annika said, standing in the woman's way. 'Did you know Sebastian Söderström?'

'You bet I bloody did,' the woman said, and attempted to get past her.

Annika blocked her way. 'Could you tell me what he was like?' she asked.

The woman took off her sunglasses. Her face bore the traces of numerous surgical interventions, mainly around her eyes. 'Sebastian Söderström was a fraud,' she said. 'He wanted to be a star, he was addicted to applause, but he didn't want to work for it. He just wanted the rewards.'

'I don't understand,' Annika said.

'He'd get an idea, trick people out of a load of money, live the high life on other people's investments until he got bored, then start something new. He'd find new investors, borrow money, polish the façade a bit and pretend to be a big star.'

'But he really wasn't?' Annika said.

'Listen,' the woman said, poking her surgically enhanced nose close to Annika. 'That was all a fuck of a long time ago.' She shoved Annika aside and left the golf club.

Annika looked out across the lawns. How should she handle this? Pretend she hadn't heard anything? Or should she write the truth, that people would rather leave their golf club than participate in the minute's silence for Sebastian Söderström?

Ice-hockey heroes, she thought. That's why I'm here. She searched the crowd.

'Can you see any sports stars?' she asked Carita, then caught sight of one of the NHL's biggest stars, a lad from Norrland who had just signed a contract with some club in the American Midwest that had landed him a quarter of a billion kronor. 'I have to get him,' she said, and forced her way through the crowd.

The ice-hockey star had some friends with him. Two had been in the team that had won bronze in the Football World Cup in 1994, and a third had made several distinctly average Swedish films.

'I'm from the *Evening Post*,' Annika said. 'Can I have a picture?'

The ice-hockey star looked at her. 'What's going on? Why are there so many people here?'

'Minute's silence for Sebastian Söderström,' Annika said, raising the camera and taking several shots. Click, click, click.

'Oh, shit,' one of the footballers said.

'Did you know him?' Annika asked.

'Course I did,' the ice-hockey star said. 'I played in the national team with him one season.'

'What are your memories of him?'

The ice-hockey player scratched his head.

Click, click, click.

'Well,' he said slowly, 'he was a good defender, in his day. I know he had a house down here somewhere, but I don't know where.'

'Somewhere called Las Estrellas de Marbella,' Annika said.

The star shook his head. 'Don't know where that is.'

'What about you?' she asked the footballers. 'Did you know Sebastian?'

They both mumbled that they hadn't.

'I play at his tennis club,' the film director said. 'Sebbe was great. If everyone was like him, the world would look very different.'

That's the one. Annika fired off a few last shots.

A group picture of the four stars, casual clothes and sunglasses, and the quote: 'If everyone was like Sebastian, the world would look very different.'

She'd done it.

'Thanks very much,' she said, and walked back towards Carita.

'I recognize him,' the interpreter said, pointing at the ice-hockey star. 'Isn't he—'

'Yes,' Annika said, putting her hand over Carita's finger. 'Let's just wait until the minute's silence is over, then we can go.'

Suddenly a man with thick white hair and a bulging stomach was standing in front of her, smiling enthusiastically. 'Annika Bengtzon?' he asked. There was no mistaking the Gothenburg accent.

'Rickard Marmén?' Annika said. 'How nice to be able to put a face to the voice.'

They shook hands warmly and he air-kissed Carita's cheek.

'Listen,' Annika said, pulling him a few steps in the direction of the car park. 'There's a couple of things I'd like to ask you. Did you know the Söderström family?'

'I'm not sure I'd say I really knew them, but I knew who they were.'

'Did Sebastian Söderström owe people a load of money?'

Rickard Marmén smiled. 'Quite possibly. But only people who could afford it.'

'I'm sorry if I'm being blunt, but it seems a lot of people are angry with him. Have they any reason to be?'

He shrugged his shoulders. 'In general, people have far too little to do down here. Which means they have a tendency to get hung up on details.'

'Did you have any dealings with him?'

Rickard Marmén laughed. 'No,' he said. 'Certainly not. I don't have that sort of money.'

Annika gazed intently at the man standing in front of her. His face was leathery; his eyes were small and bright blue. He had a week's worth of chalk-white stubble. His hair stood out like a halo. 'You've been down here for a while now, haven't you?'

'Since my twenty-third birthday.'

'Did you know that Sebastian had another child? A teenage daughter called Suzette?'

'She was here sometimes. Why?'

'When was she last around, do you know?'

Rickard Marmén stroked his beard. 'She used to go riding with Vibeke at the Cancelada Club,' he said.

'I think she was supposed to help out up there.'

Annika moved a bit closer to him and lowered her voice. 'So she was here recently?'

Rickard Marmén scratched his nose. 'I don't know,' he said. 'It's probably best that you talk to Vibeke.' He saw the questioning look on her face and went on: 'Vibeke Jensen – she owns the club. They've got a house just above it. It's—'

'I know where the Cancelada Club is,' Carita said, stepping up to Annika. 'I can show you the way. It's not far. It's just on the other side of that mountain over there.'

The murmuring around them died away. There weren't many people sitting on the terrace now. A man in a black jacket and pale trousers, who was standing at the top of the steps leading down to the artificial lake, began to speak.

'Dear members, dear guests. We're gathered here today to honour the memory of a good friend and dear colleague, a man who was an example to us all . . .'

'Who's that?' Annika whispered to Rickard Marmén.

'The new owner. He got here on Saturday, I doubt he ever even met Sebastian.'

Annika took a few pictures of the gathering. She would have to crop them later to make it look as if there were more people than there actually were.

The minute's silence began. The ducks went on swimming on the lake. A motorbike roared past the roundabout outside the club. The television cameras rolled. People glanced at each other and tried to look sad.

Annika glanced at her watch. After forty seconds the new owner had had enough and clapped his hands. 'Well, thank you, guests, members and representatives of the media,' here he actually waved at the television cameras, 'I'd just like to point out that the restaurant is open until . . .'

'Let's go,' Annika said. She thanked Rickard Marmén and headed towards the exit.

9

The road wound up the mountainside like a fat snake. It was lined with broad pavements and ornate lampposts, and every so often there was an electrical junction box or some other small building. Occasionally side-roads would slice off into the greenery of the valley.

Otherwise there was nothing but overgrown bushes and big thistles.

'Where are all the houses?' Annika asked, staring up at the mountain in fascination.

'This is one of the developments that never got going,' Carita said. 'They had grand plans, and the view's amazing, but everything ground to a halt. They never got further than building the roads. Be careful.'

Annika braked.

Ahead of her half the road had slid into the chasm below. The area around the landslide was cordoned off with a few cones and a bit of red and white tape.

'Bloody hell,' Annika said. 'Is it really safe to drive here?'

'Just not too close to the edge, that's all,' Carita said.

The carriageway had been washed away in a couple of other places. It carried on winding over the mountain, sometimes very close to the toll motorway, sometimes several hundred metres above it. The rainy weather had blown towards the Atlantic, leaving the view clear in all its dizzying glory, the sea a bright blue carpet to the left and the iron-grey Rif mountains of Africa on the horizon.

As they got closer to the riding school the road was surrounded by a half-finished golf course. Diggers, bull-dozers and lorries were laying the foundations for the same sweeping grass lawns and artificial lakes as at Los Naranjos.

'Do rich people really have nothing better to do than walk around a make-believe world trying to hit a static ball with a little metal stick?' she asked.

'They don't walk,' Carita said. 'They use a golf buggy.'

She pointed at a sign saying Club Hipico and Annika indicated and turned off to the right. The car park was full of expensive cars. They parked behind a Range Rover Sport and walked towards a low white build-ing with ornate iron railings in front of the windows. The stables were to the left, big open boxes made of dark wood with beautiful green wrought-iron detailing, shaded by huge trees. Girls with blonde ponytails walked among glossy brown thoroughbreds. A stable-lad pushing a wheelbarrow said something to one, who laughed.

Annika stopped short. 'This can't be happening,' she said. 'I recognize this place. I've been here before.'

'Are you a horsy girl?' a woman asked in Danish. She had short grey hair and red-rimmed eyes.

Annika looked at her, bewildered. 'Hööks and Kingsland both do the photography for their summer catalogues here,' the woman said. She held out her hand. 'Vibeke Jensen,' she said.

'Annika Bengtzon,' Annika said, tearing her eyes from the backdrop of those fantasy catalogues, the brochures of equestrian equipment and clothing that she and her friends had stared at endlessly when they went riding every week.

'I understand that you want to ask me about Suzette,' Vibeke Jensen said.

Annika saw that she was leaning heavily on a crutch. Not the sort you got from A&E when you have an accident, but a beautiful, if rather worn, one made of dark wood. The woman had been using it for a long time.

'Do you want me to translate?' Carita asked.

'I can handle Danish,' Annika said. 'Yes, I understand she used to ride here?'

Vibeke Jensen turned round with jerky movements. 'We can go into my office,' she said.

They walked past another block of stables. A skinny girl of about fourteen with long legs and shiny riding boots was leading an Arabian thoroughbred towards where jumps had been set out, at least one and a half metres high. She felt a rush of envy or possibly just sadness at what might have been if things had been different. She'd loved riding. And she'd been very good at it.

'Can I offer you something?'

Annika asked for a little water, Carita a glass of red wine.

They went into a small room behind a shop-cum-café. Vibeke Jensen sat down heavily, propped her crutch against the desk and stretched her bad leg out in front of her. She looked up and met Annika's gaze. 'A riding accident,' she said. 'More than forty years ago now. I've got used to it, and I can still ride.'

Annika and Carita sat down.

'Suzette was supposed to have started working here,' Vibeke Jensen said, folding her hands in front of her on the desk. They were calloused and chapped. 'But nothing came of it. In retrospect, of course, it was a blessing that she flew home.' She looked out at the stables, and her mouth quivered.

'So Suzette was here very recently, but went back to Sweden?'

Vibeke Jensen nodded. 'She called last week to say she'd changed her mind. She was going to give school another go. I have to say I thought that was a good idea.' She put her hands to her mouth. 'You'll have to forgive me,' she said.

'So you knew the family well?' Annika asked gently, not bothering to take out her notepad.

The woman's eyes roamed over the stableyard and the eucalyptus trees beyond. 'Not really,' she said. 'My's pony is here. I don't know what we'll do with it. I didn't know Sebastian or Veronica very well. She used to come riding before she had the children, but after that she was always so busy with work that she never had time for anything else. Astrid, on the other hand . . .'

She fell silent for a while.

'I got to know Astrid when I was a little girl. She and my mother used to go off to *juergas* together. She took me on outings. I liked her a lot.'

'Was it Astrid who arranged for Suzette to work here?'

Vibeke nodded. 'Astrid was very fond of the girl, and I didn't have any objections. Suzette's a decent rider and is good with the horses.' The phone on the desk rang, and she answered curtly in Spanish.

'I'd quite like to be heading home,' Carita whispered in Annika's ear. 'It's Twelfth Night, after all . . .'

Annika picked up her bag and stood up. She wasn't going to get any further here.

Vibeke put the phone down.

'Do you know when Suzette went back to Sweden?' Annika asked.

She got laboriously to her feet, leaning on her crutch. 'She called last week, Thursday I think it was. She said she was going home. I assumed she was leaving at once.'

Annika shook her hand. 'Thanks for taking the time to see us. Is it okay if I use some of your quotes in an article about the family?'

Vibeke nodded.

'Could I take a picture as well? Outside the office, with the stables in the background?'

Vibeke ran her fingers through her hair and hesitated. 'With me looking like this?' she said.

They went outside into the evening sun. The horses and stables were glowing in the slanting light.

Annika took several pictures of the woman leaning heavily on her crutch and looking across the field down towards the road. She thanked her again and turned towards the car. 'Oh, by the way,' Annika said, stopping suddenly. 'You said that Veronica was busy with work. What did she do?'

'She was a solicitor,' Vibeke said. 'She worked in an office in Gibraltar. She was the family breadwinner.'

'What about Sebastian?' Annika said, then held her breath.

Vibeke shook her head.

'She must have earned a lot of money,' Annika said, thinking of the size of the house.

At that moment her mobile rang. A number she didn't recognize. She excused herself and answered it.

'Annika Bengtzon?' an unfamiliar woman's voice said. 'You emailed me. What do you want?'

'Er,' Annika said. 'Who are you?'

'On Facebook. Lenita.'

Söderström!

'Yes, of course,' Annika said, taking a few steps towards the car park. 'Thanks for getting back to me. I

148

work on the *Evening Post*, and I was trying to get in touch with you and Suzette to ask a few questions about events in Marbella.'

'I don't know anything about it,' Lenita said. 'No one tells me anything. You'd think I'd be told, seeing as I was married to the man once upon a time.'

'It must have come as a terrible shock,' Annika said sympathetically.

'God, yes,' Lenita Söderström said. 'It's just lucky that Suzette had come home, or who knows what might have happened?'

'How has she reacted?'

'Well,' Lenita Söderström said, 'you'd think she could answer her mobile, but apparently that's too much to ask. I suppose she's not bothered to charge it, as usual.'

From the corner of her eye, Annika saw the girl with the shiny boots going over a combination jump on her beautiful thoroughbred. 'You haven't spoken to your daughter since the deaths?'

'How am I supposed to do that? She's in Spain and she's not answering her mobile. And I haven't got a number for that Jensen woman.'

Annika looked at the diminutive Dane, who was slowly walking back to her office.

'Vibeke Jensen?' she said. 'What does she have to do with anything?'

'Suzette lives with her. She couldn't stand the Witch, that Veronica, so she moved out to go and live with her employer.'

Nothing was making any sense in Annika's mind. Carita was staring at her intently.

'So you're telling me that Suzette is staying with Vibeke Jensen, the Danish woman who owns the Cancelada Club?'

'She called me the day before New Year's Eve and said

149

she was going to be moving in with the woman who owns the riding-school. It doesn't matter to me where she lives, as long as she looks after herself and doesn't cause any trouble.'

'The day before New Year's Eve,' Annika said. 'That was last Thursday, wasn't it?'

'I said to her, "If you don't want to study, you have to get a job." She can't go on thinking she can live off me for ever.'

Annika strode back towards the office.

'Can you hold on a moment?' she said, to Lenita. 'There's someone here I think you should talk to.'

She pulled the office door open, and Vibeke Jensen looked up at her in surprise. 'Lenita Söderström,' Annika said, holding out her mobile. 'She thinks Suzette is living at yours.'

The search parties gathered at dusk. They set out from a dried-up riverbed just behind Las Estrellas de Marbella, where the family had lived. The blue lights of the police cars swept across the wild oleanders and dead olive trees. People moved like shadows between the vehicles, as a man in a reflective jacket held out his arm and directed the silhouettes in different directions.

Annika was sitting beside Niklas Linde in his big BMW, watching the scene. She was lucky to be there. She had given the police officer an ultimatum: she would only tell him what she knew about Suzette if she could join in the search. Linde hadn't been able to argue.

They had stopped on a hill overlooking the riverbed. Annika pulled out the camera and opened the car door. Using it as a support, she took several long-exposure pictures. She could hear voices and the bleeping of the search team's radios. 'Do you think they're likely to find her tonight?' she asked.

'They have to try,' Linde said.

'She's been missing for six days,' Annika said. 'If she's been out here the whole time, she must be dead.'

'Do you want to talk to the officer in charge?'

'Maybe just to get a quick comment on what he thinks of the situation,' Annika said.

They rolled down towards the river. Linde parked, got out and marched up to the man in the reflective jacket. She saw them talking and gesticulating. She opened her door and moved slowly towards them, past groups of people with sticks and lamps tied to their foreheads, about to start searching for the missing girl. The ground was still warm and smelt of herbs. The wind coming off the sea was damp.

'Our man isn't an optimist,' Linde said, coming back to her. 'The toll motorway's just above here. On the far side there's the start of a huge national park that covers a vast area. I was thinking of helping with the search for a while. Do you want to come?'

Annika looked up at the stars. 'Has Suzette been formally declared missing yet?' she asked, into the darkness.

'Her mother reported her to the Western District in Stockholm an hour ago. Interpol circulated it at once. The moment Suzette Söderström goes through Passport Control, takes money out at a cashpoint or makes a call on her mobile, the alarms will go off.'

'Is Interpol really that effective?' Annika wondered.

'If she's still alive, we'll find her.'

'Do you think she is?'

The police officer didn't answer. He stopped beside her and gazed out at the moonlit riverbed. Annika concentrated on looking straight ahead, not at him. She couldn't make him out. 'Has anything new happened in the murder investigation?' she asked.

'Actually it has,' he said. 'We've got a preliminary cause of death.'

'Gas?' Annika asked.

'Not just any gas. Fentanyl.'

'Means nothing to me,' Annika said. 'Should it?'

'It's the same gas Russian special forces used to knock out the terrorists and hostages during the storming of the Dubrovka Theatre in Moscow a few years ago.'

Annika stared at him. 'So many people died,' she said.

'At least a hundred and seventeen of the hostages. Some sources claim it was even more than that. Seven hundred survived. The interesting thing is that fentanyl is spread in aerosol form, as vapour.'

'Which fits with the details of this case, from the position of the man on that big desk . . .'

He glanced at her.

'How do you know it was big?'

She was staring straight ahead again.

'Another interesting detail from the Moscow siege is that the special forces soldiers didn't need gas masks,' Linde went on. 'Each of them was injected with the antidote, a derivative of naloxone, before entering the theatre. It blocks the effects of opiates for several hours.'

Annika looked at him quizzically.

'It's used to treat addicts,' he said. 'It makes it impossible for heroin users to get a kick out of their gear. Are you coming?'

She turned towards where the search party was disappearing beneath the concrete pillars of the toll motorway. She had three articles to write. First the description of inside the House of Death, the Söderström family home, illustrated with the poor-quality photographs from her phone. They were publishable only because they were exclusive. 'You can't sell them on,' she had told Patrik. 'They *mustn't* reach the Spanish papers. I pulled a lot of strings to get in and I don't want to get anyone into trouble.'

'They're not that brilliant,' the head of news had replied.

Then she had the main story of the day: where was Suzette?

Now that the girl had been reported missing, she was being encouraged to contact her family or the nearest police station but, according to her mother, she didn't speak Spanish, could hardly speak English, and she never listened to the radio, read the papers or watched television. 'The best way of reaching her whenever she takes off is usually through MySpace, MSN or Facebook,' Lenita had said.

Suzette's mother had booked a flight early next morning with the same cowboy outfit Annika had flown with, and they had arranged to meet up for an interview that afternoon.

'Has Suzette taken off before?' Annika had asked, but Lenita had pretended not to hear her.

She hadn't even researched the third article. It was about fentanyl gas, what it was made of and its effects. Maybe she could put the facts about the gas with the pictures from inside the house and come up with something that way.

She nodded at Linde. 'Yes,' she said. 'I'd like to come along for a while.'

Thursday, 6 January

10

In a country far away, in a strange moonlit landscape, Annika was walking with Niklas Linde, looking up at the stars. The bushes around her were prickly and tall, but she wasn't scared. They were looking for something, she just couldn't remember what, and she turned to ask him if he liked horses . . .

She woke up to hear her mobile ringing. It sounded muffled and enclosed. She pulled herself up in the bed, got tangled in the sheets and tumbled out onto the floor, then grabbed for her bag and pulled her phone out just before voicemail took the call.

It was Carita Halling Gonzales. 'I can work this morning,' she said, 'but after that we're going to be celebrating Epiphany here at home. Did you want to go to the tennis club?'

Annika sat up on the floor and disentangled her feet from the sheets. The dark night was still lingering within her. Niklas Linde was still sitting beside her. 'Mm,' she said. 'That would be great.' It was already full daylight outside but she had no idea what time it was.

She took the phone from her ear to check the time – nine forty-seven – and missed Carita's next sentence.

'. . . in reception.'

'Okay,' Annika said. 'When?'

'Hello! In fifteen minutes! Were you asleep?'

'No, no,' Annika said. She clicked to end the call.

Carita certainly took her work seriously. She must really need the money.

She put her mobile back into her bag, and that was when she saw the painting. It had got a bit crumpled. She smoothed out the girl and the horse on the desk, the last thing eight-year-old My had painted before she died.

Then she hurried away to have a shower, to stop herself crying.

The tennis club was high above the sea, at the edge of a cliff and surrounded by a relatively low wall. An enormous gate of the usual over-elaborate sort blocked the entrance. It was closed and locked. Annika parked on the road, blocking the traffic in one direction, but she had come to realize that this was perfectly normal.

There was no bell on the gate, and no one answered when she and Carita shouted.

'You're sure this is the place?' Annika said.

Carita tied her belt tightly around her waist and started to walk round the property. Annika followed, with her bag and camera. At a more or less secluded spot, they heaved themselves on to the wall and jumped down into the grounds. The club was fairly small. There was one grass court and four clay. In the middle stood the clubhouse, the customary palatial affair with pinnacles and turrets, bay windows and terraces. The doors facing the sea were open.

'Hello?' Annika called, sticking her head through one of the windows.

'*Oh, God!*' A man with a mane of black hair stuck his head up from behind a desk. 'Where did you spring from?'

His English was good.

'A Swedish newspaper,' Annika said. 'We spoke yesterday, I asked if you were going to be having any sort of ceremony here in light of what's happened.'

'Ah,' the man said, getting up and brushing the dust from his knees. 'I remember. What are you doing here?'

'I'm writing about the Söderström family for my paper. I know that Sebastian put a lot of effort into his club. Can I come in?'

The man put down a sheet of paper that he must have found in one of the bottom drawers. He hesitated. 'We're closed today,' he said. 'I don't know when I'm going to open up again. I don't know who to ask.'

'Didn't Sebastian have a solicitor?' Annika asked.

The man looked away. 'Yes,' he said. 'His wife.'

Annika nodded. Of course.

Then the man let out a deep sigh, walked round the desk and opened one of the terrace doors for her and Carita. 'My name's Francis,' he said. 'Come in.'

Annika and Carita stepped into the clubhouse and introduced themselves properly. He gestured to them to walk over to the desk. Large piles of documents were heaped on top of it.

'Would you like something to drink?'

Carita asked for a beer. Francis went off to the bar and got one for Annika as well. She took a sip and it went straight to her head. She put the glass on the counter.

The whole large building was one single room, open to the eaves. On the left-hand side there was a long bar with stools and little round tables in front of it. The reception desk dominated the middle of the room, and to the right a shop sold tennis clothes and racquets.

'Do you know if Sebastian had any sort of legal representation in Sweden?'

Annika and Carita shook their heads.

'I've been looking everywhere,' Francis said, gesturing towards the papers on the reception desk. 'I can't find any deeds to the property, nothing about any debts, no indication of what he wanted to do with the club . . . He must have kept all his legal stuff somewhere else, maybe at the villa . . .'

The man's hands were trembling on the counter as he picked up a beer-mat, then dropped it again. Annika realized he was still in shock. 'What's your role here?' she asked. 'Are you the manager?'

'I'm a tennis coach,' Francis said. 'Sometimes I book people onto the courts as well if I'm not doing anything else. Sebastian's the manager.'

'How many people normally work here?'

'There are ten of us. I've told them all to come in on Monday. Do you know if they've found a will? I suppose Suzette owns the club now.'

His eyes darted round the room. 'The gym's downstairs,' he said, pointing towards the shop.

'Do you know Suzette?' Annika asked.

Francis looked at her in surprise. 'Of course I do,' he said. 'I'm her coach.'

'Coach?'

'She doesn't want to put in the work to get really good. I've tried to increase her motivation, but she's not focused enough.'

Annika blinked. 'Are we talking tennis here? Suzette plays tennis?'

Francis leaned across the bar and said, in a low, confidential voice: 'Suzette's world is governed by her emotional life, which is why it's so hard to book coaching sessions. If she can't be bothered to train, she can't be bothered, but she only knows that just ahead of each session.'

'Is she good?'

160

'I recognize myself in her. She could have made it as far as I did at the very least.'

Annika felt stupid. 'And how far was that?'

'I was ranked thirty-eighth in the world when I was nineteen.'

Annika looked more closely at him. Why hadn't she heard of him? Mind you, she probably hadn't heard of anyone ranked thirty-eighth in any sport. 'And now you work here,' she said.

Francis gave a sad little smile. 'I got fed up,' he said. 'It doesn't matter how good a player you are if you're not happy with your life. I was sent to boarding school in the USA when I was eleven. Of course it was a huge opportunity for me, but it meant I had to be away from my family. It wasn't worth that. I gave it all up when I was twenty.'

'And Suzette could be that good? Among the best in the world?'

'She's a lot like her dad, very athletic. Sebastian's a very talented tennis player as well.'

Annika didn't bother to correct his use of the present tense.

'But it's too late now,' Francis said. 'She should have focused more on her training when she was younger.'

'Have you heard that she's missing?'

Francis nodded.

'Do you know where she is?'

He shook his head.

'When did you last see her?'

He thought for a moment. 'It must have been last Thursday. She turned up and cancelled her session, said she was going to a New Year party at a friend's, that she'd be spending the night there.'

'Did she say which friend?'

The tennis coach gazed out at the courts.

161

'Amira? Was that her name? Or Samira? It's hard to keep track of those girls. It might have been Akira . . .'

'Do you know where this friend lives?'

He walked round the bar to Reception and sat down behind the desk. Annika followed him. 'Do you think she's likely to contact you? She must have had a mobile.'

Francis picked up a few sheets of paper and put them into a file. 'She tried to make a call on it while she was here, but she said it wasn't working. It made her very angry.'

'Do you think she could have been play-acting?' Annika asked.

Francis put the file down without closing the chrome clasp in the middle. 'What do you mean?'

'Could she have made up that business with the phone so that you wouldn't wonder why she wasn't answering it?'

'No,' he said, clicking the file shut. 'Suzette was never calculating in that way. She was far too impulsive. She'd never be able to keep up the pretence.'

'Do you have any idea where she could be hiding?'

Francis let his hands fall onto the piles of paper. 'Have you tried the stables? She used to spend hours there. If there was anything she obviously cared about, it was the horses.'

They drove back towards the Hotel Pyr in silence.

'So she's with Akira/Amira/Samira?' Carita eventually said.

'I doubt it,' Annika said. 'If she was planning to run away, she wouldn't have told her dad's coach where she was going to stay.'

'Do you really think she's run away?' Carita said. 'You don't think something's happened to her?'

Annika braked in the middle of a roundabout. She

162

had started to recognize the Brits who always looked the wrong way. 'For someone who's supposed to be impulsive, she seems very devious. She calls her mum and says she's going to stay with Vibeke Jensen, and she tells Vibeke Jensen that she's going back to Sweden. She tells her tennis coach that she's going to a party and will stay with a friend, and also demonstrates that her mobile doesn't work. Sounds like running-away-from-home plan A to me.'

'So what did she tell her dad?' Carita asked.

'Well,' Annika said, as she pulled out onto the motorway, 'we're never going to know, are we?'

'What if she doesn't turn up soon? Are you going to tell the police?'

'I'm going to write about it in the paper,' Annika said.

'Do you want to come round to ours this evening? We're going to a big lunch in Estepona at two o'clock, but we were thinking of doing something smaller this evening with a few neighbours, have some tapas . . .'

Annika took a moment to answer as she turned off towards the harbour. If she went, would the food appear on the invoice? 'I've got a lot to write,' she said, 'and—'

'But you still have to eat, and we'll be starting late. Come at half eight, nine, something like that. You don't have to stay the night.'

Annika pulled up in front of the hotel. 'How do I find you?'

'You need to get the right exit from a total of seven roundabouts. I'll email you detailed instructions.'

Carita opened the door, jumped out onto the tarmac and walked off on her high heels.

Annika parked and went up to her room. She'd have time for lunch and to write up the interview with Francis before Lenita Söderström was due to arrive in Puerto Banús.

Annika, or rather the *Evening Post*, had come to an arrangement with Suzette's mother. The paper would pay for her to spend three nights at the Hotel Pyr, on condition that she didn't speak to any other media in that time.

She switched on her laptop and went to the paper's homepage. The online edition was dominated by a web-TV item about a man whose nose was fourteen centimetres long. She moved on to the second most important news of the day, her article about Suzette. The murder of the Söderström family had been given its own little section of the website: 'Costa del Sol Murders'. The newsroom in Stockholm had managed to dig out an old school photograph, but presumably Suzette looked rather different now. In the picture she was smiling uncertainly at the camera, with brown curls framing her face. In the description circulated by Interpol, her hair was described as short and jet-black. Annika skimmed her text. It was pretty thin. On the other hand, the picture of the search party, which obviously hadn't found anything, was rather good. The blue lights were reflected in the concentration on people's faces. The photo reeked of night and panic.

The second piece, about the House of Death, was considerably better. Using the pictures from her mobile with facts about fentanyl gas and the storming of the Russian theatre, she had managed to come up with a fairly credible reconstruction of the family's last minutes alive.

There was the doorway where they had been found, the two young children on one side and the mother on the other. 'One important physical effect of fentanyl is apathy,' she had written. It meant that victims became lethargic, and even though they could see and register

164

everything, they didn't react. That could have been why the terrorists in the Moscow theatre hadn't fired their weapons when the building was stormed. The mother and children had been on either side of the closed door, unable to call to each other or open the door, but still aware that something terrible was happening. Then they had simply gone to sleep. Their final seconds hadn't been full of anguish. Fentanyl was a strong narcotic. It didn't cause hallucinations, anxiety or any similar response. Muscle-control simply declined and finally ceased. Victims lost consciousness, then stopped breathing. The process was rapid and would have been over in a couple of minutes.

There were the pictures of the children's rooms, the desk where Sebastian had been found, and the bed with the duvet he had used to try to save his family.

Dreadful pictures, but they were exclusive.

The minute's silence at the golf club was the third item under 'Costa del Sol Murders'. The picture of the three and a half celebrities in sunglasses was perfectly okay, with the caption, 'If everyone was like Sebbe, the world would look very different.'

She took a quick look at what the competition had produced. They were leading with the Söderström family, but with a different heading: 'The Gas Murders'.

The Madrid correspondent hadn't got anywhere near as far today. She had fewer facts about Suzette's disappearance and, of course, no pictures from inside the house. But she had already spoken to Francis, which was fairly typical. She'd have to try to squeeze Francis into the article about Suzette's mother.

In despair suddenly, she went to the bed and threw herself onto it. The best thing about staying in a hotel was that someone else cleaned up after you. It would have been nice if they could have brought up a bit of food every so often, but Officer Linde had offered to do that for her.

She remembered her dream of them walking side by side through the pitch-black national park, the thorns, the mild breeze . . .

Her mobile rang. It was Linde. 'Hello,' she said. 'I was just thinking about you.'

'We've got the burglars,' he replied abruptly. 'Can you find your own way to La Campana?'

'Have you arrested them?'

'They're dead,' he said. 'Have you been to La Campana?'

'No idea,' Annika said. 'How do you mean, dead?'

The police officer groaned. 'Okay,' he said. 'I'll pick you up. Ten minutes.'

She heard a shriek of car tyres before he ended the call.

11

The BMW's side windows were spattered with mud.

'Have you been driving off-road?' Annika asked, as she pulled on the safety-belt.

Niklas Linde didn't answer, just handed her a local Spanish paper and set off for Nueva Andalucía.

'What's this?' Annika said. 'I can't read Spanish.'

'Take a look at page seven,' the police officer said.

She turned to it and found herself staring at her own pictures from inside the Söderström family home in Las Estrellas de Marbella.

'Fuck,' Annika said, crumpling up the paper. 'I told them not to sell them to anyone else.'

'I'm thinking of doing a deal with you,' Linde said, manoeuvring the car between Porsches and cars rented for Sunday outings. 'I'll take you to the place where the Söderström burglars were found, and you can write an article about a case we're working on.'

'You're thinking of doing a deal with me,' Annika repeated. 'What makes you think I'll agree?'

'Because that way you'll get two good articles instead of none,' Linde said. 'I've done my research and found out that you're the sort of person who likes doing deals.'

She was horrified. 'What's that supposed to mean,

"the sort of person . . ."'? Who have you been talking to?'

He glanced at her. 'What is it you lot usually say? "My sources are protected by the constitution"?'

'You've been talking to Detective Inspector Q,' she said.

He grinned and turned off into a rundown working-class district. He was heading for an industrial area, a *polígono*, and stopped outside a warehouse with shutters pulled down over its doors. 'Apits Carga,' Annika read, on a sun-bleached sign above the entrance. 'What's this?' she asked.

'In here the Spanish police found seven hundred kilos of cocaine less than two weeks ago,' he said, pointing at the shuttered building. 'It was concealed in a cargo of melons from Brazil. We know that some of the shipment was intended for Scandinavia, mainly Malmö and Stockholm.'

Annika nodded. 'Your colleague mentioned something about this when I met you at that shopping centre.'

'Things have moved on since then,' Linde said. 'Now we need to pour oil on troubled waters up in Stockholm.'

'You need an article,' Annika said, 'to calm down the intended recipients.'

'Exactly. You can interview me about a big drug-smuggling operation being cracked on the Costa del Sol. A raid has been carried out and the final arrests will be made before you write the article.'

'That's not enough,' Annika said. 'I need a Swedish angle or my editor won't take it.'

'One of the men who's been caught is a Swedish citizen. Will that do?'

She hesitated, trying out the headline: 'Swede arrested in Spanish drug raid'. 'That's not going to sell many copies,' she said. 'Definitely not a lead.'

'It doesn't have to be the lead, as long as it gets into the paper.'

'Then I'll need details.'

'You'll get them.'

'Can I take a picture?'

'Go ahead.'

She pulled out her camera, opened the door and got out of the car. She took three shots of the peeling façade in portrait format, and four in landscape. Then she got back into the car. Linde drove off.

The street was narrow, the houses small and shabby. Washing hung from the balconies. The pavements were full of rickety plastic chairs, advertising hoardings and doormats. Men in caps were drinking coffee from shot glasses. Large women were carrying vegetables in flimsy plastic bags. Workmen blocked the traffic as they loaded their tools into vans.

'Looks like real people live here,' Annika said.

Linde waited as two young women crossed the street with their prams. 'The construction workers who were ordered to build Puerto Banús in the 1950s came from the north. They had to start by building their own homes. That's what we're looking at here.'

'And this is where the thieves were found?' Annika said, fishing out her notepad. 'Is it spelled the way it sounds, La Campana, with a C?'

'The truck's over there,' Linde said, turning into a large vacant plot. The furrowed ground and mass of tyre-tracks indicated that it was used as a general car park. A police cordon surrounded the far end where an old truck was parked with its back doors facing the wall. One of the rear doors was open, creaking in the wind. A car from the Policía Local was parked beside the cordon.

'Are they . . . still there?' Annika asked.

'The bodies were taken to the mortuary early this morning.'

'And this is where they were found?'

'In the driver's cab, to be precise. Shall we take a look?'

He switched off the engine, grabbed a torch and got out of the BMW. Annika followed, hoisting her bag onto her shoulder. The policeman went over to his colleague, shook his hand and exchanged greetings. Then he waved and pointed, towards her and the car, and beckoned her over. 'We can go in as long as we don't touch anything,' he said, holding up the tape so that Annika could get underneath.

The ground was uneven and hard, and she stumbled. A few clumps of grass clung to life between the potholes. Patches of cement suggested some old foundations or a roadway.

She stopped a couple of metres from the truck's rear door. Linde took a few more steps, lit the powerful torch and directed the beam inside the vehicle. It reflected back towards them off a large flat-screen television. He moved the beam and Annika watched as it lit the frame of a painting, a statue, a large globe and a rolled-up rug. On the floor of the truck sat a jewel-box and several games consoles – Annika recognized a PlayStation 3 and an Xbox. She pulled out her camera and took some pictures. 'Five lives,' she said. 'For this.'

'Seven,' Linde said. 'The thieves were killed as well, of course.'

He walked over to the left-hand side of the driver's cab, where he was out of view of his Spanish colleague.

'Is this everything that was taken?' Annika asked, following him unsteadily.

'The list isn't firm. It was put together by the cleaner,

170

and she hasn't much idea of what the art was or who it was by.'

'How did the thieves die?' Annika asked. 'Were they shot? Beaten to death?'

He shook his head. 'There were no external injuries on the bodies.'

'Could it have been the gas? Fentanyl?'

'Probably.'

'Who found them?'

'A man who lives on the other side of the street above that restaurant. He'd seen the truck standing here for several days and thought it was odd that it was still here over Epiphany. He came over to take a closer look and found them.'

Annika looked up at the cab. She could see only a dirty side-window and the edge of the roof. 'They couldn't have been visible from the outside,' she said, 'or someone would have noticed before.'

Niklas Linde stopped beside the cab and inspected it, keeping his hands by his sides. 'The cab was unlocked,' he said. 'The old man opened the driver's door. One of the thieves was in the passenger side, the other in the driver's seat. The driver tumbled out when the door was opened. The old man had a minor heart attack and had to be taken to hospital by ambulance.'

'Can we open the door?' Annika asked. 'If it's still unlocked?'

He shook his head. 'We can't touch the handle.'

'But if I climbed up,' Annika said, 'I could take a picture through the side-window?'

'Without touching anything?'

There were steps beside the wheel-arch that she could stand on. 'Can you lift me up?' she asked.

He looked amused. 'How much do you weigh?'

171

She hit his arm.

'Come on, then,' he said.

Annika let go of her bag, took a firm grip of the camera with her right hand, and stood in front of him. He put both hands round her waist, breathing on the back of her neck. 'Okay,' he said. 'Now.'

With a powerful thrust he lifted her into the air. She put one foot on a step to the cab and looked in through the side window. A narrow driver's seat and a wider passenger seat in cracked vinyl, hamburger wrappers above the dashboard by the windscreen, a map of Marbella, mud on the floor, two half-empty beer bottles in the cup-holder by the radio.

She raised the camera and fired off a series of pictures of the interior.

Then he put her down. 'Quite some place to die,' he said, still holding her.

She stood still, breathing into his shirt. He smelt of soap and grass.

'What are you doing this afternoon?' he asked.

At that moment her mobile rang in her bag by her feet. She pulled free, her cheeks glowing, bent down and grabbed the phone. It was the presenter of the radio programme *Studio Six*. 'I'd like to have you on for a debate on Monday afternoon,' the man said.

She glanced up at Linde. The way he was looking at her was more than she could handle. 'I see,' she said. 'Who with, and what about?'

'With Arne Påhlson, among others, about journalists' credibility, about how easy it is to hold those in power to account when you're sitting in their lap, about . . .'

She screwed her eyes shut. Don't get angry, don't feel insulted, don't do anything stupid. Don't give them the chance to play an outraged response on the radio.

'I'm in Spain on a job,' she said. 'I can hardly hear you. What did you say?'

'Er, about journalists' credibility, about how easy it is to—'

'Hello?' Annika said. 'Hello?'

'Hello?' the man from *Studio Six* said.

'Oh,' Annika said, holding the phone some distance away. 'He disappeared.' She ended the call and switched off her mobile. 'I've got a date,' she said, looking up at Linde again. 'With Lenita Söderström, Suzette's mother.'

'You didn't want to talk to the caller?' he asked.

'Can you drop me back at the hotel?'

They climbed back through the cordon, and Annika took a few pictures with the police car and the cordon in the foreground. She could already see the headline in tomorrow's paper: 'Sebastian's killers died here.' Then the story would be on its way off the front page.

12

Lenita Söderström checked into the hotel without Annika realizing who she was. The small woman stepped into the lobby with a brown suitcase on wheels, a coat over her arm and a slight limp, as if her shoes were chafing. She walked up to Reception and said something in laboured English, and Annika went back to the English-language edition of the local paper, *Sur*. They, too, had reprinted her pictures from inside the house. Photos: *Evening Post*.

'Annika Bengtzon?'

She'd been expecting a blonde who'd gone to seed, with tortured hair and low-slung jeans. The little woman in front of her had reading-glasses on a cord round her neck and a slightly pilled jumper. She was fifteen years older than her picture on Facebook, and introduced herself as Lenita Söderström with a sturdy handshake. 'Can we go and get some lunch?' she said. 'I'm starving.'

Annika folded the paper and left the interior shots of the Söderströms' villa on the table beside her. 'I don't know anywhere to eat round here. We can ask at the desk.'

'No need,' Lenita Söderström said. 'I've been here before.' She led the way through the doors, turned left on the street outside, past the entrance to the El Corte Inglés department store, then went down the steps into the Marina Banús shopping centre. There she stopped. Little fashion boutiques and two trendy cafés filled the ground floor. 'Well,' she said, 'I know it was here somewhere . . .'

'This will do fine,' Annika said, making for one of the cafés.

Lenita Söderström followed her hesitantly. 'Isn't it funny how the small, reasonably priced places never last?' she said. 'They always lose out to the big chains.' She sat down opposite Annika at a small, round table. Annika glanced at her as she skimmed the menu. The café specialized in organic smoothies, freshly roasted coffee and salads 'made with love'. She knew Lenita Söderström was forty-two, born the same year as Sebastian, but she seemed older. Her hair was ash-blonde, she had the beginnings of a double chin and a boyish figure.

'These new places always seem to over-complicate things,' Lenita Söderström said, putting the menu down. 'I'll have lasagne if they've got it, otherwise just a muffin. And a glass of red.'

Annika ordered two chicken stir-fries in her hesitant Spanish, plus two *agua con gas* and *una copa de vino tinto*.

Lenita Söderström sighed. 'It's so terrible not knowing where she is. It makes me so angry, so upset. The least she could do is call!'

Annika took her pen and notepad out of her bag. 'Is this the first time Suzette has disappeared? Or has she left home without saying where she was going before?'

Lenita Söderström squirmed on her chair. 'Don't all teenagers do that? And she only does it because she knows how worried I get. I can't eat, can't sleep . . .'

175

Their food arrived and Lenita Söderström tucked into the stir-fry without asking where her lasagne was. 'Suzette doesn't think of anyone but herself,' she said, between mouthfuls. 'Since she was four years old, it's been nothing but "me, me, me" with her.'

She drained her glass of wine and gestured for another.

Annika couldn't think of anything to say. The woman was stressed and wound up. This would take time.

'And Sebastian was off playing ice-hockey the whole time. We were stuck in America, unable to understand what anyone was saying. How much fun do you think that was? And with a kid who did nothing but cry.' The wine had arrived and she took a gulp.

'Where do you think Suzette might be?' Annika asked.

Lenita Söderström leaned over the table. 'All these years I've had to look after her on my own,' she said emphatically. 'Now Sebastian finally agrees to take a bit of responsibility, and what happens? She disappears after just two weeks. It's incredibly irresponsible!' She groaned and sank back in the rather too fashionable chair.

'When did you last hear from Suzette?'

'She called and said she was going to be moving in with that woman who has the stables up in the mountains.'

'And that was last Thursday?'

'After we spoke yesterday I had a look at her Facebook page. She hasn't added anything since then.'

'Do you think something might have happened to her?' Annika asked gently.

The woman's eyes filled with tears. 'I found out about Sebastian in the paper,' she said. 'Imagine finding out your ex-husband is dead from the gutter press. Do you have any idea how awful that was?'

176

Annika wondered if the gutter press in question was her own paper.

'I tried calling Suzette's mobile straight away, but it wasn't switched on. I left a message, but she hasn't called back. I don't understand why she's treating me like this.'

'You didn't talk to her on New Year's Eve?' Annika said. 'No text message at midnight, nothing like that?'

'I was on a mini-cruise with my work colleagues, so I didn't have a very good signal,' Lenita said.

'What do you do?' Annika asked.

'I'm in the hotel industry.' Lenita ordered a third glass of wine. 'I deal with the accounts, budgets, payroll. It's very demanding.' She mentioned a hotel that Annika had never heard of.

'When Suzette has gone missing before, how long is it usually before she gets in touch?'

Lenita closed her eyes, her shoulders slumped; the wine was calming her. 'A day,' she said. 'Once she was gone overnight. She slept at a friend's without telling me. After that we talked about this. About how worried I get.'

Annika had been hoping for a different answer. She'd been hoping that Suzette had got into the habit of going missing for several days without being in touch, that she was experienced and competent when it came to running away, able to cope in all weathers. That evidently wasn't so, and it was now a week since she had disappeared.

'Has Suzette ever mentioned a friend called Amira, or Samira?' she asked.

'She never tells me anything.'

'When did you realize she was missing?'

'When I spoke to the Danish woman who owns the stables,' Lenita said.

In other words, when Annika had handed her mobile to Vibeke Jensen.

'And you booked a flight down here at once?'

'It's expensive, flying abroad, but what else can you do when something like this happens?'

'What are you planning to do down here?'

'Look for my daughter,' Lenita said, and the tears overflowed.

Annika let her cry for a few minutes. Then she put her hand on the woman's arm. 'This is what we'll do,' she said. 'I'll write an article for the paper in which you'll say you're here to look for Suzette. We'll encourage her and anyone who might have had any contact with her to get in touch with the police and tell them whatever they know. I'll say that she's never gone missing like this before – that's right, isn't it?'

Lenita blew her nose on a napkin and nodded.

'I understand that Suzette's sporty,' Annika said. 'She's good at horse-riding and a promising tennis-player?'

Lenita snorted. 'Do you know what it costs for a kid to go horse-riding regularly? When I said I couldn't afford it, that Astrid showed up waving her purse. But what about getting there and back? To start with I had to go with her. It took more than an hour each way, then, when she started to go on her own, I had to keep forking out for Underground tickets and bus tickets and—'

'You said she slept at a friend's the night she didn't come home. Who are her best friends?'

Lenita gave Annika the names of four girls who were all in the same class as Suzette at school in Blackeberg.

'Did she have a boyfriend?'

'Suzette was wary of boys,' Lenita said, gesturing to the waiter. 'She could see what had happened to me.'

'Is she happy with her friends? Is she happy in Bromma?'

'Bromma's a nice suburb,' Lenita said. 'I know it isn't Marbella, but I work hard to keep things together so we can stay in Långskeppsgatan.'

'Why would she want to move to Marbella and live with her dad?'

'She was fed up of school, but I told her that if you want to make anything of your life you need an education. I can't support her for the rest of her life. And her dad won't either, even if he's rolling in money.'

'But she kept going to school?'

'Yes – it specialized in sport.' Lenita Söderström scoffed. 'What sort of an education's that, I asked her, playing tennis all day long? I thought she should have studied economics. Then she could have got a good job. She might have found something at my hotel, maybe as a temp to start with – we always need extra people over the summer, at Christmas and New Year.'

'But she moved down here to her dad so she could . . . what? Play tennis? Work?'

Lenita leaned towards Annika as a fourth glass of wine appeared. 'If you knew what he's done to me. The way he's treated me!'

Annika put her pen on her pad. 'Lenita,' she said quietly. 'Can we stop talking about you, and concentrate on Suzette instead?'

It wasn't much of an article. Fortunately she had Francis's description of Suzette to bulk out the text, because Lenita's quotes were next to useless. The picture was even worse. Lenita was standing outside El Corte Inglés. With a good deal of wishful thinking you could just about interpret her expression as upset and desperate rather than affronted and half-cut.

After Annika's pertinent but clumsy remark that she would rather talk about Suzette, Lenita had clammed up. She didn't want to have her picture taken, and it was only when Annika threatened to tear up the paper's agreement to pay the hotel bill that she relented.

She decided to wait before sending the text to Stockholm and concentrated on writing the article about the dead burglars. When she emailed it to the newsroom with the pictures, she pointed out that her photos from inside the Söderström house were in all the Spanish papers even though Patrik had promised they wouldn't be. Then she looked at the time.

Only half past six.

Maybe she should try to get hold of Suzette's school friends. None of them had their own flat or a listed phone number, but if she kept trying with various combinations of surname and postcode, she should be able to dig out their parents and their home phone numbers.

She tried the first girl, Polly Sandman.

No results.

Maybe her real name was something completely different, not Polly at all.

The second, Amanda Andersson, produced 618 results in Stockholm alone. Too many to choose from. Annika couldn't assume the girl lived in Bromma and had been born in the same year as Suzette.

The third, Sandra Holgersson, lived on Aladdinsvägen, had the same surname as her parents, and they were all registered at the same address. A phone number was listed, but no one answered. However, it *was* Twelfth Night.

The fourth girl was called Klara, but Lenita hadn't been sure of her surname. Something double-barrelled, she thought, Hermansson-Eklund or something like that. That particular combination drew a blank.

Annika got up from the computer and walked round the hotel room. Dusk was falling. The big mountain on the other side of the motorway was turning dark red in the dying rays of the sun, and the streetlamps had come on. The cars snaked slowly but relentlessly in both directions.

Maybe she should go round to see Carita and her family, after all. She had no great desire to spend another evening sitting here. She looked at the time again. An hour before she was due there. Should she have a shower? Go for a walk? Call the children?

She picked up her mobile and called Thomas, unable to bring herself to ring Sophia Fucking Bitch Grenborg's home number.

The call bounced around the satellites, one ring, two, five, six, and with each one the loneliness in the room echoed a bit louder. Finally the call went to voicemail. She clicked to cut it off without leaving a message. She went back to her laptop and stared at the screen.

Suzette hadn't been active on Facebook since last Thursday. Annika remembered the computer on the desk of the teenage bedroom next to the kitchen of the villa at Las Estrellas de Marbella. It must have been Suzette's. But she could get into her account from any computer. Annika opened her own Facebook profile.

0 Friends.

She moved to *Search* and typed in suzette söderström.

There, a direct hit.

Name: Suzette Söderström
Network: Sweden
Matches: Name

On the left-hand side was a picture of Suzette, presumably fairly recent and carefully selected. Her eyes were heavily made-up, her head was slightly tilted and her black hair was sticking out. The angles were slightly odd – it had probably been taken with a webcam.

On the right were four options: *Send Message*, *Poke!*, *View Friends* and *Add to Friends*.

She clicked on *View Friends* and let out a whistle.

Suzette had 201 friends. They filled five pages, with names and photographs in alphabetical order, then a short description of each. They were all young and from Sweden. On the first page Annika found Amanda Andersson. As she herself was now part of the Facebook community, all she had to do was click on the picture of the young Amanda Andersson and send her a message. Whoosh. Off it went into cyberspace. With a bit of luck it would result in a phone call or email.

She carried on through the list of friends, and found Klara, whose surname was Evertsson-Hedberg, and Sandra Holgersson, and sent them messages as well. On the next page she found Polly, actually Paulina Sandman, with identical jet-black hair, the same expression and tilted head as Suzette.

They'd taken the pictures at the same time, Annika thought, on the same webcam. Maybe they'd set up their accounts at the same time, too, and gathered friends together. This was Suzette's best friend.

She wrote her a message as well, slightly longer and more explicit than the others. She explained who she was, that she was writing about Suzette for the paper, that she didn't want to get anything wrong, and that it was important her friends were given the opportunity to voice their opinion.

Then she looked through the list of friends once more.

No Amira, Samira or Akira.

She tried calling Niklas Linde but got no answer, so rang Knut Garen instead.

The police didn't have any leads on Suzette, the

Norwegian explained. The physical search area had been expanded to cover a four-kilometre radius from the Söderström family home, which included parts of a rugged national park with deep ravines and steep waterfalls. They were also following up other lines of enquiry by going through her computer, speaking to her friends and neighbours, as well as to the staff at the bars of Nueva Andalucía.

She added a few lines to her article about the unsuccessful police search, explained that Suzette was a promising tennis player and that she trained regularly at her dad's club, that her coach had once been ranked thirty-eighth in the world, and Suzette had been expected to have a career at least as successful as that.

She emailed her text and the terrible picture of Lenita to the *Evening Post*.

Then she opened the email from Carita with directions to her house. She hadn't included any road names. 'Turn left after Mercadona, drive past OpenCor and follow the road round to the left . . .' On the way out to the car she stopped at Reception and asked for the number of Taxi Marbella. Just as back-up, in case she got lost.

The gate wasn't quite as showy as the one to Las Estrellas de Marbella, but it wasn't far off.

Carita Halling Gonzales's estate lay high up a mountainside with a golf course immediately below. The streetlamps formed a river of light towards the sea, where Puerto Banús spread out like an intense thousand-watt bulb in the moonlight. She pressed the security phone for house number six and waited in the car as the gates slid open.

The buildings huddled together in groups of three or four. They were all different, pink or pale blue, ochre yellow or deep red, with balustrades, terraces and decking. A swimming-pool with two waterfalls and large stone terraces faced the valley. Ornate streetlamps, like old London gas-lamps, lit the roads.

'Welcome,' Carita said, kissing her on both cheeks. 'Come in, come in! There's no need to take your shoes off – you're in España now! Come on, I'll introduce you to everyone . . .'

Having 'a few neighbours' round turned out to involve practically everyone on the estate.

'You see that couple over there?' Carita said. 'She's a maths teacher at Marbella International College, and he captains one of the yachts in the harbour. They've got two children and live just a bit further up. Nice people, but they're Brits. The people going up to them now are Swedes. Do you remember the adverts for Diesel clothing back in the 'nineties? He did them. His wife was an international model in those days. Now they live in a neighbouring development. They've got two children, a son who plays football and a daughter who's a Spanish show-jumping champion.'

Annika looked at the beautiful woman with the long, glossy hair. She was laughing as she put her hand on her husband's arm. And she had a horse.

Carita gestured towards the other end of the room. 'That woman's Swedish, a partner in a law firm in Frankfurt. He's from New Zealand and also works with boats. The young man with the dog is an estate agent from Jamaica. The older man used to run a bank in Kenya, but now he plays golf full-time. The couple over there are from Värmland – they moved down here when they sold their tyre company. But, dear me, you haven't got a drink yet.'

She bustled off and Annika was left standing beside a group of expensively dressed people holding glasses of wine. She tried talking Spanish for a short while, but after saying, 'Soy sueco', thereby introducing herself as a Swedish man, she stuck to English.

She went out onto the terrace and stood there gazing out across the harbour. The neon sign of El Corte Inglés was clearly visible.

'Ah, so you found your way all right.'

Annika spun round when she heard the thick Gothenburg accent. She grinned as broadly as if she'd just met her oldest friend. 'Rickard Marmén,' she said. 'I thought you lived in Marbella.'

'I do, but my business partner has a house up here. What do you think? Do you feel like investing?' He pointed at a sign on the next house, Se vende, for sale.

'It's all a bit too model village for my taste,' she said.

He laughed heartily.

Annika nodded towards the for-sale sign. 'How much is that going for?'

'Depends what the owner needs. He's a professional poker-player from Liverpool and he puts the sign up whenever things aren't going well. The next time he wins he takes it down again.'

'You're kidding,' Annika said. 'I thought everyone who lived here was rich.'

Rickard Marmén smiled. 'That depends on what you mean by "rich". Most people here have a lot more time than people in Sweden, for instance. The tempo's much slower.'

'Naturally,' Annika said. 'If everyone spends all day playing golf, things don't have to move quickly.'

Marmén moved closer to her and gestured towards the crowd by the bar. 'I'd say most of them have worked hard, and probably still hold down jobs.'

'So why have they moved here? For tax reasons? Or is it just the weather?'

'A lot of taxes are lower in Sweden than they are in

Spain, these days,' he said. 'I think it's more to do with wine, women and song.'

Carita sailed onto the terrace and tucked her arm under Annika's. 'My dear,' she exclaimed, 'you still haven't got a drink! *Nacho, una copa de cava, por favor . . .*' Then she leaned towards Annika and lowered her voice. 'How did you get on today? Did you get a good interview with Suzette's mother?'

Annika was given a glass of sparkling wine, which she put down at once. 'I don't think the girl's run away,' she said. 'I think something terrible has happened to her.'

'What makes you say that?' Carita asked.

'She hasn't shown any sign of life in seven days. A girl with no connections in the area, who can't speak the language, what are her chances?'

'She could be with a man,' Carita said.

'Of her own free will? When she's never even had a boyfriend? She's only just turned sixteen.'

'I was sixteen when I met Nacho,' Carita said, beckoning over a tall, thin man with a receding hairline and sensitive hands. 'Annika, this is my husband.'

They greeted each other properly, Swedish-style, with a handshake.

'I understand that you're a doctor,' Annika said in English, but the man replied in Swedish.

'Paediatrician,' he said. 'It's an incredible career, taking care of the future.'

'And you work at the hospital here in Marbella?'

He nodded. 'It's first-rate. It's just been completely renovated. I'm in the neo-natal department, working with premature babies. To my mind, that's the most important type of care of all. It repays you for decades to come. Will you excuse me?' And he slid away.

'Unbelievable,' Annika said, 'to think we haven't got

space for a man like him in Swedish society. Where did you meet?'

'At a party in Beverly Hills, at the home of a girl whose father was a scriptwriter on one of those never-ending soaps that don't make it to Sweden. Nacho was so different from all the other boys, so much calmer, so much more . . . masculine.'

'And he's from Colombia?'

'From Bogotá. Victor, his father, was chief of police. We spent a few years living there in the early 1990s, in Chía, the university city twenty kilometres north of Bogotá, on the way to Zipaquirá.' She fell silent and twirled her wine-glass.

'Why did you move?' Annika asked.

Carita paused. 'We couldn't stay,' she said eventually. 'Victor led a raid against one of the big drug syndicates that ran cocaine factories in the jungle. He was murdered immediately afterwards.'

'That's terrible,' Annika said.

Carita took a large gulp of wine. 'The Colombians are a bit unusual,' she said. 'They're not content just to kill their enemies, they wipe out whole families. There mustn't be anyone left alive to inherit anything.' She smiled sadly. 'Nacho survived,' she said, 'because we were visiting my parents in Sweden. Have you had any food? The children and I spent all afternoon preparing kebabs.' She took hold of Annika's elbow and made her way back in among the guests.

'I thought you were just going to be having a few neighbours round,' Annika said. 'This must be everyone in the neighbourhood.'

'Certainly not,' Carita said firmly. 'One in five households won't join our little association because of the membership fee, which goes into the gardener's wages, pool maintenance and the satellite television dish. Isn't that just dreadful?' She drank some more wine. 'They're not welcome here. And guess what?' She whispered in Annika's ear: 'They're all Brits.'

Racism comes in all shapes and colours, Annika thought.

Friday, 7 January

13

She was running along the beach at sunrise. The sand was firm and pale grey. Large flocks of birds she didn't recognize took off, shrieking, towards the light. She had the wind in her face and salt from the sea in her hair.

I could get used to this, she thought.

Afterwards she took a long shower and decided to have a proper breakfast, for the first time in a week.

The dining room had a tiled floor and spotlights set into the ceiling. The walls were yellow, the chairs blue, the curtains striped. She ate a slice of white bread with some ham, and a yoghurt, with coffee and a glass of juice. Then she went upstairs and called the newsroom.

Berit wasn't there yet, so she asked to talk to Patrik.

'What's happening today, then?' he said, in a tone that suggested he'd been up and about for hours.

'I told you I didn't want the pictures to be sold on,' Annika said. 'Despite that, they showed up in every Spanish paper yesterday.'

Patrik sounded affronted: 'For fuck's sake, I'm not the one who sits here trying to sell pictures abroad.'

'But I told you—'

'Do I look like a messenger? You'll have to take it up with the picture desk. What are you writing for tomorrow?'

'The burglars are dead, the stolen property's been found and Suzette's still missing. I'm starting to run out of new angles,' she said.

'The whole story's gone cold,' Patrik decided. 'Get the first plane home tomorrow morning. You can spend today tidying up anything that's left.'

'I've got something about a Swede picked up in a recent drug raid down here,' she said, thinking of her deal with Niklas Linde.

'Write it up and we'll see if we can use it. For tomorrow I want a summary of what life's like for the Swedes down there. Are they all tax-dodgers, by the way?' He sounded wistful, four thousand kilometres away in the newsroom. '"Swedes flee Costa del Sol",' he added. 'Death in Paradise. End of an era. Truckloads of possessions heading north again.'

He took an audible gulp of something, probably coffee. 'I've heard there's a Swedish estate agent down there who knows all there is to know about the Costa del Sol. His name's . . . Hang on, I've got it here somewhere . . . Rickard Marmén! Do you think you can find him yourself or shall I try to get a phone number for him?'

Oh, so Mr Marmén was an estate agent as well, was he? Of course he was.

'I think I can manage,' Annika said, leafing through her notepad until she came to his number.

'Get some really doom-laden quotes that show the whole thing's about to go under,' he said, and hung up.

She called Rickard Marmén's mobile number from the hotel phone, but got his voicemail. Must have been a late night at Carita's, she thought, and left a message asking him to call her.

Then she rang Niklas Linde.

He picked up at once.

'The Swede in the drug raid,' she said. 'I need more details.'

'I'll pick you up from the hotel at eight this evening,' he said. 'See you then.'

Her mobile rang.

'Sorry I didn't answer in time, love. How are you today?' Rickard Marmén was as cheerful as ever.

'Fine, thanks. My bosses in Stockholm have just asked me to interview you in your capacity as an estate agent. What do you think?'

'We could probably sort something out. Call in at my little boutique at lunchtime. It's opposite El Corte Inglés in Puerto Banús, the big department store that—'

'I know where it is,' Annika said. 'And lunch, that's at two o'clock?'

'Say half past,' he said.

She looked at her watch. She had four hours to kill.

The yachts were packed in along the jetties in the harbour. The lower the number of the jetty, the bigger the boats. So jetty zero had boats that looked like miniature versions of the ferries that sailed between Sweden and Finland. She walked slowly past them, licking an ice-cream. There weren't many people about, a few men carrying tools on a huge vessel, a woman polishing the rail of another.

There was a sharp breeze from the sea and little warmth from the sun. She went into the Sinatra Bar, where Niklas Linde had been the first night she called him, and ordered coffee. It was decorated in pale blue and white, with a maritime theme. The coffee wasn't particularly good. She didn't like silly little cups with two centimetres of tar at the bottom. At home she brewed a litre every morning in her French cafetière, and warmed cups of it in the microwave throughout the day.

She was actually looking forward to getting back to her flat, to the rooms she hadn't moved into properly, to the cafetière in the austere kitchen, to the stack of unread paperbacks on the living-room floor, and the children's scent in their bedclothes. She was happy to be living back on Kungsholmen island.

For some reason an image of Julia Lindholm popped into her mind. Julia had been homeless for exactly the same amount of time as Annika had. The night Annika's house had burned down, Julia had been arrested and locked up for the murder of her husband.

She looked out at the boats bobbing about in the sharp wind. Julia and Alexander were going to be stuck in the rehabilitation centre at Lejondalssjön for several more months yet. And how would they feel when they finally got back to the three-room flat on Södermalm where David had been shot?

Like moving back into a nightmare, Annika thought. I couldn't have moved back into the burned-out ruins at Vinterviksvägen.

She shivered. The bar was filling. Four blonde women were taking the first *tinto verano* of the day at one of the window tables. A few British football fans were drinking Spanish beer straight from the bottle. Two young girls were giggling over a newspaper.

Annika stood up to pay at the counter. She handed the man at the till a fifty-euro note, then turned to watch the people going past outside. He put a few coins in change by her elbow. 'Hey,' she said, pointing at the pile of shrapnel. 'Shouldn't I get a few notes as well?'

The man shrugged his shoulders. 'Maybe, maybe not,' he said, and turned away.

'Hey,' she said again, louder this time. 'I paid with a fifty-euro note.' The man was absorbed in doing something with his back to her. His muscular shoulders moved under his black T-shirt. He probably needed the money for anabolic steroids. 'Give me my change,' she said, loudly and angrily.

The bar had fallen silent now. A couple came in through the door and looked round for somewhere to sit.

'Don't come in here,' Annika said. 'They cheat people out of their change.'

'Shut up,' the man behind the counter said, tossing two twenty-euro notes at her.

'Fucking crook,' Annika said, in Swedish, picked up the notes and walked out.

When she was on the quayside her mobile rang. It was Berit. 'How's life in the sun?'

'Someone just tried to cheat me out of four hundred kronor in change in some shitty bar.'

'You give them what for. How's it going with the missing girl? I saw the mum's down there with you now. Is there anything we can use to move on with this?'

'Her friends back home in Bromma, maybe,' Annika said. 'But I've already contacted them through Facebook. They haven't got back to me.'

'Facebook?' Berit said. 'I read in the business pages that Facebook's on the way out.'

'Well, of course it is,' Annika said, 'seeing as I've finally joined. Listen, I was thinking about Julia Lindholm. Has anything happened with the review of Filip Andersson's case?'

'That'll probably take months,' Berit said. 'They've got a lot to check through. The preliminary report alone ran to over a thousand pages. It was woolly and circum- stantial, full of holes and things that weren't clear. There were people shouting about a miscarriage of justice even when the first verdict was announced.'

'Did you know Filip Andersson has a sister in the

police?' Annika said. 'Nina Hoffman – Julia Lindholm's best friend.'

'She's Filip Andersson's sister? I didn't know that.'

'Don't you think it's odd that two such criminal individuals as Filip Andersson and Yvonne Nordin should have a sister who's a cop?'

It sounded as if Berit was leafing through a paper. 'I don't know,' she said. 'To me it seems more like different sides of the same coin. Opposite reactions to the same sort of upbringing, so to speak.'

'So Nina's the white sheep of the family?'

'Stranger things have happened. Bill Clinton has a brother who's a petty crook. And my cousin Klas-Göran's done time as well.'

'Bill Clinton's brother's done time?'

'Clinton pardoned him on his last day as president, the twentieth of January 2001. Him and a hundred and thirty-nine other criminals. It's the custom for American presidents to do that. What's your sister up to, these days, by the way?'

Annika was taken aback. 'Birgitta? No idea. I don't even know where she lives.'

The silence that followed spoke volumes.

'Do you think I should try to contact Suzette's friends?' Berit eventually asked.

'It might make more sense to try Sebastian Söderström's Swedish relatives,' Annika said, breathing a sigh of relief. 'See if they have any idea where the girl might be.'

'We've already tried, but no one wants to talk.'

'What about Astrid Paulson, then? Everyone seems to be saying that she was the only person who got on well with Suzette. Maybe she's got family who might know something.'

'I'll give it a try,' Berit said. 'Have you been able to do

any work on that series of articles Patrik keeps going on about?'

'The Costa Cocaine? I haven't actually seen a single rolled-up euro note, let alone any drugs.'

They arranged to meet on Monday and ended the call.

Annika had reached the end of the quay. She was outside a shop selling bags where even the cheapest cost five hundred euros.

She turned her back on its window and looked up 'Nina H, police' on her phone. She clicked 'call' and waited to be connected, then everything went quiet. The voice that came on was metallic: *Telefonica le informa, que actualmente no es posible connectar al numero llamado. Telefonica le informa . . .* She ended the call. Telefonica was one of the big Spanish telecom companies, but why was their message cutting in on Nina Hoffman's Swedish mobile? Was Nina in Spain, or was there something wrong with the signal on her own mobile?

She tried again.

Telefonica le informa, que actualmente no es posible . . .

She gave up and looked at the time. Twenty past two.

Time to visit Rickard Marmén.

The estate agency was hidden behind a British bookshop. It wasn't much more than a hole in the wall. A dozen fairly faded advertisements for various properties were stuck in the window.

Marmén was sitting behind a desk and typing at a computer when Annika walked in. 'Ah, here you are, my dear,' he said, getting up and kissing her on both cheeks. 'Is the *Evening Post* thinking of buying an apartment in Puerto Banús?'

'Not exactly,' she said. 'How's business?'

'Fucking awful,' he said. 'There's no movement at all. It's this damn Operation Malaya.'

Annika had no idea what he was talking about, which must have shown on her face because he went on, 'One hundred and two people have been arrested for corruption in the property market down here, including the whole of Marbella's previous town council. The bribes for illegal planning permission were astonishing. The place was awash with money. The head of the highways department turned out to have three farmhouses, each of which was the size of Stockholm City Hall. He had at least a hundred racehorses and a genuine Miró above his jacuzzi.'

Annika laughed. 'And we thought it was a scandal when our old prime minister used the wrong sort of scaffolding at his country house.'

Marmén leaned back happily in his chair. 'The mayor was arrested in her bedroom where she was recuperating after her latest liposuction. Ten council workmen were busy fitting a new kitchen for her. Now every application for planning permission over the past twenty years is being investigated with a fine-tooth comb. Until that's done, the banks are refusing to authorize any mortgages. Talk about putting a dampener on the market. It'll take at least a year before things pick up. A glass of wine, perhaps?'

She shook her head. 'Tell me how the Swedish colony has reacted to the death of the Söderström family,' she said. 'Do you think it'll scare Swedes away from the Costa del Sol?'

'They've already been scared off,' Rickard Marmén said. 'Not by crime, but by the price of property. Operation Malaya has stopped prices going up even more, but you still won't find a flat in Marbella for less than three million kronor, or a terraced house for less than four. The smallest detached houses cost at least six million, and you won't get a normal family villa for under thirteen. Around Alicante you can get the same properties for around half the price.'

'Why's everything so expensive at the moment?' Annika asked.

Marmén threw out his hands. 'Because Marbella is exclusive and Alicante is common. People pay for the address. See this!' He opened a website and turned the screen towards Annika. 'This is a vacant plot with no view on the hill just below Carita's house. The owner's asking five point six million euros for it.'

Annika looked at the picture. There was a rusty lamp-post by the side of the road. A tarmac drive, lined with thistles and brambles, led down to an abandoned set of foundations in a hollow. Beyond it the undergrowth took over. 'Fifty million kronor! That must be a joke.'

'It's not,' Marmén said, turning the screen back again. 'Mind you, the owner hasn't managed to get shot of it.'

'So people aren't scared of crime?'

He became serious. 'Even if break-ins involving gas are common, this is the first time anyone has died,' he said. 'My experience is that people carry on living in the same houses, even after they've been gassed. A lot of them are in a bad way, much worse than after an ordinary break-in, but they still stay. And I don't think there are as many muggings as there are in Stockholm or as much street crime. I've got no figures for that, but it hardly ever happens.'

'But there are so many criminal gangs here,' she said, remembering Knut Garen's statistics: 420 gangs carrying out more than thirty contract killings each year in the Málaga area alone.

Marmén thought for a moment. 'Nobody notices them,' he said. 'What you see in the street are a lot of police cars, a lot of Guardia Civil, a lot of police officers on the beat or on motorbikes. That means people feel safe, not scared.'

Annika put her pen on her pad. This wasn't going to make much of an article.

'Am I disappointing you?' the estate agent asked.

She laughed. 'Not me,' she said. 'My head of news, maybe. He wanted the headline "Swedes flee Costa del Sol".'

'I don't think he's likely to be proved right,' Marmén said. 'So, how are things going for the big papers these days? Do they still pay for lunch?'

'Definitely,' Annika said.

That afternoon she was lying on the bed in her hotel room reading a Harlan Coben thriller when she fell asleep. She dreamed of Kalle and Ellen: they were missing, and she was searching for them in a sterile lunar landscape with no water or vegetation.

She felt incredibly thirsty when she woke up.

As she showered and got ready for the evening, she tried calling Nina Hoffman twice. This time the phone rang and rang until the call was cut off automatically.

She called Carita Halling Gonzales and thanked her for being so great to work with, gave her the details for the invoice, and said she would be flying home the next morning.

'We can stay in touch, can't we?' Carita said. 'Maybe you'll be down here again.'

Annika said, 'Sure', remembering Patrik's series of articles.

She was standing outside the hotel in good time.

Niklas Linde was almost half an hour late. 'Sorry, sorry,' he said, with a grin. 'I'm starting to get a bit Spanish.'

She got into the car without smiling. She didn't like being made to wait. 'Okay,' she said, slamming the door. 'How many arrests, how many suspects, where, when and how were they arrested, what does the prosecutor say, and what about the defence?'

'First I'm going to make sure you have something to eat,' he said, as he drove under the motorway.

She folded her arms over her chest. 'I'm not hungry,' she said, then realized she had lied.

Niklas Linde smiled at her. He turned off into a narrow street that led to an even narrower road that went on up the mountainside. After just a couple of minutes the car was surrounded by total darkness, which made Annika feel both relieved and nervous. She couldn't see the drop at the edge of the twisting road, but the drawback was that the view ahead was almost as bad.

'Have you been through the stolen property in the thieves' truck?' she asked, holding onto the dashboard as the car went round a right-hand hairpin.

'Everything seems to be there, apart from the safe.'

'Apart from the safe,' she echoed. 'Now, where could that have got to?'

'If it was brought out in the back of the truck along with everything else, there'd have been some evidence of it, but there was nothing.'

'What sort of evidence would a safe leave?'

'It was cemented into a brick wall in the villa. The thieves knocked the wall down to get it out. There'd have been grit, cement dust and fragments of brick somewhere in the back of the truck if it had ever been in there.'

'Maybe they put the safe in a bag?' Annika suggested.

Niklas Linde looked away from the road to stare at her instead.

'Please, the road,' Annika said, pointing in front of her.

The police officer sighed. 'It wasn't a huge safe,' he said, 'but it wasn't the sort of thing you could just chuck around. It would have taken two people to move it. I think there's another explanation.'

They drove round a jutting cliff, and a moment later a built-up area appeared on the mountainside in front of them. Row after row of white houses clung to the slope, lit by streetlamps and small neon signs. The glow from televisions flickered in windows.

'Where's this?' Annika asked.

'Istán,' Linde said. 'It means "spring". It was found-ed by the Moors in the thirteenth century. I know the woman who runs the restaurant in the square.'

They parked on a hill above the little town and walked slowly down through the cobbled streets. There was a mild breeze that smelt of herbs. Annika could see the lights of the coast twinkling in the distance, in another age, another world. The sound of running water followed them. There were drinking fountains dotted around, fed by water brought along underground channels from mountain springs.

Suddenly Annika stopped. 'I know what happened to the safe,' she said.

Linde smiled. 'Let's hear it.'

'The first time we met, you told me you'd found evidence of two vehicles and three people outside the Söderström family house. The third person didn't die in the truck. The third person wasn't interested in the stolen property, just the safe. The third person took it with them, in the other car.'

'That's probably correct,' Linde said, walking on down the street, then pushing open a saloon-style door. He ushered Annika in ahead of him, and she stepped through to find herself in a brightly lit neighbour-hood bar.

A radiantly beautiful Spanish woman with swirling hair and a low-cut top let out a cry of delight when she caught sight of Linde. She rushed over to him and kissed him warmly on both cheeks. Their Spanish sounded like the water in the channels running beneath the streets.

'This is a friend of mine, Annika,' he said in English, and the woman turned to her. Her smile faded slightly.

'*Una mesa para dos*,' she said, spinning round and heading further into the restaurant.

Annika and Linde followed her.

They were shown to the table in the far corner. The woman lit a candle with a yellow Bic lighter, gave them two dog-eared menus in Spanish and sailed off towards the bar.

'How well do you know her?' Annika asked.

The policeman's eyes twinkled. 'Fairly well,' he said, then set to studying the menu.

Annika felt strangely subdued. She picked up the laminated card and looked at the words without seeing them. She didn't like the beautiful Spanish woman. 'What's been happening in the search for Suzette?' she asked, trying to sound laid-back and unconcerned.

'It's like she's been swallowed up by the ground. According to her mobile operator, her phone hasn't been switched on since last Thursday. Would you like me to order for you?'

Annika put the menu down on the tablecloth. '*Por favor.*'

He ordered a long list of small dishes that flowed onto the table whenever the kitchen finished preparing them. He drank beer, Annika *agua con gas*.

'Shall we talk about this drug raid?' she asked, as the dishes started to empty. 'I need some meat on the bones if I'm going to write a whole article.'

Linde thought for a few moments. 'If you tell me what

happened to your finger,' he said, pointing at her left hand.

She hesitated, but saw no reason not to tell the truth. 'Two men dragged me into an alleyway and cut it open last winter,' she said. 'They told me not to snoop. They didn't like a story I was working on.'

'Do you know who they were?'

She shook her head.

'Do you want me to find out for you? Catch them and beat them up?'

She smiled at him.

'Have you got a flash on that camera?' he asked.

'Of course.'

He looked at his watch. 'Maybe you can come along on something, if you want,' he said. 'We're going to try to pick up one of the men later tonight. You'd have to stand well back and not show any identifiable police officers in your pictures.'

Her pulse rate went up a little. 'A raid?' she said. 'To-night?'

He leaned closer to her. 'Okay, this is how it is,' he said, lowering his voice, even though they had to be the only people in the restaurant who understood Swedish. 'Greco, the drugs unit of the Spanish police, had been tracking two shipments of coke that were being deliv-ered simultaneously to the harbour in Algeciras. They were both in refrigerated cargoes of fruit from South America. One was melons in the Apits warehouse in La Campana, and the other was a container of oranges from Argentina.'

'And where are the oranges now?'

He gave her a wry smile. 'Exactly,' he said. 'The oranges are on a lorry, on their way to Malmö.'

'And you've switched the contents?' Annika said.

Linde clenched his jaw. 'We've got a transmitter on the

lorry, but we haven't been able to switch the cargo. It's a gamble. My colleagues in Greco in Málaga can locate the exact position of the lorry down to ten metres. The problem is that the prospective recipients are getting nervous. They know that half the shipment has been seized, and they think there's something dodgy about the other half.'

'Okay,' Annika said, opening a fresh page in her notepad. 'Tell me what you want the article to say.'

'That Greco had been following the impounded shipment for several months . . .'

'Remind me, what does Greco stand for again?'

Linde looked annoyed. 'Does that matter? They made their move when the cargo had been unloaded and was ready for distribution, which meant they could catch both the recipients and the suppliers.'

'When did this happen?'

'Early morning, Thursday, the thirtieth of December.'

'How?'

He took a sip of beer and told her that the police had rented several units in the same *polígono* as the fruit warehouse in question. They had followed the shipment from the moment it was unloaded in the large harbour at Algeciras, a city some way west of Marbella, until it arrived in La Campana by lorry. Officers from Greco had lain in wait in the rented units, with additional support from the riot police and police marksmen, and watched as the fruit was unloaded. They had waited until the recipients showed up, then made their move.

Annika was taking a lot of notes, writing quickly. 'How many arrests?'

'Five in the warehouse. The lorry driver was arrested at his home in Estepona later the same morning. Tonight we're going to pick up the last member of the gang, one of the minor players. He usually acts as a courier, and was supposed to be driving the shipment up to Malmö via Berlin.'

Annika put her pen down. 'But how were they able to unload a whole container full of cocaine and pretend it contained melons? Doesn't anyone check that sort of thing in Customs?'

Linde burst out laughing. 'The cocaine wasn't inside the container,' he said. 'That was full of melons. A hell of a lot of melons, several tons, in fact. You can't begin to imagine the smell.'

'It was a refrigerated container, you said. That ought to keep them for at least a week.'

The policeman pointed a finger at her as if it was a pistol. 'Bullseye,' he said. 'It wasn't a refrigerated container. There were seven hundred kilos of cocaine inside the walls of the container instead of insulation.'

'And all the paperwork was in order?'

'Pure as the driven snow.' He glanced at his watch, then waved to the waitress. She sent one of the men behind the bar over with the bill.

'Let me,' Annika said, taking out her credit card.

'Carmen only takes cash,' Linde said.

'You're kidding,' Annika said. 'Her name's Carmen?'

He stood up, put his jacket on and grinned.

They walked back up the hill towards the car in silence. The sound of Spanish television, laughing voices and the clatter of crockery followed them. The cacophony leaked out onto the pavement with the light from tapas bars and open living-room windows. Two teenage boys on a moped passed them with just a few centimetres to spare, and four cats leaped up, startled, from a large bin. The wind was chilly now and Annika wished she had brought a jacket.

'Are you cold?' Linde asked, and before she had time to answer he had put his arm round her and pulled her towards him, stroking her upper arm with his other hand to warm it.

She let herself be held, leaning into him, her hip bumping against him with every step. The exhaust fumes of the moped lingered. He pulled her closer and his steps became slower, until in the end he stopped. He turned to face her, with his arms round her shoulders. She let her own hands, which she had been holding folded to her chest, fall, then put them round his back, over the rough cotton of his jacket, pulling him to her.

Yes, she thought. I want this.

He kissed her. His mouth was warm and salty and tasted of garlic. His leg slid between her thighs.

Her breathing quickened, and she let go of him.

His eyes were twinkling. 'Shall we go and catch some bad guys?' he asked, taking a step back from her but keeping his arm round her shoulders. They carried on walking.

She let her arm slide down his back to his waist. Their hips bumped against each other all the way up the long slope.

Saturday, 8 January

14

The house was on a back-street in the neighbouring town of San Pedro. It was in a corner, beside a little square lined with orange trees, two storeys high, originally white but discoloured by damp and pollution. The windows were covered with rusty black bars. The balcony on the upper floor was hung with towelling nappies put out to dry.

'The drug-runner has children?' Annika asked, in a low voice.

'He rents a room on the ground floor from the family that owns the house,' Niklas Linde replied, then left her in a doorway on the other side of the square. She pulled up the zip of the rough, oversized jacket she had been lent.

She watched the police officer walk slowly and silently along the pavement, towards his Spanish colleagues who were gathered in a side-street. The movement of his muscles was visible under his loose clothing. He can have anyone he wants, she thought, and he knows it.

The suspected drug-runner wasn't at home. Right now he was in a nightclub called Dreamers down in Puerto Banús. He had informed the Spanish police of his whereabouts, albeit unwittingly, of course. He had called a woman named Betty and tried to persuade her to meet him, but Betty was tired and cross and had turned him down. Because the officers from Greco had been bugging his mobile for four months, they had known perfectly well that Betty wouldn't go. She hated it when he called her, drunk, from various bars and hang-outs. It made her feel 'cheap'. She didn't think he showed her enough 'respect'.

Linde had told her all of this while they were sitting in the car outside one of Greco's safe-houses as the officers inside planned the impending arrest.

Annika pulled her hands up into the jacket sleeves and stamped her feet. She stared at the drug-runner's window and thought about Betty. Had they had sex in there? How had that made Betty feel? Valued and respected? She stifled a yawn.

Her flight to Stockholm would take off in eight hours.

Then she heard stumbling footsteps approaching the square. They were a mixture of dragging and tottering, as if someone was trying hard not to fall.

She retreated deeper into the doorway and took out the camera. She switched it on, holding it with the lens pointing down. She had been given strict instructions not to test the distance to the door in the darkness until the man had been arrested because the red dot of the gauge could be mistaken for the laser sight on a rifle.

Then she saw a skinny person stumbling down the street on the other side of the square. He was a fairly young man with spiked hair that looked almost blond in the faint light. He took a few steps forward, then a couple to the side, seriously drunk. He stopped outside the door and swayed.

It was a good thing Betty had stayed at home.

He spent a long time fumbling with the key before he got it into the lock.

Then she saw a series of shadows emerge from the alleyways and streets around the house.

She raised her camera.

Several plain-clothes police officers and two in uniform reached the door just before it clicked shut. A moment later the man was outside again, a Spanish policeman holding him under each arm. His feet were dragging along the ground, and his face showed an expression of total surprise. He kept twisting his head from one policeman to the other, then started to protest in a pronounced Stockholm accent. 'What the fuck's all this? Eh? Come on, lads, what are you playing at?'

Annika touched the camera button lightly to get the image in focus, so that the man was sharply depicted in the middle of the picture, then pressed it down. For an instant, the flash lit the whole square. She waited a couple of seconds, then took another picture.

'What the fuck? *Joder!*'

The drug-runner had decided he didn't want to go with the policemen. He started waving his arms and kicking, but to little effect.

'*Cabrones! Imbéciles!* Let go, for fuck's sake! *Fucking hell!*'

A few moments later he was in the back seat of a Guardia Civil car, handcuffed, with one policeman beside him, one in front and another behind the wheel.

The car disappeared down the road.

Linde appeared beside her.

'You said the Swede had already been arrested,' Annika said.

He grinned. 'He has now,' he said, then leaned over and kissed her.

'What's his name?' Annika whispered, into his teeth.

'Jocke Zarco Martinez. Are we going back to yours or mine?'

213

She pulled away and looked down at the camera. 'I'm flying home in a few hours.'

'You can do a lot in a few hours.'

She shook her head and looked up at him. 'No,' she said.

He lowered his head for a moment, then laughed. 'Come on,' he said. 'I'll drive you back to your hotel.'

He didn't hold her on the way back to the car.

They got into the BMW without a word, and drove in silence.

Far too soon he pulled up in front of the entrance.

'It's not that I don't want to,' she said.

He glanced at her. 'What is it, then?'

She decided to be completely honest. 'I daren't,' she said. 'It's been so long that I don't even know if I could.'

He laughed again, raised his hand and stroked her cheek. 'You don't have to worry,' he said. 'It's like riding a bike.'

'How long are you going to be down here?'

'Don't know. I travel back and forth quite a bit. Why?'

She had been about to ask if he was on his way back to Sweden, where he lived when he was at home, if he had anyone waiting for him. Whether he would still be here if she was sent back to write about Patrik's Costa Cocaine. But she just picked up her bag, opened the door and climbed out.

When the tail-lights disappeared round the corner of El Corte Inglés she had to bite her lip to stop herself crying.

She wrote a piece about the Swede's arrest, uploaded the photographs, sent it all to Stockholm and slept for two hours. Then she got up, packed her clothes and laptop, went down to Reception and paid for her and

214

Lenita Söderström's rooms with her personal Visa card. She left a note for Lenita saying she had gone back to Stockholm. Just in case anything happened, she left her mobile number.

She pulled out onto the motorway, which was now practically empty of vehicles, drove past the roadworks and La Cañada, and turned onto the toll motorway. Just before Torremolinos she passed a road accident. A lorry with French plates had turned over, spilling its load onto the carriageway, and she had to crawl past slowly on the hard shoulder. In the rear-view mirror she could see a Muslim woman wailing and beating her hands on her knees.

She arrived at the airport two and a half hours before her flight.

She spent an hour and a quarter trying to find the car-hire company's depot. She was sweating by the time she reached the check-in desk. In security, they went through her bag, finding things she'd forgotten about, including a shrivelled, half-eaten apple and a letter-opener with the advertising slogan '*Evening Post* – sharp and to the point'. They took the letter-opener and made her put her lip-gloss in a see-through plastic bag.

'Are you serious?' Annika asked the security guard, when he handed her the little bag. 'Do you really think I'm *not* going to blow the plane up just because my lip-gloss is in here?'

'*No comprendo*,' the guard said.

'Exactly,' Annika said, taking her deadly lip-gloss and putting it straight back in her bag. 'You really don't understand anything.'

The plane took off almost on schedule and she fell asleep at once.

She woke up at Arlanda when the wheels hit the runway. Her Harlan Coben book was on the floor and the bottle of water she'd bought from Upper Crust in the departure lounge had leaked in the seat pocket in front of her.

Confused and slightly giddy, she was swept out of the plane and into the terminal building, through deserted corridors, past Passport Control and off towards the baggage hall. She had to wait more than an hour for her case.

It was dark by the time she finally emerged from Arrivals. It was snowing, and taxi drivers from several independent companies threw themselves at her, trying to grab her case, but she snapped at them and struggled towards a Taxi Stockholm car. Over the years she had tried to be open-minded and liberal, trying all sorts of obscure little firms, but after being shouted at and turfed out once too often because she wanted to pay by card or couldn't tell them the way to her destination, she had given up.

The Taxi Stockholm driver took her case, opened the door for her, then didn't say a word. Perfect.

She tried to read the evening papers in the back seat, but started to feel sick and gave up.

At five o'clock that afternoon she unlocked the door to her as yet unfurnished flat. The rooms were big and black, and there was a faint hiss from an air-vent somewhere.

She put her case and bag on the floor and hurried round turning on lights. In every window she could see her own reflection, a hollow-eyed woman with unkempt hair and skinny arms.

She turned away from her many selves, threw herself onto the bed and grabbed the phone. She rang the head of news, and sighed quietly when Patrik answered. 'I thought Sjölander was supposed to be working,' she said. 'Isn't this your day off?'

216

'Just sorting out a few loose ends,' he said. 'What have you got?'

She shut her eyes and rested her forehead against the palm of her hand. 'I've been sitting in a plane all day, and got home three minutes ago. What do you think I've got?'

'The search for Suzette. You can check if anything's happened, can't you? Anything new about how the thieves died? A picture of the mother sitting on her missing daughter's bed hugging a stuffed toy?'

Exhaustion gave way to anger. She stood up beside the bed, holding the phone. 'At four o'clock this morning I sent an article and photographs of a Swedish citizen being arrested in a drugs raid in San Pedro outside Marbella. I think I've filled my quota of exclusives on this particular day off. If you think your new job means you can treat me like some nineteen-year-old temp, you're seriously mistaken.'

There was silence.

'Hello?' Annika said.

'Just so you know,' Patrik said, 'I've got this call on speaker-phone.'

'Excellent,' Annika said. 'In that case, your friends can note that I'm taking next week off as time owing. I've been working twenty hours a day for five days in a row. I'll be in on Monday to put in a claim for expenses.'

'What do you mean, expenses? Your ticket was bought for you.'

'Fuck you,' Annika said, and hung up.

She slumped onto the bed again, picked up the evening papers that she'd thrown on the floor and leaned back against the pillows to read them.

Her piece about the raid was there. It probably hadn't made it into the earlier regional edition, but Niklas Linde had said that wouldn't matter.

217

She studied the pictures. They were certainly dramatic. The two uniformed officers were in the foreground, the reflective strips on their jackets shining like lasers in the flash. The Swede was waving his arms and kicking in protest, and his face was more or less obscured. Linde's face was turned away and pretty much unidentifiable.

The text was short and to the point: Spanish police had crushed a cocaine-smuggling operation shipping drugs from the Costa del Sol to large parts of northern Europe; she had listed the facts about the raid in La Campana, seven hundred kilos found in a warehouse, melons from Brazil; last night's arrest was the final one in the series; charges would be laid and the trials prepared.

She let the paper fall to her lap and wondered what she felt about writing an article to order like that. Nothing much, she decided. There was always someone who stood to gain from a piece of journalism. The only difference this time was that she was fully aware of the manipulation, although she would never admit that to her bosses at the paper.

She looked through the rest of the news. A UN helicopter had crashed in Nepal. Sweden's first bed-and-breakfast for nudists was due to open in Skåne. A singer with silicon breasts had turned down the opportunity to appear in the Swedish heats of the Eurovision Song Contest, which had led to crisis talks at Swedish Television last night.

She dropped the paper onto the floor and picked up its rival. The first thing that struck her when she reached the editorial was her own picture byline from the *Evening Post* and a portrait of Jimmy Halenius. Between them hovered the picture taken outside the Järnet restaurant. 'In the hands of power,' the headline read. The text was a piece of indignant bluster, full of insinuating questions

218

such as 'How much did they really have to drink?' and 'Should those in power and those holding them to account really have an intimate relationship?', as well as 'Did Halenius neglect his duties?'

She picked up the phone and called her editor-in-chief. 'Have you seen the opposition's editorial?' she asked, without bothering to say hello.

'I've spoken to their editor-in-chief,' Anders Schyman replied. 'If they don't drop this now, we're going to lay siege to every bar in the vicinity of their offices, take pictures of all their reporters and reveal all their sources. I'll be replying in our editorial tomorrow. We will never reveal our sources, we will never surrender our expense receipts, and we will never go into any detail about what the two of you discussed.'

'Good,' Annika said.

'What did you discuss, by the way? And how much did you drink? And who the hell paid?'

She collapsed into a little ball. 'Okay,' she said. 'To take them one by one: none of your business, I drank water, and Halenius paid. Not his department.'

'How do you know him?'

She hesitated. 'I grew up with his cousin.'

'I heard you on the speaker-phone a little while ago. You really should watch your language, you know.' He hung up.

She stayed on the bed for a while, struggling against almost overwhelming self-pity. She did nothing but stand up for that fucking newspaper, and what did she get in return, apart from demands, criticism and public humiliation over her choice of dinner-partner?

She cried for something like thirty seconds, then got up and went out into the hall for her suitcase. The bathroom was equipped with a washing-machine and a tumble-dryer, so she emptied her case straight into the machine and started the quick-wash programme. She took her laptop with her into the kitchen, plugged the modem into the phone socket and prayed to God there was an Internet connection.

There was.

She sat on one of the kitchen chairs and surfed in cyberspace. Apart from the usual disasters, gossip and political squabbling, it didn't look as if anything much had happened in the world. Then she went onto her Facebook profile. She had eleven new messages: one was from Amanda Andersson, one from Sandra Holgersson, two from Klara Evertsson-Hedberg and seven from Polly Sandman. All of Suzette's friends had replied to her. Her pulse quickened as she opened the most recent message, the one from Amanda.

'I think your a gutter reporter who likes wallowing in other people's mizery,' she read.

'Learn to spell first,' Annika said out loud, and clicked to open the next, from Sandra.

'Do you really work for a newspaper? Can you get tickets for *X Factor*?'

For a moment she considered replying, then decided against it.

Klara was financially minded. She offered to give an interview for ten thousand kronor. In her second message she lowered the fee to five hundred.

Annika didn't answer her either.

Polly was the literary type, as the seven messages suggested. There were poems, reflections and thoughts about Suzette, school, boys and life in general. Annika read through them and composed a reply: 'Dear Polly, what lovely poems and thoughts. Thanks for letting me read them. If you feel like writing anything longer, I know my newspaper runs a short-story competition for teenagers up to eighteen years old. I understand that you haven't heard anything from Suzette. If you do, please feel free to contact me again.' She signed off with both her first and last name, to maintain a professional tone. She was careful not to give her mobile number – she didn't want anyone shouting at her about her ethics or asking about *X Factor* tickets.

She was about to shut down the laptop when her mobile rang. The number was withheld.

'Annika? Hi, this is Nina Hoffman.'

She stood up so quickly she hit her head on the lamp. 'Hello,' she said, rubbing the bump.

'You left a message on my voicemail a few days ago. It sounded urgent. Has something happened?'

With one hand, Annika stopped the lamp swinging and remembered the crackly Telefonica voice on Nina's mobile. 'Yes, I've tried calling you a few times. Have you been in Spain recently?'

'Er, yes. I've just had a week's holiday on Tenerife. Why?'

'I went to see Julia and Alexander,' Annika said, going out into the hall and towards her bedroom. 'We were talking about you, and Julia told me something I didn't know.'

Nina waited. 'Oh?' she said eventually.

Annika sat down on the bed. 'Filip Andersson is your brother,' she said, and noticed that her heart was beating faster. 'Why didn't you say something?'

'Like what?'

'And Yvonne Nordin was your sister.'

'You mean I'm under some kind of obligation to tell you who I happen to be related to?'

Annika tried to focus. She could see Nina in front of her, the police uniform, the brown hair in a ponytail, the straight shoulders and stiff creases, the sense of restrained power, her efficient calm that night when

221

they had stumbled upon the murder scene in Sankt Paulsgatan. *Annika, get out of here. 1617 to Control, we have a code twenty-three, possibly twenty-four, and need reinforcements. I can see two, correction, three injured, possibly deceased . . .*

'But we've talked about that night so many times,' Annika said. 'I kept going on about Filip Andersson, the murders, that I thought he might be innocent, about whether he knew David Lindholm. You listened to all my theories about David's women, Yvonne Nordin among them, you even helped me get hold of a photograph of her, and throughout all that you didn't say that they were your brother and sister. Don't you see how odd that looks?'

Nina was silent for a long while. Then she asked, 'Would you have mentioned it, if they'd been your brother and sister?'

'Of course!'

'So if you had any criminals close to you, or if you yourself had committed a crime, you'd have told me all about it straight away?'

'Absolutely.'

'You've killed someone. Why haven't you ever mentioned that?'

Now it was Annika's turn to be silent. 'That's hardly relevant,' she said at last. She hated being reminded of her ex-boyfriend. It felt like another life.

'Yes, it is, in the same way that it's relevant that my siblings are criminals.'

'This changes everything, don't you see?' Annika said. 'It feels like you've been deceiving me all along.'

'Well, I haven't,' Nina said. 'I've never lied to you.'

'You must have known that David and Filip knew each other, for instance. How long for?'

Nina let out a sigh. 'They grew up together,' she said.

'David and Filip and Yvonne and little Veronica were more like brothers and sisters than anything else. More than they ever were with me.'

Annika screwed her eyes shut and tried to fit the pieces in place.

David Lindholm, the most famous policeman in Sweden, had married the girl from Södermanland, Julia Hensen, who had grown up next door to her friend Nina Hoffman. David himself had grown up alongside Filip Andersson, who had two sisters, the insane killer Yvonne Nordin, and police officer Nina Hoffman, whose best friend Julia he had gone on to marry, even though he was simultaneously having an affair with Yvonne Nordin, and got her pregnant . . .

'How long had you known David Lindholm?' she asked.

'The first time I met David was when he lectured at Police Academy.'

'So you didn't grow up with him?'

'I suppose I must have bumped into him when I was little, and of course I knew who he was, but I didn't know him. Mum and I moved to Tenerife when I was three, and by that time Filip and Yvonne were already grown up. I ended up outside Valla when I was nine, and that's where I got to know Julia.'

'You once told me,' Annika said slowly, 'that David came up to you and Julia after that lecture at the Police Academy. Did he know who you were?'

'Obviously. I think he was extremely curious to see what had become of me.'

'But he pretended to be more interested in Julia?'

'He didn't have to pretend. I mean, he married her.'

There was a subtext of bitterness, unspoken, but it was there.

Annika rubbed her head. 'The murders on Sankt

223

Paulsgatan took place nearly five years ago. When did you realize that Filip and Yvonne were involved?'

'When Filip was arrested. That was the worst moment of my life.'

'And Yvonne? She was the one who did it, after all. When did you realize that?'

'When Filip told me, after she was dead. But I hadn't spoken to Yvonne for years before that. I lost contact with her after the abortion. She withdrew, became a bit peculiar.'

'The abortion?' Annika said, putting her hand on her forehead. 'You mean when she aborted her and David's child?'

'The same time that Julia was pregnant with Alexander,' Nina confirmed. She fell silent for a few moments. 'It's not like you think,' she said finally. 'I never meant to hide anything, but my family and childhood are a bit of an open wound for me.'

Annika didn't know what to say.

When Nina went on, her voice was thin and distant. 'I loved my mum, but she was hardly capable of looking after herself. Filip and Yvonne slipped away from her because she couldn't take care of them. I was lucky, because I had Julia's family. It's always felt like . . . like an obligation, somehow. As if I have some kind of duty to put everything right.'

Was that why you joined the police? Annika thought, but didn't say.

'Somewhere I believe in people's innate goodness,' Nina continued, her voice stronger now. 'I think everyone can change, if we're just given the chance. Mum tried, and it worked for a while, but she was too damaged for it to last.'

'Is your mum dead?' Annika asked cautiously.

'Nine years ago. She died the day after David and

Julia got married. Now all the others are gone too, apart from Filip.'

Annika was making an effort to keep up. 'You said there were four of them who were like a family?' she said. 'David, Filip, Yvonne and . . . who was the fourth?'

'Little Veronica. Veronica Paulson. But she's dead too.'

'Did you know her as well?'

Nina sighed deeply. 'Not exactly. She and her mum came to visit us on Tenerife a couple of times, but I haven't seen her since I moved back to Sweden.'

'She can't have been that old. How did she die?'

Nina sounded surprised when she replied. 'You've just been writing loads of articles about that. She was murdered a few days ago.'

Everything around Annika stopped. There was total silence inside her head and time stood still. 'What do you mean?' she said, scarcely able to breathe.

'She married that ice-hockey player,' Nina said. 'Sebastian Söderström.'

Part 2
AFTER EASTER

The Little Troll-Girl
with the Matches

She arrived at Gudagården with no shoes and wearing a tattered dress. The lady from the Child Welfare Commission shoved her out of the car. The gravel on the drive was as sharp as glass beneath her feet.

'Curtsy to your foster-mother and foster-father,' the lady said, driving her forward towards the wall of people.

She stared at the ground. The people stared at her.

'She looks like a troll,' Foster-mother said.

The lady kicked the back of her knee and forced her head down. Quick as a polecat she spun round and bit the lady's hand. Then she ran away across the gravel, cutting the soles of her feet.

After night had fallen, Foster-father pulled her down from the haystack. She landed on the stone floor hard on her hip. 'Let's see if we can't whip the Devil out of you,' he said, raising his riding-crop. And he beat her and beat her and beat her until the skin on her thighs and buttocks was in ribbons. Then he locked the door. She fell asleep in the hay and dreamed that she was lying in an anthill. The insects were eating into her legs and backside, constructing passageways under her skin, a whole society with paths and storerooms and nurseries and everything else ants needed, everything Sigrid had told her about the amazing life of ants.

When she woke up day had already broken. The hay was stuck to the scabs on her legs. She knew she needed to wash.

She found a loose plank at the back of the shed. The hole was narrow, and it was hard to get her head through, but her body slid after it, as if she was a little worm.

She had seen a lake out of the car window. It must be close by.

She took a long detour round the farm. There was nobody in sight.

She found a small beach with white sand under a large oak. She got into the water still wearing her dress and underwear. Her legs stung.

A wall-eyed boy caught sight of her when she was creeping back towards the farm. He called for Foster-father, who came rushing out, his big boots flapping. He was quick and she was weak with hunger and pain.

He tore her dress off and flayed the skin off her back as well.

'You are never, ever to run away from this farm again,' Foster-father hissed in her ear. 'If you do, I'll kill you.'

But she ran away, and he beat her, and she ran away, and he beat her.

In the end he got tired of beating her, and then she stopped running away.

She was given a room in the loft, with the baby swallows and the wasps' nests. From the crack of dawn the swallow parents would start flying in and out, bringing food to their young, gathering it in their beaks and stomachs, then vomiting it for their babies. Sigrid had told her about the amazing life of birds.

Sigrid had told her fairy tales as well. She had told her about other girls who also had a hard life, like the Little Match Girl.

'So the little girl wandered along with her little feet red and blue with cold. She was carrying a great pile of matches in an old apron and she held one bundle in her hand as she walked. No one had bought any from her all day, no one had given her a halfpenny. Hungry and frozen, she went on her way, so woebegone, poor little thing! The snowflakes fell upon her long fair hair that curled so prettily at the nape of her neck, but she certainly wasn't thinking about how nice she looked . . .'

The girl had unruly black hair that the Child Welfare Committee had cut short, so short, to get rid of the lice. She wasn't a pretty girl, she was a little troll girl. She knew that because Foster-mother had told her. She was the Troll Girl with the Matches, even though she hadn't sold matches but illicit homebrew, and it had all been going so well until Foster-mother ended up in prison and the Child Welfare Committee came to take her away.

At night she could see out through a crack in the roof, and once she saw a falling star.

The Little Match Girl had also seen a falling star in the fairy tale.

'Her old granny, the only one who had been kind to her but who was now dead, had said that when a star falls a soul goes up to God . . .'

She wondered who was going up to heaven this time, and clasped her hands together and prayed to the Lord: O Father, let it be Foster-father next time, and then Wall-eye.

And she thought that one day she herself would be a grandmother, the sort who was kind to troll girls nobody liked.

But as time passed and the darkness came, and the cold, and the harvest was brought in, and she thought her back would break, her prayers changed.

O Father, let it be me next time.

She repeated this prayer until the day the Princess came to the farm.

It was a wonderful day. The little Troll Girl had never seen anything so beautiful.

The Princess had blonde curls that hung down to her waist, and a pale-blue dress that swayed around her calves, and a doll like a fairy in her arms.

But Foster-father, who saw the temptations of the Devil in everything that was pure and lovable and beautiful, tore the dress off the girl, and her coat with the fur collar, and took away the lovely doll, and poured paraffin over the lot. As the flames rose up into the autumn sky he screamed that the sinner must burn in Hell.

The little Troll Girl was standing right at the back, watching in amazement at the Princess's despair. She lay on the gravel drive, in just her vest and pants, weeping so hard that she was shaking, until Wall-eye walked up and kicked her, and Foster-mother grabbed her by the arm and dragged her inside the house.

They installed another bed in the loft.

The Princess was scared and looked at the little Troll Girl and said something to Foster-mother in a language she didn't understand, and Foster-mother replied in the same language.

Then Foster-mother came over with her stone face and said to the little Troll Girl: 'You leave her alone, do you hear? You're a bit simple in the head, and you don't say a word.'

But that very first night the little Troll Girl got into bed beside the Princess and kept her warm when she was shaking, and told her fairy tales that Sigrid had taught her, about the Ugly Duckling and Thumbelina and the Little Match Girl, and the Princess lay there, clear-eyed, listening, and that was how she learned Swedish.

SUPREME COURT REPORT

Case no. Ö 3490-11
Stockholm, 26 April

PLAINTIFF
Filip Andersson
Representation: Sven-Göran Olin, barrister

OPPOSING
Prosecutor's Office

CASE
Appeal for retrial regarding murder and other convictions

SUPREME COURT VERDICT
The Supreme Court authorizes a retrial in Stockholm
Appeal Court case no. Ö 9487-01, and orders that this
case be reconsidered by the appeal court.
    The Supreme Court's decision to suspend sentence
stands.

Tuesday, 26 April

15

The rain was beating against the windows. Annika was standing in the kitchen stirring a pan of hot chocolate. Under the grill two slices of bread with tomato and cheese were toasting, one with ham and the other without. The cheese was spitting ominously, and she took the pan off the ceramic hob and pulled out the grill-pan. Another thirty seconds.

She peeled two clementines and opened two small pots of coconut yoghurt. She took the toasted sandwiches out and put them on separate plates, then the fruit and the yoghurts. She put the plates on the kitchen table, poured the hot chocolate into two mugs, one red, one blue, then went out through the windowless living room towards the children's rooms.

Ellen still slept with her thumb in her mouth. Thomas was seriously worried about that, and kept saying she would have to have braces when she was bigger, but Annika wasn't worried. There would be worse things to wrestle with when the children reached their teens. Braces wouldn't be a major disaster.

She crept into bed beside the little girl, took her in her arms and nuzzled her neck. 'Darling,' she whispered. 'It's time to wake up now. It's a new day.'

Ellen stretched like a cat, yawned loudly, then curled

up into a little ball beside her mother.

'I've made breakfast for you,' Annika said, stroking the hair from her daughter's forehead.

'Mmm,' the little girl said. 'Coconut yoghurt?'

'And toasted sandwiches,' Annika said. 'And hot chocolate. Don't go back to sleep or it'll get cold.'

'Mmm,' Ellen said, as her thumb drifted into her mouth again.

Annika pulled it out with a little plop. 'You know what Daddy says about your teeth,' she said.

'Daddy doesn't live here,' the little girl said, turning away, still curled into a little ball.

Annika got out of the bed and went in to see Kalle. 'Hello, sweetheart,' she said. 'Are you wide awake or still tired?'

'Tired,' he said, and yawned noisily.

'There's a toasted sandwich for you in the kitchen,' she said, pulling him to her.

He hugged her back. He was warm and a bit clammy. 'Has it got ham in it?' he asked.

'Not yours,' she said.

'Good.'

She kissed his forehead, hair and ear, laughing when he pretended to fend her off, then went back in to Ellen, who had fallen asleep again. 'Come on, you,' she said, shaking her gently. 'Your hot chocolate's getting cold.'

'Carry me,' the child said, holding her arms out.

She lifted the little body up in a single swift movement, spun round on the wooden floor with her, then jumped out into the kitchen. Her daughter was laughing. Annika put her on one of the four chairs round the table. Kalle stumbled into the kitchen in pyjamas that were too big for him. Annika steered him to the table, pulled out his chair and tucked him in at the table.

Their morning rituals had their foundation in her

fears about how vulnerable the children were. If she gave them enough love and confidence during the first hour of the day, she liked to imagine that it gave them some sort of protection against the cruel world.

Now they were sitting at the kitchen table in their pyjamas, eating their toasted sandwiches, as she drank a mug of coffee.

'Daddy's going away,' Kalle said, pushing the empty yoghurt pot aside. 'He's going to Málaga and we're going to stay with Sophia.'

Annika stared at the wall. 'Yes,' she said, 'I know.'

'Why can't we stay with you, Mummy?' he said. 'I don't want to be with her. I want you.'

She stroked his hair, and he pushed her hand away. He was a big boy now. 'It's Daddy's week,' she said. 'You know that. And I have to go to work too. I'm going to Málaga as well.'

'Are you going to work with Daddy?' Kalle asked in surprise.

'No, not really. We're just going to be in the same place.'

'Why can't we come?'

'Daddy and I are both going there to work, but not together. We've got different jobs, you know that.'

She stared into her mug of coffee and clenched her jaw. She didn't want to show how furious she was about Thomas's decision to leave the children with Sophia while he was away on business.

Then she realized that Ellen was motionless. As Annika watched, the little body started to shake with sobs. 'Oh, darling, what is it?' She took her in her arms and rocked her slowly. The little girl didn't say anything, just curled up into a foetal position and put her thumb into her mouth. Annika felt reality seeping into the kitchen and clutched the child tighter. 'Daddy's going to pick you up today,' she said. 'He'll be at home with you tonight, and if you eat your tea quickly you might have time to watch a film together afterwards.'

'*Spiderman*!' Kalle said, lighting up.

'That might be a bit too rough for Ellen,' Annika said. 'But you could take *Desmond and the Swamp Barbarians* with you, if you like.'

'But we've seen that,' Kalle said.

'It's so good, though, that it's worth watching lots of times,' Annika said, and blew into Ellen's hair. 'You'll be staying with Sophia on Tuesday, Wednesday and Thursday, and on Friday Grandma and Granddad are going to come and take you out to the island – you can play with Zico. And on the day before May Day Daddy will be home, and on Monday I'll pick you up from school and you'll be able to tell me all about what you've been doing.'

'She's horrid,' Ellen said, wiping her nose on Annika's T-shirt.

'No, she isn't,' Annika said, feeling the hypocrisy echo through her body. 'Sophia's really nice. She's very pleased that she's going to be able to look after you.'

'She only likes Daddy,' Kalle said.

Annika could feel panic building. She wiped her daughter's nose with a bit of kitchen roll and stared out at the persistent rain. At certain moments everything she said was a lie. She lied to justify her choices in life, making the children pay the price for her failures, dragging them between one home and the other. She had to bite her lip to stop herself crying. 'I know it's hard,' she said. 'I miss you too when you're not with me.'

'Why can't we be with you all the time?' Kalle asked.

'I want to be with you all the time,' Ellen said, clinging to Annika's neck so hard that she had trouble breathing. Gently she loosened the little girl's arms.

'All children have a mummy and daddy,' Annika said, 'and the best thing for children is to grow up with both of them, but if that isn't possible people have to find another way.'

Kalle was looking at her obstinately. 'Why do only the grown-ups decide?' he said. 'Why aren't children allowed to?'

She swallowed her pain and smiled at him. 'When you get bigger you can make your own decisions.'

'I'm big now.'

'You're eight years old, not that big.'

'When's big, then?'

'Big enough to decide where to live? When you're twelve, maybe.'

Kalle slumped. 'That's four more years.'

'I don't want to stay with Sophia,' Ellen said.

Annika looked at the time, then stood up, still holding her daughter. 'Okay, leave your sandwiches, I'll deal with them later. Kalle, off you go and get dressed. Ellen, go and put on the clothes we picked out last night. Your bags are packed, aren't they? You've got everything you're going to need?'

The children wandered off to their rooms.

Annika stood in her minimalist kitchen and watched them go.

They managed to leave with a quarter of an hour to spare. Annika knew that she was a Fascist when it came to punctuality, a characteristic that had been accentuated during her marriage to Thomas, who was a hopeless optimist when it came to timing.

Having fifteen minutes in hand gave them time to sing as they walked. To stop and look in shop windows and talk about things they would like. To buy two packets of sweets at the kiosk on Kungsholmstorg and promise not to open them before the film that evening.

The rain had eased and almost stopped. It was chilly, just a few degrees above freezing, but there was no wind. The clouds were resting thick and heavy on the rooftops and spires.

Annika had the children's overnight bags over her shoulders, plus her own heavy bag with her papers and laptop. More and more things had to go with the children when they shuttled between homes, and up to now Annika hadn't made them choose what to leave behind. It was no longer enough just to move new Poppy and new Chicken for the children to feel at home (old Poppy and old Chicken had gone up in flames in Vinterviksvägen): now there were favourite jeans, favourite jackets, best shoes, a few films and books that had to go with them.

Annika dropped Kalle off in the school playground with a quick goodbye hug. 'See you in a week's time. I'll pick you up as usual from after-school club, okay?'

He nodded and ran off.

Then she and Ellen went to the after-school club and left the heavy bag containing Kalle's things on the shelf marked with his name.

'Can you carry me?' Ellen asked, holding her arms up.

'No,' Annika said, adjusting Ellen's hat. 'You're too heavy. You're a big girl now. Here, hold my hand.'

They walked side by side through the underpass that connected the south and north of the island. Ellen was frowning as if she were thinking hard about something.

'Mummy,' she said, as they passed the City-Boules club. 'Will I be a mummy one day?'

'Maybe,' Annika said. 'If you want to.'

The child thought for a few moments. 'But,' she said, 'if I'm a mummy, what will you be?'

'I'll still be your mummy, but I'll be a grandma as well. For your children.'

Ellen nodded thoughtfully. 'That's right,' she said. 'And then I'll get old, and then you'll be little again, and then I'll be your mummy.'

'Will you?' Annika said, surprised.

'Because when I get old, you'll be dead, and then you'll come back.'

'Ah,' Annika said. She had a child who believed in reincarnation.

They emerged into the grey daylight next to the Hotel Amaranten and walked down Pipersgatan towards the nursery school at the White House, slipping in past the entrance to Radio Stockholm and making their way to the third floor. Annika's shoulders were aching when she finally put the heavy bag on Ellen's shelf.

The little girl took off her outdoor clothes, her scarf and boots and snowsuit. Then she put on the slippers that looked like mice and adjusted her skirt.

'I want you to have a really lovely time until I see you next Monday,' Annika said, hugging her daughter.

Ellen nodded. Her tears from earlier were forgotten. 'Mummy?' she said. 'Isn't it funny? God is real but we can't see him. But Father Christmas, we can see him but he isn't real.' Then she ran off to assembly.

The clouds had lifted a little and were now hovering a few metres above the rooftops. Annika felt as though she hadn't seen blue sky for several weeks.

In February Sweden had been hit by record-breaking high temperatures. Snowdrops and crocuses had bloomed all the way up in Ångermanland, but March had been cold and windy, with several snowstorms. Eight people froze to death in Jämtland when a bus got stranded in the snow outside Trätgärde. On one of the weeks when

243

Thomas had had the children she had been sent up to Östersund to write about the 'City of Death'. Otherwise she had been in Stockholm. She had hunkered down, running between home, school and the newsroom, and hadn't had time for anything but everyday matters.

She went down the hill at the end of Barnhusbron, breathing the exhaust fumes of Fleminggatan into her lungs. She jumped on a number-one bus out towards Stora Essingen and managed to get a seat halfway through the journey.

She reached the main entrance of the newspaper's offices at twenty past nine. She paused at the bus stop to peer through the gates of the Russian Embassy on the other side of the road. A guard wearing a hat with earmuffs was standing by the gate, stamping his feet and looking frozen. He couldn't be a day over twenty.

She always used to try to sneak into the newsroom without being noticed, walking with her head down and her shoulders hunched, slipping towards the desk used by the day-shift reporters with her back to everyone. Then she would try to come up with something to fill her schedule, a story to chase up, an old article to re-examine. Now, in this new age, that sort of thing was a waste of effort. Patrik always had a long list of things for her to go through when she arrived. It could be anything from rewrites of articles about British nurses who had systematically murdered their patients to interviews with football stars who had just had their second child. As soon as the head of news spotted her by the caretaker's desk, he would set off towards her. She usually found herself with a bundle of notes in her hand before she had even had time to take off her jacket.

The children's calm, which came from their inability to feel stressed, was still somewhere within her as she stepped into the newsroom and saw Patrik slam the phone down and come racing towards her.

'Hello, Berit,' she said, as she headed for the chair opposite her colleague.

'The Costa Cocaine,' Patrik yelled. 'We need to sketch the outline of the series.'

She brushed the hair from her face and took a deep breath.

'Looks like you're off travelling again,' Berit said, glancing up over her reading-glasses before she went back to her morning paper.

Annika put down her bag, took off her jacket and pulled out her chair.

'This is what we're going to do,' Patrik said, sitting on her desk with a handwritten sheet of paper in his hand. 'Four human-interest articles and two factual pieces. We'll start with the human stuff.' He left a dramatic pause and let his hand outline the imaginary headline in front of him. 'One: "Costa del Sol, Europe's money-laundering machine – where dirty money comes out clean". Gibraltar is apparently a real tax haven. You'll have to find a Swedish solicitor there who can explain how you turn drug-money into reputable business profits.'

Annika took out her pen and started making notes.

'Two: "Cocaine parties in Europe's Beverly Hills – the yachts, luxury cars, jet-set lifestyle". You'll need to dig out a young Swedish girl to talk about drug-fuelled parties in Puerto Banús. Ideally she'll have been arrested in a drug raid and bitterly regret what she's done. Breast implants would be an advantage.'

Annika looked up. 'How important are they?'

Patrik lost his train of thought and lowered his hand. 'What?'

'On the priority list. How important are the breasts

compared with, say, how much she regrets her jet-set lifestyle?'

He shuffled on the desk in annoyance. 'You'll have to make a decision on that when you get there. Three: "My life as a drug-runner". Contact that Swedish bloke in prison in Málaga and get him to talk about being a drug-runner.'

Jocke Martinez, Annika wrote in her pad. She'd remembered his name.

Niklas Linde had kissed her as he'd said it.

'Four: "The hero who's going to put a stop to the money-laundering". There's a seminar on international financial crime starting in Málaga tomorrow, Wednesday, and the Swedish government's going to be represented by some civil servant who's supposed to bring back everything he's learned to Stockholm. Dig him out and do some sort of glamorous article about him and how vital his work is.'

Annika put her pen down. 'That could be tricky,' she said.

Patrik stared at her. 'Of all the possible protests I expected to hear, this was way down at the bottom of the list.'

'Your heroic Swede is my ex-husband,' Annika said. 'I know you think incest is good, especially if it's kept within the family, but this feels a bit much.'

'There must be someone else, some Swedish policeman down there or something, some liaison person . . .'

She forced herself to sound neutral. 'He's there incognito,' she said.

'Someone'll be there in an official capacity.'

'He's Norwegian.'

Patrik stood up, irritated. 'God, it's all getting fucking complicated. The factual articles are easy: "This is how the drug trade works". You'll need to cover production, transport, smuggling routes, distribution and sales, but don't write too much. Keep it short and snappy. And the second: "How money-laundering works". You describe the tax haven, the methods, the companies. Same thing there, short and sharp. You'll have Lotta with you, so we'll get some pictures that are actually publishable.' He dropped a bundle of printouts in front of her computer.

'Plane tickets and hotel rooms?' Annika asked.

'You'll get the plane tickets by email today. You'll have to sort out rooms when you get there. Find somewhere cheap this time.'

'What about the gas murders?' Annika asked. 'Suzette's still missing. The third killer is still on the loose, and the safe hasn't been found.'

'That story's dead,' Patrik said.

'A missing girl?' Annika said. 'How can the story be dead?'

'She was hardly a girl. She was a fucking *emo*. Just drop it.'

Annika gulped. He wasn't worth arguing with. 'Who's Lotta?' she asked instead.

'New photographer, a temp,' Patrik said, walking back to his desk.

The chair of the local journalists' union, Eva-Britt Qvist, came marching across the newsroom, making straight for Annika.

'What does she want?' Annika whispered to Berit, who shrugged.

'Annika,' Eva-Britt Qvist said. 'I want a word with you.'

'Sure,' Annika said. 'What about?'

She held a printout towards Annika, who took it and saw that it was the article she had at the top of her bundle of printouts. 'Swedish government prepares to get tough on money-laundering,' she read, then lowered the sheet. 'Yes, and?'

'This article has been written to order at the request of the Ministry of Justice,' Eva-Britt Qvist said. 'We must make sure that this newspaper doesn't become an uncritical mouthpiece for government propaganda.'

Annika raised her eyebrows. 'But, Eva-Britt,' she said, 'surely you don't think I look like a megaphone.'

The union rep blushed. 'Well, someone has to try to maintain the ethical rules,' she said, and grabbed the printout.

'This is a good and important series of articles,' Annika said. 'It puts a new perspective on the drug trade in Sweden, shows how global finance and international crime affect us here.'

'In that case, why aren't we doing it on our own initiative? Why let the Justice Ministry commission it?'

'They're opening doors for us. As a reporter out in the field, you need friends you can call on – you know that as well as I do.'

Berit gave Annika a thumb's-up behind Eva-Britt's back. Eva-Britt Qvist had never worked as a journalist, a particularly sore point. She'd started in the archive, then worked her way up to become a secretary before she was elected as union rep.

She turned on her heel and sailed off through the newsroom.

'I thought you had serious doubts about the Costa Cocaine articles?' Berit said.

Annika smiled. 'I've changed my mind,' she said, logging into the national database. 'What are you working on today?'

'The Supreme Court has granted Filip Andersson's right to appeal,' Berit said. 'I suppose I'll have to put together a short piece about that.'

Annika lifted her head from her screen and looked at her. 'Why do you sound so sceptical?'

'I don't know,' Berit said. 'I just don't think he's innocent. I think he did carry out those murders.'

'You can't mean that,' Annika said, her fingers poised above her keyboard. 'They've identified Yvonne Nordin's fingerprints and DNA at the crime scene. They found the meat-cleaver buried behind her cottage, right where Filip Andersson said it would be. Filip's description of how Yvonne shot the victims in the legs fits as well. How can you doubt it?'

Berit took off her reading-glasses. 'It could just as easily have been Filip who buried the meat-cleaver. And the fact that he knew about the shots could be because he fired them.'

'But it still doesn't make sense,' Annika said. 'He refused to tell the truth while Yvonne was alive because it would have meant signing his own death-warrant. But as soon as she was gone he could tell the truth.'

'Or else he could begin to lie,' Berit said.

Annika shook her head. 'It was Yvonne who killed David and kidnapped Alexander. And it was Yvonne who killed those people on Sankt Paulsgatan . . .' She stopped herself and swallowed. 'They never found the amputated body parts, did they?'

Berit sighed and put her glasses back on. 'Two hands and a foot are still missing,' she said, picking up the phone to call the Supreme Court.

Annika stared off towards Sport, and the image from Sankt Paulsgatan emerged from her memory.

Nina Hoffman had been first up the stairs, then Julia, and lastly Annika, first one floor, then another. Annika had stopped on the stairs, but she still saw the scene. Her memory was dominated by the smell, sweet and heavy and thick. In the fragmented images she couldn't see any blue-trousered police legs in the way, just the dying woman, the blood on the walls, the arm without a hand. The woman, who was really little more than a girl, had crawled out into the stairwell, blood pumping from the stump of her arm, pouring over the floor and onto the stairs, splashing up the walls. The blood bright red, the walls yellow. Her hair was dark and her skull had been smashed in. Julia had thrown up in a window alcove and Nina had driven Annika out onto the street: '*Get out of here!*'

Annika shuddered. She turned back to her screen, and went into the national ID database. Gender: male. Name: Joakim Martinez. Check phonetic spellings: yes.

One result: a young man in the south of Sweden who didn't call himself Joakim and who was eighteen years old. It couldn't be him.

She blinked. There must be something wrong. Every Swede was in this database, the official national register. Either Niklas Linde had got the wrong name for the drug-runner, or he wasn't a Swedish citizen. She tried male and Martinez.

Too many results (820). Refine search.

She screwed her eyes shut.

Niklas had mentioned another name, a middle name, hadn't he?

Jocke Something Martinez.

Damn. Why hadn't she written it down?

'Are we going back to yours or mine?' he had asked, then kissed her, and that was when he had said the name.

The whole name.

Jocke Zarco Martinez?

Could that be it? How was that spelled?

She tried male and Zarco Martinez.

Two results, but the first was completely clean.

Johan Manolo Zarco Martinez, twenty-six years old, registered in Skärholmen in the south of Stockholm, *deregistered*.

She leaned towards the screen.

Deregistered?

She clicked to bring up the man's full details: *This individual has emigrated or been transferred to the register of untraceable persons*.

Of course. He'd emigrated to Spain, and his name wasn't Joakim but Johan.

Then she was struck by a thought from a dusty corner of her mind. She stared at the screen.

Zarco Martinez.

She'd seen that name before. Not heard it, because she didn't know how it was spelled, Sarco or Zharco or Charco, but she'd seen it on a screen, just like now. She was quite sure of it.

Zarco Martinez, Zarco Martinez. When, where, how?

She couldn't think of anything, and let it go.

How was she going to get in touch with Johan Manolo Zarco Martinez in some Spanish prison? Through his lawyer? And what might their name be? She smiled, took out her mobile and opened the address book. Niklas Linde, Spain. She loosened her shoulders, then pressed 'call'.

He answered at once.

'Hello,' she said, in a high voice. 'It's Annika – Annika Bengtzon, from the *Evening Post* in—'

'Hi, Annika,' he said easily. 'How are things?'

'Fine, thanks. How about you?'

'The sun's shining and I'm bright-eyed and bushy-tailed.'

'Are you in Spain, by any chance?'

'Puerto Banús, baby.'

'Great, because there's something I need help with.'

'Oh, I see. What?'

She could hear laughter and the rattle of crockery in the background. She could see him before her, suntanned and in a loose sports shirt, sunglasses and stubble. 'That guy,' she said, 'the one who was arrested that night in San Pedro . . .'

'When you didn't want to play?'

She felt her face glowing and lowered it towards the keyboard. 'That's right,' she said. 'His name is Johan Manolo Zarco Martinez, isn't it?'

'Absolutely right.'

'I'd like to interview him.'

An espresso machine was making a noise somewhere behind Linde down there in the sun. He waited for it to stop. Then she heard a wind blowing. So he was outside. It was probably hot, the wind warm and dry.

'That's going to be tricky,' he said. 'He's in prison in Málaga and I presume you're in Stockholm.'

'I'm coming down tomorrow,' Annika said, blushing furiously when he laughed.

'Really? That's interesting,' he said.

'Is he under any restrictions, or can he have visitors?'

'I think the restrictions have been lifted. He's elated. Unfortunately he doesn't know very much. He's spilled the beans on the rest of the gang who are already under arrest, but he hasn't told us anything new.'

'Do you think he'd talk to the *Evening Post*?'

Annika heard a woman's voice say something quietly in Spanish close to Linde's mobile. The police officer replied *vale* and *hasta luego*, then she heard something that sounded like a kiss.

She put her hands over her eyes.

'I doubt he'd want to be depicted as the grass of the

252

gang, if I can put it like that,' Linde said lightly, when the woman had gone.

Annika looked at the time. Was he having breakfast? Or just coffee? Who was the woman? Something serious, or just for the night?

'I'm not expecting any long confessional,' Annika said, making an effort to sound professional. 'I want to conduct a personal interview with him, about how he ended up in this position, his life on the Costa del Sol . . .'

'I can check with his lawyer, if you like. When are you arriving? Do you want to be picked up at the airport?'

She had to exert herself not to sound too happy. 'Thanks, but don't worry,' she said. 'I'll be heading straight to the international seminar about money-laundering in Málaga. There's some sort of press conference at the Palacio de Congresos at two o'clock.'

'Okay. I'll see you there. I'm going as well.'

She experienced a peculiar sensation in her stomach. 'Great,' she said. 'Maybe you could help with a few other things as well. Do you know if there's a Swedish lawyer or solicitor in Gibraltar who could explain how dirty drug money gets turned into clean business profits? Or a Swedish girl with silicon tits who'd like to tell me all about her crazy jet-set life in Puerto Banús?'

'The lawyer might be difficult, but I ought to be able to find you a few girls. How important are the breasts?'

'Absolutely vital.'

'Consider it done,' he said, and laughed.

She smiled down the phone.

'See you tomorrow,' he said, and ended the call.

He was going to be there. She was going to see him. He'd offered to pick her up from the airport. Maybe he'd kiss her again.

'Earth calling Annika,' Berit said, waving a hand in front of her face. 'Who was that?'

Annika cleared her throat and hurriedly shuffled a pile of papers. 'A policeman in Málaga,' she said.

'Knut Garen?'

'No,' Annika said. 'His Swedish colleague.'

Berit looked at her intently over the top of her glasses. 'Policemen are usually good in bed,' she said. 'It's something to do with how masculine they are. Same thing with senior ranks in the armed forces.'

Annika realized her jaw must have dropped.

'Just a little tip,' Berit said, then went back to her screen.

16

Annika wrote an article about a man who had had sex with a bicycle, a note about a miracle wrinkle cream from Britain that had just gone on sale in Sweden, then did a quick follow-up piece about a company director who had been acquitted of aggravated tax avoidance in the Court of Appeal. 'This proves what I've been saying all along,' the man thundered. 'I'm completely innocent! The verdict proves it!'

'Well,' Annika said, 'it doesn't, really. It just means that the evidence wasn't sufficient to secure a conviction. There's a significant difference.'

She ate a baguette with Camembert and ham for lunch, and drank two cups of coffee from the cafetière she and Berit had clubbed together to buy for themselves.

She checked out a rumour that a famous television celebrity had hit his girlfriend. Both the girlfriend and the celebrity were denying it vehemently. Annika drew the conclusion that the rumour was perfectly true, but let it go.

A security van had been robbed on Sveavägen in the centre of Stockholm.

A fourteen-year-old had been raped by her sports coach.

A high-jump star had said something nasty about a long-jump star. The long-jump star had replied with something even nastier.

This last item was deemed to be the most important thing that had happened all day, and was given a huge amount of space on the website. People were encouraged to write in and comment on the 'star quarrel', and were asked to tick a box and vote for which one they supported.

Once Patrik had gone to the editorial conference and was unable to throw any more notes in her direction, she took the opportunity to read up about money-laundering on the Costa del Sol. She found a fresh article from one of the morning papers in the archive. It was about Operation 'White Whale', described as the largest police crackdown in Spain to date against international money-laundering and the Mafia behind it. After eighteen months' surveillance and bugging, the police had raided several locations on the Costa del Sol, according to the paper. More than forty people had been arrested: Spaniards, Moroccans, Russians, Ukrainians, French and Finns. Seven were lawyers, and three public clerks. A Russian oil company was also involved. They had seized 251 apartments and villas, forty-two luxury cars, two planes and a yacht, as well as numerous works of art and jewellery. The amount of money that had been laundered was estimated to be at least a quarter of a billion euros, more than two billion kronor, thanks to fake companies in various tax havens, mainly Gibraltar. The money had then been filtered back into Spain and invested in construction and property companies on the Costa del Sol, described as 'the biggest tourist paradise in Europe, and its hottest property market'.

The spider at the centre of the money-laundering and fake companies was said to be a firm of solicitors in

Marbella. Its founder had taken care of legal matters and the formalities surrounding the establishment of the companies, including finding stooges to run them.

She Googled a bit more and found a company at Stureplan, in the centre of Stockholm, specializing in 'taxation law for the global economy'. It explained to her why Gibraltar in particular was so practical for 'international investors'.

Companies in Gibraltar had been free from taxation since 1967, she read. When Spain had joined the EU in 1985, the number of companies registered there had exploded. The regulations were tailor-made for foreign proprietors who didn't want anyone to know what was going on.

Annika got up restlessly, wondering at the amount of effort these people were prepared to put in. She fetched another cup of coffee.

She called Carita Halling Gonzales, but reached the interpreter's cheery tri-lingual voicemail and left a message asking if Carita would be available to interpret for the rest of the week. Then she printed out maps of the Costa del Sol, and took the virtual tour of the Palacio de Ferias y Congresos de Málaga, the congress hall that would be the venue for the press conference, and booked two rooms at the Hotel Pyr, which seemed to be the cheapest on the Costa del Sol. She wondered where all the people attending the conference would be staying, and what plane they would be on.

Finally she looked up break-ins involving gas, which she had learned were called *robo con escalamiento*, as well as *nueva andalucia* and *soederstrom*. Nothing new had been written about the gassing or the dead family in the Spanish papers.

She packed away her laptop and left the newsroom with Berit at a quarter past five.

'Do you know who Lotta is?' she asked, as they emerged from the lift on the ground floor.

'The temp photographer? Pale and blonde, the artistic type.'

Annika groaned.

'I've never worked with her,' Berit added quickly. 'She might be efficient and focused on news.'

'In the best of all possible worlds,' Annika said.

They went their separate ways outside the main entrance. Berit turned right towards the garage, Annika headed left towards the bus stop. Her mobile rang just as the number-one pulled up at the pavement.

'Annika? Hi, this is Julia.'

Julia Lindholm had got into the habit of calling every so often.

Annika felt strangely pleased about that, as if she were being allowed to look behind the scenes. She had paid another visit to Julia and Alexander in Lejondalssjön. And on another occasion Annika and Julia had gone to the cinema to see *La Vie en Rose*, about Edith Piaf.

'Hi,' she said, as she held up her monthly travel pass and climbed onto the bus. 'How are you?'

'Fine, thanks. Alexander and I are in the city. We've been to Södermalm and the flat. Mum's been there and made it really nice. Flowers everywhere, pelargoniums and African violets. We're just going to get some coffee. Do you fancy coming along?'

The bus set off with a jolt, and Annika had to grab onto an elderly man to stop herself falling over. 'Sorry,' she said, looking round for a seat, only to be met with rows of blank grey stares. At home her minimalist kitchen awaited her, with the uneaten toasted sandwiches, as well as the unmade beds. And she didn't have any food in because she was about to go to Spain. 'Sure,' she said. 'Where are you now?'

'Central Station. We're meeting Henrietta in an hour. Shall we see you at the coffee shop upstairs?'

Alexander had grown. He was taller, heavier, and his face seemed darker, maybe because his blond curls had been cut off.

'Hi,' Annika said, crouching next to him. 'My name's Annika – I don't know if you remember me? That's a nice car you've got there. Can it drive on the floor?'

He turned away and hid the toy car in his arms against Julia's legs.

'So you've started coming into the city?' she said, standing up and giving Julia a quick hug.

'We've done a bit of shopping, been to museums, and once we went to the children's theatre. They say we're making good progress. Next week we're leaving the home to live on our own, in a little house a bit closer to the centre of the village. What would you like? Something to eat?'

Julia had ordered juice for her son and two slices of Princess cake.

Annika suppressed a grimace. 'Chicken salad, please,' she said to the waitress, 'and a mineral water.'

Julia asked for a cup of tea.

Annika glanced at her from the corner of her eye. She looked completely different now compared to just a few months ago. Her hair was thicker and glossier, her movements more assured. There was depth in her eyes. She was starting to look like the police officer she had once been.

'I've finished, Mummy,' Alexander said, licking his spoon.

'Do you want to play with your car for a bit? You could go over there near the toilets, but watch out for people's legs.'

They watched as he walked slowly towards the back of the coffee shop.

'So he's talking properly now?' Annika said.

'Only with me and Henrietta, but apparently that's "normal" as well.'

They laughed.

'But things are moving in the right direction,' Annika said.

The waitress came over with the salad, water and tea. Annika unfolded a napkin and put it on her lap.

Julia picked at a nail. 'You know,' she said, 'I miss him.' She nodded towards her hands, and cleared her throat.

Annika put down her knife and fork, unsure of what to say.

'I know he treated me like shit and all that, but I really do miss him.' She looked up at Annika with moist eyes that soon moved on to Alexander and his toy car. 'You should see the pictures of him when he was little. Alexander's just like him. It's almost unnatural. We went to see David's mother a few weeks ago and had a look at some old photograph albums.'

'Does Alexander know his dad's dead?'

Julia nodded. 'He's started drawing pictures of him in Heaven. The clouds look like potatoes and the angels are stick figures with wings.'

Annika couldn't help smiling, and Julia laughed.

'Those albums,' Annika said. 'They contained photographs of David when he was little?'

'He looked so sweet, and his mum, Hannelore, was a real beauty.'

'Were there any pictures of his playmates as well? Any of the other kids he grew up with?'

Julia rested her chin on her hand and looked towards her son. He was pushing the toy car carefully around the grimy floor in front of the toilets. 'They had such a lovely house out in Djursholm,' she said. 'Well, it was Torsten's, of course. One of those big merchants' villas, with an ornate veranda, rose-beds and raked gravel paths . . .'

'Were there any pictures of Filip Andersson?'

Julia blinked and let her hand fall to the table. 'Filip Andersson? Why would he be there?'

'He and David were childhood friends,' Annika said. She didn't mention Yvonne Nordin.

Julia shook her head.

'Did David ever mention anyone called Veronica?' Annika asked. 'Veronica Paulson, or Veronica Söderström?'

Julia leaned back in her chair and peered down at the checkout on the floor below them. 'I don't think so,' she said.

'Does David's mother ever mention a Veronica? Or Filip Andersson?'

Julia sighed. 'Hannelore isn't well,' she said. 'I don't know what's wrong with her. It must be some sort of dementia, but there's something else as well. She'll soon have been in that home for twenty-five years. No, Alexander, not there. Stay between the tables.'

Annika waited in silence as Julia went over to show her son where he could play. Then she sat down again and warmed her hands on the teacup.

'How does David's mother treat you and Alexander?' Annika asked. 'Does she understand who you are?'

There was a chink of porcelain as Julia stirred her tea.

'I don't know if she recognizes us. I sometimes wonder if she's ever really understood that I'm David's wife, and Alexander his son. She used to recognize David, and she asks after him all the time. She doesn't seem to understand that he's dead.'

'So what do you do? Tell her he's gone?'

Julia nodded. 'Every time. She just stares at me, for ages, then starts talking about something completely unrelated. About things that happened in the sixties, old films and radio shows. Do you remember something called *The Breakfast Club* with Sigge Fürst?'

Annika shook her head.

'She can still sing the theme tune. She idolized Sigge Fürst. She seems to think he was German, which he wasn't.'

'But Hannelore was German, wasn't she?'

Julia nodded.

'Jewish?'

Julia tilted her head. 'Why do you ask?'

'Nina once said she came to Sweden on the white buses full of refugees after the war. And David's middle names, Ze'ev and Samuel, well, they could hardly be more Jewish.'

'She refuses to talk about it. She's never said a word about what it was like in the concentration camp.'

'Did David have any cousins or other relatives?'

Julia wrapped her cardigan more tightly round her. 'Hannelore was the only member of the family who survived.'

Annika was chewing a lettuce leaf that seemed to be swelling in her mouth. She took a gulp of water and managed to swallow it. 'What happened to David's father?'

'He's been out of the picture for the past forty years. David grew up with Torsten, Torsten Ernsten.'

'Who was he?'

'A Finnish-Swedish businessman. He and Hannelore weren't married. He used to come and go pretty much as he liked.'

'Okay,' Annika said. 'That sounds complicated, particularly out in Djursholm in the sixties. Do you have any contact with Torsten, these days?'

Julia shook her head. 'He disappeared when David was eighteen. That was when things started to go wrong for Hannelore.'

'Disappeared?'

'He went off on a business trip and never came back. Soon after that Hannelore was put in the home.'

'What sort of business trip? Where to? What business was he in?'

Julia shrugged. 'Don't know.'

Annika looked intently at her. What was this peculiar family Julia had married into? Hannelore, a German Jew, alone in the world, with a son who had been childhood friends with a famous financier and an international glamour model. The son gets murdered, the model gets murdered, and the others either join the police or become murderers. She leaned across the table. 'When you lived in Estepona,' she said, 'and David was working undercover on the Costa del Sol, did you ever meet Sebastian Söderström and his family?'

Julia stared at her, wide-eyed. 'The ice-hockey player?' she said. 'The one who died? No! Just because David was famous from television it didn't mean we socialized with other famous people. We spent all our time alone, when David wasn't away for work, of course. When he was away I was left by myself . . .' She shuddered and looked quickly at her watch.

Annika did the same. Ten minutes left until Julia was supposed to meet Henrietta.

'We should probably get going,' Julia said, standing up and taking her son's outdoor clothes from the back of his chair and heading towards the toilets. She put them on him as if he were a doll.

'It was lovely to see you,' she said, as they walked past

Annika on their way to the stairs. 'In June we're going to start spending the daytime in our flat. Maybe you could call in.'

'Of course,' Annika said automatically.

Julia took a pen and a scrap of paper out of her handbag. 'This is our home phone number,' she said, writing something on what looked like an old bus-ticket. 'We went ex-directory when David started appearing on television and everything went completely mad, with calls at all hours of day and night . . .'

She gave Annika a hug, took her son by the hand and led him down the stairs.

Annika remembered her almost untouched chicken salad and realized how hungry she was. She ate the chicken and vegetables but left the pasta: these days you were supposed to avoid carbohydrates rather than fat.

She walked home along crowded pavements with a sense of anticipation in her gut.

Wednesday, 27 April

17

Annika gasped as she stepped out of the plane. The heat and the stench of aviation fuel made her lungs burn and her eyes water.

Lotta, the photographer, appeared beside her. 'Oh!' she said in delight. 'It reminds me of Tehran. Did I mention I used to work there?'

'Yes, you did,' Annika said, hoisting her bag onto her shoulder and going down the steps towards the bus that would take them to the terminal building.

The air above the cement apron was quivering and planes in the distance looked distorted, as if they were behind uneven glass. Annika was breathing through her mouth. How hot was it? A hundred degrees?

'Everything in Tehran was extremely photogenic,' Lotta said, squeezing aboard the bus and pushing the rucksack containing her photography equipment in the face of an old lady. 'Things seem much more rigid here. I mean, you want to try to capture the expressions, the character of the buildings and people. Other cultures are so wonderful!'

Annika had already worked out that Thomas wasn't on the flight, but she checked again to make sure, although civil servants didn't fly with low-cost airlines when they were on government business.

They got their bags after just a ten-minute wait, and headed for the car-hire hall. Annika was aiming for Helle Hollis at the far end and was almost there when she realized that the photographer wasn't following her. She turned and went back. She found Lotta at the Avis counter. 'Large companies are great,' Lotta said. 'They operate everywhere, and offer a sort of continuity that I think is important when so much else around you is new.'

'Oh, I see,' Annika said. 'I thought I'd be doing the driving.'

'As a photographer I'm used to being the chauffeur.' She hired a Ford Escort, the same model Annika had had last time. They went down into the garage to find the car. Annika switched her mobile on, and found one message on voicemail. Carita Halling Gonzales said she was busy on Tuesday and Wednesday, but that she could work on Thursday, and possibly Friday.

'Let's go and check in at the hotel first,' Lotta said. 'It always feels good to get unpacked and settled before you start work.'

Annika glanced at her watch. 'The conference centre's only five minutes from here,' she said, 'and the press conference starts in three-quarters of an hour. We won't have time to get to Puerto Banús and back before then.'

Lotta raised her eyebrows. 'Who arranged such a tight schedule?'

Annika shrugged.

They found the car and squashed their luggage into the small boot. Lotta got behind the wheel, started the engine and headed for the exit. Annika opened the glove-compartment and pulled out the contract Lotta had tucked in. Avis was three times the price of Helle Hollis.

The sunlight outside the garage was blinding, eroding all shapes. Annika and Lotta fumbled for their sunglasses.

'Where do I go?' Lotta said, braking.

Annika squinted through the windscreen. Either Avis used an entirely different *salida* from Helle Hollis or the building work had proceeded at such a pace that her earlier frame of reference had gone. The only thing that was the same was the chaos of cars and people, trucks and cement-mixers. Temporary signs in yellow and red shouted directions from gantries and pillars. 'Do you want me to drive?' Annika said.

'Just tell me where to go!'

'Aim for Málaga,' Annika said, turning on the air-conditioning. 'Try to get up onto the A7, northbound. It should be the first or second exit.'

The driver of the car behind them sounded his horn. Stressed, Lotta found the wrong gear and the engine stalled. Annika shut her eyes and gritted her teeth.

The Palacio de Ferias y Congresos de Málaga turned out to be smaller than Annika had expected from the pictures on the website. The building had been thrown up in a rundown industrial area and was a futuristic affair in glass, steel and aluminium. The roof was shaped like a wave, and the walls resembled the folds of a concertina. Annika remembered the virtual tour and aimed for the smaller hall where the press conference was due to take place.

'What a clichéd building,' Lotta said, behind her. 'It strikes me that it personifies some sort of Mediterranean macho idea, with an excess of style and elaborate construction methods . . .'

'There's plenty of that down here,' Annika said, as she walked under the series of multi-coloured pipework hanging above the entrance. Lotta was right, she thought, as she entered the building. It was overblown, all cladding and lamps and orange pillars. She had to stand in a disorganized queue, then identify herself and undergo airport-style security checks.

The conference hall was on the floor above. She heard Lotta's footsteps slowing, and by the time she reached the doors the other woman had stopped.

'What is it?' Annika said, turning.

'Press conferences are never very photogenic,' she said. 'I'll go outside and try to capture the soul of the building.'

Annika looked into the hall. Blue chairs. Irregular walls of cherry-coloured wood, sharp angles, a blue podium with four chairs. The ceiling was heavily ornamented. Would anything from inside the press conference ever be published? Men in suits sitting in a row? Hardly. A picture would only be useful if anything unforeseen happened – if something caught fire or the participants started fighting.

She checked that she had her mobile handy. If anything did happen, it would probably do the job. 'Okay,' she said, taking a copy of the press release from a pile and walking into the hall.

She took a seat right at the back, switched off her mobile, and watched a sea of people file into the rows of seats. There were media representatives from all over Europe, but the order of precedence seemed to be the same as at press conferences in Stockholm.

The television teams installed themselves at the front with the unquestioning authority of those who knew they were most important. The radio journalists buzzed about in the row behind them, making a huge song and dance of putting their microphones on the podium and adjusting their digital recorders to get the sound-levels right. The newspaper photographers hung around

270

in the gangways between the seats. Behind the radio journalists sat the newspaper editors, who wanted to be seen, she knew from their studiously relaxed posture and self-important expressions. Their purpose in life was to demonstrate to their colleagues how important they were, perhaps by shouting muddled and uninteresting questions at the podium once the radio lot had finished.

She looked for Thomas but saw no sign of him.

Four men walked up behind the table on the podium: an EU commissioner, a Spanish lawyer, a Dutch lawyer and a moderator.

She groaned inwardly. Lotta had made the right decision.

The press conference was long-winded, and at one point Annika nodded off for a minute or so. It was about the co-ordination of legislation covering financial crimes throughout EU member states, everything from accounting offences to tax evasion, VAT fraud, credit-card fraud, and a duty of disclosure for banks and bureaux de change. The various countries involved first had to compare their existing legislation, work out what the differences were, then discuss who was going to change what so the bad guys couldn't go on doing as they liked by moving from one country into the next.

There must be a way of expressing that more simply, Annika thought, as she stood up with everyone else. There was still no sign of Thomas.

Then she felt a hand at the base of her spine.

'Hello,' Niklas Linde said in her ear. 'Would you mind accompanying me?'

'Am I under arrest?' Annika asked.

'Definitely,' the police officer said.

They stepped out into the vestibule outside the hall. Linde put his hands on either side of her neck and kissed

271

her, first on one cheek, then the other. 'Welcome back,' he said.

She laid her right palm over his fingertips. 'Is Knut here as well?' she asked.

'He's at the tapas bar.'

'Annika?'

The voice came from behind her. She took a deep breath. Linde let go of her. She turned. 'Hi, Thomas,' she said. He was wearing one of the new suits he had bought after the fire, dark, a bit shiny, Italian. Red tie, Rimowa briefcase, freshly polished shoes. She smiled at his tousled hair and blue eyes, but he didn't see. He was staring at the policeman beside her.

'Have you met Niklas Linde?' she said. 'He's a narcotics police officer and works down here.'

The policeman took a step forward and said, 'Good to meet you.' They shook hands and Thomas's eyes flickered back to Annika.

'Thomas is representing the Swedish Ministry of Justice,' Annika said. 'We used to be married. We have two children.'

'Well, well,' the policeman said. 'Was he the one who didn't like playing?'

Annika felt like jabbing him in the ribs with her elbow.

'Good to see you,' she said to Thomas, then, to Linde, 'Shall we go and sit down?'

Linde put a hand on her shoulder, not taking his eyes off Thomas. 'One floor down,' he said, moving his fingers to her neck and gesturing along a panelled corridor. They turned round. His palm ended up on her waist. She could feel contentment burning through her body and Thomas's stare on the back of her head.

'Recently divorced?' Linde asked, standing close to her on the escalator.

'Not particularly,' Annika said, not moving away.

Knut Garen had installed himself at a table with some chicken wings, fried baby octopus and prawns in a strong garlic sauce. He greeted her warmly.

'It's brilliant that we can do this straight away,' Annika said, sitting down opposite him, Linde beside her.

She put her pen and notepad on the table, ordered *agua con gas* and a *tortilla* with *albondigas* from the waitress.

'You know why I'm here?' she said, and the officers nodded. 'Why have drug-smuggling and money-laundering become blurred on the Costa del Sol?'

'Look at a map,' Garen said. 'An hour by boat to Morocco, Europe's very own hash plantation. Three-quarters of an hour to the Atlantic coast, where the ships turn up from South America with their cargoes of cocaine. And slap bang in the middle of it all is Gibraltar, a tax haven with no intrusive restrictions.' He popped a baby octopus into his mouth. 'It's all here,' he said. 'The raw materials, the transport network, the distributors, the tax haven, serious corruption and customers.'

'Customers?' Annika said.

'Spain has overtaken the USA as the biggest user of cocaine,' Linde said. 'One in four Spaniards over fifteen has tried it.'

'But hash is still the main drug of choice,' Garen said. 'It's estimated that a hundred and twenty thousand families in Morocco derive the whole of their income from growing hemp and producing cannabis. Do you know how they go about it?'

She shook her head. The police officer wiped his greasy octopus fingers on a napkin and picked up her pen and notepad. 'They plant the seed in the spring and the plants grow through the summer,' he said, drawing a plant with deeply lobed leaves. 'Here, right at the top, are the seeds, hidden in little pods. Between the pods and the seeds there's a fine yellow powder, a form of pollen. When the plants are harvested in the autumn they're laid out on finely woven cloths on the floor and covered with plastic. Then they're beaten with sticks to crush the seed-heads. The pollen filters through the cloth and gets collected underneath.'

The seed-head he had drawn reminded Annika of a fried egg.

Garen looked towards the entrance hall with an almost dreamy expression. 'In October and November, nights in Morocco echo to the sound of sticks beating the ground, da-dunk, da-dunk. That's the hundred and twenty thousand families crushing the seed-heads of their hemp plants. Obviously, outsiders have no idea what's making the sound.' He drummed his fingers on the table. 'It goes on all night long,' he said, 'until the plants have been beaten three times. Then they're done, and that's when the buyers show up.'

He took his fingers from the table. 'The gangs who deal in cannabis handle about twenty hash farmers each. The pollen and plants are taken to the coast where they're dried and packed into hard blocks. It's been going on like that for as long as anyone can remember.' He drank the last of his beer. 'What do you know about hashish?'

Annika took a sip of her mineral water. They used to meet up for a smoke behind the snowdrifts next to the sports ground in Hälleforsnäs. Sven always provided the hash, Sylvia Hagtorn brought the tobacco to roll it with, and Roland Larsson his grandfather's pipe. Annika always thought the pipe was a bit disgusting, with the remnants of the old man's saliva. And she didn't think much of the effect either – it just made her feel sluggish and a bit silly. She'd be giggly and desperate for sweets.

'Well, I know you smoke it,' she said, looking down at her pad.

'The pollen from the first beating is made into top-grade hash, the highest quality. We hardly ever get that in Sweden. The hash that reaches us is category three, the worst sort, the remnants from the last beating.'

Maybe that's why it never really worked for me, Annika thought. 'How does it get to Europe?' she asked.

Linde shifted on his chair. Now his leg was pressed against hers.

'It's shipped out of two small coastal towns, Nador and Asilah, in February and March,' he said.

She nodded and suddenly noticed how dry her mouth was. She didn't move her leg.

'The latest development is the so-called go-fast boats.'

She was gulping the mineral water.

'Go-fast boats are really just big barges with some-where between three and five 225-horsepower Yamaha motors on the back. Half the boat is full of fuel, the other half drugs. They go so fast that they can outrun helicopters. They dock out at sea with ships that refill their fuel tanks, then carry on, sometimes as far up as Barcelona.'

Linde held his mobile towards her with one hand. He rested the other on her knee. The phone's screen was showing a shaky film of a cheerful dark-skinned man standing in the middle of a load of shipping pallets, holding onto a wheel. The wind was pulling hard at his hair. The cameraman, whoever he was, moved the camera away from the man and did a 360-degree turn. The film had been taken on board a huge barge that was crossing the sea at very high speed. The prow was full of countless square pallets, while the stern contained several hundred cylindrical drums of fuel. Then the film returned to the man and the screen went dark.

'He doesn't look so happy now,' Linde said, pocketing his mobile. 'What you saw in the prow was three tons of hash. He and the cameraman are in prison in Granada.' He let go of her knee.

She laughed.

'The EU have done a deal with the Moroccan government,' Garen said. 'The state has marched in and destroyed millions of hectares of cannabis plants. What do you think that means for the families who depend on growing it? No bread on the table. So what do they do?'

Annika waited for the answer.

'Their plants are gone,' he said, 'but everything else is still there – staff, buyers, sellers, boats, vehicles, ships, containers, the network of contacts and distributors. So what do they do?'

'Transport and sell something else,' Annika said.

'They transport and sell cocaine,' the police officer said. 'Morocco and the Western Sahara have taken over as the transit countries for the cocaine trade, and this is the doorway to their customers. All the cocaine comes from the coca plantations in South America, and almost all of it comes through here on its way to the European market.'

'How much gets seized?'

'About ten per cent, an average of ninety kilos a day. It's estimated that a ton of cocaine reaches Europe via Spain every day.' Garen leaned towards Annika. 'And do you know what the drug gangs' biggest problem is?' he said.

'Bribing Customs officials? Finding runners? Creating new markets?'

He shook his head. 'All that's easy. The hardest thing is knowing what to do with all the cash.'

Annika looked sceptically at him. 'Hard?' she said. 'Just using notes?'

'Money-laundering is the most complicated thing they do. And we're making it harder. That's why we have seminars like this one.'

Garen ate the last of the garlic prawns. 'I have to get off to Granada,' he said. 'Are you okay with that?'

Annika looked through her notes. There were several things she was wondering about, but he had to leave and she felt terribly tired. She smiled at him. 'Thanks very much,' she said. 'This has been a huge help. I'm just wondering if you've got ideas about people I could interview. For instance, I'd like to get in touch with Jocke Martinez's lawyer . . .'

'I've looked into that,' Linde said.

'Excellent,' Garen said, getting up. 'Well, I'll leave you to it.' He kissed Annika on both cheeks and headed for the exit.

'I guess I'm picking up the tab,' she said.

18

Lotta was close to a breakdown. She'd called Annika at least a hundred times but there was something wrong with her mobile, which wouldn't connect the calls – she kept getting a Spanish voice saying something unintelligible.

'You need to dial four six before you call my number,' Annika said.

The photographer stared at her. 'Of course I dialled the country code! Is your mobile even switched on?'

Annika dug around in her bag and fished it out on the end of the hands-free earpiece. 'Sorry.'

'How could you just leave me like that?' Lotta said. 'We're supposed to be doing this series of articles together.'

'Calm down,' Annika said, switching her phone on. 'You haven't missed anything important. I've just been getting some background information. Did you get any pictures?'

'Of what? This building? Or the picturesque surroundings?' She gestured towards the windswept expanse surrounding the conference centre, the thundering motorway, the shabby industrial buildings in the background.

'We need to sit down and try to book up some interviews for tomorrow,' Annika said. 'A drug-dealer, a solicitor specializing in money-laundering, a few jet-set Swedes . . .'

Lotta looked at her uncomprehendingly. 'This has been really hard for me, getting up so early, and you just disappearing like that. I want to go to the hotel now and get unpacked, and then I need something to eat.'

Annika stared at the woman before her, her mane of blonde hair, long legs and angular shoulders. 'Unpacked?' she said. Then she remembered Anders Schyman's words of wisdom: choose your battles carefully. It was Wednesday today. They were flying home on Saturday. They had two full days in which to complete the entire series of articles. 'Sure,' she said. 'You go ahead. The Hotel Pyr is in Puerto Banús – you can see it from the motorway.'

'What?' she said. 'Aren't you coming?'

'I've got loads of work to do.'

'But—'

'With a bit of luck I'll be able to get hold of the Swedish drug-runner in prison in Málaga. One of us needs to sort that out. Shall we meet up over breakfast in the hotel early tomorrow morning? Eight o'clock?'

Lotta was about to say something else, but Annika turned away and walked towards Niklas Linde's car. Not the BMW this time, but a Jaguar.

'Is that your photographer?' he said, looking with interest at Lotta.

'No,' Annika said, as she opened the door. 'She's not mine, she's the *Evening Post*'s. You're welcome to borrow her.'

He grinned. 'I prefer reporters,' he said.

Annika waved as they drove past her in the car park. The traffic was heavy, almost static. Linde closed his window and turned up the air-conditioning. The thermometer on the dashboard said the outside temperature was twenty-nine degrees.

'Is it always this warm?' Annika said. The sweat under her breasts was starting to dampen her T-shirt.

'It'll be like this until October,' he said. 'There's never a drop of rain during the summer months.'

She took off her sunglasses and peered out at the sea. 'Has anything happened in the Sebastian Söderström case?'

He frowned. 'Have you heard what the post-mortem report said? About the thieves?'

She shook her head.

'They weren't gassed, they died from respiratory failure caused by a morphine overdose.'

Annika looked at him. His arms were chestnut-brown. 'A morphine overdose? They were addicted to morphine?'

'The morphine was in their bottles of beer.'

Annika recalled the cab of the thieves' truck: the dirty windows, the split vinyl seats, the hamburger wrappers on the dashboard, the map of Marbella, the mud on the floor, the two half-empty beer bottles . . . 'They were in the cup-holder next to the radio.'

'One-litre bottles of San Miguel,' he said. 'Screw-top.'

'So someone doctored them,' Annika said. 'That means . . .'

'. . . someone killed them. Exactly.'

'But who? And why?'

'Why do you think?'

She fell silent.

'It's actually pretty smart,' Linde said. 'You can get morphine from any hospital. The cupboards are supposed to be kept locked, but they're not hard to break into. The liquid forms have flavourings in them, so in this instance the pathologist thinks we're dealing with tablets.'

'But wouldn't it take loads of pills to actually kill someone?' Annika said.

'Someone who's not used to it would die from sixty milligrams of morphine chloride. That's either three or six tablets, depending on their strength. The amount of poison in those beer-bottles would have knocked out an elephant.'

Annika held onto the dashboard as Linde overtook a bus full of golf-playing pensioners. 'So what happened during the actual break-in, then?' she said. 'Didn't the thieves have those injections to counteract the gas?'

'A naloxone derivative, yes. Traces were found in their blood.'

'They opened the gate by using the right code. How did they know it?'

'The code that was entered was the emergency one, not the one chosen by the family. That sort of code gets sold fairly often. There have been several cases of security companies being behind large-scale break-ins – they did one in an apartment complex in Nueva Andalucía.'

Annika scratched her cheek. 'So they gassed the family,' she said, 'went inside without gas masks, smashed down the wall around the safe, carried it out to one of the vehicles, then looted the house, put everything into the truck and drove away.'

'More or less.'

'And when they thought they were home and dry they opened the bottles of beer to celebrate.'

Linde nodded.

They left the crowds on the public motorway and headed up onto the toll-road.

'But didn't those injections mean they weren't susceptible?' Annika said. 'I thought they were supposed to block the effect of tranquillizers? So how could they die of a morphine overdose?'

'The naloxone derivative only lasts an hour or two. Then the morphine kicks in. They must have got tired and parked up in La Campana for a rest.'

'I presume there are no fingerprints on the beer-bottles apart from the thieves'?'

'Correct.'

Mountains, sea and greenery flashed past. Annika shut her eyes and saw the little girl's bedroom, the un-made bed, the paints, the doll with the curly brown hair. She recalled the corridor leading to the closed door of the parents' bedroom, the floor where the children had died. 'There's something very odd about this crime,' she said. 'Don't you think?'

Linde was staring straight ahead, and didn't answer.

Then it struck her, a sudden, terrible realization. 'No one laces beer with a fatal dose of morphine in advance unless they're determined to kill the people drinking it,' Annika said.

'Quite right.'

She shivered, and he turned down the air-conditioning.

'So this was a meticulously prepared mass-murder camouflaged as a break-in,' she said. 'Do you have any idea why?'

The police officer shook his head. 'They cleaned up very carefully after them. The thieves who carried out the break-in were a risk so they were eliminated. Presumably the explanation was inside the safe, but we're unlikely ever to see that again.'

She looked out across the landscape. 'What are the Spanish police doing?'

'Nothing,' Linde said. 'The case is regarded as officially closed from a police perspective. The thieves are dead. There are a few loose ends, but there usually are.'

'You sound critical?'

He shrugged. 'I'm not formally involved in the investigation,' he said. 'I'm here to deal with the international drugs trade, not break-ins at local residential properties.'

'But you think the Spaniards were too quick to drop this?'

He shifted in his seat and cleared his throat. 'There must be some motivation for this crime that we haven't identified,' he said. 'Executing an entire family is an expression of serious brutality. The killer was making a point. We don't know which of the victims was the real target. Was it the whole family, or just one?'

'It can hardly have been the children,' Annika said, 'so that must mean one of the adults. Have you checked them out?'

Linde sighed. 'Not very thoroughly. Sebastian Söderström was a charming slacker, completely incompetent when it came to money. Veronica Söderström was a well-regarded solicitor. Astrid Paulson was practically retired, and Suzette was a schoolgirl who was about to start work at a stables.'

'Could there be something in Sebastian's shaky finances?'

'Of course, but if you don't ask any questions, you don't get any answers.'

'And what about Suzette? Have you heard anything from her at all?'

He shook his head. 'Not a thing. It's like she went up in smoke on the thirtieth of December last year.'

'Is there still any kind of active search for her?'

'Now? No.'

'Do you think she's alive?'

'There's been no sign of life from her for four months. She hasn't crossed any national boundaries, hasn't withdrawn any money, hasn't made any calls, hasn't logged into the Internet. If she's alive somewhere, she's locked up, unable to contact the outside world. So the worst of it may not be that she's dead.'

Annika sat in silence for a long minute. She thought of the picture of the girl with the sullen demeanour, her black hair and fragile face. *The worst of it may not be that she's dead*. How utterly appalling. 'But there are still things to follow up,' she said. 'Aren't there?'

He nodded. 'The person who doctored the beer.'

'He set the whole thing in motion,' Annika said. 'Hired the thieves, got hold of the gas and naloxone derivative, paid to get the villa's alarm codes, poisoned the beer, took the safe and drove off.'

'If it is a he.'

Annika gaped at him.

'The footprints found at the crime scene,' he added. 'Three pairs, two of which match the thieves' shoes. The third set were size thirty-seven.'

Few men have feet that small. 'Do you have any idea who she could be?'

He smiled. 'Oh, little Annika, you're so serious,' he said. 'I'm glad you're here again. Shall we put the gas attack behind us and talk about something more pleasant?'

'Just one last question,' she said.

He raised his right hand and brushed the hair from her face. 'There were no fingerprints and no DNA to go on. No vehicle and no witnesses.'

She could feel his touch, like scalding water. 'Just footprints,' she said.

'Just footprints,' the police officer said.

She looked down at his feet. They were huge. 'You know what they say about men with big feet?' she said.

He glanced at her, with a twinkle in his eyes. 'No,' he said. 'What?'

She relaxed and laughed, feeling her face getting

warm. She looked out at the concrete skeletons lining the motorway, and felt anticipation radiate from her stomach. 'The Swedish drug-runner,' she said, trying to sound normal. 'Does he want to talk to the *Evening Post*?'

'I spoke to his lawyer this morning. You've got an appointment to visit him in prison in Málaga at eleven tomorrow morning.'

He braked as they reached the toll-booth in Calahonda, and joined one of the queues, ending up behind a lorry from Morocco.

'What do you think the cargo is?' Annika asked.

Linde stretched out his hand again, took a gentle hold of the back of her neck, leaned across the Jaguar's central console and kissed her. The effect was electrical. The hair everywhere on her body stood on end. She kissed him back as if she were drowning, running her fingers through his hair, then tightening her grip and holding him there. She kissed him until she was short of breath and the cars behind them blew their horns.

'Are you staying at the same hotel?'

Annika nodded, feeling giddy. The car behind overtook them, its tyres squealing, and the driver gave them the finger as he passed.

'Are you in a rush to get somewhere?' she asked. 'Or have you got time to see me to my room?'

He put the car in gear and drove up to the toll-booth.

It was much easier than she had expected. There was no embarrassment, no performance-anxiety. Their clothes ended up on the floor just inside the door and he looked at her with a mixture of laughter and seriousness in his eyes, then kissed her intensely.

He stayed with her afterwards.

285

Thursday, 28 April

19

Lotta was already installed at one of the window tables when Annika got down to the dining room. The photographer had a tray laden with eggs and bacon, cereal with pink yoghurt, a glass of orange juice and another of tomato juice, bread, cheese and peppers, and two chocolate croissants.

Annika got a cup of coffee and an English morning paper and sat down beside her. From the corner of her eye she saw Niklas Linde cross the vestibule towards the main doors. They were going to meet up again that afternoon and discuss what the Swedish police were doing on the Costa del Sol to combat drugs and money-laundering.

'You've no idea what you missed last night,' Lotta said, chewing energetically on a bit of tough bread. 'I had a wonderful Spanish meal at a really authentic tapas bar down by the harbour. And you know those mountains you can see over there?' she went on. 'They're actually in Africa!'

Annika looked at her to see if she was joking. She wasn't. 'Really?' she said, opening her paper.

She could still feel Niklas's arms round her back. They had showered together that morning, which she had never done with Thomas. He always wanted to be left in peace in the bathroom.

'The amount of crime down here is terrible,' Lotta went on. 'A man in the bar said they've got the Mafia here.'

'Four hundred and twenty different versions of it,' Annika said, as she leafed through the paper.

Lotta's eyes widened. 'What?'

'Police information,' Annika said. 'They told me during my meeting with them yesterday when you were having trouble with the phone. A ton of cocaine reaches Europe via Spain every day.'

'Well,' Lotta said, 'you have to take figures like that with a pinch of salt. The police say things like that to justify their budget. What we really need is proper journalism, based on facts that we find out for ourselves. That sort of thing gets badly overlooked in newsrooms these days.'

Annika consulted her watch. 'I'm going back to my room to find out a few basic facts for myself,' she said. 'Shall we meet down here in an hour?'

She went to the buffet, grabbed some bread, cheese and ham, which she wrapped in a napkin and put into her bag.

In her room, she called Carita Halling Gonzales and told her about the planned series of articles. They arranged that Carita would go with Annika and Lotta to Málaga, and agreed to meet in the hotel lobby at nine o'clock.

She ate the bread, cheese and ham as she read the Swedish morning papers online. Then she switched off her laptop, got up and lay down on the unmade bed. She could still detect his scent on the sheets.

This isn't love, she thought. This is just because I want to do it.

*

290

The prison was located in a *polígono* not far from the airport. The building was a plain single-storey construction of concrete blocks, covered with what had once been whitewash. Now it was peeling off, grey-green from pollution and damp. It was surrounded by a wall topped with barbed wire and an electrified fence.

'Not exactly the Hilton,' Carita said, from the back seat.

It was a quarter of an hour before their allotted visiting time. They had parked in the shade, on the road that led north from the prison. According to the thermometer on the dashboard, the temperature outside was thirty-two degrees.

'Why does this man want to talk to a newspaper?' Carita asked.

'That's one of the things I want to ask him. He's obviously got some sort of motive.'

'Do you think he'll reveal something to you in exchange for something else?'

'There's not much I can do for him, except write about his case.'

'What do you know about him?' Carita asked.

'He's got a Swedish-Spanish mother and a Spanish father. He was arrested just after New Year as some sort of courier for the drugs that were seized in La Campana. I want his life story, his background, how he ended up as a drug-runner, a bit of an insight into that world.'

'The light's completely wrong,' the photographer said. 'It's far too flat. Soon there won't be any shadows at all.'

Annika looked at her. She was staring intently through the windscreen, as if she were evaluating what she could see with millimetre-precision.

'You have to get going much earlier to get any depth

291

into the pictures,' Lotta added. 'We should have been here at dawn.'

Annika took a deep breath. Lotta was basically uninterested in anything to do with their work. She hadn't asked a single question about the drug-runner or any other aspect of the articles. She turned back to Carita. 'He speaks Swedish,' Annika said, recalling the drunken swearing when he had been arrested in San Pedro. 'But none of the guards do so you'll have to do the talking before we get in. We've got authorization, but Niklas Linde warned me that they might kick up a fuss.' To Lotta, she said, 'We won't be allowed to take anything into the visitors' room. No bags or cases. They'll check our pockets for mobile phones, pens, notepads and so on, but you can try smuggling a mini-camera inside your trousers. If we're lucky, they won't have metal detectors.'

'But that's unethical!'

'The Spanish justice system doesn't decide what we publish,' Annika said. 'Anders Schyman does. We provide the material and he makes the decisions. Shall we go?' She opened the door and stepped out onto the street without waiting for an answer. It was like walking into a hairdryer. The wind swirled round her legs, blowing yellow sand around her skirt.

'This couldn't have been a prison to start with,' Carita said, shielding her eyes with a hand as she studied the mouldy façade. 'It must be some sort of adapted industrial building. A slaughterhouse, maybe. Well, he'll probably be here for a while. The Spanish judicial system is renowned for being slow. People sometimes have to wait several years before they get to trial.'

She took the opportunity to touch up her lipstick, then trotted off towards the entrance round the corner. Her blonde hair bounced rhythmically on her shoulders.

Annika had left her sunglasses in the hotel room and couldn't keep her eyes open when they stepped out into the full sun. It wasn't quite eleven o'clock, and they had to wait in the dust for several long minutes before the electronic lock on the gate whirred and they were let in to walk the few metres to the prison building.

'*Buenos días, señores,*' Carita chirruped, pushing her sunglasses onto her forehead. Annika wiped the sweat from her face with her palm and followed her in. The cool of the air-conditioning enveloped her and she wrapped her arms around herself. The door closed with a metallic clang. She sensed Lotta close behind her.

They were in a cramped reception area. In front of them there was a tall, veneered counter and to the left the arch of a metal detector. Four uniformed guards with batons and leather-belts were staring blankly at them. The only light in the little room came from a small window beside the door.

Carita started talking to one of the men, who wore a peaked cap although they were inside, and a large ring of keys on his belt. Annika heard 'Manolo Zarco Martinez' several times – clearly he wasn't Jocke here but Manolo. Carita took her passport from her handbag. The man with the cap waved both hands dramatically and raised his voice. Carita began to do the same.

'We've got authorization for two visitors,' Carita said. 'Not three.'

Annika put her passport on the counter and looked at Lotta.

'I find things like this difficult,' the photographer said. 'It's not natural for me to force myself on people in tough situations. I'll wait outside.'

Annika nodded. They'd never manage to smuggle a camera past the metal detector anyway, and even if they did, they wouldn't be able to show the man's face.

His condition for agreeing to the interview was that he would be anonymous. The best they could have got would be a silhouette of him, or the back of his head.

'Okay,' Annika said. 'Take a few shots of the prison in the meantime, something that makes it look really awful. You can imagine the headline, "This is where the Swede is being held", something like that.'

Lotta put her hands on her hips. 'I'm the photographer,' she said. 'There are loads of factors that determine whether a picture turns out well.'

'That goes without saying,' Annika told her.

'We're signed in,' Carita said, putting her leopard-print handbag on the counter. Annika stepped up, put her outsize bag beside it and signed her name on a form she didn't bother to read. 'I need to keep my pen,' she said. 'And a notepad.'

Carita shook her head. 'You can't take anything in.'

'Can't I borrow one? That's what usually happens in Sweden.'

'*Bienvenido a España*,' Carita said, stepping through the metal detector.

Annika's belt set off the alarm so she had to take it off and leave it next to the bags on the counter.

'Do you think they'll go through our things?' Annika asked quietly, glancing at the bags as she and Carita walked towards the cells.

'Bound to,' Carita said, smiling at the guard in the cap.

They went through a narrow doorway into a long, tunnel-like corridor that was even darker than the reception area. A single strip-light flickered weakly at the far end. On each side of the corridor there was a row of metal doors, the same brownish-red colour as the floor. The air-conditioning rumbled and rattled. The man with the cap held out his hand.

'*Celda numero seis.*'

Carita set off into the tunnel. The floor was slippery and she held one hand up to keep her balance. Her high heels echoed. Annika's sandals clattered and slipped. The guard's keys jangled.

'*Aquí.*' Slowly he identified the right key and unlocked the cell door at shoulder and waist height. '*Sesenta minutos,*' he said, opening the door.

They had an hour.

The cell had no window. The floor was the same colour as it was in the corridor, but the walls were darker, greyer. Annika stared into the room, at first unable to see the prisoner in his grey clothes sitting on his grey bed. She stopped short when she met his gaze from the far corner.

'Good morning,' Carita said, going to him and shaking his hand. 'My name's Carita, I'm an interpreter, but I understand that you speak Swedish.'

Johan Manolo Zarco Martinez got up slowly and reluctantly, his eyes on Annika. 'You the reporter?' he asked.

His accent was from the suburbs with a large migrant population. Annika held out her right hand. He took it and looked at her dubiously. 'My lawyer said you were pretty,' he said. 'He hasn't met you, has he?'

'Sorry to disappoint you,' Annika said. 'I'm afraid he was going on hearsay.'

'You didn't bring a beer or anything with you? They don't check that closely.'

Carita sat at the end of the bed.

A low-energy bulb in the ceiling was casting a bluish light from above, throwing deep shadows under the man's eyes and nose. Annika glanced round the cell. There was nowhere to sit apart from the bed. A faint whining sound was coming from the air-vent by the door. It was cold, but not as cold as it was in the corridor. She stayed on her feet, with her back against the door. An hour felt like eternity. 'Your name's Johan?' she asked.

'Jocke,' he said, slipping back into the shadows at the corner of the bed again. 'But you're not going to print my name, right? I don't want my picture in the paper. Mum still lives in Sweden, you know. My sister too.'

Annika knew he was almost twenty-six, but he looked younger. There was something naïve about him, something rather touching, or possibly just a bit crazy. 'What would you like me to call you in the article?' she asked. 'You can suggest a name.'

He lit up. 'Any name I like?'

Annika nodded.

'Steel Bollocks!' he yelled, then burst out laughing so hard he could hardly breathe.

She sighed and waited for the laughter to stop. 'Are you okay with . . . Andreas?'

He stopped laughing and pretended to throw up. 'No, fuck it, that's totally fucking uncool.' He thought hard for a few seconds. 'Call me Bobby.'

'That's not a Swedish name. It's English.'

He straightened his back indignantly. 'What the hell? You said I could choose!'

'A Swedish name.'

He slumped back against the wall with his arms folded. 'Fredrik,' he said.

'Fredrik,' Annika confirmed, unable to see why Fredrik was so much cooler than Andreas.

Martinez pulled his sleeves down over his hands and tucked his knees up under his chin. 'Have you any idea how long I've been in here? I've told them I was supposed to drive the gear to Stockholm so I could get a quick trial, but the bastards tricked me. I said I wanted to be transferred to Sweden, but now they're going to take me to the provincial prison in Alhaurín de la Torre. I know a guy who spent three years there before his trial. You've got to help get me out of here!'

'You're really going to have to talk to your lawyer about that,' Annika said. 'I don't have any influence over the Spanish judicial system. I'd like to interview you about how you ended up here.'

'I want guarantees,' the young man said.

'Of what?'

'That I can serve my sentence in Sweden.'

'I can't give you that sort of guarantee. All I can do is write about you in the paper, try to influence opinion . . .'

'Yes,' he said, 'That's good. Influence opinion. So they get me home again. Fuck, I can't stay here.'

Annika breathed out and sank down onto the floor. She had thirty-five minutes left. 'Shall we take it from the beginning?' she said.

She asked some general questions about his childhood and youth. It didn't sound much worse than anyone else's. The third floor of a concrete block out in Skärholmen, parents divorced, an older brother and younger sister, mum and sister still living there. He talked animatedly about his schooldays and the gang he had been in, hanging out in the shopping centre and competing to nick things. They used to sell their haul at the flea-market in the basement of Skärholmen shopping centre on Saturday mornings. His brother, who was ten years older, had started dealing hash while he was at school. He had introduced his little brother to drug-running, a career choice that had been extremely profitable until just a few short months ago.

'I started when I was too young to be charged,' Martinez said. 'It was perfect. I couldn't be charged even if I was caught, but I never got caught.'

'How did it work? What did you smuggle?'

'Coke, mostly. That's where the money is. It went really well.' He seemed genuinely happy.

'Shouldn't you have been at school?'

'My brother used to call and say I was ill. They probably just thought I was a very sickly child.' He grinned.

'What about your mum? What did you tell her?'

He shifted a bit and suddenly seemed uncomfortable. 'That I was with Dad, and Dad thought I was with Mum. They never talked to each other.'

Annika stiffened. In a flash she saw her own children in twenty years' time, sitting in a windowless cell in some foreign country, explaining how their lives had gone wrong in a similar way: 'I'm here because my parents never talked.' She dropped the subject. 'How did it work? How did you find your employers?'

He shrugged. 'First through my brother,' he said. 'Then just contacts.'

'People you knew, or people they knew, or through the employment service?'

He grinned broadly again. 'Not the employment service,' he said. 'Mates. Friends of friends.'

'Do you use drugs yourself?'

'Not much. Just occasionally. I prefer beer.'

Annika wished dearly that she'd managed to bring a pad and pen with her. Her head was starting to ache with concentration. 'Did you always run the route from Spain to Sweden?'

'I did Holland and Germany as well. The market's better there.'

'Do you remember the first time you did it?'

He laughed. 'Oh, yeah. To start with it was easy. I used to go by train, with the gear in a sports bag. The first time with rubbers was worse. It's tough when you don't know how to do it.'

Annika blinked. 'Rubbers?'

He put his head to one side and smiled. In another setting she would probably have found him quite charming. 'You think coke looks like it does in the films, then? Powder in little white bags, something like that? That's such bollocks. Coke's hard. Comes in blocks. Big as your thumb, pretty much.'

He held up his left hand to show the size he meant.

The small of her back was aching. She adjusted her position against the concrete wall.

'You practise with grapes,' he said. 'Big grapes. You have to swallow them whole without breaking the skin. They put us in a hotel room. There were eight of us. We were there two whole days, just practising. Then we moved on to swallowing rubbers and lumps of coke.'

She felt the urge to vomit rise in her gullet. 'So you swallowed condoms full of cocaine? How many?'

'I know someone who once took a whole kilo. That's probably the world record. I used to take half a kilo, which is pretty normal.'

'Isn't it dangerous?'

'You can't fly into Stockholm Arlanda any more – they're too thorough there. You go to Skavsta or Västerås. It always went okay for me. It's the west Africans who get picked up.'

'I meant in terms of your health.'

'You just have to be careful when you swallow. It's only dangerous if a rubber breaks.'

'Because then you die?'

The young man just smiled.

'But you got caught in the end,' Annika said. 'How did that happen?'

The smile disappeared as if he'd been slapped.

'It can't have come as any surprise when you got caught,' Annika said. 'All your friends had started to disappear around you. You were the last one arrested. Why didn't you run while you had the chance?'

'I shouldn't have had to,' he said. 'People ought to keep their mouths shut.'

'Are you quite sure that someone betrayed you?' Annika said. 'You don't think you could have been bugged or watched?'

He laughed, a hard, sharp sound. 'Of course I was bugged! No one ever says anything over the phone.'

'So how did you hear about your jobs?'

He fell silent.

'Anyway, you've been talking as well, haven't you?' Annika said. 'So you can get back to Sweden?'

Martinez sat up, annoyed. 'But I've only said obvious things, the things they already knew! I haven't said anything about Apits. They want me to talk about the whole fucking lot, but I don't know anything!'

'Apits,' Annika said. 'The freight company that owns the warehouse where the raid happened?'

'I'm not saying a fucking word about Apits, or about the Colombians,' the young man said, huddling on the corner of the bed again.

'Not even if it gets you a ticket home to Sweden?' Annika said.

He hunched his shoulders and wrapped his arms tightly around his legs. 'My mum and sister,' he said. 'Everyone knows where they live.'

Annika saw genuine fear in his eyes. She felt the hairs on the back of her neck stand up. 'What do you mean by that?'

He shook his head.

Annika tried to hold his gaze. 'What do you mean, everyone knows where your mum and sister live? You're worried about their safety if you say what you know?'

'I don't want to say anything else,' the young man said.

A heavy silence descended on the little cell. The ventilation unit rattled and groaned. Martinez scratched his head hard. Carita was fingering the buttons of her blouse. Annika looked at the time. Five minutes left.

'Do you know anything about other activities?' she asked. 'For instance, do you know anything about using gas in break-ins?'

The young man raised his eyebrows. 'Using gas in break-ins?'

'Do you know anyone who does that sort of thing?'

'That's those fucking Romanians,' he said. 'I don't work with Romanians.'

'You haven't heard anything about the break-in at the Söderström family home? Just after New Year. Gas was used and they all died just before you were arrested.'

There was a noise at the door. The guard was cutting the visit short by a few minutes.

The young man sat up. 'When's your article going to be in the paper? When can I get out of here?'

Annika got up from the floor on stiff legs. Carita smoothed her skirt and stood up from the bed. Only Martinez didn't move.

'*Vamos*,' the guard said bluntly.

Annika went over to the young man and held out her hand. 'I hope things sort themselves out for you,' she said, and realized that she meant it.

And before she knew what was happening, the young man had jumped up and was giving her a proper bear-hug. 'Help me,' he whispered in her ear. 'Help me get away from here.'

20

Lotta was sitting in the car, with the engine idling and the air-conditioning on.

'Málaga's a really authentic city,' she said. 'There's proper street-life, a genuine tradition of work and siesta.'

'Have you taken any pictures of the prison?' Annika asked.

The woman looked at her in surprise. 'It's not remotely photogenic,' she said. 'And the light is far too harsh.'

Annika shut her eyes for a few seconds. Pictures had to be taken, and she had an interview to write up. She dug around in her bag and took out her mobile, noting she had three missed calls, then went back out into the blinding sunlight. She switched on the mobile's camera function and walked right round the building, squinting as she took pictures every ten metres or so. When she got back to the car she opened the passenger door and leaned inside. 'There's a bar on the left,' she said. 'I'd like to sit down and write up an outline of the interview. Do you want to come along and get something to drink?'

'I was just about to suggest that,' Lotta said. 'This heat makes you so thirsty.'

Carita came up to her and said, in a low voice, 'What did he whisper to you?'

Annika looked at her in surprise. 'What do you mean?'

'Just before we left, when he hugged you. What did he say?'

Annika searched her memory. 'Nothing special,' she said. 'That he wanted help to get out.'

Carita shook her head sadly. 'Poor lad,' she said.

The bar was dark and reeked of smoke. The EU ban on smoking in bars and restaurants evidently hadn't hit home in Spain, in the way it had throughout the rest of Europe, because people were smoking everywhere.

They got a table towards the back of the room. Carita ordered a *cafe cortado*, Lotta a glass of wine, and Annika pushed the boat out with a Coca-Cola.

'When in Rome,' Lotta said. 'I like the Spanish tradition of having a glass of red with lunch. It's very civilized.'

'Don't worry,' Annika said, taking out her pen and notepad. 'I can drive us back.'

Lotta raised her eyebrows. 'Why? We're in Spain. They're not so strict as they are in Sweden.'

'If there are three of us in the car, two sober and one tipsy, who do you think should drive?'

Lotta shrugged in annoyance. 'That's so uptight,' she said. 'Anyway, you don't get tipsy after one glass of wine.'

Annika bit her tongue. She was on the point of declaring open warfare, not about anything important, just to let out some of her frustration. Instead she forced herself to smile. 'Of course,' she said.

Then she began to structure her article with keywords, scrawled notes and arrows. She put together a quick sketch of the cell and the young man, describing the smell and the damp and the shadows, then moved on to a chronological account of his life.

'The people seem a lot more genuine here than in Puerto Banús,' Lotta said. 'I took some pictures of women leading their goats to market while you were in there, their whole lives etched in their furrowed faces.'

'Yes,' Carita said. 'You won't find any of them in Puerto Banús. They can't afford to live there.'

'I wasn't expecting to find anything genuine on the Costa del Sol,' Lotta said. 'It's nothing but golf-obsessed pensioners and tax evaders. That's why it's such a nice surprise to find something real here in Málaga. It could make a really good exhibition.'

'Have you worked at the *Evening Post* long?' Carita asked.

Lotta chuckled. 'Well,' she said, 'this whole tabloid journalism business really isn't my thing. I'm an artist deep down, but everyone has to eat.'

Annika took her Coke and moved to the next table to get away from the sound of their voices. She started sketching out Martinez's offences when he was younger: the gang, the shoplifting contests, his brother dealing hash, then he himself starting to smuggle drugs while he was still legally a minor.

'It's got terribly expensive down here,' Carita was saying. 'Not just property, food costs a lot more, and the restaurants are expensive. Ordinary people can't afford to go out for Sunday lunch any more.'

Lotta sighed. 'It's so sad when tradition is forced out by commercialism. It's the same where I live, on Södermalm. Do you know Söder?'

Annika concentrated on trying to listen to the young man in the cell. Smuggling coke in sports bags on the train, his brother reporting him sick to the school, his mum thinking he was with his dad.

'It was lucky I bought my flat in time,' Lotta was saying. 'I'd never be able to afford it today.'

'Same here,' Carita said. 'I inherited some money from my parents. That was how we were able to afford the house in Nueva Andalucía.'

'So your parents are dead. How sad,' Lotta said. 'Was it long ago?'

'Eight years now. I inherited a biotech company that they'd set up.'

Annika looked up. 'A biotech company?' she said. 'What was it called?'

She remembered her former neighbour out in Djursholm, Ebba Romanova, who had set up and been bought out of a biotech company; she had got 185 million kronor for her trouble.

'Cell Impact,' Carita said. 'Why?'

'Have you ever heard of a company called ADVA Bio?' Annika asked. 'One of my neighbours used to own it.'

Carita laughed. 'I don't know anything about the biotech business. That was why I sold the company straight away.'

'You should always focus on what you know,' Lotta agreed. 'I'm going to concentrate on exhibitions from now on. That's where I feel I belong.'

Carita began to gather together the things she had spread out on the table. 'Have you had many exhibitions?' she asked, putting her sunglasses, powder and lipstick in her handbag.

'Four,' Lotta said. 'All with everyday life as their theme. I sold several of my women's portraits from Tehran.'

'Shall we go?' Carita said. She stood up without waiting for an answer.

Annika looked down at her notes. 'Two minutes,' she said.

'We'll get the car,' Carita said.

Quickly Annika thought through the end of the interview, the details about drug-smuggling, practising with swallowing whole grapes, the hard blocks of cocaine, the problem of security at Arlanda.

Her pen paused when she remembered the fear in the young man's eyes.

I'm not saying a fucking word about Apits, or about the Colombians. My mum and sister, everyone knows where they live.

She gathered together her things, drank the last of the Coke and went out into the sunshine.

The missed calls were from the newspaper, Thomas's mobile and the central exchange of the main government offices in Stockholm. She waited until she had got up to her room before she called back. It had been cleaned and the bed made. Every trace of Niklas Linde had been swept away.

She decided to return the calls in the order they had been made.

'How's it going?' Patrik snapped.

She sat on the bed. 'I've met the drug-runner who's been arrested. He's not having much fun.'

'What pictures have we got?'

She took a couple of deep breaths. There was no point in complaining about Lotta: she'd only get told off for not being able to work with other people. 'We couldn't take a camera inside the prison,' she said, 'but we've got the outside of the building. It looks like shit.'

'That works,' Patrik said. '"This is where the Swede is being held." What else are you doing today?'

'I'm meeting a Swedish police officer who's working on a massive seizure that was intended for the Swedish market.'

'Hmm,' Patrik said. 'Sounds pretty cold. What pictures will you have?'

'He's not here officially, so we'll have to sort something out.'

'Just make it fucking dramatic. What else?'

'I was at the press conference about international co-operation to stop cross-border financial crime, and I've got a decent long interview with two Scandinavian police officers about the Costa del Crime, drugs and money-laundering. I've got a good source in the police down here who can help me sort out the rest of the interviews we want.'

She refrained from saying that one and the same policeman would fulfil most of those roles.

'What about the girl spilling the beans about her jet-set lifestyle?'

'I'm still hoping to find her.'

'And she's not allowed to be anonymous.'

No, Annika had got that. Close-ups from the front were the order of the day.

One of Patrik's other phones began to ring and he hung up abruptly. She sat there with her mobile in her hand, wondering whether to call the next number.

What could Thomas want with her? They hadn't talked about meeting up.

She pressed 'call' and listened to the phone ringing. No answer. Disappointed, she let the phone sink to her lap. The room was silent. She could hear the blood rushing in her ears.

They had to learn to talk to each other. Their failure to communicate was what had caused their marriage to break down, she could see that now, not his unfaithfulness or her sniping, not because he worked too much or because she asked too much of him. She hadn't talked, and he hadn't listened.

Her head felt heavy when she recalled their phoney conversations about things that were completely irrelevant, when they would shout at each other about terrorism and integrity, circling each other in a destructive spiral that led nowhere but into the darkness.

She put her mobile down and went into the bathroom. Immediately the phone rang on the desk. She stumbled back into the bedroom.

'Annika Bengtzon? Hello, this is Jimmy Halenius. Are you busy?'

She was taken aback. They hadn't spoken since the infamous evening at the Järnet restaurant, with the ensuing pictures.

'I was on my way to the loo,' she said, still needing a pee.

There was a short, surprised pause.

'What?' Annika said.

'Was that something you'd rather carry on with or can we talk for a minute?'

'I'll manage,' Annika said.

He cleared his throat. 'How's the series of articles going?'

So, he'd been informed about it. 'Don't worry,' she said breezily. 'It'll be the perfect publicity brochure for the Justice Department.'

'Excellent. I've got some information about our friend the Kitten.'

'Really, what's she done now?'

'As you know, she was charged with three individual murders and one double homicide in a court in Boston. The trial was pretty quick, the verdict was announced yesterday. She's been sentenced to eighteen years.'

Annika blinked. 'That's all?'

'She had one of the best lawyers in the States. He got

the three murders discounted on some technicality, and she wriggled out of the double homicide by claiming self-defence.'

Annika sank onto the bed. 'So what does this mean?'

'That we can request her extradition, under suspicion of arson on your house.'

She stared at the stone floor. 'Extradition? There'll be a trial? And my name will be cleared? Will I get my insurance money?'

'Our extradition request won't be granted by the American authorities, so there won't be a trial, but the fact that charges are laid against someone else means that you'll be formally dropped from the investigation. The insurance company has already been informed. You'll get the full amount.'

The insurance company. Get the full amount.

She tried to identify some sort of emotion inside her, relief or delight, but nothing came. She was just aware of the low murmur of the air-conditioning, the background rumble of the motorway and the questions that were piling up inside her head. Will they take the flat away now? Will they let me buy it from them? When will I get the money? Thomas will get half. Or will we have to rebuild the house? I don't want to rebuild it! Can we sell the plot?

'Annika?' Jimmy Halenius said.

'Er, yes?'

'Did that picture in the paper cause you any trouble?'

She forced aside the background noise and the questions. 'I survived,' she said. 'How about you?'

'Only just,' he said. 'There was a big fuss in various parts of the building.'

Presumably he meant Rosenbad, since that was where he was calling from: the building in the centre of Stockholm that housed the prime minister's office, the cabinet office, the Justice Department and a few sections of the Foreign Office.

'Shit happens,' she said.

'So what lessons do we learn from this?'

She got up and headed towards the bathroom. 'Not to kiss in public places, and especially not when you're on duty?'

'Exactly!'

'Listen,' she said, 'I really need a pee.'

'Okay,' he said, 'I'll wait.'

She stopped mid-stride.

'You're going to stay on the line while I pee?'

'Well, you don't have to take the phone into the bath-room.'

She shook her head, put the mobile on the floor, did what she had to, then picked the phone up again. 'Are you still there?'

'So where were we?'

'Lessons for the future.'

'Right. I was wondering if you'd like to come round to mine next time.'

She sat on the edge of the bed. 'What makes you think there's going to be a next time?'

'I don't think. I'm asking. Next Friday?'

'I'll have the children,' she said.

'Tomorrow, then, or Saturday?'

She looked up at the ceiling and breathed in the smell of the room: dust, disinfectant, insecticide and some-thing unidentifiable. Could it be a lingering trace of Niklas Linde?

Did she want to see Halenius? She closed her eyes. 'I don't know,' she said. 'I don't know what I want.'

'Can I call you at the weekend?'

She opened her eyes. 'Sure.' She ended the call and

curled up on the bedspread, pulling her knees up to her chin and wrapping her arms around them. She thought about dead children, ruthless women and powerful men. She let herself be swept off into something that was warm and dangerous.

21

Lotta was waiting in the lobby at a few minutes before four. She had all her photographic equipment with her, the rucksack, a clumsy tripod and a flash so big it had its own bag.

'It's good you've got everything with you,' Annika said, 'because this is going to be a difficult shot. The police officer in question can't be recognizable, but the picture still has to be dramatic. The question is whether we doctor it instead of fussing with shadows and back-lighting and screens.'

Lotta looked at her in surprise. 'Okay, I'm the photographer here,' she said. 'I thought we'd agreed that.'

Annika put her bag on the floor. She'd fallen asleep on the bed and woken up with a headache. The limit of what she was prepared to put up with had moved considerably closer. That she was going to be meeting Niklas with a colleague from the paper was making her tense and nervous. 'This series of articles is being published in the *Evening Post*,' Annika said curtly. 'There are certain guidelines that need to be adhered to, and they're there because they work.'

'That may be true for you,' Lotta said. 'I'm here to do a good job.'

Annika picked up her bag again. 'I'll be waiting outside,' she said.

Niklas Linde arrived fifteen minutes late, true to form. Annika hurried to sit in the front seat while Lotta put her things in the boot.

'Hi,' he said, putting his hand briefly on her thigh. 'How are you?'

She took a deep breath, terrified that Lotta would see, but overjoyed at his touch. She managed a smile. 'Great,' she said.

Lotta closed the boot and Linde removed his hand. She got into the back seat and leaned forward between the front seats the way Kalle and Ellen did when they weren't strapped in.

'Lotta Svensson Bartholomeus,' she said, holding her hand out and smiling at him.

He took her hand briefly, then looked at her in the rear-view mirror. 'Niklas Linde,' he said. 'I know this doesn't look like a police car, but I can assure you it is. So I'll have to ask you to put your seatbelt on.'

Lotta actually giggled. Annika glanced at her, then looked ahead, through the windscreen. Mustn't give anything away, she thought. Lotta won't notice anything if we don't give her any reason to. She folded her arms.

He'd changed his clothes: the sports shirt had been replaced by a short-sleeved shirt of some rough material. His hair curled down onto his shoulders – she had washed it. She imagined she could still detect the smell of the cheap hotel shampoo.

'How was Jocke?' Niklas asked.

'Not too good,' Annika said. 'He's homesick.'

'That particular prison usually has that effect on people,' the police officer said, as he pulled out into the traffic.

She braced herself as they went round a bend by

holding onto the dashboard. The best defence was actually to act normally. 'I've been thinking about something,' she said. 'The name "Zarco Martinez" can't be very common?'

'You'd be surprised,' Linde said. 'It's not Andersson, exactly, but it's not Bartholomeus either. I know a few people called Zarco Martinez here in Marbella. One of them's a bloody good solicitor.'

'I've seen the name somewhere before,' Annika said. 'Before I ever heard of our little drug-smuggler.'

'Jocke's got a brother,' Linde said. 'He must be in prison somewhere because we haven't seen him for a while. His name's Nicke Zarco Martinez. They used to work together.'

The big brother who had started dealing while he was still at school. But where would Annika have come across his name? 'No,' she said. 'That's not right. Not Nicke Zarco Martinez. It was something else.'

A large bullfighting stadium slid past on the right. 'Oh!' she said. 'I've been here before.'

'You wanted pictures of the warehouse in La Campana.'

Annika turned to Lotta. 'Do you think there's any point trying to get pictures of an old drug-dealers' warehouse?'

'There's not really much to see,' Linde said. 'The container's been taken away as evidence.'

The photographer thought for a moment. 'Is it in an authentic neighbourhood?'

He glanced at her in the rear-view mirror. 'I think you could safely say so.'

Lotta nodded enthusiastically. 'Let's go, then.'

Annika looked at his profile. 'My head of news wants a heroic portrait of a Swedish police officer on the Costa del Crime. Can I write about you, or is anyone else down here at the moment?'

314

He was steering the Jaguar fast through the narrow streets. 'Knut Garen is the official Nordic representative here.'

'Yes,' Annika said, 'I know. But sometimes the Swedish police conduct operations, don't they, without actually being stationed here?'

She was thinking about David Lindholm, and Julia's description of Estepona while he had been working under cover, infiltrating some drug gang.

Linde braked and blew his horn at a cement-mixer that had stopped in the middle of a roundabout. 'At the moment I'm the only one here.'

'So what do you do, then?'

He drove up onto the pavement and passed the cement-mixer on the inside. 'I'm a co-ordinator. An observer, you could say. I'm the link between the police in Malmö and the Spanish police on a particular case affecting both countries.'

So he was stationed in Malmö.

'How active are you?'

'I follow the surveillance and am involved in the decision-making process: do we go in now? Do we wait? Shall we let the shipment through and try to get the recipient as well?'

'Like you did with the second shipment at New Year?' Annika said. 'The one with the oranges that you put a transmitter on?'

His face assumed a grim expression. 'They ditched the truck in Karlsruhe. The sides of the container had been broken open. They threw the transmitter into the Rhine.'

'Oh,' Annika said.

'A serious fuck-up,' he said. 'And I was the one who insisted that we should let it through.'

She didn't say anything for a minute or so. The streets

315

were climbing upwards, the gates growing more ornate and the walls higher.

'God, how tasteless,' Lotta said, from the back seat. 'Who on earth would want to live like this?'

People willing to pay ten million euros, Annika thought. 'Is it common to have Swedish police officers working under cover here?' she asked.

'I wouldn't say that.'

'But when it does happen, how does it come about?'

'We'd be talking about an agent who's extremely active. He infiltrates an organization, probably as a buyer. Under Swedish law we're not allowed to incite people to commit crimes, unlike in most other countries. That makes the situation a bit tricky.'

'But we do have agents like that?'

'All countries do.'

'Did you know David Lindholm?'

He cast her a quick glance of surprise. 'The TV guy? No. Why do you ask?'

'He was down here a few years ago on a fairly long undercover job.'

'When was this?'

Annika thought for a moment. Julia had been pregnant with Alexander, and the boy was four and half now. 'About five years ago,' she said. 'He lived in Estepona with his family for a while.'

Linde shook his head. 'Not a chance.'

'Yes,' Annika said. 'I'm absolutely certain. His wife hated it. David was gone for weeks at a time, and he couldn't tell her anything about what he was doing.'

Linde frowned. 'I spent all that year travelling back and forth, and I can assure you that we didn't have any independent agents from Stockholm stationed in Estepona. That's not to say he wasn't here, of course, but he wasn't working for the Swedish police if he was.'

Annika frowned. Could she have misunderstood Julia? 'Maybe he was so secret that no one knew about him,' she tried. 'Not the Nordic co-ordinator or the Spanish police.'

'That's not how it works. Everyone is always kept informed of what we're doing.' He turned left and the road sloped downward. 'Suppose we were driving from Malmö to Holland for some reason,' he went on. 'We'd have to have approval from the Danish and the German police, simply in order to cross their territory. Being so deep under cover that no one knows about it is completely out of the question. Do you recognize where we are?'

They were in an industrial district with low buildings and narrow streets. 'Yes!' she said. 'I've been here before!'

Linde sighed. 'You must have the worst sense of direction in Europe. Yes, you've definitely been here before, with me. You even took a picture of that doorway.' He leaned across her, resting his lower arm on her thigh, and opened the glove-compartment. His touch made Annika stiffen – what if Lotta noticed? He fished out a large bunch of keys, then sat up. Annika could feel his arm burning through the fabric of her skirt.

'What a charming place,' Lotta said, opening the door.

'Hang on,' Linde said. 'We can't stop here.' He put the car in gear and drove off.

'Aren't we going in?' Lotta said, looking at the closed shutters as they disappeared behind them.

'I'm fond of this car so it's a better idea to leave it round the corner.' He parked at a pedestrian crossing on the next block, switched the engine off and turned to face Lotta. 'I'd appreciate it if you took a fairly discreet camera with you. We'll all benefit from being a bit incognito.'

'Oh,' she said. 'Of course.'

'Good,' he said, taking the key from the ignition and getting out of the car.

Lotta took a camera and a small flash from the boot, and they started to walk up towards the warehouse. Annika and Linde were walking next to each other, close but without touching, up the long slope. The workshops and wholesalers had opened again after the siesta. The sound of saws cut through the air, and they had to jump to avoid a cascade of sparks from a metalwork lathe. Two men were shouting something further up the street. It was hard to tell if they were angry or happy.

'What'll happen to this particular gang?' Annika asked. 'How far have you got with the investigation?'

'Let's talk about that when we get inside.'

He stopped beside the entrance to the warehouse. Annika studied the façade. The faded sign saying 'Apits Carga' hung crookedly. The metal shutters had probably been blue once, but the paint had peeled off through weather and heavy use. The building was fairly tall compared to its neighbours, about six metres, she guessed.

Linde looked round, then crouched down, unlocked a small padlock by the wall and pulled up the metal screen. Behind it was another door, which he unlocked and slid open. 'Please,' he said, gesturing for them to hurry inside. Annika stepped into the darkness, closely followed by Lotta, and he closed the door behind them. It went pitch-black. 'Scared of the dark?' he asked.

'Actually, yes,' Lotta said.

Annika didn't answer, just breathed in the smell of sawdust and rotten fruit.

A moment later there was a click by the wall and the

warehouse was bathed in light. She raised her arm to her eyes instinctively, blinked a few times, and saw that the warehouse was equipped with the same sort of halogen floodlights you would normally see in sports stadiums or on building sites.

The warehouse was bigger than it looked from the outside. The walls had been whitewashed, with the exception of a grey rectangle of breezeblocks on the long wall at the back. Dust and spiders' webs hung in the air. Chunks of timber and fragments of plywood were scattered on the floor. A rusty saw leaned against one of the end walls. There was a pile of tools, or rather fragments of tools, in the far left-hand corner. In the right-hand corner there was a metre-high pile of sawdust.

Linde let go of the circuit-breaker and came over to her. 'You can't refer to me as your source for this,' he said, 'not even anonymously. You can write something opaque, "the police investigation indicates", something along those lines.'

She pulled her notepad out. 'Okay,' she said, and wrote *reliable sources within the Spanish police*.

Lotta had pulled out her camera and was heading enthusiastically towards the pile of tools in the far left corner.

Linde took a few steps across the concrete floor. His hair curled at his neck and his jeans were tight on his thighs. 'Apits is a haulage company,' he said. 'They ship fruit and vegetables from South America to Europe. There's no big apparatus behind it. It's all fairly small-scale. Apits Carga is the freight part of the business. We assume that Carga owns the containers and pays the shipping costs. Apits Depósito is the storage side of things, and that's the part of the business that rents this warehouse. Apits Transporte owns the articulated lorries that carry the containers north from here.'

'What does Apits stand for?' Annika asked.

'I don't actually know,' he said. 'There's nothing that resembles "Apits" in English, Spanish or any other language. "*Apios*" is the plural of celery in Spanish – that's the closest we've managed to get. We don't think it's got any significance, even if celery is a type of vegetable. The domain name apits.com has been registered, but isn't in use. It's not a first name or surname, so we're assuming it's an acronym.'

'A Place Indoors Thwarts Storms?'

'Or Airport Passenger Intelligent Transport Systems. That's a Japanese set-up for streamlining passenger check-ins at large airports. Or Analogue Proprietary Integrated Telephone System. Together with Dpits, Apits forms an integrated telephone system developed by Panasonic.'

'Not very likely, then?' Annika said.

'Not really.'

'So it stands for something completely different?'

'Anna Petter Ines Tore Sigurd. Your guess is as good as mine.'

'This is brilliant,' Lotta said. 'Good light, great atmosphere. You really get a sense of workers toiling at their machinery.'

This is good, Annika thought. We sound completely normal. Not like we spent half the night fucking.

Linde walked past her towards the grey rectangle on the far wall. 'There used to be an entrance at the back as well,' he said, pointing, 'but they bricked it up. They wanted control over anyone coming or going.'

'Who are "they"? Who owns Apits – or, rather, who's behind it?'

He let out a deep sigh. 'Gibraltar,' he said.

'So how much do you really know?'

He held out his hands.

Annika knew perfectly well that they were hard and strong. She looked down at her notepad.

'We know that the warehouse was rented on a two-year contract to Apits Depósito. We found that out when we searched the offices of the building's owners, a company in San Pedro.'

'But this has nothing to do with oranges and melons.'

'In part it does. The company ships fruit and vegetables, but only as a smokescreen for their real business.'

'Which is cocaine from South America.'

'Which is cocaine from Colombia,' Linde said.

Annika walked around the walls, looking up at the exposed roof. She could feel him following her with his eyes. 'Are the building's owners under any suspicion?'

'Discounted from the investigation entirely.' He stopped in the middle of the floor. 'This is where the container was,' he said. 'Checked through Customs in Algeciras on the twenty-ninth of December last year, with Apits Carga listed as the owner. Your little friend Jocke was supposed to have driven the contents up through Europe in a small lorry leased on a one-year contract by Apits Transporte. And that's all we know.'

She walked over to him. He didn't move. 'So how did you catch them?' He had shaved. He smelt good.

'Surveillance,' he said. 'The boys talked among themselves. Jocke seems to have been at the centre of the web. We've re-evaluated his status. It looks likely that he was the link between the distributor and the other men who were arrested.'

'He told me he never said anything important on his mobile.'

'True,' Linde said, with a grin. 'But only if you count his conversations in Spanish. One of the lads used to live in Rinkeby and Jocke didn't think we'd be able to understand what he was saying if they spoke Swedish to each other.'

'Is there any way to lower the lighting?' Lotta called.

'Lower it?' he asked, turning towards her. She was lying on the floor with her camera pressed to her nose, photographing a broken pair of plate-shears.

'A dimmer-switch or something?'

'Er, no.'

He turned to Annika and ran his finger quickly down her cleavage.

Annika opened her eyes wide and pulled a face telling him to stop. They couldn't start any rumours that she was having sex with her sources, not after the picture with Halenius. 'So the distributor is Apits and its sister companies,' she said, checking over his shoulder to make sure Lotta hadn't seen anything. She was engrossed in the plate-shears.

'Correct.'

'And the men under arrest are . . . what? Small-time gangsters?'

'Right again.'

'And the supplier is?'

'The Colombians.'

Annika looked at Lotta again. She recalled what Carita Halling Gonzales had said about her murdered father-in-law: the Colombians wipe out whole families. No one must be left to inherit anything. 'Does the Colombian Mafia have a presence here on the Costa del Sol at the moment?'

'Obviously they have representatives who make sure that the deliveries work.'

'Is it okay if I move the saw?' Lotta called from the corner.

'Not really,' Linde said.

She wanted to touch him. She wanted to put her hand on his stomach and stroke downwards, over his jeans. 'How big was the seizure?' she asked.

'What do you mean by "big"?'

She stared at her notes. 'Did everyone get excited and start cracking open the champagne?'

'Seven hundred kilos is a lot, but on average the Spanish police seize a ton every day. So it won't go down in the history books.'

Lotta got to her feet and brushed the sawdust from her dress.

Annika took a step back.

'And Apits isn't a particularly big player,' Linde said. 'But they've been established and active on the Costa del Sol for a long time. We've found information about rental contracts for trucks and warehouses going back to the mid-sixties. In other words, this is a small but very well-organized drug-distribution company. And obviously it's a good thing if such an established syndicate gets smashed, particularly from our Swedish perspective.'

'Why?'

'Because their main customers were in Holland, Germany and Sweden.'

'And this is the first time they've been caught?'

'They're bound to have had smaller shipments seized, but nothing on this scale.'

'What will it mean for them? Is this the end of the business?'

'We don't know anything about their internal state of affairs, so it's difficult to answer that.'

'Will they get trouble from the Colombians?'

'They'll have to replace what was lost, and usually both parties share the hit. Every tenth shipment is lost, and the Colombians bear that in mind in their planning. Anyway, it's like a piss in the Nile for them. But for a set-up like Apits it could be make or break.'

He took a step forward, so that he was standing right next to her, and put his lips to her ear. 'I won't be able to spend tonight with you.'

She stiffened and her pen slipped, drawing a long line across her notepad. 'Why not?'

'I have to be somewhere else.'

He walked past her towards the door, carefree and untroubled.

She stayed where she was, immobile. He's got someone else, she thought. The woman in the background at the terrace where he was having coffee when I called. *Hasta luego*, then a kiss. Or Carmen at the restaurant up in that mountain village. Or one of the girls who were laughing so hysterically when he called me from the Sinatra Bar the first night I was here last time . . .

'Is there anything else you want to know?' he asked.

Who is she? Annika thought. 'Jocke Martinez,' she said. 'How did he get his information from the distributors?'

He opened the door a crack and looked out, then closed it again. 'That's one of our biggest stumbling blocks,' he said. 'We don't know how Martinez communicated with his employers, and we don't know how Apits communicated with the Colombians.'

'If they didn't use the phone, did they write letters? Emails? Did they meet at various tapas bars and exchange coded messages in folded newspapers?'

'We had Martinez under surveillance. He didn't meet anyone we can link to the supply chain. We haven't found any written evidence, and nothing on the harddrive of his personal computer. But he could have gone to an Internet café and received messages under the alias

Horny Finnish Housewife on some online message-board that we don't know about.'

'Did he often go to Internet cafés?'

'This was a really great place,' Lotta said, stopping beside the police officer with a smile.

'Never,' Linde said. 'By the way, I've found you a party girl. She says she wants to speak out in the paper as a warning to others.'

'Great,' Annika said, forcing herself to smile. 'Thanks a lot.'

'Come on. I'll drive you back to your hotel.'

22

Lotta dashed to sit in the front seat. She was talking enthusiastically to Linde about how much she had appreciated the bare setting of the warehouse, the harsh shadows, the worn tools.

Annika sat in the back trying to get a grip on her feelings.

Somewhere else.

Obviously.

What had she been expecting? That he'd move into the flat on Agnegatan?

She stared out of the window. Gates and walls and rooftops rushed past. No, she thought. I wasn't expecting him to move in with me, but I did think he'd be with me for the few nights I'm here.

Then a terrible thought: He didn't think I was any good in bed. She shut her eyes. Tried to pull herself together. I thought it was good, and that's what matters. He can think what he likes. I don't regret it. She stifled a sob.

'What do you say, Annika?'

She met his gaze in the rear-view mirror. 'What?' she said.

'Do you agree that art is much more real than journalism?'

She looked out of the window again. 'That's an impossible question,' she said. 'What does "more real" mean? It's like asking, "What's special about a fish?" and getting the answer, "It can't ride a bike."'

Linde burst out laughing.

'What I mean is that art creates an experience inside you as a viewer, whereas newspapers only report other people's experiences,' Lotta said.

'That's crap,' Annika said. 'Do you mean you never experience anything when you read a newspaper or watch the news on television? When children are gassed to death? Or teenage girls vanish without a trace? Or dictators are toppled and people get democracy?'

'That's not what I meant,' Lotta said, sounding hurt.

'So what did you mean? That people will be more affected by your photographs of those plate-shears than reading about little children dying of fentanyl-gas poisoning on the floor of the landing outside their mother's bedroom door?'

The silence in the car was deafening. The only thing she could hear was her own agitated breathing.

Oh, God, she thought. I'm doing it again. Going into battle for the most ridiculous things instead of talking about the real problems. There must be something wrong with me. 'Sorry,' she said. 'I've got the most awful headache.'

'Here in Spain there are lots of fun pills,' Linde said. 'Do you want me to stop at a *farmacia*?'

'I've got some paracetamol in my room,' she said.

They passed the bullfighting arena on the left and Annika could just make out the motorway below. Thank God they were nearly there.

They sat in silence until they pulled up in front of the Hotel Pyr.

'Give me a call before you leave,' he said, with a smile, through the open window.

She slammed the door and forced herself to smile back.

Lotta went straight up to her room without looking at Annika.

Fine, Annika thought. She went back out onto the street and set off towards the department store, turned right towards the harbour and went into McDonald's. She'd had enough of spending the evenings starving in her hotel room. She ordered a quarter-pounder with cheese, carrot sticks and mineral water, then sat at a window table.

It was relatively calm around her. A few kids were laughing near the counter. Two smartly dressed women were talking confidentially over a couple of muffins. At the table in front of her a man in a suit, white shirt and tie sat next to a teenager in a wheelchair. The boy seemed to have cerebral palsy. His arms, hands, feet and legs were contorted, and jerked uncontrollably. Annika made an effort not to stare at him, which was hard when he was sitting right in front of her. She picked at her carrots and drank the water.

The dad was talking to his son in low, soft Spanish, feeding him fries and holding a cup with a straw for him to drink from. The boy tried to say something, which his father evidently understood, because he laughed conspiratorially, then said, '*Sí, sí, claro.*'

The door opened and an elegant woman and a girl of about five walked in. The woman lit up when she caught sight of the father and son. She skipped between the tables, holding the little girl with one hand and shopping bags from D&G and Versace in the other. She went over to the table, kissed the man on the lips and the boy on the cheek, and said something that made all four of them laugh.

Without thinking, Annika got up from her table and walked towards the door. She bumped into tables on the way, bruising her legs, but the pain was in her chest. There was so much love in the world, if you only knew how to find it. And what did she choose to do? Fight pathetic little battles with everyone, obsessed with the idea of winning, of being *right*, of showing off and getting recognition.

Some British girls were coming along the pavement towards her, with loud voices, Zara bags and peeling noses. She wiped her tears with the back of her hand and walked quickly, head down, towards El Corte Inglés. She stopped outside the department store and looked up at the hotel. She didn't want to be alone in her room, waiting for someone to call.

I have to be somewhere else.

She looked in the other direction, and remembered that Rickard Marmén's estate agency was just round the corner. Maybe he was still there.

She turned right, past the British bookshop, and saw that the lights were still on. She tried the door, but it was locked. The office was empty, but a bluish reflection on the wall behind the desk told her that the computer was still on.

She knocked on the glass.

Marmén poked his head through a doorway at the back of the room. He seemed to say something, but Annika couldn't make out what. He vanished again, but re-appeared a moment later with a key in his hand. 'Annika Bengtzon, our favourite representative of the Swedish press,' he said, holding the door open. 'Welcome!'

Annika smiled and air-kissed him on both cheeks.

'And what can we do for you this evening?' he asked.

'I don't suppose you've any new lives for sale?' she said, walking into the shop.

'But, my dear, we don't sell anything else here. Dreams and new lives are our speciality. Did you have anything particular in mind? Marble floors, wild vines on the terrace? Four bathrooms, each with a sea view?'

She laughed, and her spirits rose. She sat down on one of the chairs in front of his desk. There was a large dustball by the desk-leg. The window was smeared. Marmén locked the door again and came to sit next to her on the other chair. 'What's wrong with the life you've already got?'

Annika decided to blank the question. 'I'm here to write some articles about drug-trafficking and money-laundering,' she said, 'so right now things aren't too bad. The title of the series is "The Costa Cocaine".'

'How exciting. Glass of wine?'

Annika shook her head.

He stood up anyway, then fetched a bottle of red wine and two glasses. 'You can keep me company,' he said. 'How are you getting on with the cocaine?' He poured some rioja into both glasses.

'I've got a bit more to do before I go back home,' she said.

'I can't help you there, I'm afraid,' he said. 'Drugs are one of the few things I've never dealt in. I've got no contacts at all. Cheers!'

He drank with his eyes closed.

Annika tasted the wine and put the glass to one side. 'Has business picked up?' she asked.

'If it was static before,' he said, 'it's going backwards now. The mortgage companies are demanding that buyers have a fifty per cent deposit in cash, even if there's already planning permission. Only the drug barons have that sort of money, and although there are a lot of them, they can't keep the whole market afloat. Prices are falling, so people would rather sit it out than

330

sell. I'm thinking of opening a lettings agency instead. That's what people are doing, these days, leasing their property in the hope that things will pick up—'

Annika interrupted his tale of woe. 'The drug-barons pay cash?' she said.

'If there's one thing they've got plenty of it's cash. You said you were writing about money-laundering? Building large, expensive houses is one way of cleaning up dirty money.'

Annika looked at the man beside her. She really shouldn't be remotely surprised. 'So you know how money-laundering works?'

Marmén smiled a very sad smile. 'Sadly I've never been blessed with any dirty money that needed laundering,' he said, 'but knowing how the washing-machine works is no great secret.'

'Would you mind telling me?'

'What do you want to know?'

She pulled her pen and notepad from her bag. He re-filled his glass.

'So they buy property?' she said.

He nodded. 'The laws are constantly being tightened,' he said. 'Nowadays you can't just waltz into a bank with a sack full of dollars – the police will be there before you can say "deposit account". The banks and financial institutions have a duty to report anything suspicious. You have to be able to explain that you acquired the money legally.'

'So you buy a house?'

'Or you buy a plot and build a house. As much as possible gets paid in cash. It's no problem for the builder to roll up at his bank with a bundle of notes because he can explain that it came from building a house. He'll have receipts for pipes, cement and bricks. And then the house is there, all finished, and can be sold for X million euros. The drug-baron can prove that he got the money from selling a house perfectly legally. And then the money is back in the system.'

'They must build a lot of houses,' Annika said.

'And they must have a lot of luxury yachts that they sail about in,' Marmén said. 'That's why Gibraltar is so useful.'

Annika put down her pen. 'I read about something called "Operation White Whale",' she said. 'Some huge crackdown where loads of crooks were arrested, and more than two hundred and fifty villas seized. Apparently they used solicitors and companies in Gibraltar.'

Marmén nodded enthusiastically and drained his second glass. 'That's it exactly!'

Annika was taking notes. 'So how does it work? The money-launderer sets up a company in Gibraltar,' she said, drawing a circle in the middle of her page. 'Then what?'

'Several companies,' Marmén said patiently, reaching over and moving her notepad to his own lap. He drew several smaller circles around the first one. 'The barons feed money into a few of the companies, then start sending invoices to each other. For rent, perhaps, or consultancy services, import and export of goods, everything between Heaven and Earth.'

'But none of it's actually real?' Annika asked. 'All the invoices are false?'

He poured some more wine. 'Are you sure you don't want any?'

Annika pointed at the circles. 'When all the invoices are there, it's perfectly all right that the money is there as well?' she asked.

'Hey presto,' Marmén said. 'Dirty drug money has become lovely clean company profits, all of it audited and signed off by solicitors and bankers and accountants.

And Gibraltar is completely tax-free, which, of course, is wonderfully practical!'

'But doesn't anyone check to make sure that it's all above board?'

'Of course. The solicitors and bankers and accountants.'

'Solicitors and bankers and accountants in Gibraltar?'

'Exactly.'

She was starting to realize why Patrik had been so keen for her to interview someone practising there. 'You don't happen to know a Swedish solicitor I could interview?'

'In Gibraltar?' He rolled the wine around his mouth as he thought. Then he swallowed loudly. 'Not a Swede,' he said, 'but a Dane.'

'Does he launder money?'

'Like I said, not for me. Would you like me to call him?'

'If you wouldn't mind.'

She went through to the toilet while Marmén, swaying slightly, made his way round his desk and dialled a number with the prefix 350. There was no loo paper and the washbasin had dark-grey tide-marks. He had evidently cut back on cleaning costs.

She stood and looked at her reflection as she heard his voice rising and falling out in the shop. It was obvious that she had been crying. Her eyes were red and her lashes were like spiders' legs, with the clumped mascara. She was incredibly tired.

Then she heard the telephone being hung up out in the office. She dutifully flushed some water into the basin and went back out to Marmén.

'Stig Seidenfaden will see you in his office first thing tomorrow,' the estate agent said. 'Do you feel like heading down to the harbour for a bite to eat?'

She smiled, but felt ready to collapse. 'Thanks,' she said, 'but I've already eaten. Now I need to go and write an article.'

He tutted. 'All work and no play makes Jack a dull boy,' he said.

'Oh,' Annika said, 'I think you're pretty good fun.'

'I was thinking more of you,' he said seriously, as he switched off his computer.

They headed out through the door together. Marmén pulled down the obligatory metal shutter and secured it with a padlock to a hook in the pavement. 'Let me know if there's anything else you need help with,' he said, then waved and disappeared into the alleyways leading to the harbour.

The lobby was empty. There wasn't even any sign of the receptionist.

Annika hurried up to her room without meeting anyone. Best of all, there was no sign of Lotta. Relieved, she slumped onto the bed. That's how I see things, she thought. If I can avoid confrontation, if I don't have to talk and explain myself, then I've won. If I can talk about work, and make use of other people's expertise, I feel good. As long as someone answers my questions and does as I say, my anxiety fades away.

She straightened her back.

And that's not very healthy, she thought. It might even be worthy of its own diagnosis. What if I'm mentally ill?

Maybe she ought to see a shrink after all – her friend Anne Snapphane had been trying to persuade her to do so for long enough. Or she could try to change her behaviour. Make an effort to be more accommodating, even with people who didn't do as she said. How hard could that be?

She stood up and walked around the room restlessly.

People with far worse problems than hers managed to fit in. They had the capacity to appreciate love – it happened all over the place, all the time. It happened in damp prison cells, where men were locked away because they were scared for their closest relatives. It happened in half-empty hamburger joints, where people with a disabled child stuck together and loved each other.

She sat on the bed again and pulled her bag onto her lap. She took out her mobile and paused with it in her hand. She had to let Lotta know they would be going to Gibraltar early the next morning. The question was whether she should call her or send a text. She hesitated for half a second, then decided to text. First she clicked to check the list of missed calls.

Thomas's number was second on the list, after the government office.

It was now a quarter past eight. She pressed 'call'.

The phone rang, once, twice, three times, four . . . 'Hello, Thomas here . . .'

She had to clear her throat. 'Er, hello,' she said. 'It's me.'

'Hi! Hello!' he said. 'How are you?'

A double greeting. He was surprised to hear from her. 'I saw you called me,' she said. 'Some time this morning?'

'Yes, I did! Can you hold on?'

She heard him say something in English in the background. 'That's better,' he said. 'I'm outside now.'

'Where are you?'

'At the hotel, the Parador. A golf resort right by the sea, and right under the flight-path to the airport. If you hear something that sounds like the Third World War, it'll be the easyJet flight from London bringing a load of British tourists on a package holiday to Torremolinos—'
The rest of his words were drowned in the roar of a

plane coming in to land. 'That was it,' he said, and she couldn't help laughing. He must have had some wine – he wasn't usually so light-hearted.

'Did you want anything in particular when you rang?' she asked feebly, transferring responsibility for the call to him.

'Er, yes,' he said. 'I had a call from the insurance company this morning. Do you remember that damage assessor, Zachrisson?'

A small man with a wide, dishonest smile, in a glass-walled, high-rise office with chrome furniture. 'How could I forget?' she said.

'He said we're going to get the money. Do you know if anything's happened?'

She laughed with relief. It really was true. 'They've identified the person who did it,' she said. 'It's a woman who's in prison in the US. She's not going to be extradited, so there won't be a trial, but any suspicions against us have been dropped.'

She said 'us' rather than 'me', but he didn't protest. 'That's brilliant,' he said simply.

She gulped, then said: 'Do you want to celebrate?'

'Celebrate?'

'What are you doing tomorrow evening?'

'The negotiations are due to finish at four or so. We were going to have dinner.'

She bit her lip, making it bleed. 'Okay,' she said, embarrassed. 'Of course.'

There were a few long moments of silence. She put her hand over her eyes.

'It's just the Scandinavian delegation, though,' he said. 'The Norwegians have come along for the ride as usual, taking part in all the things they like about the EU but refusing to pay for any of it.' He fell silent.

'I could interview you about how the negotiations have gone,' Annika said.

'It might be a bit hard to summarize without—'

'You can just say that the discussions have been very rewarding, that you're making good progress and that everything's going as well as can be expected.'

He thought for a moment, then made up his mind. 'They can manage without me. Where shall we meet?'

She had to stifle a squeal of joy. 'I'm staying in Puerto Banús,' she said, trying to sound focused. 'Have you ever been here?'

'Once, with my parents, when I was fourteen. Where are you staying?'

She gave him the name of the hotel and some basic directions. They arranged to meet in the lobby at eight. Then they hung up, and she remembered that she was supposed to be writing something, but she was feeling so tired that she pulled off her skirt and top and crept under the covers, her mind full of confused but hopeful thoughts, and fell asleep just as the lights came on along the motorway.

Friday, 29 April

23

Dawn came later to the west of Spain than to any other part of Europe, a political decision by the Spanish authorities. They had decided that the whole of the Spanish mainland should share the same time zone as the rest of Europe, one hour ahead of Greenwich Mean Time, which made no geographic sense. Annika was standing on the beach in shorts, a hooded jacket and trainers, watching the sun rise over Puerto Banús at half past seven in the morning. The same sun was shining on the other side of the sea, hitting the red mountains of Morocco, but there it was only half past five.

She looked out across the water for a while. Her last day at work on the Costa del Sol. She would be flying home early the following morning. She hadn't written up a single word of any of the interviews she had conducted. All of the material existed only as fragmentary notes in her pad or as digital information on her mobile. It would take days to go through it and structure it into anything that was publishable. And none of the articles felt particularly interesting. She hadn't had time for what she'd been hoping to do: check out the members of the Söderström family.

There has to be a motive for this crime that we haven't identified. Executing an entire family is an expression of serious fucking brutality. The killer was making a point. We don't know which of the victims was the real target. Sebastian Söderström was a charming slacker. Veronica Söderström was a well-regarded solicitor. If you don't ask any questions, you don't get any answers. Suzette vanished without trace on 30 December last year. The worst of it may not be that she's dead.

The wind had got up during the night. It had changed direction, and the air was cooler now. She was freezing in her skimpy shorts.

Gibraltar was going to be a nightmare. They needed pictures from there, and they'd have to get some good shots of the Swedish girl who was going to spill the beans about her jet-set lifestyle. She might be the only person they could print a picture of in any of the articles. It all depended on whether the solicitor was willing to be photographed.

She wasn't going to win any prizes for her journalism with any of this, she knew. Mind you, her articles never would. She covered the wrong subject areas in the wrong medium. Heavy politics with a shaky handheld television camera was a cast-iron way of getting nominated for an award, as were sensitive articles in one of the morning papers about children or old people threatened by council cuts, and war, of course. War was actually easiest. You just needed an old man holding a white flag on some road in Iraq and you'd get Picture of the Year.

She raised her face towards the blood-red sun for a minute or so, then turned back towards the hotel. If she was in luck, she'd have time for breakfast before Lotta came down.

They bumped into each other outside the lifts. Lotta got out of one just as Annika was about to get into the

342

other. 'Britain hasn't signed up to the Schengen Agreement,' Annika said, 'so you'll need your passport. We'll set off in half an hour.'

The doors closed and she was carried up to the third floor.

She showered, got dressed, gathered her things together and wondered how she was going to persuade Lotta to take some photos. It was ridiculous, she thought, that the most troublesome part of an already difficult assignment was working out how to get the photographer to do her job.

She knew Patrik was expecting an utterly corrupt solicitor, Swedish, obviously, who was prepared to have his name and photograph printed alongside an article in which he explained how many billions he had laundered for the drugs Mafia. She doubted that Rickard Marmén's acquaintance would volunteer that sort of information. This had every chance of being a truly excruciating interview.

How nice of you to see me. Tell me, have you been bought off by the Mafia? Oh, really? And how do you feel about the colleagues who have taken their money?

She would just have to let him explain how the set-up with companies hidden from official oversight worked, and ask if he saw any dangers or shortcomings with it, then bulk out the article with Rickard Marmén's description of how money-laundering worked. She would have to stitch it all together so that the Dane was the personification of an activity he didn't actually represent, ideally in such a way that the paper wouldn't get sued.

She could hear Anders Schyman's voice in her head: *It's just a question of how you frame the article.*

She left her room, closed the door and headed towards the lifts.

*

343

Lotta had even more equipment with her than she'd had the previous day: the rucksack with her camera and lenses, a large flash, a tripod for the camera and another for the flash, a circular screen to direct the light and another bag whose contents Annika couldn't guess at. 'Do you really think you need to take all that?' she asked.

Lotta didn't answer, just carried it purposefully to the car, first the rucksack, then the two tripods, and finally the screen and the bag.

'We only need fairly straightforward pictures,' Annika said. 'Really just four. A general view of Gibraltar, a shot of Main Street, a portrait of the solicitor and one of the girl in Estepona.'

Lotta got into the car and started the engine. Annika got into the passenger seat with her bag on her lap. She pulled out a bundle of notes and printouts, and set to work. She knew she would end up feeling car-sick, but it would be worth it to avoid having to talk.

Lotta drove up onto the N340, then turned right towards the toll-motorway. She didn't say a word until they were halfway to Estepona. 'Your outburst yesterday was completely unacceptable,' she said, gripping the steering-wheel so tightly that her knuckles were white.

'Not now,' Annika said, without looking up from her papers. 'Not on the motorway.'

The drive was shorter than she had dared to hope. They arrived at La Línea, the Spanish border-town that had practically merged with Gibraltar, after just half an hour. They drove along a four-lane highway that followed the coast, with the vast Rock rising up in front of them, 430 metres straight up from the sea, according to Annika's printouts from Wikipedia.

'Try to find somewhere to park,' Annika said. 'It's

supposed to be really difficult to drive across the border, and there's no guarantee that they'll let us through at all seeing as we're in a hire car.'

'I'm going to take good pictures, and for that I need good equipment. I can't drag everything with me so I'll have to take the car across.'

'To get the pictures we need, you don't need all that studio equipment,' Annika said.

Lotta braked sharply. The cars in front of them formed a lengthy queue.

Annika sighed. They waited for a minute. Two minutes. Five minutes.

She opened the door and got out. 'I'll go and see what's happened.'

It was considerably cooler here than in Marbella. The sea on her right was the Atlantic, and the water beyond the Rock was the Mediterranean; the wind was coming from the Atlantic. She was glad she'd decided to wear her jeans and a sweater.

She walked past car after car, some hundred metres, until she could see where the queue started. Then she turned and went back. Lotta had moved about four metres. She got back into the car.

'This is the queue for the border-crossing into Gibraltar,' she said. 'We can probably expect to sit here for a couple of hours if we're going to drive across. At least.'

'You don't respect my integrity as a photographer,' Lotta said. 'I have to feel happy to put my name to everything I produce. You tell me to take a nondescript picture of an ugly prison when it would actually be possible to take a really dramatic photograph of the same thing.'

Annika swallowed hard. 'Maybe,' she said, 'but it's the ugly prison that's important for the article. It doesn't matter that there are loads of women with goats and furrowed faces around us because, right now, we're here to write about drugs and money-laundering.'

'I'm not talking about women with furrowed faces, I only took those pictures so I had something to do while I was waiting. Of course it's possible to take good pictures of a prison, but you have to follow the light – you have to work with the picture. Be there at dawn and dusk, see how the colours change . . .'

'So why weren't you there, then?' Annika asked.

'You're the one who makes all the decisions! You're the one who says when we're going somewhere and where we're going. You treat me like I'm your secretary.'

'Have I stopped you taking the initiative? Have I said no on any occasion that you've suggested something? You've got exactly what you wanted every time you've opened your mouth!'

Lotta looked down at her hands and tried to suppress a sob. 'This isn't easy,' she said. 'I'm completely new to this and you're Annika Bengtzon. Do you really think I dare suggest to you what we should do?'

Annika heard herself gasp. '"You're Annika Bengtzon"? What the hell's that supposed to mean?'

'Everyone knows how you treat temps. Do you think I wanted to come on this job and spend four days in your company?'

Annika stuffed her papers into her bag, opened the car door and got out.

'Where are you going?' Lotta shouted.

'Take whatever fucking pictures you want to. I'm going to interview the solicitor. See you at the airport tomorrow morning.' She slammed the door and marched off towards the border with her bag over her shoulder.

*

There was no queue to cross the border on foot. She showed her passport and left the Spanish side, walked ten metres or so across no man's land and entered the British border-post.

The building looked like an Underground station in some London suburb. The ceiling was low and arched, the floor grey-blue, the walls concrete. There were a few tired pot plants, a Coca-Cola machine, and a machine selling disgusting chocolate. A sweaty, red-faced man was sitting at a desk and gave her passport a desultory glance as she walked past.

She stopped at the tourist information office at the end of the tunnel, and asked for a map with City Mill Lane marked on it.

'Go over the runway,' the tourist guide said, pointing through the door, 'then up to the left, over the draw-bridge, in through the city walls, and you'll be in Main Street. When you get to the Plaza turn left again, and City Mill Lane is a bit further up the Rock.'

She said thank you, went out of the door, and found herself in Great Britain, on Winston Churchill Avenue. She hoisted her bag onto her shoulder, and began to cross a landing strip that stretched from one body of water to the other.

This was where Veronica Söderström had worked. She had crossed this border every day, crossed this landing strip to get to work. Or did she usually drive? Did she sit in that long queue, or had she found some way of avoiding it? Why on earth had she put up with it?

There had to be a very good reason why she had established her office in Gibraltar.

The number of people crossing the landing strip was fairly small. There was a cold side-wind blowing from the Atlantic, and she hunched her shoulders and pulled her sleeves down over her fingers. Her pulse slowed. She forced Lotta's words from her mind: *Do you think I wanted to spend four days in your company?*

She was trembling as if she were actually freezing.

In front of her there were some hideous apartment blocks, with washing hanging off them. There might be a lot of money here, she thought, but it doesn't show in the look of the place.

The centre of the city was older, better looked after, and seriously commercialized. Main Street had ornate benches that no one was sitting on, elaborate lampposts and rubbish bins, and hundreds of tax-free shops for tourists. It was a kaleidoscope of jewellers and off-licences, fashion boutiques, department stores, mobile-phone shops, toyshops and, thank God, camera shops.

She went into one and asked for a decent digital camera with a wide-angle lens and a simple zoom, a large memory and a charged battery.

I can use it to take pictures of the children afterwards, she thought. After all, I'll soon have the insurance money.

She sat on one of the ornate benches outside the shop and skimmed through the English-language instructions. It was as simple as she had hoped. Point and click. The camera automatically adjusted everything, from the aperture to shutter speed and focus. She dropped it into her bag with the rest of her clutter and carried on along Main Street.

Ten minutes later she found City Mill Lane, a narrow, winding street with no pavements that clambered up the western side of the Rock. She set off up the road, soon out of breath, thanks to her heavy bag. The noise from Main Street died away and soon there was total silence up among the buildings. She smelt dust and sausages.

Number thirty-four was a brown door between a travel agent and a barber.

*

The Danish solicitor, Stig Seidenfaden, had a modest office on the second floor of the old building in City Mill Lane. He received her with a formal bow and showed her into a small conference room where tea and scones had been laid out.

'So you're a good friend of Rickard Marmén,' he said, looking at her with interest. 'How long have you known each other?'

Annika sat down on one side of the table, and Stig Seidenfaden sat down at the end. 'We meet up for dinner every now and then,' she said vaguely. 'Rickard often helps me with contacts.'

A secretary came in with a sugar-bowl, which she put on the table, then glided out silently and closed the door.

There was a short and slightly oppressive silence once she had left. Annika looked around. Three windows filled almost the whole of the wall facing the street. You could see right into the building opposite: a conference room similar to the one she was sitting in. It was very quiet. The sun, creeping through the top few centimetres of the window, was making the dust dance near the ceiling.

Stig Seidenfaden cleared his throat and leaned forward across the table. 'Rickard told me that you were interested in interviewing a Scandinavian solicitor in Gibraltar,' he said. 'There aren't many of us and, of course, one of our number died last winter.'

'You mean Veronica Söderström?' Annika said.

The man nodded. 'We tend to stick together, us Nordic types down here in the sun. Rickard's friends are my friends. How can I help you?'

'Did you know Veronica Söderström?'

Stig Seidenfaden poured some tea from the pot and sighed. 'We weren't close friends, but naturally we knew each other. Some tea?'

Annika moved her cup and the solicitor filled it. The

china was delicate, decorated with roses and a gold rim. The saucer was chipped. 'What sort of law did she specialize in?'

The solicitor looked rather surprised. 'Her practice was somewhat broader than mine. She dealt with business cases and crime. She was also authorized to work as a public notary, I seem to recall. I provide corporate services.'

'Business and tax?' Annika said.

He nodded.

'Can you explain how the tax system in Gibraltar works?'

He nodded again and stirred his tea. 'People have been able to register tax-free companies here since 1967,' he said, 'but it wasn't until Spain joined the EU in 1985 that things started to take off.'

She had taken out her pen and pad and was making notes. 'Is anyone allowed to register a company here?'

The solicitor leaned back in his chair, holding the small handle of the teacup tightly and sticking his little finger out. 'There are certain criteria that need to be fulfilled. The working capital of the company has to be over a hundred British pounds.' He paused to give her time to write it down. 'No resident of Gibraltar is allowed to be the ultimate owner of the company. The company is only allowed to conduct its business here if all its income is derived from sources outside Gibraltar.'

She glanced at the man, at his serious expression and bulging stomach.

Was this why Veronica Söderström had travelled to Gibraltar every day? To uphold some sort of washed-out British business morality in a make-believe country on the edge of Africa?

'The company must have its official address here, and keep its register of shareholders here. Lastly, the pro-

350

prietor must be able to attest to his good standing and financial status.'

She made an effort to look interested. 'Who provides those references?'

'They have to be given by a bank, a solicitor or an accountant.'

Annika nodded. This was what Marmén had been saying.

'And there's no official oversight of companies registered here?'

'All information is treated as confidential, and isn't entered on any public register.'

'And there are no taxes?'

'There's no income tax here, no tax on company profits, no stamp duty on the transfer of shares, and no taxation at source. The only thing that's obligatory is a fixed tax of two hundred and twenty-five British pounds each year.'

Annika couldn't help shaking her head. 'It seems remarkable,' she said, 'that something can work like this in modern-day Europe.'

'Not for much longer,' the solicitor said. 'The rules are changing. This system's coming to an end. The EU is putting a stop to it.' He sipped his tea. 'But there'll be alternative solutions,' he said. 'There always are.'

'Will there be any more transparency after 2010?'

'I can't imagine there would be,' the solicitor said. 'Have you tried the scones? My wife made them.'

'Your wife?'

'And secretary.'

He spread some marmalade on one. It crunched as he bit into it.

'I've spoken to people who describe Gibraltar as the biggest money-laundering machine in Europe,' Annika said. 'What's your opinion?'

The solicitor chewed his scone, picked up a napkin and wiped crumbs from the corners of his mouth. 'I'm a solicitor,' he said, 'not a prosecutor. I have to trust my clients. If they say that a source of income is legitimate, then it isn't my job to question that information. But I only provide references when I can personally guarantee the good standing of my client.'

'Do you see any dangers with this system?'

'It wasn't constructed by lawyers,' he said. 'We just make sure that it's adhered to. Any solicitors who actively participate in money-laundering, who set up fake companies and slalom around the legislation – well, I dissociate myself entirely from them.'

'Do you know of any like that?'

He smiled. 'Even if I did, do you think I'd tell you?'

She smiled back politely. 'I doubt it. Would it be all right if I took a picture of you?'

He raised his eyebrows. 'Yes,' he said, 'I suppose so. Where? Here?'

'In your office, perhaps? With some files and documents in the background?' Usually it was best to avoid pictures of men sitting behind desks, but in this case it would serve a purpose. The reader would see the files, wonder what they contained and hear the washing-machine rumbling in the background.

He shook his head. 'I don't let anyone in there,' he said.

Smart man. She took out the camera, switched it on and held the viewfinder up to her right eye. It looked a bit odd. There was a pot-plant in the background, and the solicitor was sitting directly between her and it. As a result, a plant seemed to be growing out of the top of his head.

'Perhaps we could move closer to the window,' she said. 'For the light.'

She positioned the man beside one of the windowsills, with his profile facing the glass. Then she stood in front of him. The daylight was soft and indirect. Half of his face was clearly visible, the other half in shadow. The effect was rather striking.

She took several pictures of him sitting at the table as well, and then she was done. They stepped out into the little hallway again, and the secretary-wife materialized on silent feet to ask if everything had gone all right. She spoke English with a British accent.

'Very well,' Annika said politely. 'And thank you for the scones. They were delicious.' Then she remembered she hadn't had one. 'Veronica Söderström,' she said quickly. 'Where was her office?'

'I suppose it's still there,' Stig Seidenfaden said. 'It's in Tareq's Passage. Opposite the church.'

Annika did up the zip on her bag, shook his hand and thanked him.

'Say hello to Rickard,' Stig Seidenfaden called down the stairs after her.

24

The stream of people on Main Street had thickened into a dark mass. The street led vaguely uphill, and she took out the camera and stood on one of the benches. Using the telephoto lens she compressed the crowd still further, then took a few portrait shots and several in landscape.

There, enough establishing shots.

She stood there for a few minutes trying to identify a suitable subject for a photograph: a young man with broad shoulders and jeans that clung to his thighs. He was walking up Main Street with his arm round his girlfriend. He was even wearing a sports shirt.

'Hello,' Annika said, going up to him with her hand out.

Taken by surprise, the couple stopped and shook her outstretched hand: an instinctive reaction in Westerners. Annika explained that she was a photographer, and asked if she could take a picture of the young man from behind: she needed an anonymous picture of a young man to illustrate a newspaper article.

The man seemed pleased, but his girlfriend was unhappy. 'What's the point of that?' she said.

'What sort of article?' the young man asked.

'It's for a Swedish paper, the *Evening Post*,' she said. 'Have you ever seen it?'

He hadn't.

Annika positioned him so he was facing a dark-grey building, asked him to spread his legs, hook his fingers in the waist of his jeans, and put most of his weight on his right leg.

He was almost a carbon copy of Niklas Linde.

She took a series of shots, then asked him to turn his head slightly to the left. The sun was hitting his hair and back, putting his profile in shadow. It would do as an anonymous picture of the heroic Swedish police officer on the Costa del Sol.

She thanked him for his help.

'When can I see the picture?' the young man asked, with interest.

'Keep an eye on the online edition of the Swedish *Evening Post*,' Annika said.

She put the camera away and made her way to the church. It was white, and looked like all the churches in Pedro Almodóvar's films. In front of it was a small square. On the far side there were two alleyways, each entered through an archway: Giro's Passage to the right, and Tareq's Passage on the left.

She headed left. The archway led straight through the building at the end and into a narrow alley. She was met by the deafening roar of a huge air-conditioning unit and stood there at a loss. The old buildings lining the alleyway were poorly maintained. Electricity cables hung like lianas between the windows. Water and drainage pipes had been stuck to the outside of the buildings, making them look misshapen. All the shutters on the windows of the lowest two floors were closed and padlocked.

She walked further down the alley and found a door with a entry-phone but no identifying label. Round the corner there was a small brass sign:

VS Counselling
Barrister – Solicitor – Commissioner for Oaths
International Legal Services
International Corporate Services

VS: Veronica Söderström.

But where was the entrance?

She walked on another ten metres, passing an estate agency that looked closed, and a chemist that was just opening, and stopped to think. What had Veronica Söderström spent all her time doing in this run-down building?

Had she fought to defend those let down by society? People who had been wrongly convicted? Had she arranged contracts worth billions for the fishing industry?

Or had she laundered money?

If you don't ask any questions, you don't get any answers.

She looked down at her clothes. Trainers, jeans and a sweater from H&M: there was no way she could pass as a chief executive or international investor. She walked determinedly towards the unlabelled entry-phone, pressed the button and held it down. Eventually an intercom came to life with a great deal of crackling.

'Yes, what is it?' a voice said, in an American accent. It sounded young, male and annoyed.

'Hello, my name's Annika Bengtzon, and I need some help with a legal problem,' she said. 'Can I come up?'

The phone was still making a noise. The irritated young man hadn't hung up.

'A legal problem?' he said. 'I can't help you with that. I'm very sorry.'

Annika didn't believe him. He didn't sound the slightest bit sorry.

'I can go somewhere else,' Annika said, 'but Veronica would have wanted me to come here first.'

Another silence. More crackling.

'You knew Veronica?'

'I'm their stable manager. I look after My's pony.'

The lock clicked.

She hurried to push the door open and stepped into a pitch-black stairwell. The door closed behind her and she blinked a few times to get her eyes used to the dark. Then she saw a luminous red button just to her left. She pressed it and the lights came on with an audible click.

A naked bulb cast an uncertain light over a small entrance hall. A narrow staircase led up steeply in front of her. The walls and ceiling had seen better days. The floor must have been beautiful once upon a time: under a layer of dirt she could make out a blue, white and brown mosaic.

There were two doors, one on the right, one on the left. They were both barred and padlocked. She headed for the stairs and started climbing them, almost literally.

There didn't seem to be any other businesses in the building. The doors on the first floor were barred as well.

The office of VS Counselling was right at the top, on the second floor. On the door there was a brass sign similar to the one down in the street. She couldn't see a bell and knocked so hard her knuckles hurt.

The door opened so abruptly that she had to take a step back.

'Good morning,' she said shyly, holding out her hand. 'Thanks for seeing me.'

The man really was very young. He was dressed in

357

a neatly ironed shirt and tie, suit trousers and polished leather shoes. His expression softened as he looked her up and down. She evidently wasn't a threat. 'Henry Hollister,' he said, sounding rather less irritated now.

'I've never needed legal advice before. This all feels rather strange.'

'Come in,' he said, stepping aside to let her into the office.

It looked like an old flat that hadn't been changed very much to adapt it to its new function. The doors were all open, three small rooms to the right, a kitchen straight ahead and a larger room to the left. It was completely quiet. The place seemed deserted, apart from the young American. Annika could smell coffee and unaired fabrics.

'Can I offer you anything to drink?' Henry Hollister asked.

'No, thanks, I'm fine,' Annika said.

The young man showed her into the large room on the left. It was a conference room, very similar to Stig Seidenfaden's. Solicitors in Gibraltar evidently never saw people in their own offices.

They sat down opposite one another. Henry Hollister frowned deeply and folded his hands on the table. 'Well,' he said, 'how can I help you?'

'I'm not actually the one who needs help,' Annika said. 'It's my brother. He's been arrested for possession of drugs, hash.'

There was a silence. The man blinked several times.

'Possession of hash?' he said. 'Where?'

'In Puerto Banús,' Annika said.

'But possession isn't a punishable offence under Spanish law.'

Shit, shit, shit. She hadn't known that. 'The police have accused him of intending to supply,' she said.

358

'How much cannabis are we talking about?'

'Four kilos,' she hazarded.

The young man blinked again and leaned back in his chair. 'Well,' he said, 'it would be hard to claim that amount was all for personal use. I'm sorry, but this isn't something that I—'

Annika leaned across the table and grasped his hand. 'You've got to help me,' she said. 'He's in prison in Málaga, in a *polígono* right next to the airport.'

Henry Hollister pulled his hand away in horror. 'I know that prison,' he said, 'but I can't help you. I'm not a solicitor, just a legal assistant. I'm not qualified for active work, just holding the fort for the time being.'

'Holding the fort?'

'Yes, until the new owner arrives.'

'Has the firm been sold?'

'It's been transferred within the holding company.'

Really? *Transferred within the holding company.* She sniffed. 'Spanish legal procedures take for ever, and my brother's going to be shut away in there for years if I don't do something. How long will I have to wait?'

'The only thing outstanding is some sort of legal formality before the new owner can come down. It might take another month, six weeks . . .'

'Why can't he be here sooner?'

The young man looked uncomfortable. 'I don't actually know.'

Annika let out a deep sigh. 'It was so tragic about Veronica,' she said. 'Imagine if that terrible break-in had never happened. She'd have sorted this out in no time.'

'Do you really think that?' he said, clearly puzzled. 'I never heard of her doing any work on minor felonies in Spain.'

'Really? I thought she did. She was always away so much. What did she spend her days doing?'

'Veronica was a business solicitor. She spent most of her time on contracts and negotiations for international companies.'

'Oh,' Annika said, trying to sound disappointed. 'I always thought she defended innocent people, like my brother. That's what it says on the sign downstairs, "Legal Services".'

Henry Hollister's mouth curled into a slight grimace. 'You've no idea what accusations get made against international companies,' he said. 'The authorities are so suspicious of successful businesses in this part of the world. It's quite different from the USA, where I come from. There, free enterprise is encouraged.'

'What sort of companies did she work with most?'

'Import-export,' Henry Hollister said. He leaned towards her. 'How did you say you knew Veronica, again?'

Her feet were starting to itch. 'I look after My's pony. We haven't found a buyer for it yet. I ride it every day so it doesn't lose its condition. It's a lovely animal – have you ever seen it?'

The American stood up. 'I'm sorry,' he said, 'but I can't help you.'

She sighed unhappily. 'I suppose I'll have to try somewhere else. Do you know of any good criminal law firms?'

'I'm sorry,' the man repeated.

She smiled, tried to put a bit of extra sparkle into her eyes, then held out her hand. 'Thanks for seeing me,' she said.

Suddenly he looked worried. 'Listen,' he said, 'don't tell anyone you were here talking to me. Call and book an appointment to see the new owner once he's settled in.'

She pretended to be surprised. 'Okay,' she said, 'no problem.'

They went out into the cramped hallway. On the wall outside the conference room an ornate degree certificate was framed behind glass. *The Faculty of Law at the University of Oxford.* Veronica's.

'If you know anyone who'd like to buy a really lovely pony, call the stables,' she said, and closed the door behind her.

The light had gone out and the stairwell was as dark as before. She felt along the wall and found the switch. Then she hurried quietly down the stairs.

25

In the street she stopped, out of breath, as if she'd been rushing upstairs, not down. Then she took a last look up at the building and hurried away. She stopped outside the closed estate agency and fished her pen and notepad out of her bag. She sat on the pavement and jotted down what she had found out during her conversation with the young American.

Veronica had studied law at Oxford University. She was primarily a business solicitor, even if the sign on the wall mentioned legal services. She had never worked on Spanish criminal cases. She had handled contracts and negotiations for international businesses involved in import-export. These international conglomerates were evidently the subject of 'accusations' every now and then. Perhaps that was when Veronica's legal services had come into the picture.

After her death the firm had been transferred 'within the holding company'. So a company with a number of proprietors now controlled Veronica Söderström's law firm, unless it had always done so. The new owner, a man, was waiting for some sort of formality before he could 'come down' and take over the running of the firm. Come down from where?

For the time being the office was manned by an

American legal assistant who was clearly so bored that he let people in off the street, which he had presumably been instructed not to do. That much was clear from his parting remark. His smart appearance suggested sporadic contact with the outside world, or he would have been wearing jeans and a sweatshirt. Did the holding company pay unannounced visits to the office?

The building housing the office was a mystery in itself. Why was most of it shut up and abandoned? She'd read on Wikipedia that property prices here had gone through the roof. Ordinary people who worked in Gibraltar almost always lived on the Spanish side of the border, in La Línea, where housing costs were a third of what they were in Gibraltar.

She glanced up at the window of the closed estate agency. It looked as if it hadn't been open for a while. There was a little row of dead insects along the ledge.

She got up, brushed the dust from her backside, and leaned forward to check out the cost of property in Gibraltar. There wasn't much to choose from in the window, just faded pictures of a handful of villas and apartments, with little information and obviously no addresses. Carita had told her that Spanish houses might be on sale with ten different estate agents at the same time. No one ever had exclusive rights, so the agents always concealed the addresses in an effort to stop others muscling in.

She glanced at the pictures and realized that none of the houses or flats were in Gibraltar: they were like all the others on the Costa del Sol.

Then she stiffened. She thought her eyes were deceiving her. She took a step closer to the window and wiped the dust from the glass.

Existing Freehold Villa.
Ideal Family Home. Ideal Investment.

The picture of the villa was faded and had slightly curled corners, as if it had been there for a while. There was no indication of where it was or its price, but Annika recognized it. A mixture of two and three floors, terraces and balconies, bay windows, pillars and arches, curved balcony rails and ornate iron balustrades. At the top there was a tower with arched windows. The pool, the light, the mountainside in the background.

It was the Söderström family home in Nueva Andalucía.

The picture had to be several years old because the trees were much smaller than she remembered, and there was a cement-mixer in the bottom corner.

She moved towards the door to see if there was any indication of opening hours. Nothing. Just a brass sign referring visitors to a website.

A Place in the Sun
Your Real Estate Agents on the Coast
Visit us at www.aplaceinthesun.se

She stared at the sign and read the last line twice.

Why would an estate agent in Gibraltar have a Swedish domain address?

She took out her notepad and wrote it down. Then she moved back to the window to see if the villa had a reference number.

It didn't.

It wasn't surprising that it was for sale, she thought. Obviously the executors would have to sell it, like the pony. But why not use a newer picture? Unless the picture had been there since the Söderström family had bought the villa. Veronica worked just round the corner, so obviously she must have walked past and looked in the window. Maybe that was how she'd found it. Maybe she'd bought it through this estate agent, and they'd just never got round to removing the picture from the window.

She looked at her watch. It was time to head to Estepona.

She didn't have a car.

The bus station in La Línea was in the Plaza de Europa, a roundabout just a couple of blocks from the border. There were buses leaving for Estepona all the time, the next one due to set off in ten minutes. She bought a ticket at the counter, just as the bus rolled into the station. It was noisy and belched diesel. She climbed on board and smelt oil and disinfectant. The seats were stripy blue velour and there were grubby curtains at the windows. She had a sudden flashback to the school-bus that used to take her from Hälleforsnäs into Flen and on to Katrineholm.

Just like the school-bus, the Spanish local service was slow, calling at every stop. A distance that would have taken fifteen minutes by car took an hour and a half. Outside Marina de Casares she dozed off, waking when a boy with a surfboard got on in Bahía Dorada.

The road wound along the coast. The surface of the water was white from the wind. The sky was bright blue and free of clouds. She could tell they were approaching Estepona.

It was hardly the city's fault that Julia had thought it was so awful, she thought, as the bus turned off towards the harbour.

The main street followed the beach. Palms and orange trees lined the road, and the wind was pulling at the treetops. The sunbeds on the beach were empty, but people had started to gather for lunch at the restaurants by the shore. She suddenly realized how hungry she was.

The young jet-setting Swede she was going to meet was called Wilma. Niklas Linde had texted her the girl's mobile number. She got off the bus at Avenida de

España, pulled out her notepad and mobile, then called the number.

Wilma answered straight away, very excited about the chance to 'tell her story in the paper', as she put it. They arranged to meet in the beach restaurant below the bus station.

'Annika Bengtzon?'

Annika looked up from the menu and knew at once that the series of articles had been saved.

Wilma fulfilled all of Patrik's criteria: young, blonde, too much makeup and a pair of seriously enlarged breasts. Annika stood up and they shook hands. 'It's great you were able to see me at such short notice,' she said.

'Well, you want to do your bit, don't you?' Wilma said, sitting down opposite her.

All the men in the restaurant were staring at them.

'What would you like?' Annika said. 'Have whatever you want.'

'Have you tried the *almejas*? They're a sort of mussel they catch out on the reef. Or *mejillones*? They're a bit bigger. They've got shellfish here you've never seen before.' Wilma closed her menu authoritatively. 'Shall I order for you?' she asked, evidently not expecting to be contradicted. She leaned back and waved to the waiter. Her nipples were clearly visible through her tight T-shirt.

'*Camarero, queremos mariscos a la plancha, con mucho ajo y hierbas. Y una botella de vino blanco de la casa, por favor!*'

'Goodness,' Annika said. 'Where did you learn to speak so fluently?'

The girl looked at her in surprise. 'At school,' she said. 'Why?'

Annika took out her notepad and pen. 'How old are you?' she asked.

'I'll be twenty in July.'

'You know I got your name from Niklas Linde?' Annika said. 'He said you wouldn't mind telling me about life down here on the Costa del Sol.'

'I want to warn other people,' Wilma said, smiling warmly at the waiter as he put a misted bottle of white wine and two glasses on their table. '*Gracias, señor, quiero probarlo.*'

She rolled the wine around her mouth in a practised gesture, then nodded in approval. The waiter filled their glasses and glided away.

'It might look like life down here is all bars and night-clubs and guys with flashy cars, but there's a completely different side of the Costa del Sol,' Wilma said, sipping her wine. 'The drug-dealers want to get rid of as much of their stash as possible down here,' she went on. 'That saves them the hassle of transport, and losing any of it on the way up through Europe. You don't drink wine?'

Annika looked up. The girl was a walking, talking headline-generator. She just had to sit here taking dictation. 'Er, yes, I'm just not thirsty.' She had a symbolic sip. The wine was unpleasantly sharp.

'You *loca*!' Wilma said. 'You don't drink wine because you're thirsty! It's incredibly easy for young girls to be charmed by the good-looking guys down here. They've got big yachts and fast cars, and use girls as disposable goods. I see it time after time, Swedish girls turning up here thinking they're going to marry a millionaire and live the high-life in some huge villa in Nueva Andalucía, but all that ever happens is that they get hooked on coke and end up nervous wrecks.'

'What about you?' Annika said. 'Have you tried cocaine?'

Wilma nodded. 'Yes,' she said, 'and I bitterly regret it. I got picked up in a raid back in February, but that

367

probably saved me. Talk about a warning! As luck would have it, I was questioned by Niklas Linde, and he put me on the right track. I mean, he's just brilliant. Do you know him?'

Annika picked up her glass and swigged. 'No,' she said. 'I've just interviewed him a couple of times.'

'It actually makes you feel a lot safer knowing the Swedish police have such competent officers.'

'Can you tell me about the raid?'

'It was a private party down by the harbour in Puerto Banús, in rooms above one of the clubs. The police came in at half past two with sniffer-dogs and everything, and searched everyone. It was horrible, but actually really good at the same time.'

'Are you going to be charged?'

She shook her head. 'I only had a few grams for personal use.'

Ah, yes, Annika thought. Possession alone wasn't a punishable offence. 'So what were you doing at the party? What attracted you to that lifestyle?'

The waiter came over with their food, an enormous dish laden with grilled shellfish, swimming in oil, garlic and herbs.

'*Ah, qué bueno!*' Wilma exclaimed in delight, clapping her hands. She set about the food.

Annika peered suspiciously at the prawns, mussels and lobsters. She wasn't fond of shellfish, and would much rather have meatballs with lingonberry sauce if she was given the option. She prodded a prawn tentatively.

'I felt special, chosen,' Wilma said. 'Imagine, little me allowed to be here with all the beautiful and famous people. Princess Madeleine's been – she stayed at the Marbella Club. I never met her, obviously, but I got to know a lot of other celebrities.'

'Did you know Sebastian Söderström?' Annika asked, trying not to sound too eager.

Wilma wolfed down half of a small lobster and nodded enthusiastically. 'It was so awful what happened to him. Who could have imagined it? We were at his daughter's birthday party a week or so before they died.'

Annika let the prawn drop. 'You went to a child's party?' She couldn't see Wilma eating birthday cake in My's bedroom.

'No, you *loca*, it wasn't the little girl's birthday. The other one, Suzette.'

'When? Where?'

'Actually in the same place that got raided a few weeks later. Above one of the nightclubs by the harbour. If you buy four bottles of vodka you're automatically allowed to use it. It's very popular.'

'And that's what Suzette did to celebrate her birthday?'

'No, *loca*, it was her dad. He wanted Suzette to make friends, so he invited the lot of us, all the younger ones. Sebbe was always so generous, champagne, champagne, champagne all night long.'

'Did you get to know Suzette?'

Wilma let out a deep sigh. 'Well,' she said, 'that young lady really didn't want to be there. She sat in a corner trying not to talk to anyone. I don't know when she left, but after a while she just disappeared.'

'And when was this?'

'Just after Christmas. Boxing Day, I think. There were a few girls snorting lines in the toilet and Sebastian was furious. He was really anti-drugs, and he threw them all out, just like that . . .'

'You know Suzette's missing?'

Wilma gathered together the last of the mussels. 'I read about it. It's just so awful.'

'Have you any idea where she could be?'

'No.'

'Did she have any friends?'

'I really don't know. I only saw her that once.'

'So she never used to hang around the harbour partying?'

Wilma shook her head firmly. 'Maybe once or twice, but she wasn't a party animal. If she was, I'd have known about it.' She drank the last of her wine and refilled her glass.

'So what do you do now?' Annika asked. 'Do you work, or study?'

'Work,' Wilma said. 'I'm a consultant. I help Scandinavian companies to set up on the Costa del Sol.'

Annika stared at her. 'You?' she said. 'Help Scandinavian companies? What with?'

'Finance, and getting established,' she said.

Annika tried to focus her thoughts. 'And business is good?'

'Are you kidding? I know every rich old man on the whole Costa del Sol.'

Wilma leaned forward so that Annika was confronted with her massive cleavage. 'There's just one simple rule,' she said, in a low voice. 'Never sleep with them. Because then they lose all respect for you.'

Annika drank what was left in her glass and ordered a mineral water. Wilma finished the rest of the bottle.

Annika asked some dutiful questions about Wilma's background and childhood (Vikingshill outside Stockholm, parents IT consultants, two younger brothers), then asked what advice she had for young women who wanted to try their luck abroad, what they should look out for and what they should focus on.

When the plates had been cleared, Annika said, 'Shall we take some pictures? Maybe down on the beach?'

Wilma was thrilled. 'That's a brilliant idea! How lucky that I've got my bikini with me!' She pulled a tiny piece of cloth from her handbag and dangled it in Annika's face.

'Great,' Annika said. 'We'll try some with the bikini, and some with clothes. Then the editors up in Stockholm can decide what works best.' She paid the bill. The restaurant seemed basic, with its woven raffia roof and open sides, but their meal had cost more than her plane-ticket.

They went down to the beach. Wilma wanted to start with the bikini shots, and Annika didn't object. She pulled off her T-shirt and Annika noted that the scars from her surgery were in her armpits. She slipped on the bikini top, wiggled her hips until the thong was in place, then posed cheerily on a sunbed with Estepona in the background. They wouldn't be able to use any of those pictures, but Annika snapped a sequence to keep Patrik happy.

'We should probably take a few of you looking more serious as well,' she said.

Wilma suddenly looked as stern as anyone wearing a minuscule bikini possibly could.

'And now a few with clothes on.' She told Wilma to walk along the shore with her heels in her hand, gazing out to sea with a thoughtful expression. It all worked very well. The sun looked hot and merciless, and Wilma was alone and vulnerable on the long, white beach.

They said goodbye outside the bus station and Annika sat down to wait for the next bus to Puerto Banús.

26

There was no sign of Lotta in the hotel lobby. Annika had no interest in any further confrontations on the subject of photography, so she went quickly to her room.

It was a quarter past six. She dropped her bag on the floor. An hour and forty-five minutes before she was due to meet Thomas. The thought made her stomach knot. She lay down and pulled the bedspread over her head. She remained there, quite still, for a while, listening to her own heartbeat. She and Thomas hadn't sat down to talk to each other since the divorce. On one occasion he had come up to the flat in Agnegatan, that Sunday evening after she'd got back from Spain the first time. It had been a rather strained meeting. Annika had been keen to make a good impression and the children had rushed round like mad things, chasing each other through the rooms, yelling and laughing, until Thomas had told them to behave. He'd thought the flat was 'nice'. She'd said it was 'nice of him to call in'.

She'd cried for ages that evening, and now she was going to meet him again.

She looked at the time: an hour and half to go.

She pushed off the bedspread, got up, sat down at her laptop, logged into the hotel network and surfed randomly around the Swedish news sites. The *Evening*

Post was leading with earth-shattering news: 'Ten fine wines to make your May Day party go with a swing'. And there was me thinking it depended on the people you were with, she thought.

Below the wine story there were two financial articles: the first expressed outrage at how careful with his money Ingvar Kamprad, the founder of Ikea, was; the second was horrified that this year's Swedish Eurovision entry was using a private plane for a publicity tour. It wasn't entirely clear which of these was most deplorable.

The other evening paper was running with 'Pay-day shopping in the sun!', then 'How to escape the luxury gap'. She gave up and went into her Facebook page. It had been a while since she had last logged in. She had eight new messages, all of them from Polly Sandman, Suzette's best friend back in Blackeberg. Most were long musings about life, death and love, but occasionally Polly wrote short messages or just wanted the answer to a specific question.

Annika worked through them from the top, which meant she read the most recent one first. It contained a short, blunt question: 'Is the moon full at the same time all over the world?'

Annika blinked at the screen. She didn't actually know. It couldn't be, could it? Maybe it could. She made a mental note to find out.

The next message was a long story about a reality soap-star who became an astronaut.

The third consisted of three sentences: 'Suzette's mum has sold their flat. She's thrown out all Suzette's things. I don't know where she's moved to.'

Annika read the message twice and felt her throat tighten. Suzette meant nothing. She was in the process of being erased. Everything she had been, thought and liked was being wiped away, and nobody cared. The message was dated 16 April. I really must keep a closer eye on this inbox, she thought.

The following three messages all contained gloomy poems about missing friends.

The penultimate one was short, just two sentences: 'I've had a really weird email. I think it's from Suzette.'

Annika's heart started to pound.

I think it's from Suzette.

She glanced quickly at the bottom of the page: Polly Sandman was online. She clicked on Chat, which brought up Facebook's own instant message facility, and typed 'Hi, Polly, Annika Bengtzon here! What was the weird email you got? Why do you think it's from Suzette?'

She sent the message, then stared at the screen. Rolle in Mellösa wanted to add her as a friend. It was a few seconds before she realized that Rolle in Mellösa was Roland Larsson, the boy who had had a crush on her at school, Jimmy Halenius's cousin. She stared at the screen and wondered if he was serious. How many grown men voluntarily spent their free time on this sort of thing? On the other hand people spent their working lives helping fraudulent businessmen to avoid tax by registering companies in places like Gibraltar.

She clicked to accept Roland as her friend, then looked at the time. Maybe Polly wasn't at her computer. Maybe it was just on in her room while she was out with her friends or something.

The chat-box pinged. 'Do you believe in messages from the other side? In the olden days the dead used to speak through spirits. Maybe they use email these days.' Annika replied briefly and bluntly: 'Not a chance. What did she say?'

There was a short pause. Then: 'The message was from Gunnar Larsson. There was nothing in it.'

374

Annika's pulse slowed. What was this nonsense? 'Gunnar Larsson?' she wrote back. 'Who's he?'

The reply came quick as a flash. 'That's a secret.'

'Polly,' Annika wrote, deciding to be dramatic. 'If this has anything to do with Suzette, you have to tell me. It could be a matter of life and death.'

It was several minutes before the reply arrived. 'Gunnar Larsson was our maths teacher in year nine. He was so stupid and old that Suzette and I wanted to play a trick on him. We set up an email account for him, then sent dirty emails to some of the girls in the class. We don't know exactly what happened, but Gunnar Larsson had to leave the school.'

Annika read the message twice. 'He was fired because of the emails you sent?' she asked.

'Don't know. He was only a supply teacher, so maybe he had to leave anyway. But we got really scared. We swore we'd never tell anyone about Gunnar Larsson's emails.'

Annika's heart speeded up again. 'And now Mr Gunnar Larsson has got in touch?'

It was eight minutes before the answer came. Annika had time to chew off most of her thumbnail.

'Only me and Suzette know the password to Mr Gunnar Larsson's email. I have to go, we're going out for dinner. Bye for now!' She went offline.

Annika stared at the screen with a faint buzz in her ears. A blank email from a hotmail address? That it had come from hotmail meant the sender had had to know the password for the account. That it was empty suggested they were in a hurry. It didn't necessarily mean anything, but it might be a sign of life.

She clicked to open Polly's last message, which turned out to be the start of the story about the reality soap-star/astronaut.

Annika sat in front of her laptop for a minute or so. Then she wrote a short reply: 'Here's my mobile number. If Gunnar Larsson emails you again, I want you to call me.'

She typed her mobile number, sent the message and shut down her laptop. She'd have to hurry if she wanted a shower.

He was standing in the lobby with his back to the lifts, wearing the same suit as when she had bumped into him at the conference centre, the slightly shiny Italian one that fitted so well across his hips. She walked up behind him, breathing in the smell of his aftershave. He had showered, too, and shaved. 'Hello,' she said quietly.

He turned and ran his eyes over her. No direct sign of appreciation, but no attempt to distance himself either. 'Hello,' he said. 'Shall we go?'

She walked past him and out onto the street. She was wearing her jeans and the old sweater, and had her bag with her, as usual. She had brought her best dress with her to Spain, a bright red, sleeveless thing she'd bought on impulse in the Christmas sales, but she'd had Niklas Linde in mind when she'd packed it, not Thomas. She had put it on earlier, but felt overdressed. As if she were trying too hard.

He had his hire car parked outside the hotel. He unlocked it by remote, then opened the passenger door for her.

'Where are we going?' she asked.

'I've booked a table at a place just above here.'

'Not in Istán?'

'What?' he said, clearly confused.

'Nothing,' she said.

He got in beside her, just as he had done hundreds of times before, fumbling with the key and checking the

376

gears were in neutral, then pausing a moment before turning the key. Breathed out, tested the accelerator, looked in the rear-view mirror, and forgot to release the handbrake before pulling away.

He headed up towards Nueva Andalucía. She was looking straight ahead through the windscreen, intensely aware of his presence: long arms and legs, narrow fingers, broad shoulders. She shivered and wrapped her arms round herself.

'The porter at the hotel recommended this place, and gave me directions,' he said. 'Apparently they specialize in grilled meat. I assumed you wouldn't want fish or shellfish.'

She didn't answer.

They swept past the bullfighting arena.

'How are your articles going?' he asked.

This was what they always did. Skirted around the important things. Said stuff that never meant anything. 'Fine, thanks,' she said. 'Not enough time, a lazy photographer, too little preparation, but it'll probably work out okay. How about you?'

He sighed. 'This whole business, trying to co-ordinate economic legislation throughout Europe, is a much bigger task than I'd thought. I'm going to be on secondment to the department for a while. It feels good to be entrusted with something of this significance by the heads of the department.'

Why did he always have to tell her how fucking important and talented he was?

They sat in silence as the car climbed upwards. They were on a different road from the one she had driven along with Niklas Linde, so at least they weren't on their way towards La Campana. The sun was low, colouring the walls red. Bougainvillaea tumbled over fences and rooftops, glowing like fire in the sunset.

'I've been thinking,' she said. 'We have to try to make sure we get on well, you and I, for the children's sake.'

He glanced at her, but said nothing.

'I interviewed a guy yesterday,' she went on. 'He's twenty-six years old and he's locked up in a windowless concrete cell in Málaga. He'll be lucky to get out before he's thirty, and there was no need for him to end up there in the first place.'

Thomas didn't respond, and turned into a large car park outside a place called El Picadero. 'The porter told me this place used to be a ranch once upon a time,' he said. 'There were horses here until just a few years ago, in fact. I thought you might like it.'

The restaurant was a long, low building with flame-coloured tiles and a large covered terrace stretching the entire length of the front. Lanterns with candles were hanging under the roof.

'Do you want to sit outside?'

She nodded.

They got a table for two at some distance from the door.

'I've been doing some thinking as well,' Thomas said, once they had sat down and ordered water and wine. He played with his napkin and shuffled his feet restlessly under the table, as he always had when he was worried or nervous about something. 'It was wrong of me not to say anything about Sophia,' he said. 'You knew about it, and I wish you'd said something, but it wasn't your fault that things turned out the way they did. Not exclusively, anyway.'

Annika looked at the tablecloth. She knew what he meant, and how hard it had been for him to say it. That was the closest she would get to an apology.

Evidently he hadn't finished, because his feet were still shuffling about. 'That's why I think we should be honest.'

She nodded, agreeing.

'So you can tell me . . .'

She blinked.

'. . . if you were ever with anyone else.'

'Never,' she said. 'Not with anyone, not once.'

The waiter arrived with their drinks. Thomas tasted the wine. Annika took a thirsty gulp of her mineral water.

'How about afterwards?' he said, when the waiter had disappeared.

The only man she had been with was Niklas Linde.

'That policeman?' Thomas said. 'Or Halenius?'

The old fury poured out. She stood up, her chair jabbing into the diner behind her. 'You've got a nerve!' she said. 'Cross-examining me about who I've slept with the moment you get a chance.' I can walk back to the hotel, she found herself thinking. I can ask for directions. It can't be more than five kilometres.

The other diners were looking at her curiously. The man she had rammed her chair into moved forward.

She was about to do it again: run away from confrontation and hide her head in the sand. She blushed and sat down. 'Sorry,' she said.

'Those people over there are Swedish,' he said, nodding towards a table by the entrance. 'They would have heard you even if they're deaf.'

'Sorry,' she repeated.

The waiter appeared beside them and asked if they were ready to order. They hurriedly picked up their menus. 'Apparently the steak is what we should have,' Thomas said. 'It gets cooked at the table on a red-hot stone. It's supposed to be really good.'

Annika closed her menu without answering.

Thomas ordered a few starters, and *carne a la Piedra*.

The waiter disappeared.

'The children,' Annika said. 'We have to put aside any disagreements. We have to be able to talk to each other without it always being so fucking volatile. For the children's sake.'

'I've been thinking about that too,' he said. 'How different things are now. We used to share the children, but now I'm the only one taking responsibility.'

'No, Thomas,' she said. 'While we were married I looked after the children and you looked after your career. Not at the start, but once I was on leave you left me to it. Whereas *now* we're sharing responsibility, the two of us.'

His astonishment was written across his face.

Annika stared at him. He'd started to get some grey hairs by his temples. The wrinkles around his eyes were more clearly defined than before. He'd put on weight as well. Maybe Sophia Fucking Bitch Grenborg baked cakes. Thomas had a weakness for cake.

Silence descended. A cricket started to chirrup in the grass alongside them. Others answered it from some distance away. A dog barked.

The waiter arrived with their starters, one plate of finely sliced ham, and another with cheese and walnuts.

'I thought we could share them,' Thomas said. 'Have you tried this? *Jamón ibérico bellota*, the best in the world.'

They ate without talking. Annika wolfed down the ham, the cheese and endive salad with walnuts in a Gorgonzola cream. She drank water and, for once, a whole glass of wine.

The darkness was getting thicker, and soon formed a wall around them.

'Have I told you what Ellen said the other day when we were on our way to her school?' she asked. '"When I get old, you'll be dead, and then you'll come back."'

Thomas laughed. 'We have a daughter who believes in reincarnation.'

'Exactly.'

'I wonder if she had a previous life, and who she might have been?'

'Mahatma Gandhi?' Annika suggested.

'Well, not Josef Stalin, anyway,' Thomas said. 'She's far too scared of blood.'

They chuckled.

At that moment his mobile rang. He pulled it out of his inside pocket, peered at the screen, then stood up and turned his back on her.

'Hi, Kalle,' he said, walking out to the car park.

She watched him, deflated.

Their son was calling him, but he didn't want the boy to know that he was having dinner with her because it would be too complicated to explain to Sophia.

She got up and threw her napkin onto her chair. There had to be some limit to the humiliation. She was expected to sit there and tell him who she was sleeping with, but he couldn't even own up to the fact that they were having dinner together.

She'd made it a couple of metres into the car park when Thomas caught sight of her.

'I miss you too, Kalle,' he said. 'Do you know who's coming now? There's someone here who I think would like to talk to you.'

She stopped mid-stride. He was standing four or five metres away, holding the phone out to her. She practically ran towards it. 'Kalle?' she said.

'Mummy?'

Warmth welled inside her, bringing tears to her eyes. 'Hi, Kalle, how are you?'

'Mummy, guess what! I've lost a tooth!'

She laughed and stopped a tear with a finger just

below her eyelashes. 'Wow, another! How many is that now?'

'Loads! Do you think the tooth fairy knows the way to Grev Turegatan?'

'Leave it in a glass of water and you'll see that it's turned into a gold coin by tomorrow morning.'

'Mummy?'

'Yes?'

'When are you coming home?'

'Tomorrow. And I'll see you on Monday when I pick you up from after-school club.'

'I miss you, Mummy.'

'And I miss you too. Is Ellen still up?'

'She's asleep – she's just a baby.'

'Well, you should be asleep too. Sleep well, now. I love you.'

She waited for the words he usually said at the end of every phone-call: 'I love you, Mummy, you're the best mummy in the whole *wooorld*.' They didn't come.

'Mummy?'

'Yes?'

'Are you going to marry Daddy again?'

She saw Thomas walking around the car park the way he did when he got nervous. He never could stand still. 'No, darling, I'm not. Here comes Daddy, so you can say night-night to him as well.' She passed the phone to Thomas and went back to her chair. It was completely dark now. The warmth of the day was still lingering, and the wind had died down. Thomas ended the call and put away his mobile.

The waiter removed their starters and came back with a frame on which he placed a red-hot stone slab. Then he laid out thin slices of marbled T-bone steak and vegetables, and three different sauces, and showed them how to melt fat directly on the stone, then fry the meat.

It hissed and crackled, smoked and steamed.

Annika was enchanted by the flame burning beneath the frame, and the crackling from the stone.

'I miss you sometimes,' Thomas said.

She thought he was going to say something else, but he didn't. 'Why?' she said eventually.

He put another slice of meat on the stone. 'You never went with the flow. You always said what you thought. I was never very happy when I was discussing anything with you, but I always ended up wiser.'

Thomas fried and sliced the meat, fried and sliced.

She was still full from their starters.

The flame under the frame flickered and went out.

The waiter came and took their empty plates away.

Neither of them wanted dessert or coffee. Thomas picked up the bill and paid with a credit card she'd never seen before. He signed with his usual looping signature, and left a ten-euro note as a tip.

'Is the state footing the bill for this?' she asked.

'Hardly,' he said. 'I don't want to end up in the *Evening Post*.'

She laughed.

'It's my private account,' he said. 'We have a joint one for food, travel and other shared expenses . . .'

Annika turned towards the darkness. She really didn't give a shit about their shared account.

He saw her reaction. 'Sometimes I wonder if you and I tried hard enough,' he said.

She shivered: it was getting cold now. She was pleased she'd put on her ugly old sweater. 'Shall we go?' she said.

'Maybe we could get a drink somewhere,' he said. 'Somewhere down by the harbour.'

'I don't think so,' she said. 'I'm pretty tired.'

They left the restaurant and walked out into the car park. There were hardly any cars left.

'Do you miss me?' he asked. 'At all, ever?'

All the time, she thought. Every day. Whenever I'm alone. Or do I? She took a deep breath. 'I don't know,' she said. 'Not as much now. At the start it was awful. The fact that you were gone was like a black hole inside me. It was like you'd died.' She stopped beside the car. 'It would probably have felt better if you had died, because then at least I'd have had the right to grieve.'

'I never wanted that,' he said. 'I never meant to hurt you.'

'You should have thought of that before,' she said.

'I know,' he said.

They got into the car and drove in silence through the streets of Nueva Andalucía. The sky was dark and starless – clouds had rolled in from the Atlantic during the evening.

'It was on a night like this that the Söderström family were gassed to death,' Annika said. 'A cloudy night, but colder. They had the heating on in all the bedrooms.'

'Are you sure you don't want to come and have a drink? A beer, maybe, or just a coffee?'

'Maybe a beer,' Annika said.

They parked at the Hotel Pyr and walked down to the harbour. Crowds of people were milling about in the streets. They shuffled slowly out of the way whenever a Lamborghini wanted to get through. The row of bars and nightclubs lining the quayside were pumping out light and music. Thomas was heading towards the Sinatra Bar.

'Can't we walk out onto the pier?' Annika asked.

She didn't want to run into Niklas Linde and his girls.

They walked past the lighthouse and carried on along the breakwater. The wind was cold and Thomas did up his jacket. Annika stuck her hands into the pockets of

384

her jeans. They were walking close to one another without actually touching.

'There's a lot I wish I'd done differently,' Thomas said, into the wind. 'I wasn't thinking about the consequences. I was just thinking that you were so cold and difficult and emotionless.'

'She was the easy way out,' Annika said. 'You do have a tendency to just *end up* doing things.'

He stopped, without looking at her. To the south-west there were scattered lights on the shore of Africa.

'I know I made mistakes,' Annika said. 'I was running away too. And I'm pretty sure we could have sorted things out, if we'd tried to get help.'

Now he turned to her. 'Do you think it's too late?' he asked.

At first she thought she'd misheard him, that the wind was playing tricks on her. 'Too late?'

He put his hand on her cheek and kissed her.

At first she was completely rigid. His lips were soft and cold. 'Come on,' he said, in a low voice. He took her hand and led her back towards the lights on the quayside.

She went with him, her fingers laced in his, and it struck her that he had always held her hand in this way – imagine forgetting something like that. She moved closer to him because her injured forefinger was hurting.

They walked round the harbour and back towards the hotel, along streets that quickly became empty and cold when the music and lights no longer reached them.

The reception desk was unmanned, the sound of a television coming from the little office behind. They walked quickly and silently through the lobby and got into the furthest lift. Annika pressed the button for the third floor and Thomas brushed her hair aside. She caught sight of her reflection in the mirror as he kissed her earlobe.

Her room was completely dark. Thomas turned on the ceiling light. 'I want to look at you,' he said. 'See if I remember you right.'

Does he fantasize about me? she wondered.

She pulled off her sweater and T-shirt, and her bra caught in the bottom of the sweater. She was wearing the red one, the one she had bought to go with the smart dress she'd chosen not to wear.

He put his hand on her shoulder, stroked her arm, cupped his hands around her breasts. The way he used to. The way he knew she liked.

She undid his shirt, following her fumbling fingers with her eyes, button by button. Then she looked up at him. His eyes, oh, how she loved his eyes.

'You know,' he said, 'I've really missed you.'

Me too, she thought. Every time things are silent around me, every time I'm alone, that's when I miss you.

He undid her bra and put it on the bedside table. Unbuttoned her jeans and stroked her backside. 'You've lost weight,' he said.

He's remembering wrong, she thought. Sophia's just sturdier than me.

She pulled off his shirt and let it fall to the floor. He'd developed a bit of a belly. She put her hand under his navel and left it there for a moment. The way she used to.

Afterwards he fell asleep on his back with his arms stretched out, but Annika lay awake with her head on his shoulder, staring into the darkness.

Saturday, 30 April

27

Annika paid for her and Lotta's rooms, then headed straight out onto the street with her suitcase. She waited on the pavement for a few minutes. There was still a chill in the air: the sun hadn't yet risen above the Sierra Blanca.

Her plane left at ten o'clock, and Thomas's at a quarter to four. He was going to drive her to the airport, then fetch his things from the Parador. It felt as though nothing odd or unpleasant had ever happened between them. The divorce was just a bad dream. Everything was the way it always had been, and now they were going home to the children and the flat on Kungsholmen. There'd be loads of washing to do and they'd have to remember to get some milk. Her parents-in-law would be waiting for them on the island and . . .

Suddenly she felt short of breath. Her chest was tight and the sounds of traffic faded. She fumbled for her suitcase and sat down on it gingerly, leaning forward so she could breathe better.

His hire car glided up alongside her. 'What's up?' he asked, jumping out. 'Aren't you feeling well?'

She waved a hand dismissively.

'No, no,' she said. 'I just felt a bit dizzy. It's nothing.'

They hadn't made love that morning. He hadn't

showered. He hadn't borrowed her toothbrush – he'd never dream of doing something so unhygienic.

He looked at her with genuine concern in those wonderful eyes, bright blue. She took his hand, allowing herself to be pulled up and led to the passenger seat. He brushed her hair from her face and engaged her seatbelt. Then he put her suitcase into the boot, closed it and made sure it was properly shut. He went round to the driver's side, got in and smiled. His hair had fallen across his forehead and his shirt was open at the neck.

She made an effort to smile back.

'I don't regret it,' he said.

Not yet, she thought. 'Me neither,' she said.

Then he pulled away.

The motorway was almost deserted. Once they reached the toll-road they didn't see any other vehicles. They sat in silence beside one another. Thomas was concentrating on driving and Annika was staring out to sea. She couldn't see Africa – it was too misty. At this rate they'd be at the airport in half an hour. She would get out of the car and kiss him rather tentatively, then go inside the Pablo Ruiz Picasso terminal and the sliding doors would close behind her. The illusion would be over.

Their flights would take off, then there'd be baggage reclaim and the taxis with their fixed rates. And she'd be sitting up in her three-room flat on Agnegatan and he'd be taking the last boat out to Vaxholm to his parents' summer-house in the archipelago, where Sophia and the children would be waiting for him, Kalle and Ellen clingy and expectant, Sophia warm and cooing. This car journey would feel strange and incomprehensible.

She noticed a smell of old socks – they were passing the San Miguel brewery that was right next to the airport.

It was almost over.

Thomas headed up the ramp for *salidas*, departures. The airport was utterly chaotic, no matter what time of day it was. An official in a fluorescent yellow jacket waved them towards an empty space a few metres from the terminal doors.

She took a deep breath.

'Are you feeling better?'

His expression was open and bright. He wished her well, she was sure of that. 'I'm fine,' she said, and brushed his hair from his forehead, the blond fringe that he hardly ever bothered to comb. She leaned over and kissed him lightly.

'Let me help you with your case,' he said.

'There's no need,' she said, but he'd already opened the door and got out, and was on his way round to the boot.

She followed him, her legs heavy as lead, and took her case, and he kissed her forehead.

'I'll call you,' he said, as though he really meant it, and she smiled, then turned round and headed towards the doors.

When they slid shut behind her she stopped.

It was all gone.

Annika drifted round the shops until it was time for her flight. She bought sweets and toys for the children, wine and spirits for herself, even though she would never drink any of it, and a travel-pack of lipsticks from Dior that she would probably never use.

Lotta was waiting by the gate. She had her rucksack containing her camera, but she must have checked in the rest of her equipment. Annika sat down beside her without saying anything.

Lotta started and moved a few centimetres away from her.

'Don't worry,' Annika said. 'I only bite when there's a full moon.'

'I know I haven't done very well,' Lotta said, sounding terrified.

Annika looked at her. Her expression was scared yet defiant. Lotta had spoken to someone. She'd probably called the paper and demanded to speak to Pelle, head of images, or Schyman himself, and the conversation couldn't have gone well. Now she felt even more unfairly treated, but would have to swallow a whole load of shit if she wanted to keep her job.

'The articles are all sorted,' Annika said, picking up a copy of the previous day's *Daily Mail*. She held it in front of her without reading a word until they boarded.

They were sitting next to each other. Annika took the window seat. Because she hadn't slept for more than an hour last night, she fell asleep as soon as the plane had got into the air, and didn't wake until they were on their descent into Arlanda.

The baggage carousel spat out Lotta's bags, all five, before Annika's little suitcase appeared. 'I'd be grateful if you didn't mention our collaboration to anyone at the paper,' Lotta said, once she'd piled all her things onto a trolley.

Annika looked at her, trying to work out what she felt about the pale young woman. She couldn't summon up anything but indifference. 'What collaboration?' she said.

Lotta headed off to Customs.

Annika watched her disappear along the corridor, with its vast portraits of famous Swedes welcoming visitors to their home town.

She bought the evening papers in the arrivals hall and read them as she ate a fairly unpleasant salad in a Seven-

392

Eleven. Then she took the express train into Stockholm and decided to walk from the station.

The sky was steel-grey and there was rain in the air. The wind was damp and cold, and cut to her bones. She struggled across Kungsbron towards Fleminggatan. The small wheels on the suitcase kept catching in the grit on the pavements and in the end she gave up and carried it. By the time she reached her flat her arm was numb.

She put the case on the hall floor and decided to put off unpacking it, just as she always did. Instead she went into her bedroom and found herself transfixed by the framed drawing of the girl and the horse that hung over her bed. Little My, eight years old, who was left to mourn her? What trace had she left on the world?

Annika lay down on the bed. With her eyes open, she listened to the sound of the building breathing. First the big noises, the ones indicating people. Water running through the pipes. Someone flushing a toilet. Voices from a radio. Then she closed her eyes and listened for other sounds. The quiet hum of the central heating, the creaking of the hundred-year-old beams, the soft whistling of wind through windows and air-vents.

Thomas was probably on the plane now. It would just have taken off and Spain would be disappearing below him, the mountains speckled with olive trees, the villages standing out white against the red soil.

Maybe Suzette was still alive. Who else could have send that empty email from Mr Gunnar Larsson?

Suddenly she was struck by a thought that made her sit bolt upright. What if Larsson himself had hacked the account? What if Suzette hadn't been trying to send a message, but the teacher, bitter at being sacked, had wanted to take revenge on those responsible?

If he had suddenly been sacked because of the emails, his employers must have confronted him with them. He

393

would have seen the address so he might have gone to hotmail and tried to crack the password. It wasn't brain surgery. She'd done it herself.

She leaped out of bed, ran into the hall, pulled her laptop from her bag and went into the kitchen, the only place she had an Internet connection.

Her computer booted up and she went straight to her Facebook page.

No new messages. And Polly Sandman wasn't online.

She went into hotmail and typed in the account name Mr-Gunnar-Larsson. She started with the obvious passwords: polly.

Invalid ID or password. Please try again using your full Yahoo! ID.

suzette

Invalid ID or password. Please try again using your full Yahoo! ID.

blackeberg

Invalid ID or password. Please try again using your full Yahoo! ID.

She wondered how many attempts she could make before the site shut her out. Maybe there was no limit.

She gave up and went back to her Facebook page. She wrote to Polly, asking if she thought Gunnar Larsson could have cracked their password.

She hadn't called Niklas Linde before she'd left. He had asked her to – it had been the last thing he'd said before she'd got out of his car that day. Maybe he'd had something to say to her, something he couldn't say with Lotta listening.

She clenched her fists, fingernails digging into her palms.

Then she logged into the national ID register and searched for Niklas Linde without specifying any particular geographic area.

Too many results (ca. 170). Please refine the search terms.

She removed the phonetic search option, to remove anyone called Lind or Lindh, and searched again.

Ten hits, eight of them with the surname Linde. Four lived in Skåne, one had been deregistered and had moved to Switzerland, and three were registered in the Stockholm area.

She looked at their dates of birth, and immediately saw her Niklas.

Linde, Bo NIKLAS Yngve
Registered address: ÄNGSLYCKEVÄGEN 73,
245 62 HJÄRUP
Region: 12 SKÅNE
Council district: 30 STAFFANSTORP
Parish: 06 UPPÅKRA

He was thirty-six.

She tried a new search, looking for the surname, Linde, the postcode 245 62, and gender: female.

Bingo. Three results at the same address.

Linde, Anna MARIA, thirty-three.

Linde, Kajsa ELENA, ten.

Linde, Alva NATALIE, three.

His wife, and two daughters. Did he have any sons?

She performed a third search, Linde, male, postcode. Bingo again.

Linde, Bo OSCAR, eight.

She stared at the name in front of her. A boy, like Kalle. Oscar. Presumably he was busy losing his teeth and calling to tell his dad, who was away working on the Costa del Sol in Spain.

Nice work, Niklas. A wife and three kids in Hjärup, wherever the hell that was. Somewhere outside Malmö, at a guess. A proper little idyll, presumably. Ängs-lyckevägen – 'happy meadow way', indeed.

Her mobile rang in her bag. She got up from the kitchen chair, stubbing her toe on the table, and limped out into the hall.

'Annika?'

It was Niklas Linde.

She glanced quickly at the computer: was there some way he could have traced her searches? Probably, but that could hardly be why he was calling. 'Hello,' she said. 'I'm back in Stockholm.'

'Listen,' he said. He sounded abrupt. 'Can you talk?'

She went back to the kitchen table and clicked to get rid of the national ID database and the details of Niklas Linde's family. 'Sure,' she said, putting all her weight on one foot with the other in the air. The little toe hurt like hell.

'It's about Johan Zarco Martinez, the Swede you met in prison in Málaga on Thursday.'

'Okay.'

'Can I ask you what you talked about?'

'Of course, but I don't know if I'll answer. Not because it was anything particularly secret, but you know how it is, confidentiality of sources, integrity and—'

'He's dead,' Niklas Linde said. 'He was found dead in his cell this morning.'

Annika slid down onto a chair, weak at the knees. 'Dead? How?'

'There's going to be a post-mortem, but the doctor was able to identify a couple of things straight away. His pupils were myotic, extremely small. That's charac-teristic of a morphine overdose.'

Annika shook her head as if she were trying to clear her thoughts. 'Morphine? But how could he get hold of that, stuck in prison?'

'That's what I was going to ask you. You were one of the last people to visit him. Did he ask for drugs when you were there?'

Her heart was thudding now, and her palms were clammy. 'No,' she said nervously. 'He did say he wasn't very fond of cocaine. He said he preferred beer.' She nodded to herself. 'Yes, that was it,' she said. 'He asked if we had any beer with us. He said it was pretty easy to smuggle it in.'

'But you didn't have any beer with you?'

'Of course not.'

'What did Carita say during the interview?'

'Nothing much. She interpreted and got us in, but obviously Jocke could speak Swedish.'

'What did she say afterwards?'

Annika took a deep breath. 'Nothing. Well, actually, she asked me what he had whispered to me right at the end, just as we were leaving.'

'What *did* he whisper?'

'Nothing much. He hugged me and asked me to help him get out of there. I didn't answer because there was nothing I could say.'

'Why did Carita ask about that?'

'No idea.'

'Were you working with Carita yesterday?'

'Yesterday . . . What – Friday? No, I was doing interviews in Gibraltar and Estepona, in Danish and Swedish. Why do you ask?'

Niklas Linde fell silent. The line crackled and hissed. Eventually he said, 'Carita Halling Gonzales visited Johan Zarco Martinez in prison yesterday afternoon. Because she was already registered as a visitor, they saw no reason to stop her going in.'

'Are you absolutely certain it was morphine? It couldn't have been something else?' She was feeling dizzy and sick.

'Unless one of the guards supplied Jocke with the morphine, it must have been Carita. She's the only person who had the opportunity. Jocke had no contact with the other prisoners, and he didn't have any other visitors.'

'That's impossible,' she said. 'I've been to her house. I *know* her. She's vain, anti-British and seriously in love with her husband . . . But what does she say? Haven't you spoken to her?'

'We'll put out a warrant for her with Interpol as soon as the post-mortem has been conducted.'

'Why? Has she gone missing?'

'The house is shut up. Her husband wasn't at work this morning.'

'So the whole family has gone? The children as well?'

'Did Carita say anything to you about her background, her family?'

'How do you mean?'

'The first place we look is with relatives and close friends.'

Annika could hear her own voice from far away, as if someone else was using it. 'She grew up in Beverly Hills, and met her husband, Nacho, there. He's a paediatrician, from Colombia. They lived in Bogotá in the early 1990s. Her father-in-law, Victor I think his name was, was chief of police there and was murdered by the Mafia, and they had to leave, because the Mafia wipes out the whole family so there's no one left to inherit . . .'

'Anything else?'

She screwed her eyes shut.

'Her parents ran a biotech company, Cell Impact. When they died she inherited the business and sold it straight away because she didn't know anything about that sort of thing. They used the money from the sale of the business to buy the house in Nueva Andalucía.'

'You may be called in by my colleagues in Stockholm for a more formal interview at some point, but that's enough for now. Well, take care . . .'

Annika stood up. 'Wait a moment,' she said. 'Has the death been made public? Can we write about it in the paper?'

'You'll have to check with the Foreign Ministry press office. Nothing I've told you is official, as I hope you appreciate.'

'One more thing,' Annika said, before she changed her mind. 'Why didn't you tell me you were married?'

There was complete silence on the line.

'Oh, Annika,' he said. 'Are you disappointed?'

She cleared her throat. 'No,' she said. 'I feel dirty.' There were limits. She was never going to turn into a Sophia Fucking Bitch Grenborg.

'Maria knows,' he said. 'Not everything, and no names, but that doesn't matter. I'll never leave her. She knows that too.'

You're deceiving yourself, she thought. One day you'll meet someone you can't resist, and then she'll be left standing, your wife, in Ängslyckevägen, all alone with her empathy and tolerance.

More silence on the line.

I ought to tell him about Suzette, she thought. About the email, and the fact that she might be alive.

'Was there anything else?' Niklas Linde asked.

Annika didn't answer.

'Well, then, take care.' He hung up.

28

She stayed where she was, paralysed. She felt like throwing up or crying or maybe both at once.

Carita Halling Gonzales visited Johan Zarco Martinez in prison yesterday afternoon . . . We'll put out a warrant for her with Interpol as soon as the postmortem has been conducted.

It just wasn't possible. The Colombian Mafia didn't carry leopard-print handbags and wear high heels.

Beer. Morphine. Dead men.

Size thirty-seven shoes. Few men have feet that small.

She got up and went to the sink, turned on the cold water and drank straight from the tap. She closed her eyes and let the water wash over her face, run down her neck and under her collar.

Who was she to decide whether or not someone was a criminal? The two Nordic police officers had recommended Carita Halling Gonzales because they, too, had used her as an interpreter.

She turned off the tap, tore off some kitchen paper and wiped her neck.

Criminals some way up the hierarchy probably looked just like anyone else. Lipstick, high heels and a leopard-print handbag: why not?

She sat down at the kitchen table again. She closed

her eyes, saw the villa in Nueva Andalucía and tried to understand what had happened there that night. She tried to see Carita pumping gas into the house and stepping over the dead bodies of the children . . .

She let the thought go. It was impossible.

Could there have been any misunderstanding?

Was Carita the victim of some sort of conspiracy?

Or was she mad?

No, not mad, obsessed. You don't kill eight people unless there's a very great deal at stake. Or do you? Even if you simultaneously love your family and get upset because your British neighbours won't contribute to the pool-maintenance guy's wages?

She got up and drank some more water, this time from a glass.

Carita had been extremely clever. Carved out a quite brilliant position for herself. By interpreting at police interrogations she knew exactly what anyone under arrest had said. By allying herself to Annika she had managed to get an insight into the work of the inquiry.

And she herself was responsible for Carita gaining access to the prison.

She jumped when her mobile rang. Number withheld, presumably the paper. Probably Patrik.

'Yes,' she said. 'I'm home.'

'Er, hello, this is Jimmy Halenius.'

Oh, fuck! Not him as well.

'Hello,' she said flatly.

'Is this a bad time?'

'Someone I interviewed on Thursday has just been found dead in his prison cell, and I've just found out that the interpreter I used is probably a killer for the Colombian Mafia,' she said.

'Oh, shit,' Jimmy Halenius said. 'Which prison?'

'Málaga.'

'Zarco Martinez? Bloody hell. We've just requested his extradition.'

'Too late now,' Annika said.

'And the Mafia killer?'

'A woman who worked as an interpreter for the police in Málaga.'

'Oh, shit,' he said again. 'Would you like to come round and have dinner with me this evening?'

'I've got some writing to do,' Annika said. 'If I can get permission from the Foreign Ministry, Zarco Martinez will probably be the lead story tomorrow.'

'I understand,' Jimmy Halenius said. 'Good luck with the Foreign Ministry. You'll need it.'

She put her mobile down and stared at her laptop. She couldn't write about Carita. It was too tenuous. Besides, there wasn't even a formal warrant out for her arrest yet. She'd count herself lucky if she found anyone who could confirm that the young man was dead. She wouldn't be able to get verification of the cause of death or his last visitor, Carita.

And she couldn't make any direct link to the murder of the Söderström family either.

Annika stretched her back and scratched her head.

Where could they have gone? They couldn't go back to Colombia: the whole family had been forced to flee, hadn't they? They'd had to abandon the good life in a cosy suburb there when Nacho's father, the chief of police, was murdered by the Mafia. And the Mafia wiped out entire families, so that no one was left to inherit anything . . .

She could suddenly see Carita before her, outside the house, that rainy day when the policeman had let them in, when she had first become aware that there was another daughter, a girl called Suzette.

'Another child?' Carita had said, eyes wide, her face completely white.

She had noted Carita's reaction, but had thought she was just upset at the whole story.

You didn't kill them all, Annika thought. There was someone left, an heir. A serious miscalculation. She had to take a walk round the flat, into the children's rooms, stroking the sheets on their beds. Then she roused her laptop and went onto Google.

Carita's father-in-law, the murdered chief of police, maybe he was on some Spanish-language page, held up as a hero of democracy. Victor? Victor Gonzales?

She got 965,000 results.

She tried *victor gonzales policia bogota*.

The number of hits shrank to 179,000.

She pushed the computer away and looked at the time. She ought to phone Patrik and tell him about Martinez. If nothing earth-shattering had happened in the world of television, if no one had tripped over during a live broadcast or something equally serious, his death would probably be the lead story, assuming she could get the story confirmed. She did a quick calculation. What were the chances of anyone else finding out about the death and getting confirmation of it before she did? Zero, pretty much. So there was no reason to call Patrik until she had something to offer him.

She reached for her bag and pulled out the notepad where she'd jotted down the main points of her interview inside the prison. She leafed through her scribbled notes as she reached for an apple that had seen better days. Then she picked up her mobile and dialled the press office at the Foreign Ministry. She took a big bite, leafing back through the interview with Wilma in Estepona, and her visit to Gibraltar. There was a click on the line

403

and a woman answered. 'You've reached the press office of the Foreign Ministry, can you hold?'

'How long for?' Annika asked, but the woman had already put her on hold. There was a hiss on the line, like distant tinnitus.

She sighed loudly and hoped someone could hear her at the other end. She would use the prison interview tomorrow: news had to come before any series of articles. She picked up the pad again and carried on leafing through it.

Was there anything else she could use now?

Her eyes fell on a web address she had jotted down. The closed estate agency, with the Söderström family villa in the window.

There was a click on the line.

'Hello?' Annika said.

No answer, just more tinnitus.

She put the apple down, pulled her laptop towards her and typed www.aplaceinthesun.se into the address box of Internet Explorer.

She took another bite while the computer did its thing.

Welcome to A Place in the Sun, your Real Estate Agent on the Coast!

The website was like those of all the other estate agents she had looked at when she had checked house prices and properties around the world, albeit perhaps a little more basic. This was no big agency. The logo was in the top left corner, brash and ugly. Maybe there was some information about the family's villa.

Another click on the line.

'Hello? Hello!'

On the left, beneath the logo, there was a list of subsections: *Home*, *Property Search*, *New Developments*, *About Us*, *Contact*. She clicked on *Property*

Search to look for villas in Nueva Andalucía, but the link led nowhere.

'Foreign Ministry press office, can you hold?'

'Hello?' Annika said. 'I've already been on hold—'

There was another click and the buzzing resumed.

She threw the apple-core into the sink's waste-disposal unit. Stuck-up diplomats, she thought, and clicked on the *About Us* link.

She found herself looking at the usual opening drivel in English: buying a property in Spain is a dream for a lot of people but it's also a serious investment. So you need the very best advice and guidance from an established company. Since we opened our first office on the Costa del Sol in 1968, we've helped thousands of people to find a new home on the Spanish coast . . .

She clicked to get off the page, and found herself on the contact page instead. She was about to close the window when she spotted the agents' email addresses:

astrid.paulson@aplaceinthesun.se

ernesto.zarco.martinez@aplaceinthesun.se

Her skin broke out in goosebumps all over her body.

Astrid Paulson.

Ernesto Zarco Martinez.

Astrid Paulson was Veronica Söderström's mother's name. It could hardly be a coincidence, two women with the same name just round the corner from the office of the daughter of one.

Had Astrid Paulson been an estate agent? And who was this Zarco Martinez?

She hung up, leaving the woman at the Foreign Ministry to her fate.

She Googled ernesto zarco martinez, and got 133,000 results. Hopeless.

She stared at the screen until her eyes started to water, searching hard in her memory.

She'd seen this very name somewhere before, but with something else added. Another name, perhaps, or an address?

She thought for a while, then opened the search box for the laptop's own hard-drive. She clicked to search for documents ('word processing, spreadsheet, etc.'), and used the advanced search to look for a word or phrase in a document. Then she searched the entire hard-drive for Ernesto Zarco Martinez, with capital letters in the right places just to be on the safe side. It would take a while, but if she'd ever written that particular combination of names, the search function would find it.

A happy little dog appeared on the screen, wagging its tail as the computer searched. She went out to the bathroom, had a pee, washed her hands and face, and returned to the laptop. The dog was wagging its tail. No results so far. She went through to the landline in her bedroom.

'Foreign Ministry press office, can you hold?'

'No!' she said loudly. 'Absolutely not! If you won't talk I'm going to write my article anyway!'

There was stunned silence at the other end, no tinnitus.

'Er, what's this concerning?'

'Are you aware that a Swedish citizen has died in prison in Málaga?'

The person at the Foreign Ministry drew a deep breath. 'We haven't received any information to that effect.'

'That's as may be, but I happen to know that this death has occurred.' She gave the woman all the facts about the case, and said she would call back in an hour for confirmation. That ought to get them moving.

Then she went back to the kitchen.

One result.

She felt her pulse quicken as she clicked to open the document.

It was an old website that had been cluttering the laptop's memory, in temporary Internet files, a page from a company search on the national database that she must have made ages ago. It was about Advice Investment Management AB, described as providing 'financial advice and business development and associated activities, but nothing that could legally be deemed to be banking or credit-related'. She scanned down the page. The company had two full board-members, Lena Yvonne Nordin from Huddinge, and Niklas Ernesto Zarco Martinez from Skärholmen. One deputy director was listed: David Ze'ev Lindholm from Bondegatan in Stockholm.

She forced herself to breathe calmly and steadily.

She recognized the image in front of her. This was where she had seen the name Zarco Martinez before. She knew exactly where it was from: her research into the bizarre business activities of the murdered police officer, David Lindholm.

Niklas Ernesto Zarco Martinez from Skärholmen was known as Nicke in Sweden and Ernesto in Spain. So he was Johan Zarco Martinez's elder brother, and he had run a business with Yvonne Nordin, the triple-murderer from Sankt Paulsgatan.

She went back to her search: the dog with the wagging tail had found another two results containing the name in question, then stopped. He had evidently finished.

The first was a company record for a defunct clean-ing business in Skärholmen. It had been run by Lena Yvonne Nordin and Niklas Ernesto Zarco Martinez.

The second was a record from the national ID data-base.

Niklas Ernesto Zarco Martinez – deregistered. De-ceased.

He had died on Christmas Eve eighteen months ago.

She nodded to herself. That's right. She remembered the search now that she saw it again.

Suddenly she was trembling. There was a connection between the Zarco Martinez brothers, Yvonne Nordin, David Lindholm and Astrid Paulson, Veronica Söderström's mother: they had run companies together, worked together, and now they were all dead, all in a violent or destructive way.

Then a thought popped into her head and she went back to the website again, www.aplaceinthesun.se. She looked at the garish logo in the left-hand corner, the words set out vertically inside a beaming sun.

A
Place
In
The
Sun

She read the initials, from the top down, and felt the room start to spin.

Apits.

Niklas Linde had been wrong. The drug business on the Costa del Sol, Apits, didn't mean Airport Passenger Intelligent Transport Systems, or Analogue Proprietary Integrated Telephone System. It meant A Place in the Sun.

Part 3
AFTER WHITSUN

The Angel at Gudagården

To start with there was only sky and meadows. Air and space and wind.

There were Mother's strong arms and the scented bed-linen. The pattern of the scrubbed floor-tiles , the shimmering water of the lake, and singing in the evenings.

He has opened the pearly gates
So that I may come in,
Through His blood he has saved me
To keep me with Him.

She had no early memories of Father. He was there at a distance, always on the edge of her vision, because he was so tied to the earth: land, farm, winds. She herself was always slightly elevated, without any real contact with the ground, and that was because she was an angel.

That was what Mother always said.

'You're my little angel,' she said, or *Du bist mein Engel*, because Mother always spoke her own language, the Angels' Language.

And she would float and dance over Gudagården like the blessed child she was, conceived without sin with the approbation of the Lord. Father didn't like her talking to the other children on the farm, but she did anyway, because God talks to everyone, and He sees and hears everything. And everyone was kind and friendly towards her, smiled and said nice things, because, of course, she was the preacher's daughter. Everyone except the Troll Girl.

It was a mystery.

The Angel was a bit scared of the Troll Girl. Not very scared, because as an angel she was the servant of the Lord, and no one could be safer than God's host of children, but the Troll Girl hid her voice and had narrow black eyes that could see round corners.

The only person the Troll Girl was prepared to show her voice to was the Princess, the most beautiful of all princesses in the whole world. In fact she was almost an angel too, because she could actually speak the Angels' Language. She had heard the girls talking to each other up under the roof where they lived; they only spoke when they thought no one was listening, and the Princess told stories about the Castle Among the Clouds, and the Troll Girl talked about the Little Match Girl who froze to death and became a falling star in the sky.

But the Troll Girl's weasel eyes saw her on the stairs and she drove her away with hard fists.

Then came the day when Wall-eye put his hand on the Princess for the first time. The Troll Girl hit him on the head with a stone and he let go of the Princess and rushed after the Troll Girl, who hid right at the back of the tool-shed.

And the Angel, she saw it all, and she knew that the task of angels is to protect and help, so she followed them into the shed and saw how Wall-eye found a knife and circled round the Troll Girl with the blade sticking out.

'Thou shalt not kill,' she said, in her high, clear angel's voice, and Wall-eye looked in her direction, angry.

'Get out of here,' he said.

But angels help people in need, even troll girls, so she took another step into the tool-shed.

'Honour thy father and thy mother: that thy days may be long upon thy land,' she said.

'Ma's dead and Dad's been locked up to dry out. That's why I'm in this hell-hole,' Wall-eye said, his voice cracking.

'We should fear and love God that we may not harm our neighbour's life or cause him suffering, but help and defend him in every danger and need,' the Angel said, going up to him and taking hold of the knife.

Wall-eye sniffed, let go of it and ran for the door.

It was completely quiet once the boy had disappeared. The dust danced in the rays of sunlight. The Troll Girl was staring at her open-mouthed, and then she let the Angel hear her voice. 'Why did you do that?' she asked, and all of a sudden the Angel felt bashful.

'Thou shalt love the Lord thy God with all thy heart,' she said, 'and thy neighbour as thyself. So Jesus says.'

The Troll Girl took a step towards her and her eyes narrowed. 'Are you a bit simple?'

The Angel shook her head.

And from that day on she was allowed to go with the Troll Girl and the Princess wherever they went around the farm. Father and Mother didn't want her to join in with the sowing and reaping, but she replied with the words of the Lord, 'In the sweat of thy face shalt thou eat bread,' and they let her be. Together they whirled round, between the mist's frosty down, at rest and play, and the Angel learned of other worlds, where there was a great man who lost a mighty war, and cold nights in damp cellars where drunken men bought drink and love. Yes, they did everything together, through summers, autumns, winters and springs, until that night in August when the terrible thing happened and the Troll Girl and the Princess vanished from Gudagården for ever, and the Angel's long journey towards the underworld began.

—— Original Message ——

TT NEWSFLASH: Filip Andersson cleared.
Press Conference: Lawyer Sven-Göran Olin's office
Skeppsbron 28, at 10.30 a.m.

(nnnn)

Tuesday, 14 June

29

It felt as if summer would never arrive. There hadn't been a single day when the air had been mild. The north winds had the whole country in a cast-iron grip, and the weather-forecasters had nothing good to say.

Annika pulled her jacket tighter round herself as she headed for the bus. Rain was lingering in the treetops. She passed the billboards for that day's papers outside a Seven-Eleven: 'HOW TO GET AWAY TO THE SUN' and 'RAIN FORECAST FOR MIDSUMMER'. Sadly her paper had the negative message, and their competitors the optimistic one. So there was no doubt who was going to win the circulation war today.

She missed the bus and waited in the doorway of number 32 Hantverkargatan to escape the rain that had now decided to fall. She looked up at the arched doorway above her head: this was where she and Thomas had lived together for several years. It seemed so unreal, like something she'd read about or seen in a film.

He hadn't been in touch since the Costa del Sol. 'I'll call you,' was the last thing he had said when he'd dropped her off at the airport, and he had looked as if he meant it, but he hadn't.

She hadn't called either. In fact she had bought

Kalle a mobile phone and taught him how to charge it so that she wouldn't have to call the flat on Grev Turegatan when she wanted to say goodnight to the children.

She missed them already, even though she had had them for the Whit weekend and had only just dropped them off at their schools.

She hadn't heard anything from Niklas Linde either, but she hadn't been expecting to.

Not even Jimmy Halenius had called, but that was probably down to a mass break-out from Österåker Prison, which had had serious political consequences. Obviously, all the opposition parties were calling for the justice minister's resignation, as if he had personally driven the bulldozer through the wall of the prison. It looked as if he'd survive, as usual, thanks to a few tactical appointments and a large dose of natural political talent.

The bus pulled up and she scrambled on board. She had to stand all the way to Gjörwellsgatan.

Tore the caretaker made straight for her when she came through the door. 'You didn't fill up the car the last time you borrowed it,' he said, standing squarely in front of her.

Her mobile rang and she fished it up at the end of the hands-free cable and checked the screen: a number she didn't recognize.

'Do you think I'm some kind of errand boy with nothing better to do than clear up after you?' he said.

'Hello?' Annika said, into the phone.

'Annika? Hi! It's Polly.' The voice was high-pitched and bright, like a little girl's. She closed her eyes to shut out the whining caretaker. Polly: Polly Sandman, Suzette's friend. She'd never heard her voice before, just exchanged emails with her.

418

'Hello,' she said, turning away from Tore and walking towards the newsroom. 'How are you?'

'Next time you want a car from here you can whistle for it!' Tore shouted after her.

'You said I should call you,' Polly said, 'if Suzette got in touch.'

Annika stopped in the middle of the newsroom. Patrik caught sight of her from the newsdesk and leaped to his feet, bouncing towards her with a bundle of notes in his hand.

'Has she?' Annika asked. 'She's been in touch?'

'As Mr Gunnar Larsson,' Polly said. 'This time she wrote a message as well.'

'Press conference at Skeppsbron, half an hour,' Patrik said, handing her a printout from the bundle. 'You're going at once, with Steven.'

'What?' Annika said, taking the earpiece out. 'Who's Steven?'

'Filip Andersson's been released. New temp photographer.'

'Hello?' Polly said in the earpiece.

Annika put it back in. 'Can we meet up?' she asked. 'Bring your laptop or a printout of the message. Where will you be at lunchtime?'

Polly mentioned a café on Drottninggatan, right in the city centre. Annika had never heard of it, which probably meant it was terribly trendy. She saw a tall man, very young, festooned with camera cases, rushing towards her. 'Hi, I'm Steven.'

She dropped her mobile into her bag and shook hands with him. 'I suppose we should set off at once,' she said, glancing at the printout of the newsflash from the agency that Patrik had given her: 28 Skeppsbron. In Gamla stan, then, with parking spaces on the quayside opposite the building.

'I don't drive,' Steven said.

Great, Annika thought, and made for the caretaker's desk.

'No chance,' Tore said, when he saw her coming towards him. 'You need to learn to fill the tank before you try that again.'

'It's your job to fill the tank, and it's my job to think,' Annika said. 'Get me a car.' She got the shabby old Volvo he usually gave her.

'What do we want from this press conference?' the photographer asked, as Annika drove out of the car park. 'Dramatic or formal? Who's the victim? Who's the hero? Is there a bad guy?'

She glanced at him to see if he was making fun of her, but he seemed deadly serious. 'I suppose Filip Andersson's the victim, and the lawyer's the hero,' she said, 'but neither of them looks particularly good in their respective roles. Filip Andersson's like a gangster and Sven-Göran Olin is a cuddly old uncle.'

'And the bad guy is a well-dressed man with a suntan and trustworthy blue eyes?'

'The bad guy is an ordinary-looking woman who was shot by the police in the forest outside Garphyttan in December last year. Called Yvonne.'

The rain had stopped. She crept through the heavy traffic in the city centre and parked on the quayside at Skeppsbron, paying 260 kronor for two hours. It would have been cheaper to take a taxi.

She wondered how long the press conference would last. If it looked like it was going to drag on she'd abandon it. Her meeting with Polly in the café was more important, no matter what Patrik might say.

It might be a false alarm, she thought. It doesn't necessarily have to be a sign of life from Suzette. Polly was prone to dramatizing.

The legal firm's waiting room was already stuffed with journalists, television cameras and radio transmitters, which surprised Annika. It had been fairly clear since last winter that Filip Andersson was going to be released. I suppose they're here to get a look at him, she thought.

She forced her way through the room and found an empty chair next to the lavatories. The various sections of that day's illustrious broadsheet lay on the arm. She sat down with a sigh and opened the culture section. She flicked through it without reading anything until she got to page four, where she was brought up short. The double-page spread was dominated by a review of a photography exhibition at Kulturhuset, entitled 'The Other Side of the Costa del Sol'. The photographer, Lotta Svensson Bartholomeus, was praised for having 'captured and sensitively documented the underbelly of the over-exploited Costa del Sol: the women on their way to market, craftsmen's abandoned tools . . .' The article was illustrated by a close-up of the plate-shears from the drug warehouse in La Campana.

Who'd have thought it, Annika mused, and put the paper down.

She looked straight ahead for a few minutes with a growing sense of unease in the pit of her stomach. Then she picked up the culture section again and studied the strange picture, remembering Lotta's assertion that art was more real than journalism. There was something about this that she didn't understand, that much was clear. How, in principle, could a broken pair of plate-shears on a warehouse floor be interesting? What was she missing? She lacked the capacity to see anything exceptional in it.

She folded that section of the paper into a hard little bundle and stuffed it under her chair, then got up and waited until the doors to the conference room were opened. There was an immediate crush in the doorway. She heard Sven-Göran Olin urging everyone to calm down. She stayed where she was until most people had gone in, then went through the doors and stood just inside them.

Up at the front, by an ordinary table with three chairs on the other side, the photographers, television people and radio journalists were jostling for position. She could see Steven in the crush – he was much taller than all the others.

She tried to catch a glimpse of the exonerated murderer. He wasn't there yet.

Her unease showed no sign of letting up.

Filip Andersson had been locked up for five years for a grotesque crime that he hadn't committed. Was it possible to emerge from something like that in a healthy mental state, or did you have to be Nelson Mandela to cope with it?

She realized she was about to get an answer because a door at the far end of the room opened and Filip Andersson came in, dressed in dark trousers and a white shirt. The sporadic clicking of the photographers turned into a torrent, the television lamps came on, casting a blue sheen over the whole room, and reporters performed animated pieces to camera.

Andersson didn't look at any of them. He sank onto one of the three chairs and stared ahead without blinking. Annika craned her neck to get a better view. He'd lost weight since they'd met in the visitors' room in Kumla Prison last autumn. His hair had been cut, and he'd shaved. Sven-Göran Olin sat down beside him, and finally a young woman came in and sat on the chair at the end.

'It is with great pleasure,' the lawyer began, 'that we have today received the decision of the Swedish Court of Appeal to exonerate Filip Andersson entirely of all three cases of murder on Sankt Paulsgatan.'

The camera clicking subsided slightly. The radio journalists sat down.

'Filip Andersson has been locked up for over five years,' the lawyer went on. 'As I pointed out when the verdict of the City Court was announced, he was found guilty on very weak evidence on both occasions. Everyone involved in the case seemed to be mainly pre-occupied with making things easy for themselves.'

By now there was complete silence in the room.

Annika looked at the man's face for signs of emotion, relief, sadness, joy or bitterness, but she couldn't identify anything. His face was utterly blank, his eyes staring fixedly at a point slightly above the heads of the crowd. His shoulders seemed broader – maybe he'd been exercising in anticipation of his release.

'A judgment of this sort means that we have simultaneously more and less faith in the legal system,' Sven-Göran Olin said. 'That it is possible to raise an appeal and put things right in retrospect is positive. But at the same time it is very troubling that such mis-carriages of justice can occur.'

You could have heard a pin drop. Annika studied her colleagues. They were all staring at Filip Andersson, their faces showing disappointment and uncertainty. What could they make of this in their papers?

Filip Andersson was pretty terrible in the role of victim. He didn't have a cute family gathered round him with cake and children's drawings, no beautiful wife holding his hand and gazing in gratitude at the cameras with tears in her eyes. He looked what he was: a slightly overweight, unscrupulous financier who had been in the wrong place at the wrong time. There was no way they'd be able to drum up much sympathy for him among their readers.

'Since the chancellor of justice has rejected our application, today we will be submitting a claim for damages against the Swedish state,' Sven-Göran Olin said. 'Filip Andersson is claiming twelve million kronor, five million of which represent reparations for the suffering caused, and seven million his loss of income.'

The woman beside him stood up and started handing out printed documents, presumably copies of the claim.

There was murmuring in the room. A record-breaking claim for damages wasn't going to make the public feel particularly sympathetic.

'Filip Andersson, how does it feel to be free?' a radio journalist shouted.

Sven-Göran Olin leaned towards the microphone again. 'My client would prefer not to comment at the present time,' he said.

'So why's he here, then?' someone shouted angrily.

'Olin forced him,' someone replied. 'He's conducted the whole case *pro bono*, and this is the payoff.'

Annika didn't think the lawyer was getting much return on his investment, although he hadn't had to do a great deal. It had been her articles about Yvonne Nordin that had set the ball rolling, and the attorney general herself had requested the judicial review.

The woman distributing the documents had reached the back of the room, and handed one to Annika. Annika leaned towards her and whispered in her ear: 'Can I have an exclusive interview with Filip? My name's Annika Bengtzon. I wrote the articles about Yvonne Nordin which—'

'Filip Andersson isn't making any comment,' the

woman said expressionlessly. 'Not now, not to any-one.'

The other reporters were frowning at her as if she'd just tried to jump the queue in the Co-op.

She glanced anxiously at the time. If she couldn't get any comment, the whole morning would have been wasted. It was impossible to write an article for the evening tabloids about a man who had nothing to say.

The journalists began to drift away. She stood aside and pretended not to see her colleagues as they streamed out into the hall. 'If he wants that amount in damages, he could at least have the sense to speak out about those lost years,' a woman in the crowd said, as she passed.

Filip Andersson got up. He was still pretty large. Annika slid to one side and made her way towards him along the wall. The young woman who had passed round the printouts opened the door at the end of the room. Sven-Göran Olin slipped out first. Filip Andersson began to walk towards the door.

'Filip!' Annika said in a loud voice. 'Filip Andersson!'

He stopped in the doorway and turned. His gaze landed directly on her.

Did he recognize her? Surely he must – he couldn't have received that many visitors in prison.

'What are you going to do next?' she asked loudly. 'What are your plans?'

Incredibly slowly, he raised his left forefinger, then bent it several times, as if he were waving at her.

His left forefinger. Waving.

A shiver of terror ran down her spine.

Suddenly she was back in that alleyway again, in Yxsmedsgränd in Gamla stan, that Wednesday night after she'd visited him in Kumla Prison. She had been on her way home when two masked men had dragged her into a doorway. One had leaned over her, and the eyes staring at her through the holes of the balaclava had been as pale as glass. The other had held the point of a knife a centimetre from her left eye. *Leave David in peace. It's over. No more poking about.* Then they had grabbed her left hand, pulled off her glove. She felt again the terrible pain that had run from her hand up her arm and into her chest. *Next time we'll cut your children instead.* The cold of the cobblestones against her cheek, her thundering heartbeat in her ears as she'd watched their heavy boots disappear down the alley.

She met Filip Andersson's gaze, took a step back and unconsciously hid her left hand behind her back.

Filip Andersson saw the gesture and smiled, then turned and disappeared from the room in the same way as he had arrived.

Her hand was still burning as she headed back to the car. The scar on her index finger was throbbing again – she hadn't noticed it since the coldest days of the previous winter. She put her hand into her jacket pocket and hunched her shoulders against the wind.

'He doesn't seem particularly humble,' Steven said. 'Perhaps you wouldn't be, though, if you'd been locked up for five years when you were innocent.'

'No one's saying he's innocent,' Annika said. 'The only thing the Court of Appeal has concluded is that there wasn't sufficient evidence to convict him. There's a huge difference.'

Steven fell silent again.

I'm too hard on temps, she thought. It serves me right that they don't want to work with me.

'I'm not going back to the newsroom,' she said, trying

426

to sound a bit gentler. 'You'll have to take a taxi, I'm afraid.' He didn't seem upset. Probably glad to get shot of me, she thought, as she paid 260 kronor for another two hours. She'd leave the car where it was as there were no parking spaces on Drottninggatan.

30

Polly hadn't arrived when Annika clambered onto an extremely high bar-stool next to a table with a rolled-steel top and LED lights. She tried to order a *caffé latte* from a waitress with a silver stud in her nose, but the girl snapped that it was self-service. Not that trendy, then. She decided to skip the latte.

The place reminded her of the inside of a factory in some futuristic horror film. There were rusty lumps of iron on the walls for decoration, many of them wrapped in loops of multi-coloured neon. The coffee machine hissed, and she could hear a dishwasher in the kitchen, with the clatter of crockery. The music throbbing from the speakers made the German industrial metal of Rammstein sound like singalong Euro-pop.

Her finger ached. It could hardly have been a coincidence. He had waved to her with the same finger that had been cut on the night after she had met him in prison.

She put her hand back into her pocket.

The café was filling – it was getting towards lunchtime. A surprising number of the customers seemed to be civil servants from the government ministries and office blocks in the city centre, to judge by their conservative appearance: white shirts and dark trousers, exactly like Filip Andersson at the press conference.

She shivered.

If Filip Andersson had ordered the knife attack that evening, he had been quick off the mark. It hadn't been more than a few hours after her visit to him in Kumla. He must have been extremely keen to stop her snooping about in David Lindholm's past. Why? The two men had run a business together. David had had an affair with his sister, and got her pregnant. He had been Filip Andersson's trustee at Kumla, which involved providing support and acting as middleman for lifers.

There was obviously something she wasn't supposed to find out, something she didn't already know. David had had a lot of dark sides.

Annika remembered Nina Hoffman's description of how he had treated Julia. David Lindholm had kept his wife locked in their apartment for up to a week at a time. On other occasions he had thrown her out naked into the stairwell, until she had become so ill that she'd had to go to A&E. He was notoriously unfaithful, disappeared for weeks without saying where he had been, shouted at her, calling her a whore and a slut . . .

What if Polly didn't show up? She drummed the fingers of her right hand on the metal tabletop.

David had been an extremely contradictory character. While he had been a pig of a husband, he had somehow become one of Sweden's most famous and respected police officers. She knew he had been violent, from the investigations into complaints made against him at the start of his career in the police. She remembered Timmo Koivisto, a former drug addict she had met at the Vårtuna rehab centre: he had told her that David had smashed his head into a lavatory wall, leaving him with permanent injuries. Timmo Koivisto had been a dealer right at the bottom of the food-chain. He had supported his own habit by ripping off his employers and cutting the gear with icing sugar, then charging extra and pocketing the difference.

'Why did he do it? Why did David beat you up like that?' Annika had asked.

'They wanted to show me that I could never get away,' Timmo Koivisto had said. 'Wherever I went, they would find me.'

And who were 'they'? Annika had asked. Was he talking about some sort of drugs Mafia?

'That's one way of describing them,' he had replied.

She looked around the nightmarish décor. She was in the right place, wasn't she?

To make sure, she took out her notepad and checked. Yes, this was it.

David Lindholm, drugs Mafia, the murders in Sankt Paulsgatan, Filip Andersson arranging for her finger to be damaged . . .

'Annika?'

She looked up and saw a blonde girl with a rucksack and padded jacket standing next to the table. 'Polly?'

The girl sat down opposite and shrugged off her rucksack. 'I know,' she said, leaning across the table so Annika could hear her. 'I don't look like my picture on Facebook any more. I've thought about changing it, but for some reason I don't want to. We took our pictures together, Suzette and me, and if I change it, it'll be like another bit of her vanishing.'

She seemed so grown-up. 'And now you think she's got in touch?' Annika said.

Polly nodded. 'Do you want anything? I can go and get it.'

Annika took out her purse and handed Polly a hundred-kronor note. 'Just a glass of water for me, please.'

The girl went off to the counter, which was actually a

430

rusty metal table. Annika watched her. She must be six-teen, maybe seventeen, but seemed older. She returned with a glass of water, ice and lemon, and a cup of green tea for herself. She looked rather apologetic. 'I know it was a bit silly of me,' she said. 'What I said last time.'

Annika arched an eyebrow.

'When I asked if you thought there was email in Heaven. Of course there isn't, I know that. I suppose I was just hoping . . .' She struggled onto a stool. She wasn't particularly tall, about the same height as Annika. 'This time I know it's for real. Suz is alive,' she said, calm and focused.

'Have you got your computer with you?' Annika asked.

Polly pulled a laptop out of her rucksack. 'I'm in a bit of a hurry,' she said. 'We've got a student council meeting.'

She started the laptop up, logged in, did a bit of clicking, then turned the screen towards Annika. It was covered with a picture of a smiling, black-haired girl hugging a chestnut horse. 'There's free Wi-Fi here,' Polly said. 'Hang on, I'll log in.'

'That's a lovely picture of Suzette,' Annika said.

'The horse's name is Sultan – he was her favourite. The riding-school's sold him now.'

The screen flickered and a hotmail page appeared below Windows Live. A banner at the top advertised some science magazine. Immediately below that, on the right-hand side, she saw the email address for Gunnar Larsson. The darker blue marker on the left was highlighting 'sent'. There were two messages. They had been sent to Polly's yahoo address, the first at the end of March, and the second at 14.37 the previous day, 13 June.

'So this is Gunnar Larsson's email account,' Annika

said. 'The one you and Suzette set up to send dirty messages to girls in your class.'

Polly nodded. 'We deleted all the messages after Gunnar left,' she said, shamefaced.

'But you kept the account?'

'We didn't know how to close it down.'

Annika clicked on the first message, from March. Empty.

Then she clicked on the one from the day before.

Hi Polly, you cant tell anyone about this email. You cant say anything to mum and DEFINITELY NOT the police. Theres no internet at the farm so i havent been able to email. Im at an internet cafe now. They dont know where i am, and Fatima would be furious if she knew I was writing.

Im with Amira. Ive been here since new year. Ive got my own horse called Larache. Hes lovely, a mix of English and Arabian thoroughbred. Is Adde with anyone else? Dont tell Adde ive been in touch. You can answer this but I dont know when ill read it. We only go places like Asilah, but not very often.

Big hug from suz

Annika read the message twice. Evidently it had been written on a fairly basic keyboard, without any Swedish characters. Asilah sounded like a place . . . It seemed vaguely familiar. Where had she heard its name before?

'Do you think it's genuine?' she asked. 'Is this how Suzette usually expresses herself?'

Polly took a sip of her green tea and nodded. 'She always writes *big hug*, and Suz with a small s.'

'Who are the people she mentions? Fatima, Amira and Adde?'

A shadow passed quickly over Polly's face, unless Annika was imagining it.

'Amira's Suz's best friend. That's what she used to say, as if those of us here at home didn't count. I think Fatima's her mother. Adde is Suz's boyfriend. Well, maybe not boyfriend, they weren't really together. It was mostly that Suz had a crush on him. Adde's always got loads of girls . . .'

'What about Amira?' Annika asked. 'How come she's Suz's best friend?'

'Her summer friend. Suz spent a lot of time on their farm when she was little. They're the same age.'

'Where? In Spain?'

Polly shook her head. 'Morocco. They've got a farm there.'

'Do you know where it is? The place she mentions, Asilah?'

Polly shrugged and pushed her cup aside.

'But how do they talk to each other?' Annika asked. 'They speak French and Arabic in Morocco, and Suzette couldn't really speak English, could she?'

Polly looked indignant. 'Of course she can speak English.'

'Does she speak English with Amira?'

Polly shook her head and turned the laptop round to face her.

'Swedish, obviously.'

'Hang on,' Annika said. 'Can I forward this to my own email?'

Polly hesitated. 'No,' she said. 'I promised to tell you if she got in touch. I have to go now.'

'They speak Swedish to each other? How come?'

'Amira's half Swedish, isn't she? Her dad's from Sweden. Her surname's Lindholm.'

All the noise around Annika faded. 'Lindholm?' she

said. 'Her dad's surname is Lindholm? Do you know what his first name is?'

Polly put her laptop back in her rucksack and shrugged again. 'No idea. I don't think he lives on the farm.'

'Could his name be David? Do you know if he was a policeman?'

The girl was pulling her rucksack back on now. 'Can I ask you something?' she said.

'Of course you can,' Annika said.

'Don't say anything about this to anyone. Promise.'

Annika looked at the serious young woman with the blonde hair, so different from the heavily made-up, black-haired girl on Facebook. 'I won't say anything,' she said. 'And I won't write anything either. I promise.'

They shook hands, then Polly disappeared out of the door.

Annika gave her two minutes, then followed her. She left the noise of the hellish café behind her with a sigh of relief.

Suzette was alive; she was on a farm somewhere in the Moroccan countryside, where there was a girl of the same age whose surname was Lindholm.

She stopped on the street, fished out her mobile, called International Directory Enquiries and asked to be put through to the Swedish Embassy in Rabat, Morocco.

An automated answerphone message clicked in. A long harangue in French mostly explained the opening hours for the visa section, and telephone times for other business. Annika had trouble keeping up – her French was almost as bad as her Spanish – but it was already too late to get any information that day. She'd have to try again tomorrow.

She looked towards Kungsholmen. She ought to go back to the paper and tell them that Filip Andersson

434

wasn't talking. People were sweeping past her, bumping into her, catching her bag, standing on her toes, hurrying, hurrying, hurrying to lunch or the dry-cleaner or a meeting. Buses squealed and cars splashed through muddy puddles.

She looked towards Hamngatan. Writing up that worthless press conference would take thirty seconds. She raised her mobile and dialled Julia Lindholm's home number on Bondegatan.

She and Alexander were in, and Annika was more than welcome to pay them a visit.

Their flat was on the third floor of a rather dull 1960s block. The stairwell was dark and smelt musty. The only thing that looked new was the sign saying LINDHOLM on the letterbox. The police must have smashed the old one when they broke into the flat after David was murdered, Annika thought.

She rang the bell and heard a distant ding-dong echo on the other side of the wall.

'Welcome,' Julia said, throwing the door wide. 'How lovely of you to come and see us! Isn't it, Alexander?'

The boy, who had grown at a phenomenal rate during the spring, was standing in the doorway to his room. He didn't answer.

Annika dropped her bag in the hall and hung her jacket on a hook. Then she went over to Alexander and crouched beside him. 'Hello, Alexander,' she said. 'Is it nice being able to play in your own room again?'

He went into it and closed the door.

'He'll start back at his old nursery school next week,' Julia said. 'The therapists have decided he's ready. Have you been here before?'

Annika shook her head.

'There's not much to see, but my parents have re-decorated and made it nice while Alexander and I were at Lejongården. This is the kitchen.'

She gestured towards a very ordinary sixties-style kitchen with painted cupboards and a scratched stainless-steel worktop.

'It suits the building well,' Annika said.

'Yes, doesn't it? I really like it. And here's the living room . . .'

It had oak parquet-flooring, a television and windows facing in two directions. 'We haven't got a balcony,' Julia said, 'which is a bit of a shame. It's really the only thing I wish was different. My bedroom . . .' She opened the door to the room where her husband had been murdered. The bed was neatly made. The curtains were open. If David had done errands for the Mafia in return for money, he hadn't spent it on his home, Annika thought.

'I know what you're thinking,' Julia said. 'How can I sleep in here?'

Annika took a deep breath and was about to protest, but breathed out instead.

'He's gone, but we're still here. There's no way round that,' Julia said. 'Have you had lunch?'

Annika shook her head.

'I was thinking of doing meatballs and mashed potato. Frozen meatballs and instant mash, but it does the job. Would you like some?'

'Thanks, yes.'

They went back out into the hall. Annika could hear banging from inside Alexander's room.

'He's decided to build a flying saucer,' Julia said. 'The therapists say I should let him do what he wants.'

Annika sat down at the kitchen table while Julia got out a packet of powdered potato and a bag of meat-

436

balls. 'How's he getting on?' Annika asked.

Julia took a while to answer. 'He isn't the same boy as before, although I don't really know what I was expecting. After all, he was a whole year younger then.' She stopped, holding a spatula in front of her face. 'You know what?' she said. 'It doesn't really matter. I'm just so grateful that I've got him back.' She went back to the meatballs. They were soon sizzling in a frying-pan with some melted margarine. The sound was soothing and homely, the kitchen freshly painted and tidy, and Julia was humming bits of an unidentifiable song.

This ought to feel nice, Annika thought, but something about it jars. The irregular banging sounds coming from the boy's room, perhaps, or possibly the Spartan furnishings. Maybe it was just the echo of all David's lies. He had never been under cover on the Costa del Sol. But there was no such thing as ghosts.

'How are you managing financially?' she asked, trying not to sound too intrusive.

'The flat's freehold, and we inherited that, but there were no savings. David had life insurance, payable to those he left behind, and that's me, Alexander and Hannelore, of course. It was actually quite a lot of money, so that's what we're living off at the moment.'

'What do you think you might do? Go back to the police?'

Julia shook her head. 'I want to study architecture. If I'm careful, the insurance money will last until I graduate.' She measured some water into a saucepan and put it on the stove.

'Can I ask you something else?' Annika said. 'Do you know if David had any connection to Morocco?'

Julia looked up at her in surprise. 'Morocco? No, none at all. Why would he have?'

437

'He never mentioned Morocco? Or if he knew anyone there?'

'Why do you ask?'

Annika took her time answering. 'He might have relatives there.'

Julia got the butter out of the fridge and a whisk from the cutlery drawer, poured some milk into a mug, added a large knob of butter and put it into the microwave, set it to two minutes and pressed start. 'The only time he ever mentioned Morocco was when he talked about his stepfather, Torsten. He disappeared in Morocco when David was in his late teens.'

Annika sat still, searching her memory. Julia had said something about the missing stepfather on some earlier occasion. 'Did he ever find out what happened to him?'

Julia got out three plates, glasses and cutlery. 'I don't think he ever really got over it. They were very close. He never knew his own father, so Torsten meant a great deal to him.' She stopped. 'It was the winter before David applied to Police Academy,' she said.

Annika took the plates and laid the table. 'When you lived in Estepona, could David have gone to Morocco to look for Torsten?'

'No,' Julia said. 'It was all such a long time ago. I can't imagine that he did.'

The microwave bleeped three times. The milk was hot, the butter melted. The water was boiling on the stove and Julia poured the potato powder into the buttery milk and stirred it energetically with the whisk. 'Alexander! Lunch is ready!'

He emerged from his room at once and stopped in front of Annika. 'You're in my place,' he said. His voice was surprisingly low-pitched, not at all as Annika remembered it from that night in the forest all that time ago.

438

'You can sit here, Alexander,' Julia said, pointing to the place at the end of the table.

The child's face contorted into a grimace and he howled. He collapsed, his upper body jerking, his hands and feet banging the floor, as he screamed. Annika backed away in horror. Julia seemed neither surprised nor concerned, just picked him up and rocked him in her arms until the tantrum had passed. 'Today you can sit in this seat,' she said, putting him on the chair at the end of the table.

He fired a hostile glare at Annika, then grabbed his knife and fork and set about the meatballs. 'Ketchup?' he asked, between mouthfuls.

'Not today,' Julia said.

Annika ate in silence. Sure, her children were angry sometimes, but she'd never seen anything like that in such a small child.

'Can I get down now?' he said, when he'd finished.

'Say thank you for the food and clear your plate away,' Julia said.

'Thanks for the food,' he said, then leaped off the chair, picked up his glass, cutlery and plate in a somewhat un-steady grasp, then took them to the draining-board.

He left the kitchen without a backward glance, went into his room and shut the door.

'The seven years I spent as a beat officer make it easier,' Julia said, with a sad smile. 'Coffee?'

Annika looked at the time. 'I should probably get going,' she said. 'By the way, do you have any contact with your mother-in-law?'

Julia filled a kettle with water and got out a jar of coffee. 'Not much,' she said. 'We brought her here last weekend, but she just wandered about looking for David. It was all a bit weird, so I don't think we'll be doing that again in a hurry.'

439

'Which care-home is she in?'

'Ramsmora.'

'Where's that?'

'In Nacka. I know it's not far, but we haven't got a car and it's a bit tricky getting there on public transport. We don't visit her very often.'

'Would you mind if I went to see her?' Annika said.

'Why would you want to do that?'

Annika decided to be honest. 'Do you remember me asking if you'd ever heard the name Veronica Söderström or Astrid Paulson?'

Julia nodded. 'She was that ice-hockey player's wife.' She measured some coffee into a machine and pressed the start button.

'I have reason to believe that David met her when they were children,' Annika said. 'You've never talked to Nina about that?'

Julia shook her head in bewilderment. 'Why would I?'

'Nina once told me that they grew up together, David and Filip Andersson, Yvonne Nordin and Veronica Paulson.'

Julia started at the mention of Yvonne's name.

'We've talked about this before,' Annika said. 'That they were like siblings. It means their parents must have known each other, or at least their mothers. Have you ever heard of a woman called Astrid Paulson?'

'Wasn't she one of the people murdered in Spain last winter?'

'That's right,' Annika said. 'She was Veronica Söderström's mother. Have you ever heard her name in any other context?'

Julia shook her head.

'Astrid Paulson, Nina's mother and your mother-in-law, Hannelore, all knew each other.'

'Did they?'

'Nina, Yvonne and Filip's mother was called Siv. You knew her, didn't you?'

Julia put two mugs on the table. 'She died soon after we got married. I always felt rather sorry for Siv. She was a fairly severe alcoholic. You take it black, don't you?'

'Yes, thanks. David's real father, Klas Lindholm, what happened to him?'

'They divorced before David was a year old,' she said, sitting down at the table. 'He moved away, I don't know where. They didn't have any contact after that. He died a few years ago. David didn't go to the funeral.'

'Do you know if he went on to have another family?'

'David inherited an old Saab and a summer cottage outside Kramfors when he died. He was the only heir.'

'Do you know if he used to go to Morocco?'

Julia raised her eyebrows. 'You're really banging on about Morocco. What's this about?'

Annika felt herself flush. 'I've heard about someone called Lindholm who's supposed to be living in Morocco, and I was wondering if it could be a relative.'

'Hardly,' Julia said. 'Lindholm's a very common name. There's one in the next building – we're always getting each other's post.'

'Mummy?' Alexander was standing in the kitchen doorway.

'Yes, darling, what is it?'

'My flying saucer's finished.'

Julia lit up. 'How lovely! I must have a look. Would you like to see it too, Annika?'

'If I'm allowed to?' Annika said.

Alexander nodded.

They went into the boy's room, next to Julia's. Half of the floor was covered with a huge pile of plywood and chipboard, all nailed together. A few sticks, probably broom-handles originally, poked up towards the ceiling.

Julia clapped her hands in delight. 'That's wonderful!' she said. 'I'm sure you could fly all the way to the moon in it.'

Alexander regarded her solemnly. 'I need to get higher than that,' he said. 'All the way to the stars.'

'What do you want to go there for?' Annika asked.

He gave her a look of utter surprise. 'To see Daddy, of course.'

31

Annika picked up the car from Skeppsbron. The parking-ticket had expired and she had been given a 500-kronor fine. She tossed the penalty notice into her bag, called Directory Enquiries, and asked for a text containing the phone number and directions to the care-home in Nacka.

Alexander's stare was still burning inside her.

She started the car. Slowly she steered towards Slussen and turned off onto Stadsgårdsleden. The traffic was heavy and sluggish. It had stopped raining, but the sludge on the road spattered the windows and she still had to keep the windscreen-wipers on.

There was a sixteen-year-old girl called Amira Lindholm in Morocco, on a farm outside Asilah.

Torsten Ernsten, David Lindholm's stepfather, had disappeared in Morocco.

As she was passing Skurusundet she thought the sky looked a bit brighter to the east, where she was heading.

She carried on along the motorway towards Gustavs-berg.

Where had she heard the name Asilah?

Who could have mentioned it to her?

Suddenly she heard Niklas Linde's voice in her head.

It was saying something, and she was taking notes, something she hadn't used in her article because it hadn't seemed relevant, but what was it?

It gets shipped out of two small coastal towns, Nador and Asilah, in February and March.

They had been talking about the cannabis produced by the hash farmers in Morocco. They had been sitting in the tapas bar in the conference centre in Málaga, and Niklas Linde had been pressing his leg against hers under the table.

She realized a moment too late that she'd missed the turning. She had to take the next exit instead, then turned round and drove straight to Ramsmora care-home.

The building was long and low, and seemed to have been renovated in the 1990s. It was painted a glossy pink, which didn't suit it, and was framed with rustling birches.

She pulled up in the visitors' car park and breathed out. She really didn't drive anything like enough, regardless of what Tore the caretaker might think, and was always tense when she was forced to.

She had closed the car door and was on her way to the entrance when her mobile rang. It was Berit Hamrin. 'I'm sorry,' she said. 'I didn't mean you to have to go to that press conference.'

'What press conference?' Annika asked, before she remembered Filip Andersson.

'I had to go to the dentist this morning or I'd have gone. Did he say anything?'

'Not a thing,' Annika said, remembering his little wave.

'You know I don't think he's innocent.'

Annika didn't answer, and carried on towards the entrance.

444

'Where are you?' Berit asked.

'I'm going to visit a confused old lady. She's a German Jew, and came here on the white buses after the war.'

'She's German?' Berit said. 'And came to Sweden on the white buses? You must have misunderstood.'

Annika stopped. 'What do you mean?'

'The white buses picked up Scandinavians who were held in German concentration camps, Danes and Norwegians. There weren't any Germans.'

'Are you sure?' Annika said.

'It was claimed that the buses were going to rescue other nationalities as well, but that turned out to be a lie. The only Germans who got anywhere near those white buses were dying prisoners who were moved between various camps. Almost all of them died.'

Annika looked up at the tops of the trees. She really shouldn't be surprised. Nothing about these families seemed to be either true or normal.

'Why did you ask?' Berit wondered.

'I'll tell you later,' Annika said. 'I'll be back in a couple of hours.'

She reached the door, scraped the mud from her shoes and stepped inside the care-home.

There was strip-lighting in the ceiling of the lobby, reflecting off the polished linoleum floor. A few pictures of indeterminate subject matter hung on the plastered walls, and there was a sharp smell of disinfectant.

She stopped and listened.

Two corridors led off from the entrance hall, one straight ahead and the other to the right. She couldn't see anyone, but somewhere she could hear voices. To the left she could just make out a dining room through a half-open door. She walked over and pushed it open. Two women in their fifties turned towards her. They fell silent at once.

'Hello,' Annika said. 'I'd like to visit Hannelore Lindholm. Which room does she live in?'

They looked at each other and whispered something. Then one went off towards the kitchen while the other came towards her.

'My name's Annika Bengtzon,' Annika said, holding out her hand and smiling. 'I know Julia and Alexander. Julia told me that Hannelore visited them at home in Bondegatan last weekend and—'

'I know who you are,' the woman said. 'I'm Barbro, the manager. We do read the papers at Ramsmora. You found Alexander.' She was very red under her nose, as if she had a cold and had been blowing her nose too much. 'Are you going to send something to the paper?'

People generally couldn't tell the difference between the various types of article in the daily papers: long, explanatory reports, incisive interviews, sharply focused news stories, diaries, notes, op-ed pieces or adverts. For a lot of people, including Barbro, it was all just something you sent in.

'No,' Annika said. 'I'm not going to write anything. I'd just like to see Hannelore and talk to her.'

'About what?'

Annika adjusted her bag on her shoulder. 'Do I have to tell you?'

The woman blushed. 'This way,' she said. She led the way through the lobby and carried on straight ahead. Annika followed behind. 'At Ramsmora, we focus on a number of particular areas,' she said, over her shoulder. 'We have forty-eight apartments in total. We strive to make the atmosphere as homely as possible. We have a care-home section, some sheltered housing and a section for people suffering from dementia. That's where we are now.'

The walls were pink, with a painted row of darker

pink flowers along the middle. After a few metres the corridor opened out and became wider, with a carpet on the floor. There were groups of armchairs and small tables placed at regular intervals along one wall. The other contained a series of doors, some open, others shut.

'So Hannelore Lindholm has been diagnosed with dementia?'

'I can't discuss the medical details of our residents,' Barbro said, stopping at one of the closed doors and knocking on it. She pulled it open and went in without waiting for an answer. 'Hannelore,' she said, far too loudly, as if the old lady was hard of hearing. 'You've got a visitor.'

Then she let Annika into the room. She remained standing there with her hand on the door-handle.

'Thanks,' Annika said. 'I'll be able to find my own way out.'

Barbro hesitated, then walked out and closed the door.

To her right Annika saw a bathroom, and to her left a rudimentary kitchen. The rest of the flat consisted of a single room that was seriously over-furnished. A heavy, cracked-leather sofa, an ornate writing-desk, bookcases made of yew, and a narrow bed in the corner closest to the kitchen. The furniture looked exposed and out of place on the yellow linoleum floor.

A woman with long white hair was standing by the window, fiddling with a pot-plant. She didn't seem to have noticed that Annika was in the room.

Annika cleared her throat loudly.

No reaction.

'Mrs Lindholm?' Annika said. 'Hannelore? My name's Annika Bengtzon. I've come to talk to you.'

The woman cast a surprisingly alert glance over her shoulder. 'What do you want, then?' she asked, in a completely normal tone, as she turned her attention back to the plant.

'I'd like to talk to you about Astrid and Siv,' Annika said.

The woman's hands stopped in the middle of what they were doing. She turned round. Annika noticed that her hands were full of brown leaves. She was strikingly attractive.

'Is Astrid here?' she asked.

She had no trace of a German accent. On the contrary, she had the same Södermanland accent as Annika.

'No,' Annika said. 'She's not here at the moment. Shall we sit down?'

Hannelore Lindholm hesitated. 'I just have to get rid of this rubbish first,' she said, heading for the little kitchen.

Annika pulled off her jacket and dropped it with her bag on the floor by the door, then went over to the sofa and armchairs.

'When is Astrid coming?' the old woman asked expectantly.

'Astrid won't be coming again,' Annika said, sitting down in one of the armchairs. 'Perhaps you could tell me a bit about her.'

'Where is she?'

Hannelore was tall and slender, her back bent but her shoulders straight. Her hair had been carefully washed and brushed. Her eyes were large and bright blue, and the look on her face reminded Annika of a surprised doll. She had rouge on her cheeks.

She had walked round the flat on Bondegatan looking for David, even though she had been told countless times that he was dead. There was no point in Annika telling her Astrid was dead, when she might already have been told and forgotten.

'She's on the Costa del Sol,' Annika said, because she didn't know if the bodies had been moved or, if so, where to.

Hannelore Lindholm sat down on the sofa. 'She's so happy there,' she said. 'Does she still have the estate agency?'

'Oh, yes,' Annika said.

Hannelore laughed. 'Astrid's so courageous,' she said. 'She's always the one who dares to do all the dangerous things.' She smiled and nodded for emphasis.

'What sort of thing does Astrid dare to do?' Annika asked.

The answer came promptly and easily. 'Jump off the biggest haystack. Ride the wild bull.' Hannelore laughed again. 'She's crazy!'

The laughter died. Annika waited. Nothing else followed.

'Where did Astrid jump off the haystacks?' Annika asked.

The surprised expression returned to Hannelore's face. 'At Gudagården, of course! She's already there when I arrive. She's the only one who's kind to me.' She leaned over an antique table and lowered her voice. 'Astrid's a very good person,' she said quietly. 'She always looks after anyone who's weak or scared. She's not a little troll girl at all.'

The old woman was completely confused. Maybe it would be better if she asked some easier questions. 'Could you tell me a bit about yourself?' Annika asked.

Hannelore looked up, then glanced around the cramped room. 'I live in a castle,' she said. 'In a castle high above the clouds. I dance in *die Halle* for all the animals.' She raised her arms and made graceful gestures in the air, her hands floating as she closed her eyes. There was something enchanting about her expression, as if there really was another reality concealed within Swedish geriatric care, another room besides this one in Ramsmora care-home. Annika looked at her for a long time, until she started to feel a bit uncomfortable.

'Where are your parents?' she asked.

The woman froze and she opened her eyes. 'I'm not allowed to talk about Mother and Father,' she said. She looked frightened.

'Why not?'

'Onkel Gunnar and Tante Helga have forbidden it.' She tucked her hands under her armpits.

'But you can tell me,' Annika said.

She shook her head vigorously. 'He'll hit me even more if I ever say anything about Mother and Father,' she said.

'Who will?'

'Onkel Gunnar.' Her voice was a monotone now, and she stared in front of her as she spoke. 'I came to Sweden on the white buses that Count Folke Bernadotte and the Swedish Red Cross so generously put at the disposal of those in need,' she recited.

'But that isn't true, is it?' Annika said.

Hannelore Lindholm glanced at her but said nothing.

'They forced you to lie, didn't they? Why?'

The woman blinked as though she were about to start crying. 'Because Father was an officer,' she said, in a very thin voice.

'An officer? A German officer during the war?'

She nodded.

'That castle you used to dance in, what sort of place was that? Was it a real castle?'

She nodded again. 'Berghof,' she said, in the same little voice.

Annika started. She wasn't great at history, but she'd seen almost every episode of the miniseries *Band of*

Brothers. 'But that was Hitler's home in Bavaria,' she said. 'The one they used to call the Eagle's Nest.'

Hannelore wrapped her arms round her knees and hid her face against her legs.

Annika looked at the woman, her soft white hair flowing over her legs. Her hands were clenched around her lower arms, white hands with blue veins and pale pink nails.

Hannelore Lindholm wasn't Jewish, Annika realized. She had never been in a German concentration camp. On the contrary, she was the daughter of a Nazi officer, so high up that the family had visited Berghof at least once. Her Jewish background was a retrospective fabrication put together by the people she called Onkel and Tante. Who were they? Annika had never studied German, but those sounded like family titles. Were Gunnar and Helga distant relatives who had taken her in after the war? And who thought it sounded better and nobler to look after a poor Jewish girl who had survived a concentration camp than the daughter of a senior Nazi officer?

But why had she given her son Jewish names, David Ze'ev Samuel? Was that a way of repaying some kind of psychological debt?

Unless the boy's father, the elusive Mr Lindholm, had chosen the boy's names? And he might have been Jewish, of course . . .

The woman was rocking on the sofa in a slightly odd way.

'Can you tell me about Siv?' Annika asked.

Hannelore stopped rocking. She straightened her back, her shoulders relaxed and her arms let go. Her vision cleared and she looked at Annika. 'Is Siv here?' she asked.

'No,' Annika said, 'she's in Södermanland.'

She seemed content with the answer. She nodded in agreement, looking slightly concerned. 'Poor Siv,' she said.

'Why's that?' Annika asked.

Hannelore leaned towards Annika. 'She's so easily taken in. She really believes in God and Heaven and all the other things that Onkel Gunnar preaches. When I first arrived at Gudagården she actually thought she was an angel, because that was what Tante Helga called her. How silly!'

Annika was studying her thoughtfully. Hannelore Lindholm didn't seem to have any difficulty in remembering her childhood. In fact, it seemed as if she was still there. What she was saying was probably true.

The girls had grown up together on a farm somewhere, presumably in Södermanland because Hannelore had the same accent as her. They had shared the same childhood experiences. Something that had happened back then had bound them together so tightly that they had stayed in touch when they were grown-up.

'What happened at Gudagården?' Annika asked, watching the woman's reaction carefully.

Hannelore Lindholm blinked. 'Happened?'

'When did you move away from there?'

Hannelore Lindholm got up from the sofa so quickly that she knocked over the antique table. She went to the window and began picking at the plant again, roughly now.

The question had upset her. Annika went after her and put her hands on the old woman's. 'Come and sit on the sofa,' she said. 'Let's talk about Siv and Astrid.'

The doll's eyes met Annika's. 'Is Astrid here?' Hannelore asked.

Annika led her back to the leather sofa. 'I'd like to talk about Torsten,' she said.

'Torsten isn't here,' Hannelore said.

'No, I know,' Annika said. 'He's in Morocco. What's he doing there?'

Hannelore was fiddling with her skirt. Her lips moved, but no sound came out.

'Does Torsten often go to Morocco? What does he do there? Do you know?'

Hannelore started singing, something monotonous and incomprehensible, maybe in German.

'Don't you want to talk about Torsten? Has he upset you?'

She stopped singing. 'Torsten never came home,' she said. 'He went to the farm and never came back.'

Annika felt the hair on the back of her neck stand up.

Theres no internet at the farm so i havent been able to email.

'Where is the farm?' she asked. 'Who's at the farm?'

Hannelore Lindholm was staring straight ahead without moving.

Annika waited for a long time, trying to understand the limits of Hannelore Lindholm's memory.

Julia had said she had been taken into care after Torsten disappeared. She seemed to remember that he hadn't come back after his last trip. How long ago could that have been? David had been a teenager, and he would have been forty-three now. Twenty-five years ago, when Hannelore would have been about forty-five. Maybe she still had memories from that time.

He went to the farm and never came back.

'Is David in Morocco as well?' she asked.

Hannelore Lindholm brightened. 'No, no,' she said. 'He's coming to get me soon. We'll be going home.' She got up and went over to one of the bookcases, opened one of the doors and started to pile the books on the floor in front of it.

'Hannelore,' Annika said, going over to her, 'come and sit on the sofa. David's not here yet. We'll have to wait a bit longer.'

She nodded and left the books where they were on the linoleum. 'David doesn't have an easy life,' she said. 'All the other children have a father.'

Annika got her to sit down again, and sat beside her on the sofa. 'Why doesn't David have a father?' she asked.

Now Hannelore picked angrily at her cardigan. 'They got cross with each other. He shouted at Astrid. Is David coming soon? He should be here by now, shouldn't he?'

Annika could hear footsteps and voices in the corridor, the clatter of crockery on a trolley. She took a deep breath and looked directly at Hannelore. 'Can you tell me about Fatima?'

The woman gazed at her uncomprehendingly. 'Who?'

Annika waited a few seconds before she replied. 'Fatima's at the farm,' she finally said. 'With Amira.'

Hannelore's eyes darted round the room.

Annika waited, then asked, 'Can you tell me about Julia?'

The old woman's hands fumbled with her skirt.

'Alexander, do you remember him? David's son?'

There was a knock on the door and Barbro stuck her head into the room. 'How's it going?' she asked, looking inquisitively at Annika.

'We're just having a chat,' Annika said, rather sharply. 'We'd appreciate it if we could be left in peace.'

Barbro came into the room and closed the door behind her. 'It's time for your medicine,' she said, unlocking a cabinet in the bathroom.

'I don't want my medicine,' Hannelore said. 'It makes my head feel so fuzzy.'

The manager took something from the cabinet and

454

locked it again, then came out into the room and went to the sink. 'Don't throw dead leaves into the drainer,' she said clearly and slowly. 'Just remember that we have to come and clean up after you.' She filled a glass with water, then went over to the old lady.

Hannelore sighed, took the pill and swallowed it with a sip of water.

'Well done,' Barbro said in her loud voice, for people who were hard of hearing.

She turned to Annika. 'I'll have to ask you to leave now,' she said. 'Hannelore needs to rest.'

Annika glanced at her watch. It was time for her to be getting back anyway.

Hannelore went to sit on the bed with a look of resignation in her doll's eyes. Annika followed her and took her hand. 'Thanks very much for the chat,' she said.

Hannelore peered at her. 'Who are you?' she asked.

Annika patted her hand, then went over to her bag, slung it onto her shoulder and put her jacket over her arm. 'Julia and Alexander send their love,' she said. 'They'll come and see you again soon.'

Hannelore was gazing at the window and didn't seem to hear her.

32

It had started to rain again. Annika ran out to the car, discovered she had forgotten to lock it, and threw herself into the driving seat, tossing her bag onto the seat beside her.

She pulled out her mobile and checked the screen: one missed call, from Patrik's mobile.

The head of news would have to wait.

She closed her eyes and thought. The rain was drumming on the roof of the car and streaming down the windscreen.

Hannelore, Astrid and Siv had grown up together on a farm in Södermanland called Gudagården. The patriarch was called Gunnar, and he hadn't been above beating children. Hannelore was the daughter of a Nazi, and related to the farmers, who were hypocrites of the highest order: they had beaten the little girl into lying about her past.

The three girls had grown up and stayed in touch with each other. Their children in turn were like brothers and sisters: David and Filip, Yvonne and Veronica, and little Nina.

She started the car and drove onto the motorway as she dialled the number.

Nina Hoffman answered at once, as she usually did, and gave her full name.

There was no noise in the background, so Annika assumed she was at home or in her office. At least she wasn't in a patrol car or in some noisy custody-suite corridor.

'I was at the press conference when your brother was released,' Annika said. 'Do you know what he's going to do now?'

'I'm grateful for what you've done, but I don't owe you anything,' Nina Hoffman said. 'You'll have to ask Filip what he's planning to do next.'

Annika slowed down and pulled into the inside lane. 'Okay,' she said. 'On a completely different subject, do you know anything about a farm in Morocco?'

The windscreen-wipers were going at top speed. Nina didn't answer.

'Hello?' Annika said. 'Hello? Nina?'

'Yes, I'm here.'

'I've just been to see Hannelore Lindholm,' she said. 'I talked to her about your mum, and Veronica Söderström's mother, Astrid.'

'What on earth for? Why do you want to go poking about in our family? Can't you just leave us alone?' She didn't sound upset, just determined. 'Hannelore is a sick, confused old woman. You've got nothing to—'

'Nina,' Annika interrupted. 'Did your mother ever mention a farm in Morocco?'

There was a hissing sound on the line.

Nina was silent for a few seconds. 'Why do you want to know?'

'I know there's a farm somewhere outside Asilah in northern Morocco, and it's got something to do with Astrid Paulson, David Lindholm and all the rest of you.'

'What do you mean by "all the rest of you"?'

'A woman called Fatima, with a daughter called Amira? Ever heard of them?'

There was a click, then complete silence on the line. Nina Hoffman had hung up.

Annika bit the inside of her cheek. Damn. Nina knew something and she didn't want to talk about it.

A lorry pulled alongside her, spattering the windscreen with sludge.

Annika put down her mobile and tried to concentrate on driving.

Tore had left for the day, thank goodness. She handed the car keys back to the evening-shift caretaker, telling him the car needed filling and could do with a wash. Then she got out a claim form for the day's expenses, wrote down the cost of the car park, as well as the parking fine. They were supposed to pay any fines themselves, but there was no harm in trying . . .

'How much do you want about Filip Andersson?' Annika asked, as she passed the news desk.

'Did you get an exclusive?' Patrik asked.

'Nope.'

The head of news pushed back his chair. 'Where have you been all day?'

Annika stopped beside him, taken aback. 'Checking a few things,' she said. 'Why?'

'Not the things you should have been checking,' he said, putting his hand on a bundle of notes beside his computer. 'How are we supposed to publish a paper if the reporters don't show up for work?'

She made up her mind not to get angry. 'Give me the notes,' she said. 'What is it – some television celebrity burping during a live broadcast? Or has the man with the world's longest nose got hay-fever?'

Patrik grabbed the edge of his desk and wheeled himself towards it without answering.

'Oh, well,' Annika said. 'It can't have been that important, then.'

She went over to the day shift's table and took out her laptop. She opened an ordinary Word document, gathered her thoughts, then started to type up what she had learned during the day. She started at the end, with Nina not wanting to talk to her, then Hannelore and her confused childhood memories, Julia and Alexander and their brittle existence, and then she reached Suzette. She stopped, and saw in her mind's eye the photo on Polly's computer of the black-haired girl with her arms around the horse, the radiance in her eyes and smile.

'Annika? Can you come into my office for a moment?'

The editor-in-chief, Anders Schyman, was standing in the doorway to his glass box.

'What?' Annika said. 'Right now?'

'Preferably.'

'Sure,' she said, logging out of the network to avoid having her password changed, a nightmare that seemed to be the new game among night editors with too little to do. She left her jacket on top of her bag on a spare table, and followed him inside the box.

'Close the door.'

She slid it shut. 'Has something happened?' she asked.

'Sit down,' he said, pointing at a chair.

Annika remained standing, and didn't say anything. Schyman sat down behind his desk. 'How do you think it's working, you being a reporter?'

She looked at him intently, trying to work out what he wanted. 'Okay,' she said. 'It's quite fun. It's not exactly rocket science, not with Patrik at the news desk.'

'I've received a number of worrying reports about the way you treat your colleagues,' he said.

Annika stiffened.

'Patrik says you come and go as you please. You can't behave like that. He has a responsibility to me and the management team, and he has to be able to rely on you being at work during the hours you're paid for.'

She folded her arms. 'He's been in here telling tales,' she said. 'He's annoyed because I didn't rush back to his little notes quickly enough.'

'Patrik's not the only one who's fed up with your attitude. One of the temp photographers called me in tears when you were in Spain on that job about the Costa Cocaine. She said you'd abandoned her outside a conference centre, gone off with some man and not come back to the hotel all night. Then you went around by yourself, taking your own pictures, instead of working with her.'

Annika took a deep breath. 'Nothing I wanted was "photogenic" enough so she refused point blank to get her camera out. And I had my hands full. I couldn't sit there holding Lotta's hand, listening to her telling me how clever she'd been in Tehran.'

The editor-in-chief raised a hand. 'She's been getting great reviews for her exhibition at Kulturhuset,' he said, 'so she can't be completely without talent.'

'Those were the pictures she was running round taking instead of doing her job,' Annika said.

Schyman's elbows landed heavily on the desk. 'You have to think about the way you act,' he said. 'Your behaviour towards Patrik has been terrible ever since his first day as head of news. Almost as bad as some of the others were towards you when you were head of crime. Patrik doesn't want you on his shift any more, and I can't say I blame him. So I've agreed to transfer you.'

Annika wanted to sit down, but stood where she was, paralysed. 'What do you mean?' she asked.

'Have you got any idea of where I can put you?'

'Are you serious?'

Anders Schyman sighed. 'Are you interested in a free-lance contract?'

She gasped. 'What the fuck is this? Are you *firing* me?'

The editor-in-chief got up, squeezed round his desk, pulled out one of the visitors' chairs and said, 'Sit down.'

Annika sat. The chair was lower than she'd expected and she jarred the base of her spine as she landed.

'Can you see how Patrik might have had trouble handling you?'

Her instinct was to argue, pointing out Patrik's overhasty decisions and journalistic incompetence, his superficial judgements about news and his poor instincts, but instead she said nothing.

'Do you want to work nights again?' the editor-in-chief asked. 'Or be a sub-editor? In charge of the letters page? Or something online? A news anchor on the web? How about that?'

How could she possibly be a problem? She managed to bring home all the news editors' odd stories – she found missing children in forests and uncovered terrorists, Nobel killers and Yugoslavian Mafia gangs . . . 'I think you're being bloody ungrateful,' she said. 'You make it sound like I spend all day sitting around drinking coffee, but I bring in more stories than anyone else.'

'I'm not questioning your competence, just your attitude.'

'My *attitude*? Is that more important than the fact I come up with the goods? Haven't you got enough yes-men around you?'

The editor-in-chief's face darkened. 'This isn't a question of me wanting people who don't contradict me—'

'Of course it is. You're just like every other male boss.

461

You want well-behaved girl reporters who are cute and friendly and always do whatever anyone tells them. And I'm never going to be like that.'

Silence descended on the room.

'What's going to happen to me?' Annika asked. 'Honestly?'

Anders Schyman bit his lower lip. 'I've always defended you,' he said. 'Hell, I've gone further than that. I've gone into battle for you. The chairman of the board wanted to get rid of you, but I put my own job on the line to keep you.'

'Oh, my heart bleeds,' Annika said. 'If the board ever gets to overrule you and starts hiring and firing staff, you're finished as a boss, and you know it. You don't have to pretend with me.'

Silence descended again.

'Are you interested in what I've spent the day doing,' Annika asked, 'instead of following up Patrik's little notes?'

Anders Schyman didn't answer.

'You remember the fatal gassing in Nueva Andalucía? The missing sixteen-year-old girl, Suzette Söderström?'

He nodded.

'I think she's alive. I think she's being held prisoner on a farm in Morocco. I've been going round talking to people who might have information about that farm and where it might be, how she came to be there, who else might be there and—'

Schyman put his hands over his face and groaned. 'Annika, Annika, Annika,' he said. 'There was a sabotage alarm out at the nuclear power station in Oskarshamn this afternoon, and we didn't have a reporter we could send.'

'I heard about that on the car radio,' Annika said. 'It turned out to be nothing. A welder who had a trace of explosives on a plastic bag with an IFK Norrköping logo on it.'

'But we didn't know that to start with. The fact remains that we didn't have a reporter to keep an eye on the story.'

Annika stared at him. 'Well, that's hardly *my* fault! I'm not the one who's just got rid of half the staff!'

Anders Schyman stood up. 'We aren't going to get any further,' he said. 'I'll give you the rest of the week to think about where you want to be transferred.'

Annika remained seated, with a dizzying sense of freefall. Then she forced herself to get up, left the glass box and closed the door without looking back.

Patrik stared at her as she walked across the floor of the newsroom. Of course he knew what they had been discussing. He must be on top of the world.

She couldn't bring herself to look at him, just went to her laptop and tried to hold back the tears burning inside her.

There were other places she could work. There had to be some other media company in Sweden that was willing to employ her. And she could manage without a job for a while, with the insurance money she was about to get. At the end of June she would finally be getting compensation for her burned-out house, six million kronor plus a quarter of a million for contents. Admittedly, Thomas would get half of that, but the plot would also be put up for sale and ought to bring in another couple of million. She'd checked online: there was only one vacant building-plot in the whole of Danderyd, and that was on the market for 4.4 million.

Maybe getting fired wasn't such a tragedy after all.

Maybe it could be the start of something new, something good.

Maybe it would be a good idea to go freelance. Then

she could do exactly what she wanted without anyone else interfering . . .

But she wanted to feel she belonged somewhere. She wanted her own chair, her own pigeon-hole in the post-room.

She sat down, shut her eyes and took several deep breaths, then logged in and opened up the document she had been writing. She had reached Suzette's email, and tried to re-create it from memory.

You can't tell anyone about this email. Not Mum, and not the police. There's no internet at the farm so I haven't been able to email. Fatima would be furious if she knew I was writing.

I'm with Amira. I've been here since New Year. I've got my own horse, called Larache. He's a mix of English and Arabian thoroughbred. Don't tell Adde I've been in touch. You can answer this but I don't know when I'll read it. We only go places like Asilah, not very often.

Big hug from suz

She read it through twice. It was ridiculous that the paper wasn't interested in Suzette's story. Why were girls with horses so boring? Besides, something bigger was going on underneath, something shady and out of reach, about Astrid and Siv and Hannelore and their families, something whose extent she was only just starting to appreciate.

'What did Schyman want?'

Patrik was standing beside her, unable to conceal his triumph.

'To wish me a happy birthday,' Annika said. 'You know perfectly well what he wanted. He told me you want to get rid of me.'

The head of news sat on her desk, on top of her notes. 'You're a good reporter, Annika,' he said. 'If only you could learn to—'

'Spare us both,' Annika said, grabbing her notepad. 'I'd like to get on with what I was doing.'

Patrik got up reluctantly. 'Shouldn't you go home? Tomorrow's another day.'

She made a decision. 'I'm not feeling well,' she said, 'so I won't be coming in at all tomorrow. I need to see the doctor – it's probably streptococcus.'

He looked at her sceptically, but said nothing and went back to his desk.

Annika clicked to close the Word document and went onto the net instead. There were flights from Stockholm to Málaga every morning. There were boats between Algeciras and Tangier all the time: she'd discovered that from the adverts along the Costa del Sol motorways. There was bound to be some way of getting from Tangier to Asilah – Morocco couldn't be that big.

She went onto Google Maps and typed in *asilah morocco*. A couple of seconds later she was staring at a satellite image of a town on the Atlantic coast of north Africa. It was probably fifty or sixty kilometres from Tangier. She took a couple of quick breaths and glanced over at Schyman's glass box. It was dark: he must have gone home without her noticing.

She hesitated for a second or two, then went to the booking page for the early-morning flight to Málaga. There were a few seats left on the plane, departing at six forty-five.

Falling Through the Sky

The Angel hit the ground with a thud once the Troll Girl and the Princess had disappeared. She was confined to bed with a fever and strange blisters on her hands, and was prescribed liniment for her chest and the prayers of the congregation.

Father and the farm workers searched the surrounding area for three days and three nights. Then the runaways were reported to the Child Welfare Commission. The girls were officially declared missing, but not Wall-eye. He was no longer a ward, since he had come of age the previous month.

The silence at Gudagården was extensive. Father took on the task of retribution, and mortified his own flesh in penance, as well as that of the farm workers. This wasn't well received. People had tolerated him beating the foster-children, but adult farmhands didn't take kindly to being whipped by their master.

Soon Father and the Angel were left to deal with the sowing and reaping on their own. Despite Father's prayers for the Lord's assistance, they didn't manage to lift the potatoes before the first frost.

Not a word was heard from the runaways, so Father took in more foster-children. He didn't want any more girls who would run away, just boys of working age. And he got the worst ones, the ones no one else wanted, and he whipped the exhortations of the Lord God into them until their backs bled. Then he worked them until they couldn't even think of dissent. He no longer searched for any who ran away, merely left them to the Lord's Mercy and the Flames of Hell.

The Angel was fourteen when Gregorius came to the farm. He was very different from all the other boys because he was dark, thin and quietly spoken; he never started fights and he wasn't boastful or noisy. He smiled his strange smile and inspired respect among the gang of boys, possibly even fear. Those who chose to pick on him woke up with strange injuries or had peculiar accidents.

The Angel was drawn to him like a moth to a flame and, like a careless insect, her wings were burned so badly that she was never able to fly again.

She was fifteen years and eight months old when Mother realized she was pregnant, and by that time Gregorius had been gone from the farm many weeks. Father beat her legs, back and crotch to shreds, intending to whip the sin out of her wicked body, but all he succeeded in doing was giving her scars that stayed with her for the rest of her life. Then she was locked away in the loft where the Troll Girl and Princess had been made to sleep, beneath the frost-engraved glass of the attic window. And, like her predecessors, she climbed over the roof tiles and down the fire ladder as soon as her wounds had healed enough for her to run.

She made her way to the road under cover of darkness, through the village and out onto the main highway. Early that morning she got a lift with a lorry-driver who was going all the way to Gnesta. He asked what a little girl like her was doing out on the road so early in the morning. She said she didn't want to talk about it, and he said he wouldn't say anything if he could be a bit friendly with her. And, of course, the damage was already done so she saw no real harm in letting him have his way.

Her wounds stung when he took her, and she felt the earth close above her head, never to open again.

He drove her to Mölnbo. From there she got a lift on a milk-truck that was on its way to Södertälje.

By then it was evening and she was very hungry.

She spent the night in a hollow next to the railway track, shivering like a dog, but she knew that there wasn't far left to go because the Troll Girl had told her about her mother. She had been out on licence for a long time, and she wanted to take care of her daughter, but the Child Welfare Commission had said no: they thought it was better for the Troll Girl to be raised in the Righteousness and Discipline of the Lord at Gudagården.

What no one knew was that sometimes the Troll Mother would come and visit her little girl, always at night when the roof was clear of snow and the child could use the fire ladder, and the Angel knew her address.

How she was going to find it in the big city of Stockholm was something to which she had given no thought but it wasn't too difficult. A cab driver took her to 28 Tyska brinken, in return for the same payment as the lorry driver from Mölnbo. Then she rang the doorbell.

The Princess opened it. It took her several seconds to recognize the Fallen Angel.

They looked after her on the truckle-bed in the kitchen for several weeks. Her wounds were infected, she fell into a fever and the child in her belly wasn't well. But in the autumn, just before the child was due, the Troll Girl took them all, her mother and the Princess and the Fallen Angel, to the cinema to see an almost new film from America.

The Troll Girl had already watched it several times, and knew all the dialogue off by heart. It was called *A Place in the Sun*, and it was about a poor young man who went to work for his rich relatives, and fell in love with a beautiful girl, and he was prepared to do anything for her sake, even murder someone. The film was terribly sad and the Angel wept for the pregnant girl, Al, for the handsome, weak George, his love for the divine Angela, and because he was unjustly executed in the electric chair.

Afterwards they went to a café, drank coffee and ate buns.

They didn't say much, but they were all thinking how unfair life was.

The Troll Girl paid the bill and gave the waitress a generous tip.

Before they got up from the table she leaned forward and took the others' hands in hers. Her voice was low and dark and her troll eyes were black as she prophesied their future. 'We deserve a place in the sun,' she said. 'Each and every one of us, and all of our nearest and dearest. And that's what we shall have, I promise you that.'

The words burned their way into the Angel's body, and then the first contraction came.

The little boy was born at dawn the following morning.

Wednesday, 15 June

33

She didn't bother going to bed. She stayed at the paper, printing out everything she knew about Hannelore, Astrid, Siv and their children, about Carita Halling Gonzales and all she had done; she read up about Algeciras, Morocco and Asilah; she thought through what she needed to do, and when it was half past two she went home to pack. She took just a bag containing her laptop, the camera from Gibraltar, her toothbrush and a change of underwear. At four o'clock she got a taxi to the airport, boarded the plane and slept like a log.

She woke up as they were landing and tried at once to call the Swedish Embassy in Rabat. Another long harangue in French, which she thought meant they weren't answering the phone yet.

She went straight from the plane to the car-rental desks on the floor below. There were more people there than ever before so she presumed the tourist season had started. She moved quickly and easily through the crowd because she had no luggage this time.

She hired a Ford Escort from Helle Hollis, found her way out of the increasingly chaotic airport, and saw they had built a vast Ikea warehouse next to the motorway since she was last there, unless she hadn't noticed it before.

It wasn't as hot as she had been expecting: the thermometer on the dashboard said twenty-six degrees. The sunlight was hazy and dull, strong enough to make her squint. She drove west, past Torremolinos and Fuengirola, then turned up onto the toll-motorway and speeded up. The landscape had changed since she was last there. The verdant vegetation was gone. Everything looked yellow-brown and burned, with just a few hints of dark olive-green.

Soon the signs for 'Tickets Ceuta Tanger' began to appear along the side of the road. She passed the Hotel Pyr in Puerto Banús on her left. The roadworks were still going on and she had to slow down in front of the hotel. She peered up at the third floor and tried to work out which room had been hers.

To her right the huge walls surrounding the villas of Nueva Andalucía rose up. She turned off the motorway and headed upwards, past the bullfighting arena.

'You need to get the right exit from a total of seven roundabouts,' Carita had said, when she'd invited her to that party.

She made one mistake and had to go back to Plaza de Miragolf, but after that she got it right.

The gateway was less ostentatious than she remembered it, unless she was just starting to get used to them. What a terrible thought. She pressed various buttons until house number twenty opened the gate without asking any questions. She drove in.

The development Carita Halling Gonzales had lived in had looked like a model village that evening, and it made the same impression in daylight. The houses clambered up the mountainside, a pastiche of a southern Spanish mountain village. The waterfall by the pool burbled, the bushes were in bloom and the glass of the lampposts sparkled.

She parked outside *casa numero seis*, wound the window down and looked at the house. There were white aluminium shutters over all the windows. Blue and white police tape hung from the terraces and balconies of all three floors.

Annika switched the engine off, got the camera out of her bag and stepped into the sunshine. She stood beside the car for several minutes, just studying the house. There was no movement anywhere around her. No sound apart from the waterfall. It was as if all the houses had been abandoned, not just Carita's.

She adjusted the focus and took a few pictures, some general shots of the area and some of Carita's cordoned-off house. She hesitated, then climbed onto a raised flowerbed and took some pictures of the terrace behind the cordon. As long as she was standing on the flowerbed she wasn't guilty of trespass. At least, she hoped not.

The terrace was as she remembered it. It was where she had stood talking to Rickard Marmén that evening. The potted plants were still there. A hose on a timer led along the edge of the terrace from the tap. The plants would survive long after their owners had vanished.

She jumped down from the flowerbed and went to ring the bells of other houses on the estate: she didn't want to waste the opportunity to use the well-worn headline 'A Town in Fear'. She got no answer. She found the pool-maintenance man and asked if he knew where the Halling Gonzales family had gone.

No, he didn't keep tabs on the residents. They came and went all the time, or they rented out their houses. It was pretty much impossible to know who was where. She asked when the police had been there and was told that it was a while ago now, some time after Easter. He didn't know anything about any of that, he added.

She thanked him and walked back to the car, looking

475

up at the houses and trying to work out which was number twenty. Someone was definitely at home there because they had let her through the gates.

The house was apricot-coloured, and was one of a row on the far side of the pool. The woman who opened the door had the same quintessential Scandinavian look as Carita: bleached hair, a dark tan, a bit of a facelift and gold sandals. Annika didn't recognize her from the party last winter.

Her name was Tuula, she was Finnish, and had nothing but good to say about Carita Halling Gonzales. Carita had been on the committee that looked after things for the residents, and she kept everyone informed about the meetings, increases in ground-rent and shared activities. Her children had never thrown the sunbeds into the pool, which wasn't something you could say of the British brats and their parents. Imagine having people like that here! Carita was always the person who called the water company when there was no water, or the electricity company when there was a power-cut, because she spoke fluent Spanish.

'And garbage collections,' Tuula said. 'Who'll call the council about the rubbish now?'

'Apparently Carita is under suspicion for a serious crime,' Annika said, trying to look concerned.

Tuula merely snorted. 'The Spanish police,' she said. 'Everyone knows what they're like. Lazy and corrupt to the core. Everything is all *mañana*, *mañana* in this country. They're probably only blaming her because she's foreign.'

Annika thanked her and went back towards the pool. The Finnish woman's reaction was hardly surprising. Even the worst criminals had their supporters. There were still people who thought Pol Pot had been a really great guy.

476

She stopped to look out over the golf-course that spread across the valley below, then took out her mobile, found the number and called Knut Garen. He answered on the fifth ring. 'I'm just calling to say that I'm on the Costa del Sol, and I'm planning to write about Carita Halling Gonzales,' Annika said. 'Does anyone know where she's gone yet?'

'No,' Knut Garen said. 'The Spanish police have been checking the passenger lists of all planes and ferries, but she must have got out another way.'

'Could she still be in Spain?'

'If she is, the whole family must have access to a completely different identity, with different schools, homes and bank accounts. We don't consider that very likely. What are you planning to say?'

'Anything I can get confirmed – by you, for instance. Has her arrest warrant with Interpol been made public?'

'Not yet,' Garen said.

She bit her lip. That had been a mistake.

'But it might well be made public this afternoon. The Spanish police got the results of some DNA tests back from England yesterday, and they've linked her to the gassing in Nueva Andalucía just after New Year.'

Annika's pulse quickened. 'Linked her how?'

'The safe and the other vehicle used in the break-in have been found.'

'Where?'

'The long-stay car park at Málaga Airport.'

Annika was walking back to her car. Very smart of Carita. If she'd abandoned the car by the side of the road or in the middle of nowhere, someone would have noticed it sooner or later. A car could be left for ages in the unmanned long-stay car park of a large airport without anyone thinking it odd.

'Was there anything in the safe?'

'It had been blown open. It was empty, apart from a few traces of the explosives. But inside the car they found strands of hair and flakes of skin, and yesterday it was confirmed that they match Carita Halling Gonzales's DNA.'

'You had something to compare it to?'

'From the search of her house,' Garen said. 'I think they got the DNA from her toothbrush.'

Annika looked up at the house. Poor Jocke Zarco Martinez must have been party to a great deal of information. Carita had sacrificed her whole lifestyle to kill him. She hadn't even taken her toothbrush with her when she'd run.

Then she remembered a thought that had occurred to her during the night. 'I didn't see any broken walls in the Söderström family home,' she said. 'Where was the safe?'

'There were safes in all the bedrooms. This one was in a room on the ground floor.'

She frowned. She hadn't known there were more bedrooms downstairs, other than Suzette's.

'Whose room was it in?'

'Astrid Paulson's.'

She blinked. Of course. 'What could she have had in there that was so valuable?'

'Cash, deeds, documents, diamonds, codes, sensitive information. Take your pick.'

Annika rubbed her forehead. Of course Astrid's safe would be the most interesting in the house. Not Veronica the money-launderer's, or Sebastian the financial disaster's, but Astrid's. She'd come first; she'd started her own business; she'd been running an estate agency on the Costa del Sol since 1968. 'How much of this can I write?'

'The head of the preliminary investigation will make the formal decision to arrest Carita Halling Gonzales in her absence this afternoon. At the moment there's a warrant out for her for the manslaughter of Zarco Martinez. We know she gave him the morphine, but it's not clear that she intended to murder him. But as of this afternoon those suspicions will be expanded to cover eight cases of murder. And when that happens, any restrictions on reporting will be lifted. I wouldn't expect anything else.'

Annika took her notepad and pen from her bag and scribbled down the information. 'Eight cases?'

'The family in the house, plus the thieves and Zarco Martinez. Now that we know how it all fits together, the prosecutor can assume she meant to kill him.'

'Can I call and get it confirmed later on this afternoon?'

'Of course you can.'

They were silent for a moment.

'Why?' Annika finally asked. 'Why did she do it?'

Garen didn't answer.

'But you knew her,' Annika said. 'You worked with her. What was her motive?'

The police officer sounded weary. 'Money, I assume,' he said. 'Status and recognition, maybe, a life of luxury . . .'

Annika looked up at the terrace, with its blossoming hibiscus bushes. 'But why choose to become a criminal? I mean, she didn't have anything like that in her background. Quite the contrary, with a father-in-law who was chief of police in Bogotá.'

Garen coughed. 'Yes,' he said. 'We checked out what you said about her background. It wasn't entirely correct. Her father-in-law, Victor Gonzales, was one of Colombia's biggest cocaine barons. He, his wife and daughters were executed by another cartel fifteen years ago. They blew up his cocaine lab and burned his house down.'

Annika could feel her cheeks burning, not just because of the sun. 'But Nacho and Carita survived,' she said, 'because they were in Sweden visiting her parents.'

Garen sighed. 'Fifteen years ago both of Carita Halling's parents were in prison in the USA. They used to run a company called Cell Impact. Then it went bankrupt, but to avoid scandal they started falsifying invoices and cooking the books.'

Bloody hell! She really had been gullible. 'But now they're dead?' Annika said.

'Our colleagues in Sweden have spoken to them,' Knut Garen said. 'They live in a small village outside Borlänge. They haven't had any contact with Carita since they were released from prison, and that was ten years ago.'

Annika closed her eyes. Had the interpreter spoken a single word of truth during all the days they'd spent together? Yes: her father-in-law's name and the fact that he had been murdered, and her parents' company. She probably had grown up in Beverly Hills, and maybe she did meet her husband in the way she described. And her love for him and the children wasn't necessarily a lie. Annika recalled Carita's twittering presentation of her guests at the party, how pleased and proud she had sounded when she spoke about them. *His wife was an international model, their daughter's a Spanish show-jumping champion. She's a partner in a law firm in Frankfurt, he used to run a bank in Kenya* . . . 'Do you think you'll find her?'

'People who are used to daylight usually pop up sooner or later. Terrorists and freedom fighters are different. They can spend for ever hiding away in caves.

But Carita Halling Gonzales wants to go out for meals in restaurants, send her children to good schools.'

'Did she carry out the murders of her own volition? Or was she contracted, or forced, to do it?'

'The murders link Zarco Martinez, the Apits organization and the Söderström family,' Garen said. 'But we don't know what Carita Halling Gonzales's motive was. We're hoping to find out when we catch her.'

Annika thanked him for his help and ended the call. She had forgotten to ask about Niklas Linde.

34

There was a traffic-jam through San Pedro de Alcántara, but after that the traffic flowed fairly freely. She passed through the unjustly maligned town of Estepona with no problem. As she reached the top of the hill by the junction for Torreguadiaro, the Rock of Gibraltar rose from the sea in front of her, like a huge iceberg. Immediately behind it she could make out the Rif mountains of Africa through the mist.

Then all the road signs began to appear in two languages, Spanish and Arabic.

Algeciras was a messy city, quite different from the neat, picturesque places she had visited so far in Andalucía. The ornate Arabic script rushing past her only heightened her sense of unfamiliarity. She wondered how she was going to find the harbour, then saw that the word 'PUERTO', harbour, was painted on the tarmac of the motorway.

Low palm trees lined the six-lane *autostrada*. She followed the arrows, which led her onto an island with a forest of huge cranes. Cargo ships crowded the quays as far as she could see. Thousands of containers were stacked up, being loaded or unloaded in a sort of chaos that reminded her of an anthill. On Wikipedia she had read that Algeciras was the sixteenth busiest port in the world. She wondered what the fifteen busier ones looked like.

She parked the car by the Estación Marítia and headed towards the Terminal de Pasajeros. It reminded her of the Silja Line Terminal in Stockholm's Freeport, if a bit less organized. There seemed to be a number of different companies that sailed to Tangier. Large boards announced departures and arrivals, just like in an airport. She saw that she had missed one boat to Tangier by a couple of minutes. The next wasn't for nearly an hour. She bit her lip. It was already after two o'clock. The crossing to Morocco would take a couple of hours, then she had to get through Customs and find a way to get further south. She had read online that there were trains and bus-taxis, *grand taxis*, between the cities.

She bought a ticket and took the escalator up to the departure hall. The Sala de Embarque was built entirely of speckled grey granite, and was the size of a football pitch. She checked in, no, she didn't have any luggage, and was told that Passport Control would be open in a quarter of an hour and that she could go aboard then. The cafeteria was available in the meantime, the man said, pointing to a door on the far side of the football pitch.

It was almost as big, and just as deserted. She ordered a *café cortado* and a *bocadillo con jamón serrano y manchego* from a waitress with a gold stud in her nose; she was wearing pink underwear. She couldn't help noticing this because the girl's jeans were slung so low that her belt was at the same level as her backside.

She was seriously hungry. As she had been asleep on the plane she had missed the chance to buy one of the airline's gluey sandwiches. She devoured the large baguette in three minutes flat. Then she tried calling the embassy in Rabat again. This time the French voice told her that telephone hours were over for today.

Instead she rang Rickard Marmén.

He picked up at once. 'Annika!' he said cheerfully. 'Have you managed to find a new life that suits you?'

'I decided to keep the old one,' she said. 'I'm in the middle of doing it up, actually. Listen, have you ever done any property deals in Morocco?'

'Can you hold on a moment?' He said something in Spanish to someone next to him.

'Morocco?' he said, when he came back. 'Sure. Morocco's an up-and-coming country. What did you have in mind? I've got two villas overlooking the sea outside Tangier, and several nice projects off plan.'

She clenched her left fist in triumph. 'Are there any property registers in Morocco? Public ones?'

If he was surprised by the question, he didn't show it. 'Yes,' he said, 'there are, but only in printed form. You can look at them all you like, but you have to do it in person. They haven't been computerized. And they're in French, Spanish and Arabic.'

She bit her lip. 'If I have a name and a city, is there any way of finding out where that person lives?'

'Hmm,' Marmén said. 'You want to find an address in Morocco?'

'If possible.'

'And you've got the name of the person, and you know which city they live in?'

'Exactly.'

'Well, you could try going through a *muqaddam*.'

'A what?'

'The local civil servant. There's one in charge of each district. They distribute voting cards, keep a record of who lives where, sign applications for ID cards and so on.'

She closed her eyes and breathed out. She would have bought a house off Rickard Marmén just to make him happy. 'On a completely different subject,' she said, 'what do you know about Asilah in Morocco?'

'A sleepy little dump, although they restored the medina fairly recently. It's supposed to be quite smart.'

'Would there be a *muqaddam* there?'

'In Asilah? Bound to be.'

'And how do I find him?'

'It's probably no harder than finding the police station. Just ask someone. And if you go to Asilah, be sure to try the food at Casa García. You do like Spanish food, don't you? It's on the main road into the city, looking out over the harbour. Well, I need to get going, love. Was there anything else?'

'I'll be in touch if I make a mess of the renovations.'

'You'll be more than welcome.'

When Passport Control opened she was at the front of the non-existent queue. She got a stamp and was ushered into a glass corridor that hung high above the harbour. Beneath her, dozens of lorries were heading onto or off one of the ferries.

She had to show her passport once more before she was allowed to board the ship, when she was assailed by déjà vu: a school trip to Finland in the mid-1980s. She seemed to recognize everything, from the tired blue carpet to the duty-free shop and the bar with its maritime theme.

She walked about the various decks, and concluded that she and the lorry drivers, who all seemed to know each other, were the only passengers.

Outside the women's lavatory on deck six she discovered why her surroundings seemed so familiar: the fire-drill instructions were in Finnish. The ship had previously worked the Stockholm–Helsinki route.

With a dull clanking the ferry pulled out and began to head towards Africa with long, lurching rolls. Annika settled down in the bar.

They passed several ships in the seaway as they followed the Spanish coastline westwards. She saw towns and villages, sandy beaches, olive plantations and wind turbines. It had just occurred to her that she was travelling along the new Iron Curtain, between the first world and the third, when suddenly she felt ill. She had forgotten that she was always seasick, no matter how insignificant the swell.

Quickly she took out her laptop, to have something else to think about. She moved to a table with a plug-socket in the wall alongside it, then opened a new document and wrote a news article about the gassings in Nueva Andalucía, which were on their way to being cleared up. Interpol had issued a warrant for the arrest of a Swedish woman living on the Costa del Sol in Spain on suspicion of eight counts of murder. Sebastian Söderström and his family had been among the victims.

She referred to Knut Garen as her source, in his capacity as Nordic police representative on the Costa del Sol. She wrote that the suspect and her family had disappeared from their home without trace, and that the police believed they had fled the country. She mentioned that the car had been found at Málaga Airport, with DNA evidence, the expanded arrest warrant and Interpol. She also mentioned the link to Johan Zarco Martinez's death, that the suspect had been the last person to visit him in prison before he died. The article was short and concise. She saved it, then looked at the time.

Ninety minutes until they docked.

She opened another new document and wrote an

article about Carita Halling Gonzales. Any decision to publish the name and picture of a suspected criminal wasn't hers to make: it was down to the person legally accountable for the paper's publication. She thought for a moment, then decided to call Carita 'the Swedish jet-setter'. She wrote that 'the Swedish jet-setter' had lived in the well-to-do district of Nueva Andalucía (anywhere that wasn't a suburb full of concrete high-rises was a 'well-to-do district' in evening-tabloid jargon), and that she had worked as a translator and interpreter, occasionally for the media and the Spanish police. She described the woman's social life with her friends, how she had been active in the local residents' association. She quoted Tuula, the Finnish neighbour, anonymously. Then she saved the file to the hard-drive, clicked to close the document and looked out across the sea.

The strait was narrower. The mountains were so close to the ship that she felt she could touch both continents at the same time if she stretched out her arms. She was still feeling sick.

She opened the article she had already started about how Carita Halling Gonzales had set about carrying out the mass murder in Nueva Andalucía, a long, detailed description of what had happened that night in early January.

She described how the woman had planned the murders of the Söderström family and the two Romanian crooks. How she had got hold of gas, beer and morphine, how she had stolen or bought the codes for the alarm, and recruited the unfortunate criminals. How they had driven up to the villa along roads wet with rain, injected themselves with the naloxone derivative, then headed to the ventilation unit at the back of the house, with a gas canister, a lump-hammer and a crowbar . . .

She wrote of how the thieves had loosened a pipe from the fresh-air intake and attached it to the gas canister, then turned the valve and listened to the hiss as the gas poured into the house. Then they had waited. The gas alarm had gone off. Lights had come on in the bedrooms. Could the cries of the dying children be heard beside the ventilation unit at the back of the house?

She went back to her old articles and reread them.

One effect of fentanyl poisoning was lethargy. The mother and two children had been found lying on either side of a closed bedroom door, unable to cry out to each other or open it, yet still fully conscious. They had been dead within minutes.

No, there probably hadn't been any cries.

Annika looked up at the horizon to try to suppress her nausea. The ferry had left the Mediterranean and entered the Atlantic.

She got up and bought a bottle of mineral water, then carried on with her article.

They had broken in through the terrace door. The gas-alarm was shrieking but everything else was silent. Then they had switched off the alarm, the hardest part of the job over. Now they had plenty of time.

They began by stealing the safe, a time-consuming and noisy job, then carried it out to the woman's car. She had driven off, with the safe in the boot, and probably the gas canister, which hadn't been found.

The car, and the remains of the safe, were dumped in the airport car park.

The thieves had stripped the villa of art, rugs and jewellery. They hadn't known they had just four hours to live.

Annika saved and then closed the document. The ferry was swinging south, leaving Spain and Europe behind, and was rapidly approaching the Moroccan coast. The sun had passed behind some clouds and the sea was grey. Rain hung heavily above the Rif mountains. She could make out buildings along the shore, tall and white, as well as a number of cranes.

She closed her laptop. She received a message on her mobile from Meditel, a mobile operator, welcoming her to Morocco. She put everything away in her bag and went out on deck. The wind tugged at her hair. She felt better immediately.

The construction boom from the Costa del Sol seemed to have spread across the strait. She could see people on the beaches, cars on the roads, shops with big plate-glass windows. She had never been to Africa before, but this was nothing like she'd been expecting.

The ferry slowed, the deck and walls shaking as it approached the quayside. She looked at her watch: they'd been late leaving Algeciras and the crossing had taken almost half an hour longer than the promised two hours. It was now a quarter to five. She paced about restlessly, hoping that the *muqaddam* observed the Spanish custom and stayed open for part of the evening.

The lorry drivers and workmen gathered on deck five, chatting to each other in a mixture of French, Spanish and Arabic. None of them seemed to be in any great hurry. She positioned herself strategically beside the door through which she had entered the ship, hoping to get off quickly, but nothing happened. There was a lot of banging and crashing below her, and she presumed that gangways and ramps were being fixed in place.

Then the door opened – not the one she was standing next to, but the corresponding one on the other side. She ground her teeth in frustration but went meekly to the back of the queue.

It took ages.

First she had to fill in a form, listing all her personal details, her profession and her address in Morocco, the purpose of her visit and how long she was planning to stay. She knew better than to say she was a journalist, and put 'writer' as her profession. Two Customs officials and two border guards were checking all passports and travel documents with irritating thoroughness.

'What do you write?' one of the customs officials asked suspiciously in English, fingering the laptop in her bag.

'Textbooks for schoolchildren,' Annika said.

They let her through without any further questions. She had to go down two decks, across the car deck and along a narrow metal corridor to reach the gangway. She stepped ashore in Morocco and took a deep breath. The air smelt of sea and burned rubber.

She was channelled into a glass corridor, like the one she had walked through to reach the ship in Algeciras, surrounded by a similar view of articulated trucks, containers and cranes. She stopped inside the terminal building, sat down on a bench in the arrivals hall and called Knut Garen. Meditel worked fine: the police officer sounded as if he was next door.

'The arrest warrant has been made public,' he confirmed. That was all Annika needed.

She took out her laptop and connected to the Internet on her mobile. It would probably cost a fortune, but she opened her usual Outlook Explorer page and composed a new message to Anders Schyman. Using Bluetooth, she sent off all three articles about Carita Halling Gonzales: the arrest warrant, her as a person, and the crime, plus one of the pictures she had taken outside the prison in Málaga on her mobile when they had visited Martinez. Carita was in one of the pictures, albeit only in the corner, but you could see that she was blonde, carrying a leopard-print handbag and wearing high heels. The 'Swedish jet-setter' in person.

Finally she attached two pictures of the area where Carita had lived, one general shot with the pool and waterfall in the foreground, and then one of the house with the police cordon. In the email she included some captions for the pictures, explained briefly what had happened, gave Carita's full name and told Schyman that her parents lived outside Borlänge. She said he could do what he liked with the articles.

It took for ever to send the email. She was worried the connection would fail and she'd have to start all over again, but it didn't, and eventually the pictures and articles had been whisked into cyberspace. She breathed out and packed everything away.

That's for all those damned notes, she thought, as she walked out of the terminal building.

35

The sky was overcast but the light was sharp. She squinted up towards the city, which sprawled up the mountainside. How to get to Asilah?

'Taxi?' an older man in blue jeans and a greyish-blue jacket asked, as he leaned against the outside wall.

'Asilah?' she said quizzically.

'Twenty-five euros,' the man said.

Twenty-five euros? All the way to Asilah? That was less than half what she'd paid to get to Arlanda Airport that morning. 'Okay,' she said.

'My car is over here,' he said, in heavily accented English.

She followed the man towards a car park alongside the terminal. His neat haircut and relaxed gait reminded her of someone she knew – Thomas's dad, maybe? He walked to a yellow Mercedes with a taxi-sign on the roof, opened the door to the back seat, and closed it after she had got in.

'So you're going to Asilah?' the man said, glancing at her in the rear-view mirror. 'It's a very nice little city.'

She put her bag beside her on the vinyl seat. 'Will it take long to get there? I'm in a bit of a hurry.'

'Not long at all. This is a very good car. It's been to Rabat, Casablanca, the Sahara, all over the world!'

He started the engine and steered through the harbour with a practised hand, then out into the streets of Tangier. It was just like Marbella, Annika thought. The streets were lined with palms. Modern white buildings rose up towards the sky, and there were bars, cafés and car-rental companies along the pavements.

'A million people live in Tangier now,' the taxi-driver said. 'Everything's new. Europeans come over here and buy up the land. They build hotels and golf courses and shopping centres. It's very good business for people here, legal business. Very good.'

She watched the buildings sweep past and decided not to ask about the illegal business. She presumed part of it consisted of what Knut Garen had identified: the hash plantations up in the mountains, and the distribution chain leading to Europe.

How on earth had Suzette managed to get into the country without a passport? The check on the ferry had been rigorous. Annika had rarely had to answer questions about her occupation and the purpose of her visit before. How had Suzette, at just sixteen, with no money, managed to get through without Customs and the border guards sounding the alarm?

'This is a very good place to live,' the driver said. 'The atmosphere is relaxed, good food, good weather.'

They were driving through a residential district with a forest of television aerials and satellite dishes on the roofs. She saw women on their way to shops and markets, some with their hair covered, others without. They passed petrol stations, mobile-phone shops and a large football stadium that was still under construction. The residential housing thinned out and industrial buildings took its place. They passed a Hotel Ibis, a large Volvo showroom and a Scania dealer.

Suzette had been here for several summers, driving

along this road, looking out at the fields, car show-rooms and petrol stations, sitting in her grandmother's arms and playing with her friend Amira. For her Africa had been perfectly normal.

'The factories produce goods for the European market,' the driver said, pointing. 'Moroccan workers are much cheaper than Europeans.' He gestured to the other side of the road, to a thin line of trees along the shore. 'Families come out here at weekends,' he said. 'They cook on open fires, read books, play with their children.'

'How come you speak such good English?' she asked. 'Have you lived in England?'

He cast a quick glance at her in the rear-view mirror. 'Never,' he said.

'Did you learn it at school?'

'No.'

'So you've got English friends?'

He didn't answer, and she didn't ask any more questions.

They were heading south along the coastal road. It clung to the Atlantic: to her right Annika could see vast sandy beaches, completely deserted. To her left there were rolling fields and hills, soft and friendly, nowhere near as harsh and dramatic as the Mediterranean coast of the Costa del Sol. There seemed to be flowers every-where, an overwhelming display of blossom.

The man carried on talking, telling her how people from Qatar had discovered the Moroccan coast and had started buying up land and building huge villas with big pools, and other things that were probably perfectly true but not terribly interesting. She shut out his voice and looked at the landscape.

How was she going to find a *muqaddam* in Asilah? Where could she start? Who should she ask?

Then she looked at the man behind the wheel and slapped her forehead: God, she was stupid! She had the best guide in the world sitting right in front of her. 'Excuse me,' she said, 'but do you know if there's a *muqaddam* in Asilah?'

He looked at her in the rear-view mirror. 'A what?'

She tried to make the word sound right. 'A *muqaddam*?'

'Ah, a *muqaddam*!' He swallowed all the vowels, pronouncing the word as *mqdm*. 'Of course there's a *muqaddam* in Asilah.'

She looked at the time. Half past six. 'Does he have an office?'

'Sure.'

'How late is it open?'

'Until five o'clock.'

Her spirits sank. Oh, well, if the driver could help her find the office, she could book into a hotel and go back there first thing in the morning. . .

'We'll probably make it in time,' the driver said. 'We're only a few kilometres from Asilah now.'

She looked at him in astonishment, then at the time again. It had just gone half past six. 'But didn't you say the office closed at five?'

The man's eyes twinkled in the rear-view mirror. 'You didn't put your watch back when you got off the boat, did you? It's half past four here.'

She'd completely forgotten that there was a two-hour time difference between Spain and Morocco, even though they were on the same longitude. She adjusted her watch. As she raised her head, she saw the sign for Casa García rush past. That was the restaurant Rickard Marmén had recommended. They must have reached Asilah.

A moment later the driver slowed.

'Can you help me?' she asked. 'I need to ask the *muqaddam* something, and my French is really bad.'

He pulled into a car park, pulled up and turned to face her. 'You want to ask about someone?'

'A woman called Fatima. She lives on a farm somewhere near here.'

He nodded, and looked as though he were thinking. Then he asked, 'Whereabouts?'

'That's the problem. I don't really know. Do you think the *muqaddam* would?'

He nodded, more firmly this time. 'Her name is Fatima? If Fatima lives on a farm near Asilah, then the *muqaddam* will know.' He switched off the engine. 'We'll park here, and walk to the *muqaddam*.'

They followed a sign showing the way to the Quartier Administratif. Annika stayed half a metre behind the man, letting him set the pace. He wasn't walking very quickly. They reached a pedestrian street with low residential buildings on both sides. There were pots of flowers and herbs along the pavement. The driver stopped a man dressed in white and asked something in Arabic. The man answered and pointed, the driver nodded, the man bowed, then they talked and talked and talked. Eventually they moved on.

'That green door up ahead,' the driver said, raising his hand. 'Fatima? On a farm near Asilah? Does she have a husband?'

'I think he might be dead,' Annika said.

The driver walked up to the green door and knocked. Without waiting for an answer he pushed it open and stepped into darkness. Annika was unsure whether or not to follow him. She decided it would be best to wait outside.

The driver went along a dark hallway, then into a room on the left at the far end. A triangle of light fell onto the floor when the door opened. Then it shrank and disappeared as the door was slowly closed. She heard him greet someone, then a stream of Arabic. She shifted her weight from one foot to the other.

Some young boys were playing on a bicycle a bit further down the street. They became shy when they saw her watching them, so she turned away. A girl with plaits wearing a school uniform walked past with a pink school-bag on her back. A woman in a long dress, her hair covered, strolled along on the other side, talking animatedly into a mobile phone.

The door off the hallway opened and Annika turned as the triangle of light reappeared. The taxi-driver came towards her, with a man in traditional Arab dress behind him.

'Muhammad, the *muqaddam* in Asilah,' the driver said, taking a position beside Annika, as though he were about to introduce her. Annika's mouth was dry. How did you say hello in Arabic?

But the *muqaddam* held out his hand and said softly: '*Bonjour, madame.*'

Annika took his hand. '*Bonjour*,' she muttered, embarrassed.

'Muhammad knows Fatima's farm,' the driver said. 'It's up in the mountains.'

'*C'est une ferme très grande*,' the Arab man said in his gentle voice. '*Les routes sont très mauvaises. Vous avez besoin d'une grosse voiture pour y aller.*'

'What?' Annika said, bewildered.

'The roads are bad,' the driver said. 'You need a big car. He's explained to me where the farm is. Do you want me to drive you?'

'One more question. Fatima's husband, does he live on the farm too?' she asked, looking at the *muqaddam*.

The driver translated. The civil servant shook his

497

head, then raised and lowered his hands. 'He's dead,' the driver said.

'What was his name?'

More gestures, more shakes of the head.

'He was European.'

Annika looked at the driver. 'Yes,' she said. 'I'd be very grateful if you could drive me to the farm.'

'Another twenty-five euros.'

'You drive a hard bargain.'

'But first I need to eat,' he said.

The thought of food made her feel weak at the knees. The only thing she'd had all day was the baguette in the café at the ferry terminal in Algeciras. 'Okay,' she said.

They thanked the civil servant for his help. He went back inside the building and locked the door. It was five o'clock.

The taxi-driver, whose name also turned out to be Muhammad, thanked her for her offer of dinner, but politely declined. Annika watched him sit down in a local bar, where he immediately struck up a conversation with some other men in grey-blue jackets.

She walked round the corner and got a table in the Spanish restaurant, Casa García. They would take an hour for dinner, Muhammad had decreed, so she ordered a starter (*jamón ibérico*), main course (*pollo a la plancha*) and dessert (*flan*). Afterwards she was so full she could hardly move. She paid by card, then walked towards the medina, the old centre of the city. She wasn't worried that Muhammad would disappear – she hadn't paid him anything.

The sun was sinking quickly into the sea. She stopped at the north gate of the city and looked out over the small harbour. Colourful little fishing-boats were bobbing up and down in the shelter of the jetty. This was supposed to be one of Morocco's main shipping ports for cannabis? She had trouble believing that.

But, of course, she couldn't see the go-fast boats that Knut Garen and Niklas Linde had told her about. And it wasn't certain that they'd use the main harbour in the centre of the city to load a cargo of hash. She went for a walk among the thousand-year-old buildings within the city walls. They had been freshly painted, and looked as if they had gone up the day before.

The taxi driver, Muhammad, was waiting for her in the car. She slid into the back seat. He started the engine and drove out of the city. 'You got some good food?' he asked.

'Very good,' she said.

'Morocco has very good food, good couscous.'

She didn't tell him she'd eaten at a Spanish restaurant.

Asilah disappeared behind them, drowning in the setting sun. The car headed east, across a railway line and under a motorway. Then the tarmac came to an end, replaced by a gravel track. Muhammad braked, turned the headlights on and steered the big Mercedes over the rough surface. The track was visible in front of the car as a slightly paler strip through the dusk, and she could make out bushes, crops and rocks along the side of the road.

When the last light of the motorway had disappeared behind a ridge, darkness closed around them. Muhammad wound his window all the way up, as if he wanted to shut it out.

'Is it far?' Annika asked, wondering if it would have been better to wait until morning before setting out for the farm.

'No,' he said, 'but the road is bad. You have to be careful with the car.'

She leaned back in the seat and stared into the darkness. She could see nothing but the vague outline of her face reflected in the window.

What had made David come here, to this godforsaken part of the world? Had he been shaken about in bad cars on even worse roads to get out to some little farm in the Moroccan outback? Had Suzette come this way recently?

Suddenly a scene from a film popped into her head, *La Vie en Rose*, which she'd seen at the cinema with Julia a few months ago. The boxer, Marcel, is sitting with Edith Piaf in a restaurant in New York, telling her about the pig farm he owns in Morocco. His wife looks after it while he travels the world, boxing and sleeping with French singers.

She shut her eyes and let herself be shaken and jolted by the potholes and stones. Men go out into the world while their wives stay at home to feed the pigs. She leaned her head back and fell asleep.

36

'Madame? Madame! We're here!'

She sat up with a jerk. The driver had turned to face her. He looked tired. It was half past eight. They had been driving for two hours. She rubbed her eyes, getting mascara on her knuckles.

The night was as impenetrably pitch-black as before, but above a hill to her right something was brightly lit.

A bright yellow spaceship was hovering against the sky.

'What's that?' she said, staring up at it.

'That's the farm.'

'That thing?'

She wound down her window. The wind blew into the car, bringing with it sand and pollen, and blowing her hair about. 'Can you drive closer?'

'Right up to it?'

'Yes, please.'

Muhammad put the car into gear and slowly began to drive the last stretch towards the farm.

Annika gaped, fascinated, at the bizarre sight in front of her.

Of course, it wasn't a spaceship. It was a yellow wall that was several metres high, enclosing a very large area, all brightly illuminated by powerful halogen floodlights.

'Are you sure?' she asked dubiously. She'd been expecting a little farm with a few sheep and a couple of horses.

'This is the farm where Fatima lives, according to the *muqaddam*.'

'Christ,' Annika said.

The car stopped with a slight jolt in front of a large grey iron gate. The wall was crowned with a spiral of thick barbed wire. The floodlights were mounted along the top every ten metres, and two shone down directly on the gate. She could see an entry-phone and a surveillance camera. It looked more like Kumla Prison than a farm.

'Where exactly are we?' she asked.

'Between Souk el Had el Rharbia and Souk Trine de Sidi el Yamani.'

'Hmm,' Annika said. 'Are there any other houses nearby?'

'No other houses. An hour ago we passed a little village. There might be more houses in other directions.'

'How far are we from Asilah?'

'Forty kilometres, maybe a bit more.'

'Up in the mountains?'

'Up in the mountains, but not too high. Good farmland in Asilah.'

She took a deep breath and opened the door. She'd come all this way so the least she could do was find out if anyone was at home.

The driver cleared his throat. She paused.

Payment, of course.

She sat down again in the back seat, and Muhammad switched on the little light in the roof so she could find her purse. She dug it out of her bag and pulled out three twenty-euro notes.

'Don't have any change,' he said quickly.

She smiled at him. 'It's a tip,' she said. 'Can you wait until you see that I've been let in?'

He nodded enthusiastically. 'Of course.'

She got out of the car, hung her bag on her shoulder, carefully closed the door and turned to the wall.

Muhammad had stopped ten metres or so from the gate. She started walking. The track sloped upwards, and the surface was poor. She blinked and squinted under the floodlights, then heard something buzz and saw the surveillance camera zoom in on her.

She reached the gate. It was shiny, as if it had just been smartened up with gloss paint. She touched the smooth surface gingerly with a finger. Then she went to the entry-phone and pressed the button next to it.

Ten seconds passed.

She was about to press it again when the speaker crackled. '*Oui?*'

She cleared her throat quietly and licked her lips, trying to summon the French she had learned at school. '*Je m'appelle Annika Bengtzon. Je voudrais parler avec Fatima.*'

The speaker clicked, then was silent.

She stood by the wall, increasingly aware of the sound of her own breathing. The floodlights hummed. In the bushes, just out of reach of the lights, she could hear animals and the wind.

She looked over her shoulder. The taxi was still there.

Muhammad met her gaze. 'Problem?' he asked.

'I don't know,' she said. 'I think so.'

'Do you want a lift back to Tangier? Fifty euros.'

You've got to drive back anyway, Annika thought, pressing the button by the phone again.

The speaker crackled into life at once this time. '*Oui?*' More annoyed.

'*Je veux parler avec Suzette aussi.*' I want to speak to Suzette as well.

The speaker hissed and crackled: they hadn't switched it off.

'*Je sais qu'elle est ici.*' I know she's here.

'Maybe they've gone to bed?' Muhammad said.

Hardly, Annika thought, looking up at the surveillance camera. They were still up: there was no doubt whatever about that.

The speaker clicked and was silent.

'I need to go now. Long way to Tangier.'

Annika hesitated. Apart from the rustling in the bushes, there was nothing but silence.

Maybe it would be as well to drive back and try again in the morning, in daylight.

She turned to walk back to the taxi, but at that moment there was a clang from the wall and the gate started to open. Another floodlight became visible through the gap, shining right into her eyes and forcing her to put a hand in front of her face. She squinted and waited, then held her breath and walked through the gap in the gate. At once it began to close. She was seized by sheer panic. Then there was a loud click as the lock snapped shut and there was no longer any point in thinking about retreating.

The floodlight shining in her face went out. She blinked against the darkness, still blind from the bright light. She heard Muhammad start his taxi, then turn round and drive off.

Two men were standing in front of her. One was in his fifties, the other a boy in his late teens. They were both armed with some sort of automatic weapon. The guns were pointing straight at her.

She took a step back, her sight still affected by the floodlight. She could see various versions of it floating

504

in front of her vision as pink balls of light. She tried to blink them away and see what was behind them. A yard, she thought. She was standing on gravel.

'*Pardon*,' she said. '*Je ne veux pas causer des problèmes.*'

The older man said something to the younger one in Arabic. The boy came over to her and pointed at her bag with his gun. '*Laissez le sac.*'

She put it on the ground.

'*Donnez-le moi.*'

She pushed it towards him with her foot.

The older man took a step closer to her as the boy bent down and tipped the contents out onto the gravel. He poked through them with the barrel of his gun. Annika wondered if the lens of the camera would survive.

'*Venez par ici*,' the older man said, pointing with his gun. He wanted her to go with him. The boy gathered her things back into her bag and slung it over his shoulder. She wasn't getting it back.

She took a few cautious steps forward, now able to make out the shapes of buildings and vehicles. As she had assumed, she was walking across a large, walled yard. There were buildings in two directions, in front of her and off to the left. She looked up at the building in front and gasped. It was a residential house, and it was huge. Thirty metres long, three storeys high, with balustrades and balconies on both top floors. There were lights on in several of the upper windows, but they were faint, as though filtered through heavy curtains. A small lantern glowed above the door on the ground floor.

The older man was walking in front of her, and the young lad behind. It looked as if they were heading for the illuminated door.

The man knocked lightly and it opened, like a black

hole. '*Entrez*,' the man said, gesturing with his gun again.

She could hear her heartbeat pounding in her ears and gulped hard. Then she stepped through the door. The darkness was solid but the air light. She was in a large hall, a big, open space.

'*À droite.*'

She had to think for a moment, then turned right.

A door opened in front of her. She got a light shove in the back and stumbled into a room containing a desk and an old chair.

'*Attendez ici.*'

The door closed behind her. She heard a key turn in the lock.

She breathed out. At least it wasn't pitch-black in here. A small table-lamp was shining on the desk.

There had to be someone here called Fatima, or they wouldn't have let her in. And as soon as she had mentioned Suzette's name the gate had opened.

She took a few steps to a window hidden behind closed curtains. She pushed one aside to look out, but couldn't see anything. It took her a few seconds to realize that there were closed shutters on the outside.

Then she heard a rattle from the lock. She let go of the curtain as if she'd burned her hand and quickly went back to the spot in the middle of the room where the armed man had left her.

A woman in her fifties wearing traditional black clothing came into the room. She said something into the hall and closed the door behind her. Then she turned towards Annika. She was tall, almost one metre eighty, had neatly made-up black eyes and large rings on her fingers. 'You wanted to talk to me?' she said in perfect Oxford English.

'Are you Fatima?' Annika asked.

'I'm Fatima.'

'My name is Annika Bengtzon,' Annika said. 'I'm from Sweden. I work for a newspaper there, called—'

'I know who you are.' Fatima walked round the desk and sat down on the old chair. 'Why have you come?' Her eyes showed that she was used to giving orders.

Annika had to make a real effort to stand her ground and not back away. At least I'm in the right place. She knows who I am. So she also knows what I do. 'I'm a journalist,' she said. 'I want answers to some questions.'

Fatima's face didn't move a muscle. 'Why would I answer your questions?'

'Why not? If you have nothing to hide?'

Fatima looked at her intently for a whole minute. 'Maybe you can give *me* some answers,' she eventually said.

'Me?' Annika said. 'What about?'

'Where's Filip?'

Annika stared at her. 'Filip?' she said. 'Filip Andersson?'

Fatima gave a curt nod.

Annika cleared her throat. It was no secret that she'd attended the press conference after his release. She had nothing to lose by answering. 'He was released from Kumla Prison yesterday morning. I saw him at his lawyer's office on Skeppsbron in Stockholm yesterday, just before lunchtime. I haven't seen him since then.' She paused. 'I have no idea where he is now.'

'What time did you see him in Stockholm?'

Annika thought for a moment. 'Approximately a quarter to twelve,' she said.

'Does he have a passport?'

'A passport?' Were prisoners allowed passports? She'd once written an article about a prisoner who hadn't been allowed to attend his mother's funeral in Scotland. The young man had been desperate, but the rules were inflexible. His passport had been seized when he had gone inside, and that applied to anyone who was sentenced to serve twelve months or more. See paragraph twelve of the Passport Act. It was out of the question that anyone sentenced to life would have a passport. And getting a new passport took five working days, she knew that, because she had tried to get the process speeded up herself a few years ago and failed. He might be able to get hold of a provisional travel document out at Arlanda – Anne Snapphane had managed to do that once when she was going on a charter holiday to Turkey.

She shook her head. 'Not an ordinary passport,' she said. 'Possible a provisional one.'

'Is Sweden part of the Schengen Agreement?'

Annika nodded.

'So he can travel within Europe on a national ID card?'

She nodded again.

Fatima got up from the chair, went to the door, opened it and said something in Arabic. Then she closed the door again. 'Do you know him?' she asked. 'You know what sort of man he is?'

Annika hid her finger behind her back. 'I interviewed him once, but I don't know him.'

Fatima sat down behind the desk again.

'I've answered several questions now,' Annika said. 'Can I ask one in return?'

Fatima didn't move. Annika took that as a yes.

'Is Suzette here?'

The woman didn't even blink. 'What makes you think she'd be here?'

The woman didn't ask who Suzette was. Which meant that she had to know.

Annika thought hard about her answer. She couldn't let on that Suzette had managed to write an email because that would get her into trouble. 'Suzette has a very good friend called Amira. She's told her friends about her, it's no great secret. Amira lives on a farm with horses outside Asilah. If you know who I am, then you know that I write articles. I've written about Suzette. I've was very affected by what's happened to her. I wanted to find her.'

There was a knock on the door, and Fatima went to open it. Annika heard voices muttering in Arabic. Fatima stepped outside and closed the door.

Annika waited five minutes, then the woman was back. 'We'll talk more tomorrow. You'll stay here as our guest. Ahmed will show you to your room.'

She disappeared and the young man stood in the doorway. He handed Annika her bag, empty except for her toothbrush, notepad, pens and the change of underwear. They had taken her laptop, mobile phone and camera. '*Suivez-moi*,' he said. Annika took her almost empty bag and followed him.

They walked through the dark hall to a stone staircase on the left-hand side. It led up steeply through the floors, and ended at a heavy wooden door. The young man pushed it open and they emerged into a poorly lit corridor.

'*Allez*,' he said, then followed her almost the entire length of the corridor. He stopped beside a narrow door on the left. '*Ici*,' he said.

Annika stepped inside the room and felt the door close behind her.

She turned to ask how long she would be kept there, only to hear a key turn in the lock.

Death on the Beach

Wall-eye was a bit simple. People said his father had once hit him so hard across the face when he was little that his eye had been dislodged and one ear deafened, but that might just have been talk. He was among the first foster-children to arrive at Gudagården, and he never made much fuss.

He had just one weakness. He couldn't stay away from the girls, especially not the Princess. He would hide among the reeds when they bathed, he creep up on them from behind and squeeze their breasts and backsides, then press up to them and rub himself against them.

The Troll Girl always had to keep an eye on him so he couldn't get at the Princess.

The girls were thirteen and fourteen on the evening when the Princess didn't manage to get away. He caught her on the beach where the reeds were at their thickest, ripped off her bathing-suit and put his hand over her mouth. He took her with such a frenzy that the violence and sand tore at her organs and left her drenched in blood.

The Troll Girl and the Angel had been to the local shop, to buy sugar and salt, and when they got back to the beach he was pulling on his trousers, facing away from them, towards the water. The Princess was lying, apparently lifeless, at his feet. The Troll Girl moved silently and, quick as lightning, quick as the weasel she was, she picked up a stone, ran up and hit him on the head. She didn't stop hitting him. The Angel stood there, mouth open in a silent scream, as the Troll Girl hit him and hit him and hit him, until the blood stopped running and the grey sludge from his shattered skull lay strewn over the sand.

'Get spades and bandages,' she told the Angel, as she carried the Princess to the water to wash her.

And the Angel ran to Mother in the kitchen, with the

sugar and salt, and asked if they could sleep in the hayloft that night, and they could, and then she dragged the spades and the little crowbar all the way down to the lake, and she and the Troll Girl spent all that night digging a suitably narrow but deep grave behind the big oak-tree on the shore. First they cleared the dead leaves and twigs away, and the sand was soft and easy to dig, but the tree's roots were hard as steel and the Angel had to fetch an axe. It was almost light by the time they had finished. The Princess had recovered a little and they all joined in to drag the limp body into the grave. One of Wall-eye's shirt-sleeves got caught on a tree-root, so the Troll Girl had to clamber down into the grave and pull it loose. The corpse fell on top of her and the others had to help her climb out.

They shovelled the blood and brains in first, then filled the hole with roots, soil and sand. They scattered leaves and twigs over the top.

They sat and wept together, out of fear and exhaustion, in a tight huddle on the sand by the lake below Gudagården, and promised each other they would never tell.

The Princess was fourteen, and the Troll Girl was thirteen, and the Angel, she was only ten.

And for the three of us I have had this book printed, just the three copies, one each.

And all this, every single word, is true. Because the Angel is me.

Thursday, 16 June

37

Annika woke up with the sun shining in her face. It was oppressively hot in the little room. After hours of torment she had eventually managed to fall asleep with her clothes on, lying on the narrow bed that filled half of the floor.

She sat up wearily and squinted out at the sunlight. It was pouring in through a pair of small-paned french windows that weren't shuttered. She got up to open them but they were locked. There was a pair of thin yellow curtains hanging on either side of the glass, and she pulled them closed in a vain attempt to shut out the heat.

She was desperate to pee. She went over to the narrow door and tried the handle.

Locked.

She sat on the bed again, brushed some locks of sweaty hair from her forehead, and looked at the time. Half past six. She took off her jacket; the T-shirt under it was soaked with sweat.

Last night she hadn't been able to find a light-switch and had had to feel her way to the bed, where she had curled up in the darkness. Now she could see why. There was no electric light in the room. One wall was taken up by the bed she was sitting on, and the other by a large, solid wooden desk with a lantern and a box of matches on top. A rickety chair stood in front.

What sort of room was this? A guest room? A nursery? Servants' quarters? Or was it a cell?

Right now it was definitely the latter.

She got to her feet, went to the door and banged on it as hard as she could with her right fist. 'Let me out!' she shouted in Swedish. 'For fuck's sake, I need to go to the toilet! Hello! Can you hear me?'

She stopped banging and put her ear to the door. All she could hear was her own heartbeat. She waited five minutes, then sat down on the bed again.

She had to pee. She'd just have to do it on the floor if that was the only option.

Then it occurred to her to look under the bed. Sure enough, there was an enamel pot under it. Almost exactly the same as the one her grandmother had kept at Lyckebo, her cottage in the woods near Hosjön, where there were no drains. She pulled it out and shrugged off her jeans. Afterwards she pushed it back under the bed, close to the wall.

She sat on the chair by the desk.

The house was silent.

Her grandmother had never met Kalle and Ellen. Her children had never peed in an enamel pot in a draughty cottage beside the waters of Hosjön. When she got the money from the insurance company she was going to buy a place in the forest in Södermanland.

She got up to bang on the door again, but stopped herself. They weren't going to let her out just because she kept banging. And beating her hands to shreds wasn't a particularly constructive thing to do.

Her bag was on the floor beside the desk. She picked it up and took out her notepad and a pen. She chewed the pen and thought. The woman called Fatima knew Filip Andersson and that he'd been released from Kumla. Her questions about his passport meant she thought he was going somewhere. She hadn't shown any surprise when Annika mentioned Suzette so the girl was here, or Fatima knew where she was being hidden.

The farm she was in was large and wealthy. The little she had seen of the buildings and walls was well maintained.

Annika got up and went to the french windows, drew the curtains and looked out.

She couldn't see much, just the yard she had crossed the previous evening, the inside of the wall and the hillsides beyond. She was at the very top of the large house. To the right was the smaller building that presumably contained stables and outhouses.

Then she saw a young woman in a headscarf emerge from the outhouse, in the company of two young boys. Could that be Amira? She pressed her nose to the glass. No, this woman was much older: she must be more like twenty-five. She was holding one child in each hand and was walking towards the gate through which she herself had come the night before.

Outside the walls, as far as she could see, stretched vast fields of verdant vegetation. She couldn't make out the shape of the leaves, but she was sure they weren't potatoes. On Wikipedia she had read that *Cannabis sativa* was a hardy, fast-growing plant that could survive in most climates and at altitudes of up to three thousand metres above sea level. As far as the European market was concerned, most of it was grown among the Rif mountains of northern Morocco.

Annika recalled Knut Garen's telling description of the rhythmic drumming that echoed through the Moroccan mountains in the autumn months, da-dunk,

517

da-dunk, as the pollen from the cannabis plants was beaten out between layers of fine cloth.

There was a rattle from the lock and the young man from the previous day appeared in the doorway with a gun. '*Suivez-moi.*'

She put her notepad and pen back into her bag and went with him.

'*Laissez-le ici.*'

He wanted her to leave her bag. So she wasn't going anywhere, and would be coming back here. Unless?

'*Où allons-nous?*' she asked. Where are we going? Her French really was pretty awful.

He didn't answer.

'*Qu'est-ce que vous faites maintenant?*' What are you doing now?

'*Ne vous inquiétez pas,*' he said. No need for her to worry.

They went down a different staircase, first Annika, then the young man with the gun. It was a much broader flight of stairs than the one they had come up the previous evening. It was covered with thick carpet, and led down to the first floor of the house. They were in a large stone hall with doors in three directions, all of them closed and barred. The doors and walls were all dark and richly ornamented – there was even some gilding. Heavy stone and bronze statues stood in various alcoves. In place of the fourth wall, a well of light reached from the ground floor all the way up to the eaves. The staircase carried on downwards: she could see to the front door she had come through the night before.

The young man stopped outside a large pair of double-doors on the left-hand side, opened one and ushered her in. She noted that there was a large key in the lock. She heard the door close behind her, then the click of the lock.

She was in a library. The walls were covered with built-in bookcases that held masses of books, leather-bound and modern. There was both Arabic and Latin lettering on the spines.

There was no other way out.

She went over to the three windows and tried opening them, one after the other. They were all locked.

She stopped in the middle of the floor, between two upholstered sofas in blood-red leather. Beside her was an ornate marble-topped table with a solid bronze ash-tray on it. She kicked the table, hurting her toe.

In one corner there was an old table with four chairs and a tray laid with breakfast for one. They weren't going to let her starve. She went to the table and looked suspiciously at the food. She recognized pitta bread, and the vegetables alongside it, but the hummus in the middle looked dodgy. She sat down, picked up the fork, tasted it and decided it was actually pretty good. It was flavoured with garlic and parsley. She ate everything, washing it down with sweetened tea.

She had just finished the tea when the lock rattled.

Her stomach lurched. She didn't want to go back to the stifling cell upstairs.

But it wasn't the young man with the gun. It was a slender girl with big eyes and jet-black hair. Annika gasped.

'Ha!' the girl said. 'I'm starting to understand the language. I thought they said they were going to give you breakfast in the library, and I was right.' She closed the door carefully behind her and leaned against it, her eyes shining with curiosity. 'Is it true that you work for a newspaper?'

Annika nodded. 'And you're Suzette?'

The girl smiled broadly. She was wearing jeans, a T-shirt and trainers. 'What are you doing here?' she asked.

Annika studied the sixteen-year-old. She was clearly happy and healthy, didn't seem to have been suffering. 'I wanted to see if you were here. A lot of people are looking for you.'

Her face darkened. 'No one cares,' she said. 'Not really.'

'Your mum's really worried about you.'

The girl walked away from the door and threw herself onto one of the leather sofas. 'She only cares about her pathetic job. I just got in the way, and I cost too much money.'

She half lay on the sofa with one leg dangling over the armrest. Annika sat in silence and waited for the girl's curiosity to build up again.

'No one knows I'm here. How did you know?'

Suzette was evidently aware that she was being kept hidden. She probably wasn't supposed to be in the library.

'The most important question is probably *why* you're here,' Annika said. 'And how you got here.'

Suzette shrugged her shoulders and smiled. 'Do you want to interview me?'

'If you want to be interviewed.'

'Ha!' She threw her head back. 'Fatima would never agree to that. I'm not allowed to tell anyone where I am.'

'Why not?' Annika asked. 'Are you a prisoner?'

Suzette picked at her fingernails, but she was still smiling. 'Fatima came to get me,' she said. 'She told me to tell everyone I was going somewhere else, and then we came here.'

Whatever the reason the girl was being kept out of the way, it didn't seem to be anything that bothered her: that much was abundantly clear. What she was saying was probably true. Francis, the tennis coach, had said that Suzette was too disorganized to plan any sort of disappearing act.

'But you didn't have your passport with you,' Annika said.

Suzette sat up on the sofa, annoyed, dropping her trainers to the floor. 'Fatima's got her own boats, hasn't she? She doesn't have to go through Passport Control. She uses her own private harbour.'

Is that so? Annika thought. 'And you've been here ever since?'

The girl nodded.

'Do you want to be here?'

She stopped nodding and sat still. 'You know what happened?' she asked, her eyes filling with tears. 'The gas?'

Annika got up from the breakfast table and went to sit on the sofa opposite Suzette. 'Yes,' she said. 'I wrote about it in the paper.'

The tears overflowed. 'They were, like, so cute. Leo could be really annoying, but he was so little. My was lovely, really lovely. She loved horses, just like me . . .' Suzette put her hands to her face and wept for several minutes. Annika sat quietly and waited for her to stop. In the end she wiped her eyes and nose with the back of her hands and looked at Annika. Her makeup was smeared all over her cheeks.

'Hang on, I'll get you something to wipe your face,' Annika said, and fetched her unused linen napkin from the breakfast tray.

Suzette blew her nose loudly and wiped the mascara from her cheeks. 'And Grandma as well,' she said. 'She was my best friend.'

Annika sat down again. 'Astrid, you mean?'

'She always said I was her little princess, even though she wasn't my real grandma.' She blew her nose again. 'She brought me here the first time. The farm was our special place.'

Annika tried to sound calm and neutral. 'So you and Astrid used to come here together?'

Suzette nodded.

'What for?'

'Grandma knows Fatima well. They do *bizniz* together. And Amira's the same age as me, and she's had her own horse since she was four. We used to come and stay here every summer.'

'Isn't it difficult talking to Amira?' Annika asked, even though she knew the answer.

'She speaks Swedish because her dad's Swedish. She had Swedish nannies when she was little, and Grandma used to send her Swedish children's videos.' Suzette laughed. 'Imagine, sending *Seacrow Island* to Morocco!'

Annika leaned forward. 'What's Amira's father's name?'

Suzette frowned. 'He's dead. I never met him. But her mum's name is Fatima and her sisters are Maryam and Sabrina, and Maryam is married to Abbas, and they've got the cutest little children in the world, two boys. But Sabrina's not here at the moment because she's studying at Harvard, and Amira's going there as well, as soon as she's finished her International Baccalaureate exams.'

Annika tried to look as if it was perfectly normal to study at Harvard. 'Did Maryam go there as well?'

'No, she did two years in Cambridge, like Fatima, but she wanted to come home and get married to Abbas, so obviously that's what she did. Fatima doesn't make anyone do anything. She doesn't force me either, because I don't like studying. I've got a horse of my own, Larache. He's a mix of English and Arabian thoroughbred, and he's the sweetest horse in the world. I want to work with animals and horses, and Fatima thinks that's a good idea.' She nodded to emphasize the point. 'You don't have to be top of the class,' she said. 'I help Zine and Ahmed – the foreman and his son.'

'Did Grandma Astrid think it was okay, you working with horses?'

The nodding was even more intense. 'Of course she did. I mean, Grandma grew up on a farm, even if they weren't very nice to her there.'

Annika leaned back in the chair and tried to calm down. 'Did Grandma tell you what it was like when she was little?'

Suzette lay down on the sofa again and threw both legs over the armrest. 'Sometimes. Her stories were all pretty sad . . .' Then she leaped to her feet. 'There's a book about Grandma and her friends.' She spun round and ran to one of the bookcases in the corner behind the breakfast table.

'A book?' Annika said, turning to see what she was doing.

Suzette was running her hands over the spines of the books. 'It was here somewhere . . . Got it!' She held up a thin, stitched pamphlet with a white cover, no picture or other decoration, just the title and name of the author. 'They've got all the Emil and Pippi and Goldie books,' she said, 'but this is pretty much the only adult book in Swedish.' She handed it to Annika. 'I've read it. It's a bit weird.'

Annika stared at it.

A Place in the Sun
by
Siv Hoffman

'And you found this here? In the bookcase?' She opened the imprint page. Printed by a vanity press twenty years ago. Nina's mother had evidently had ambitions to become a writer.

'It was where I just found it. There's no proper system, not like the school library. Everything's all mixed up . . .'

There was a noise from the door. Annika and Suzette stiffened. Annika sucked in her stomach and slid the book inside her jeans, then pulled her top over it, hoping it didn't show.

The young man called Ahmed came into the library, holding his gun in front of him. His eyes opened wide and he shouted something at Suzette in Arabic. She got up, quick as a flash, and slipped past him onto the stone landing. '*Allez!*' he shouted angrily at Annika. '*Dépêchez-vous!*'

'Yeah, yeah,' she muttered. He wanted her to hurry.

It was considerably cooler in the room now. Someone must have aired it. Which meant that it must be possible to open the window. They had also left a jug of water and a glass on the desk.

The footsteps faded down the corridor and she pulled the book from her jeans and put it on the blanket. Then she crouched to look under the bed. Someone had emptied and rinsed the pot.

She sat at the desk and took out her notepad and pen. Quickly she wrote down what Suzette had told her, filling in the gaps with her own thoughts and conclusions. Fatima had secretly collected Suzette. She must have known that something was likely to happen, and had wanted to get Suzette away from the Costa del Sol without anyone knowing. Why? Because she liked the girl, maybe. Because Suzette was her daughter's best friend. Or did she have some other, less noble, reason? Was Suzette a hostage? In exchange for what? And from whom?

Her next thought made her stop writing.

If Fatima knew that Suzette needed to be saved, she must also have known that the Söderström family were in danger. She could be mixed up in the murders herself.

Maybe she was the person who had ordered them to be carried out.

Suddenly the walls felt even more restrictive.

Annika put her pen down and got up to try the door. Still locked, of course.

What if they didn't let her out again?

What if they kept her here for ever?

Who knew where she was?

No one, except Muhammad, the taxi-driver from Tangier.

She felt her throat tighten and the classic symptoms of an approaching panic attack: tunnel vision, tingling in her fingers, utter terror.

She stumbled to the bed and lay down on her stomach, facing away to the side.

There's no danger, she tried to persuade herself. If they really did want me dead, they'd already have killed me. Or they wouldn't have let me in in the first place. Fatima may grow dope, but she's not a murderer. That's why she picked up Suzette. Fatima cares about people . . .

She lay there without moving for a long time, concentrating on breathing normally.

She should have grown out of these panic attacks by now.

She got up cautiously and went to the window. It was still locked.

She couldn't see anyone outside. The skies had darkened: black clouds had rolled in from the Atlantic. They were going to have some rain.

She looked down towards the building below her. The top floor, where she was now, was more sparsely decorated than the rest of the house, which suggested it was for servants, or had been added later. The middle floor seemed to be the main social part of the house. She didn't have much sense of what was on the ground floor, but from the outside it had looked much more basic than the floor above. On the way to Asilah she had seen similar farms. Maybe this was the way houses were built in Morocco: you started with a fairly basic ground floor, then added to it as your finances allowed.

The building was huge, at least a thousand square metres. And parts of it were extremely lavishly appointed. This was a wealthy farm. It was quite clear that Fatima belonged to the premier league of hash farmers.

It was starting to get darker inside the room now.

She sat down at the desk, picked up the pen from where it had fallen to the floor, and started to make a list of the farm's inhabitants.

How many people lived here? To start with, Fatima and her three daughters: Maryam, Sabrina and Amira. Maryam was married to Abbas, and had two little boys. They were probably who she had seen from the window that morning. Sabrina was at college in Boston. Zine, the foreman, and Ahmed, his son, must be the men with the guns.

Then there had to be servants: people who emptied chamber pots and worked in the fields. Zine the foreman had to have someone to be foreman over, after all.

She put her pen down and sat on the bed. She pulled out the book that Suzette had given her in the library, Siv Hoffman's labour of love, *A Place in the Sun*. She pulled the pillow out from under the blanket and put it against the wall to cushion her back.

She opened the first chapter and started to read.

As she read about *The Princess in the Castle Among*

the Clouds, The Little Troll Girl with the Matches, The Angel at Gudagården, Falling through the Sky, Death on the Beach, and other strange tales, the Atlantic rain lashed the window-panes and the wind tore at the plants in the fields around the farm.

38

In the afternoon it was so dark in the room that she had to light the little lamp so she could finish the book. She read the last page and didn't know what to think. Could that really have happened, or was it just a piece of fiction with literary pretensions?

A flash of lightning followed by a clap of thunder made her get up and look out at the mountains. They were completely black. More lightning chased across the sky, to the sound of rumbles and cracks. What would she do if a bolt hit the house and set it on fire?

She recalled the smoke and flames on the other side of her bedroom door in Djursholm, how she had opened the window and lowered the children in the bedclothes. Here she was trapped like a rat in a trap.

A terrifying crack of thunder shook the whole house, almost making her lose her balance. She screamed, took the three paces to the door and yanked at the handle. It was as unresponsive and solid as the door of a bank-vault.

She ran to the window and peered intently at the lock on the french windows. They opened outwards. The lock was part of the handle, in the middle of the windows, at waist-height. She pushed at it, hard. It didn't move.

She looked down at the farm. The lights had gone out. A power cut.

She tried to calm herself. She'd never been scared of lightning before.

The house was made of stone and the roof was tiled, so it couldn't be particularly flammable.

But it wasn't the weather that was her main problem: it was her own foolhardiness.

She sat on the bed again and tried to think carefully.

Schyman knew she was on the Costa del Sol, as long as he had received the email with her articles. It wasn't absolutely certain that they'd got through.

If there was any kind of search for her, then passenger lists and Passport Control would show that she had entered Morocco. At least they'd know which country she was in.

Her service provider's list of calls made on her mobile would show that she had called Rickard Marmén, and he could lead them to the *muqaddam* in Asilah. And he, in turn, could tell them that she had been asking about Fatima's farm.

So she hadn't disappeared without trace, even if it had been incredibly stupid not to tell anyone where she was going.

There was a crack of thunder above her head and she ducked instinctively.

How long would it be before anyone started looking?

Monday at the earliest, when she was supposed to pick up the children.

There was another crash, not thunder this time but something else, a shorter, sharper noise from below.

She went to the window, leaned forward and peered down at the yard. The little lantern was reflecting off the glass so she moved it aside and blew it out. Then she huddled up and peered out through the bars of the window. The gate in the wall was half open. The metal at the bottom was warped and smoking.

She frowned. The metal gate was actually smoking.

The bang had been an explosion. Someone had blown the lock off the gate.

She saw movement in the yard, black figures sliding through grey sheets of rain. Two, no, three moving towards the house. Then something flared and she heard a different sort of noise.

She gasped. They had guns and were using them.

She fought an intense impulse to crawl away and hide under the bed. Instead she pulled her dark jacket on over her pale T-shirt so as not to be seen. She pulled the hood over her hair and cupped her hands against the glass.

There was more noise, several shots this time, and fire was returned from somewhere inside the house. She heard a scream and one of the shadows fell: one of the intruders. Zine or his son must have hit him.

The two other shadows zigzagged across the yard, now firing constantly. The flashes from the barrels lit them so she could see their faces.

They were Europeans.

Another man fell, the one closest to the house. She saw him land on his back immediately below her window.

The remaining man stopped, pulled himself up to his full height, and seemed to be thinking. Then he walked calmly towards the house and disappeared from Annika's field of vision. She waited, and after a short while he reappeared. He had someone else with him, a man or a child, and was dragging him by the hair into the middle of the yard where he let go. The youth lay squirming on the ground – it looked as if he had been hit by one of the shots.

Annika caught a glimpse of his face, contorted by pain and fear. It was Ahmed, the foreman's son. The black-clad man leaned forward, aimed the barrel of his gun at the boy's head and fired. Ahmed twitched, then lay still. Annika thought she was going to throw up.

The gunfire ceased. That must mean the foreman had been disarmed as well, and was possibly dead.

The man stayed where he was in the yard. She saw him lift his head and study the building in front of him, and leaped back into the room so he wouldn't see her in the window.

She waited a minute before she dared to look out again.

The man was gone.

She heard a shout from one of the floors below her, then more screaming.

Suzette, she thought, the little boys, Amira. Oh, God, he's going from room to room, shooting everyone.

Her pulse was racing and she assumed she was about to die. Soon he would have worked his way through the lower floors and then he would come up to where she was.

She forced away her panic. Shouting and screaming, which she had been on the verge of doing, would be stupid.

She had to get out of there. Breaking the window was out of the question: there were forty little leaded panes of glass in each side so she'd never be able to squeeze out. She had to find a way to open the french windows and get down to the ground.

She had used bedclothes before and survived. And at least there wasn't a fire this time.

She tried throwing herself at the window-frame but lacked force because she didn't have enough space to take a proper run-up.

Then she glanced at the desk and knew what to do. She pushed it towards the windows, got up on top of it, shuffled forward so that her feet reached the lock, pulled her knees back as far as possible, then kicked as hard as she could. The thunder rumbled. The doors creaked and the desk moved back a bit. She took aim again and kicked four more times. Then she had to get down and push the desk back into place.

After the seventh kick the door flew open with a crash. The thunder answered. Rain swept into the room and she was drenched in an instant. In two swift movements she tore down the pale-yellow curtains. She pulled the sheets off the bed, noting to her relief that they were made of decent linen. Fingers trembling, she tied them together with reef knots – thank God she'd been in the Scouts. She attached one end firmly to the balcony railing, and tossed the other over the edge.

It stretched almost to the ground, swaying in the gusts of rain.

Would the rain make the fabric slippery?

Probably.

She hesitated.

Maybe it was better to stay in the room. Maybe the man wouldn't come up this far.

At that moment she heard another shot below. She took three deep breaths, then stepped out onto the little balcony and climbed over the edge.

It was a very long way to the ground.

She crouched on the other side of the railing, grabbed the curtain and tested to see if it would hold. It did. The rain lashed at her face, making it hard to see. Well, she didn't need to look, not downwards at any rate, just needed to lower herself down the wall until she reached the ground. As long as she could get over her fear of heights . . .

She let go of the balcony railing and almost fell straight away. She was breathing so hard that it drowned the claps of thunder. She clung on for dear life and realized she had to let go with one hand. She eased her grip. The fabric burned her palms. Then her feet touched the wall. She steadied herself and began to lower herself down, one step, two steps, another step, far too big. She made it past the first knot, past the next floor, as her arms started to ache. She passed the second knot. She must be halfway now. Her arms were getting numb so she loosened her hold a fraction, then the third knot, and she lost her grip. She tumbled to the ground and landed awkwardly on one foot. The gravel cut into her lower arms. She lay there quite still, just listening. The rain was still pouring down and she was soaked to the skin. Her ankle hurt badly.

She could hear voices. From inside the house.

She sat up. It seemed lighter on the ground than it had been up in her room. She could see the stable-block as a dark shape maybe thirty or forty metres away. The mangled gate was creaking in the wind far behind her, and off to one side, in front of her, the door to the house was open.

With a twisted ankle she wasn't going to be able to run away from anyone. Getting out through the gate and hiding among the hash plants was one option, if she could make it that far. The stable was closer, but then she'd have to go right across the open yard, and she didn't know if it would be unlocked.

She heard a child's heartrending scream from inside the house. She looked towards the open door.

There was a faint light on the floor above.

Swaying slightly, she got to her feet. Just a couple of metres away from her lay one of the men who had been shot, staring up at the sky. The rain was falling on his open eyes.

She limped over to him. She recognized those eyes. Pale, they had laughed at her as they cut into her left forefinger.

The man's gun was by his side, some sort of automatic rifle that she'd only ever seen before in American action films. She picked it up. It was astonishingly heavy.

Ahmed lay ten metres away. Half of his head had been blown off. She looked away.

In a flash of lightning she saw something move by the gate. She stiffened, staring intently through the veils of rain towards the opening in the wall.

Then she saw it again. She was quite sure. It was the shape of a person running past the shattered gate.

Her legs crumpled and she dropped the gun. Oh, God, oh, God, just don't let them shoot me.

On all fours she crawled towards the wall of the house, got to her feet, then ran at a crouch towards the doorway with adrenalin pounding in her ears.

By the entrance she stopped and peered inside the hall. She couldn't see anything, and threw herself into the darkness of the house, pressing her back to the wall. She slumped down, gasping, and put a hand over her mouth to muffle the sound. The thunder rumbled on. The child was crying. She glanced out through the doorway but couldn't see anyone outside.

She couldn't stay where she was. She got up and tried to put weight on her foot. It hurt badly, but it was just about bearable.

As quietly as she could she moved away from the front door towards the stairs. She grabbed the banister and peered upwards.

The voices were coming from one of the rooms up there. She could hear a man's voice, then a woman's. She couldn't make out what they were saying, but it sounded like English.

She went up a few steps.

'You emptied the accounts in Gibraltar. Where's the money?' The man's voice, almost shouting.

'Yes, I emptied them,' Fatima replied, her voice thick with fear. 'I warned her about the raids in Algeciras, but Astrid wouldn't listen. I knew what was coming, and I saved what I could.'

Annika took several more steps.

'You sold us out,' the man said. 'You wanted to force us to use your supply chain, with your grotesque over-pricing. When Astrid refused you tried to get rid of us.'

She recognized the voice. It belonged to Filip Andersson.

Annika used the banister to heave herself up the last few steps. The stone landing of the smartest floor of the building was in darkness. The voices were coming from the room next to the library where she had had breakfast. She looked down at the thick carpet under her feet: it seemed to run the whole length of the hall-way.

'The police had you all under surveillance,' Fatima said. 'I warned Astrid, but she refused to listen. She said she had no choice.'

The double-doors were ajar, letting a thin strip of light out into the hallway. Annika moved along the wall to squint through the gap between the door and its frame into a large sitting room. Filip Andersson was standing with his back to the door. A white shirt collar stuck out from inside his black waterproof jacket. A pool of water had formed by his feet.

'Of course she felt under pressure,' Filip Andersson

said. 'She'd withdrawn the money to finance that fucking tennis club.'

Annika moved so she could see more of the room. It was dimly lit by a candelabrum, with two candles, and two oil-lamps. At the far end of the room Fatima was sitting on a flowery chintz sofa with a little boy in her arms. One of her grandchildren, of course. Suzette and another girl, presumably Amira, were sitting together in an armchair, holding each other's hands. They were terrified. Two other women were standing in front of them, presumably servants, crying. Beside them stood a man and the woman she had seen in the yard that morning. She was holding the other little boy: Maryam and her husband, Abbas, with one of their sons.

It looked as if Filip Andersson had gathered together everyone he could find and ordered them into the sitting room. No one seemed to have been shot or injured.

'You shouldn't have brought in such big shipments,' Fatima said. 'You should have let me handle it.'

'And you should have kept your hands off the Gibraltar accounts. Where's the money?'

Fatima didn't answer.

'I'll count to ten,' Filip Andersson said. 'Then I'll start with the kid in your lap. One.'

Annika pulled back. There was a rushing sound in her ears and her hands were trembling. What should she do? Call someone? There must be a phone somewhere. She hadn't seen one, or any phone lines leading to the house.

She looked down the stairs: nothing but darkness.

'Two.'

Annika realized what Filip Andersson was about to do. He was going to kill all of them, regardless of whether or not he got the money. The little boys,

Suzette, Amira, the weeping servants: he was going to shoot them all just as he had executed Ahmed.

What should she do?

'Three.'

He wasn't standing far from the door, two, two and half metres.

She looked round the hallway.

It was dark: she could hardly make out anything.

She limped quickly towards the library and blinked at the shadows inside.

She heard his voice from within the sitting room.

'Four.'

She focused her eyes and looked round the room, at the leather sofas, the books and the table. The tray was gone.

Then she saw the bronze ashtray on the marble table between the sofas.

She limped over and picked it up. It was just as solid and heavy as it looked. Her foot hurt even more as she limped back towards with the door with it in her hands.

'Five. Where's the money?'

'It's not your money, Filip. We can come to an agreement, you and me. Put the gun down and let the children and servants go. Then we can sit down and work out a solution.'

'Six. I negotiate my way. Try asking Astrid. Ask her who owns all her cherished fucking codes and records and company deeds, these days. Seven.'

Annika hopped back towards the sitting room on one leg.

'Filip, there's been more than enough death and misery now.'

'Eight.'

'Okay, Filip, I'll tell you where the money is.'

Annika peered into the room again. Filip Andersson was heading across the floor towards Fatima and the child, with light, almost playful steps.

He's enjoying this, she thought. He's going to do it.

'Nine.'

She'd only get one chance.

Annika raised the ashtray above her head, took a deep breath, then rushed into the room. Filip Andersson was three metres away. The muscles in her arms ached, and pain shot up her leg every time her foot hit the floor.

One of the weeping women saw her and screamed.

With all the strength she could muster she smashed the ashtray into Filip Andersson's head.

The man had noticed her in the corner of his eye. He turned round just as the bronze ashtray hit him.

Annika saw at once that she had failed.

The ashtray didn't hit him on the back of the head, but on his ear and shoulder. He staggered and dropped his gun but remained standing.

'What the . . . ?'

Annika threw herself forward and grabbed the gun, the same as the one lying beside the dead man outside. She tried to shove it away, towards the others, but Filip Andersson was faster than her. He grabbed the weapon from her and kicked her, and she ended up on her back beneath him. He aimed the gun at her forehead. She saw his face twitch as he recognized her.

'What the fuck are you doing here?' he said, sounding genuinely surprised.

Annika couldn't bring herself to answer. She was close to peeing in terror.

Filip Andersson put a hand to his ear, and found blood on his fingers. She saw the surprise fade from his face as fury took over. 'I warned you,' he said. 'You really shouldn't stick your nose into things that are none of your fucking business.'

He took off the safety catch and aimed the barrel at her forehead, just as she'd seen him do with Ahmed, and she thought about the fact that she had two children, that he mustn't do it.

Then his head exploded.

The women screamed as the sound of the shot rolled round the room.

Annika stared at the body swaying above her, the joints loose, as if it had no skeleton. In a panic she scrambled backwards with her hands so that it wouldn't land on her when it fell. It hit the Persian carpet with a soft thud. Andersson's shoes ended up right next to her face.

The two servants' screams rose to a falsetto. Suzette and Amira were clutching each other in the armchair, and Fatima put her hand over the child's eyes. They were all staring at the door and Annika turned her head to see what they were looking at. She saw a shadow in the darkness out in the hallway.

She shuffled away from the body, away from the door, and bumped into a statue, knocking it over.

A figure walked into the room with an automatic rifle in its hands. It was the same gun Annika had picked up but then dropped in the yard. The barrel was smoking.

Suzette and Amira screamed.

Annika looked up at the person holding the gun, at her sharp profile and shoulders, the wet ponytail and pointed chin.

'They're going to kill us,' Suzette screamed. 'They're going to gas us all.'

The woman didn't seem to hear her. She put the gun down and went over to the dead man. She knelt beside him and stroked his hand, which was still clasped around the trigger. 'Sorry,' she whispered. 'Sorry, Filip, but this has to stop.'

Then she slumped to the floor and wept.

Abbas rushed over and grabbed the gun, took the safety-catch off and aimed it at the intruder.

Annika got to her feet and stood in front of the woman with her hands stretched out. 'Don't shoot her!' she cried. 'Leave her alone. She's a police officer. Her name's Nina Hoffman.'

39

The storm passed. A warm wind began to blow. It swept in through the open front door, up the stairs, through the stone hallway and into the sitting room, the library and all the other open rooms in the house.

Fatima stood up and handed the child she had been holding in her lap to Suzette and Amira. She went to the dead man on the rug and looked at him for a long minute. He was lying on his front, with his arms close to his sides, and the gun to his right. The back of his head was gone. The women had stopped screaming. No one said anything. Not even the children were whimpering.

Then she looked up at Annika and Nina. 'Are there any more men here?'

Annika cleared her throat and tried to catch Nina's eye, but the police officer was staring at the floor and seemed not to have heard the question.

'There are two out in the yard,' Annika said.

'Zine and Ahmed?'

'Ahmed's out there,' Annika said. 'I haven't seen Zine.'

Fatima nodded towards her and Nina. 'You two,' she said. 'Take the body downstairs and put it by the stable wall. Then you're to come back up here, roll this carpet up and leave it on the floor of the washroom behind the kitchen. Then check which other carpets up here need washing, roll them up and leave them against the back wall of the washroom.'

Annika looked at her in astonishment. Fatima returned her gaze without moving a muscle. Then she turned to her son-in-law. Abbas was still standing there with Nina's gun raised and ready to fire.

'Abbas,' she said, 'get the electricity running again. Then you're to gather all the guns together and lock them up where they should be. Then get the digger out, and the small trailer. Girls!' She turned to Suzette and Amira. 'Take the boys to the kitchen. Get them something to eat. Then take them up to my bedroom and read them a story. Try to get them to sleep.'

Amira was the first to move. She put her nephew on the floor, heaved herself out of the armchair, took Suzette's hand and helped her up, then went to her sister and took the youngest boy from her arms. Abbas put the safety-catch back on the gun, hung it over his shoulder, leaned over and pulled Filip's gun from him and left the room.

Then Nina moved. She went to the head of the corpse and crouched down. 'We won't be able to carry him,' she said in English. 'We need some help, or we'll have to clean all the other carpets in the house as well.'

'Amira,' Fatima said to the girl, who went out quickly with the child in her arms and disappeared down the stairs.

Then Fatima said something to the servants in Arabic, and they left the room with Suzette.

Annika couldn't bear to look at the corpse and turned away.

Amira came back with a bin-liner and handed it to Nina, who quickly pulled it over the dead man's head and tied the handles firmly round his neck. 'Okay, let's turn him over first,' she said to Annika, who did as she said.

'Grab his legs.'

Annika did as she was told, simultaneously empty and full to bursting. In spite of the gloom the contours of the furniture were crystal-clear, the colours sharp. He would have shot her, wouldn't he?

His body really was incredibly heavy. They couldn't manage to lift the whole thing at once, so pulled it with its back dragging on the thick carpets until they reached the staircase.

At that moment the power came back on and the stone hallway was lit by ornate chandeliers and lamps.

Nina swung the legs over the edge of the top step.

'You go first and pull. I'll keep hold of the head and try to stop the bag coming off.'

Annika pulled the feet and trousers. The body slid down fairly easily, a couple of times she had to grab its stomach to slow it down.

The yard was illuminated by huge floodlights. They lowered the head to the ground and each pulled one of the legs. The bag split and blood seeped out.

The two black-clad men who had run in through the gates with Filip Andersson were lying where they had fallen, hit by several shots to the chest. Ahmed had been moved: Annika could see the dark patch where his head had been lying, clearly visible in the brightly lit yard.

'You can put him straight on the trailer,' Abbas said.

He pointed to a tractor with a scoop at the front and a digger at the back. Behind the digger a small trailer had been hooked up to it.

'We'll need help,' Nina said.

Together they managed to get the heavy body onto the trailer.

Without saying anything they went back towards the black-clad bodies. Abbas took the arms and Nina and Annika a leg each.

'Where's Zine?' Annika asked, once they'd put the two men on top of Filip Andersson.

'He's alive, but he's lost a lot of blood. The only person here with the same blood-type is Ahmed, and he's dead.'

Fatima came out into the yard in a black garment.

Abbas climbed up into the tractor, started the engine and drove off towards the fields. Fatima stopped beside them and watched the vehicle disappear over the brow of the hill.

'They'll never be found,' Annika said. 'Just like Torsten. That's right, isn't it?'

Fatima closed her eyes, but said nothing.

'What did Torsten do?' Annika asked.

'What didn't he do? He deserved to die.'

'Who killed him?'

'David.' Fatima walked back towards the house.

Annika heard the sound of the tractor fade and disappear.

At that moment the lights in the yard went out.

She went back into the house and up the stairs to bring down the blood-stained rugs.

The crops were rustling in the fields outside the walls. Annika sat on the steps leading up to the house. Her eyes settled on the dark patch of gravel where the life had run out of the man with pale eyes. Nina sat down beside her.

'I recognized him,' Annika said, pointing to the dark patch. 'He was the one who cut my finger open.'

The stars was sparkling and twinkling, clearer than Annika had ever seen them before. She felt shaky and oddly exhilarated.

They sat in silence for a long time.

'How are you feeling?' Annika asked eventually, to the woman next to her.

Nina picked up some stones, weighed them in her hand, then let them fall again. 'Numb,' she said. 'I'd never shot anyone before. It was much easier than I'd expected.' She raised her arms and aimed an imaginary gun, closed one eye and squeezed the trigger. 'It's hard to aim an AK-47,' she said, letting her arms fall. 'This one had a long barrel, or I don't think I would have dared. I went down on one knee and shot him from below because a bullet of that calibre could easily pass through the body and I didn't want to hit anyone behind him . . .'

'You got it just right,' Annika said.

Nina glanced at her. 'I was aiming for his body,' she said. 'The barrel must have moved. It was pure luck I didn't hit anyone else by mistake.'

Annika was relieved that the woman was a police officer, used to handling violent situations and trained to use firearms. 'Why did you come?'

Nina replied, in a quiet, focused voice, 'Filip came to see me on Tuesday, at lunchtime. He wanted a passport. I asked him where he was going. "The Costa del Sol," he said, "to sort out some business that's gone wrong." I told him he could fly using just his national ID card, and then he got angry. I told him he'd have to go to the passport office, and that I'd try to speed up his application . . .'

She looked out into the darkness and wrapped her arms around herself. 'That evening he called and asked if I knew where the farm was. "Astrid was always so secretive about that farm," he said. I said I didn't know what he was talking about. "Stop being so sanctimonious," he said. "It's time you did something useful. There's only us left now. Apart from the kid." I didn't know what he meant.'

She fell silent and lowered her eyes to the gravel.

'Then he said "I bet you anything she's at the farm," and hung up. That was the last time I spoke to him.'

Annika waited in silence.

'I wanted to talk to him,' Nina went on. 'I got the plane to Málaga this morning. That's why I came, to talk some sense into him.'

'But how did you find your way here?'

Nina took a deep breath and glanced at Annika. 'Through you,' she said. 'You called that afternoon and asked the same thing as Filip, what I knew about the farm, but you told me where it was. In Morocco, outside Asilah. I went to the *muqaddam*, and he said I was the second white woman in two days who'd come to see him with the same question. When did you get here?'

'Yesterday evening. They locked me up straight away.'

Nina rubbed her forehead and suddenly looked very tired. 'They knew Filip was on his way. They probably just wanted you out of the way until it was all over.' She sat for a long while without saying anything. Eventually she said, 'I'll never be able to talk to anyone about this.'

Annika couldn't think of a response. She tried to imagine what Nina was feeling.

Was she remembering all the times she had visited her brother in Kumla Prison? Was she thinking about the big brother who used to lift her up to the ceiling at Christmas and birthdays? Or could she no longer see beyond the criminal who had been on the point of killing even more people?

'He was going to shoot me,' Annika said. 'You saved everyone.'

'I'm the last one left. It was up to me to put everything right.'

*

Amira came out and asked if they wanted anything to eat. Her Swedish was clear and fluent, with hardly any trace of an accent.

Annika didn't think she'd be able to keep anything down, but she got up and followed the girl inside the house, across the open hall and down a long corridor. The kitchen was huge. It filled the whole of the eastern end of the ground floor. There were twenty-four chairs round a rustic wooden table in the middle of the floor, with space for more if need be. There was cheese and fruit, lamb, vegetables and a dish of cold couscous.

Annika and Nina sat down and helped themselves. Annika managed to swallow some vegetables and drank several glasses of water. She felt dizzy and shaky, her palms were blistered and her ankle hurt.

When they had finished, Fatima appeared. 'You two,' she said, nodding to Annika and Nina. 'Come with me.'

She went into the hall, up the stairs and into the library. She sat down on one of the leather sofas, and indicated that Annika and Nina should sit opposite.

'I understand that you're Filip's sister,' she said, to Nina.

Nina raised her chin. 'Yes,' she said.

'I've heard a lot about you,' Fatima said.

Nina didn't reply.

Fatima waited. No one said anything. Annika realized she was holding her breath. 'You're a police officer,' Fatima said at last. 'Like David.'

'Yes, but not like David. I've never been mixed up in the business, not like David and Filip and the others.'

Fatima nodded. 'That's what David said. You were the only one who got away.'

Nina cleared her throat. 'Why are you talking about my job? This has nothing to do with it.'

547

'You're a police officer, and you killed your brother. I've got ten witnesses.'

Nina didn't answer.

'Are you going to go to your superiors and confess what you've done?'

Nina looked away.

'Are you going to report him missing?'

'No.'

'Never?'

'No.'

Fatima looked at her intently. Nina didn't move. 'The other men, do they have families?'

'I don't know,' Nina said. 'Someone will probably notice they're missing.'

'Can they be traced here?'

'I presume they flew to Málaga and got their guns there. Filip didn't have a passport, so my guess is that they chartered a boat and paid cash. I saw a car outside, an old Seat. The passenger door had been broken open.'

Fatima nodded. 'They must have stolen it. Abbas has already taken care of it.'

Annika looked down at her blistered hands. Filip Andersson and his thugs would never be traced to Morocco. They had already been buried alongside Torsten in some distant corner of the farm. They'd never be heard of again. She shuddered. Were more bodies buried out there? 'Where's Carita Halling Gonzales?' she suddenly asked, looking straight at Fatima. 'Do you know?'

Fatima raised her eyebrows. 'She's taken off, I don't know where.'

'Why did she kill the entire Söderström family?' Annika asked.

The woman's eyes narrowed. 'You're a journalist,' she

said. 'Your job is to poke about in other people's affairs. Are you going to write about my farm?'

Annika straightened her back. 'I'm going to do my job,' she said. 'I'm going to write that Suzette is alive. I want to interview her, and let her decide how much she wants to say about her new life. I'd like to quote you as well, if you'll agree to that.'

'What about what happened here today?'

Annika blinked.

'You could have run away,' Fatima said, 'but you chose to come back. No one forced you to intervene.' She said nothing for a time, then sighed. 'Carita Halling Gonzales was Filip's eyes and ears on the Costa del Sol while he was in prison in Sweden,' she said. 'As the years went by she became sloppy. Åstrid was able to embezzle large amounts of money, and shipments were delayed and seized. When Filip realized the extent of it, he gave Carita an ultimatum: her family or Astrid's.'

'That's terrible,' Annika muttered.

Fatima pulled a face. 'It's not the first time Carita Halling Gonzales has tidied up. Do you know why you were let into this farm?'

Annika shook her head, unable to say anything.

'Do you believe in God, Annika Bengtzon?'

She gulped. 'Not exactly.'

Fatima put her hands together on her lap. 'Well,' she said, 'you're fairly secular in Sweden. Do you respect people who believe?'

Annika nodded.

'Then you understand that my God is the most important thing in my life. More important than my children and my family, my property and my work.'

Annika didn't answer.

'According to my faith a man can have four wives. I was his first, and he took one other. That's how I see my marriage. I'm well aware of Western practices and traditions, and I expect you to accept mine.'

Annika waited silently for her to go on.

'My husband and I, we had only daughters. But with his second wife he had a son, Alexander. You saved him, my husband's child, his only son. So I am in your debt, and that is why you were let in.'

'I didn't think Muslim women were allowed to marry Christian men,' Nina said.

Fatima was clearly surprised. 'David converted to Islam. Didn't you know?'

She stood up. Nina and Annika followed suit. 'You can stay here tonight,' she said. 'Abbas will drive you to Tangier tomorrow morning.'

She turned to Annika. 'My duty is done, as far as Suzette is concerned,' she said. 'She can decide for herself if she wants to be interviewed. I believe in free will. God isn't an obligation but a gift.'

Then she slumped. 'You're free to talk about what you've done here at the farm this evening,' she said. 'I don't make threats and I would never use force. I leave it up to your judgement to take responsibility for your own actions.'

Some women started to sing in another part of the house.

'The window in your room is broken,' Fatima said to Annika. 'Amira will show you both to another bedroom. You'll find her still in the kitchen.' She waved them away with her hand, and from the corner of her eye Annika saw her turn towards the darkness outside the window.

40

Annika was given back her laptop, camera and phone. To her surprise she saw that she had a full signal on her mobile.

'Mum installed a mast,' Amira said. 'We've got our own power plant as well, with solar cells and wind turbines. It's enough for the house and the stable, but not when we have to light up the walls with the flood-lights. Then it gets all weird and dark, like it was last night.'

'How's Zine?' Annika asked.

Amira's beautiful face twitched. 'He died,' she said. 'The funeral's tomorrow. This way. There are some back stairs.'

She led them up the same narrow stone staircase that Annika and Ahmed had gone up the previous night. The lamps in the walls were much brighter now that the floodlights on the wall weren't on. 'The window in your room's broken,' she said to Annika.

'I know. My bag's in there. Can I go and get it?'

She nodded. 'The door's open. Suzette and I have pre-pared the big room for you. It's much nicer, and it's got lights. Here's the bathroom.' She gestured to a door be-side her.

Annika and Nina glanced at each other, then stepped

into the bedroom they would be sharing. Annika made sure the door was left ajar. No one locked it.

The room was certainly a lot bigger than her previous cell. It had two large beds, with lamps, a big desk, two armchairs and lights in the ceiling.

'I'm going to have a shower,' Nina said. She disappeared into the bathroom.

Annika put her things down on one of the beds and went out into the corridor, back to her former cell. When she opened the door, the floor was soaked. The french windows were swinging slowly in the wind. The mattress was hanging off the bed from when she had pulled off the sheets, but her bag was still on the end of it. She splashed through the water and picked it up. Beneath it was the white book with the black lettering on the cover.

A Place in the Sun, by Siv Hoffman.

She picked up the book and put it into her bag, then went back to the bedroom.

She left the door ajar, sat on the bed and checked her mobile. It must have been on the whole time, because the battery was low and she had three missed calls. Thomas, then Anders Schyman, then Thomas again.

She had two new voicemails. The first was from her editor-in-chief, and it was short and to the point: 'I assume you didn't send those articles from your sickbed. Call me.'

The second was from Thomas, slow and hesitant: 'Hello, Annika, it's me . . . Well, I know I said I'd call you . . . well, you know . . . but I've been doing a lot of thinking, Annika, I really have, and I was wondering . . . can you call me? Soon? When you get this. Call my mobile, that would be best. Okay. 'Bye . . .'

She clicked to end the message and held the phone to her chest.

How strange he'd sounded. Surely nothing had happened to the children. He would have said if it had, wouldn't he?

She sat still for a moment, listening, as the water ran in the shower. Quickly she closed the door, then sat on the bed again, took a few quick breaths and pressed 'call'. 'I got your message,' she said quietly, when he answered.

'Good, hi, thanks for getting back to me,' he said, sounding very official. 'Can you hold on a moment?'

'Sure,' Annika said.

The water stopped in the bathroom. There was a clatter at the other end of the line, then a door closing, and now there was an echo, as if Thomas had gone out into the stairwell.

'Hello? Annika?'

'Yes, I'm here.'

'Listen, this isn't a good time, but I've been doing a lot of thinking and I really want to talk to you. Can we meet up?'

She cleared her throat and heard the toilet flush on the other side of the wall. 'I'm not in Stockholm,' she said. 'What do you want to talk about?'

'I think this is a big mistake,' he said.

Annika closed her eyes. 'What's a mistake?'

'The divorce,' he said quietly.

She opened her eyes, then her mouth, but no words came out.

'Annika?'

Nina came into the room with a towel round her hair and another wrapped round her body. 'There's not much hot water left,' she said.

'Where are you?' he asked.

'Away on a job,' she said. 'Your message sounded so urgent that I wanted to call straight away. Can I call you when I get back to Stockholm?'

'Sure.'

They were silent.

Nina unrolled her turban and shook her hair loose. She put the wet towel over the armchair and stood in the middle of the room.

'One last thing,' Annika said. 'Are you standing in the stairwell on Grev Turegatan?'

'Er, yes. Why?'

She rubbed her eyes with her fingertips. So he was sitting at home, all cosy with his new partner, then, when his ex-wife called, he had crept out into the stairwell to tell her he regretted getting divorced. 'Nothing,' she said. 'I'll be in touch.'

They hung up.

'It didn't help,' Nina said. 'I still feel just as filthy.'

She seemed as together as she always was.

Annika switched off her mobile: she didn't have her charger with her and needed to save the battery. Then she reached for her bag and pulled out the white book. 'Suzette found this in the library,' she said. She went over to Nina's bed and put it in front of her. 'Have you seen it before?'

'"*A Place in the Sun*, by Siv Hoffman",' Nina read, as she picked it up. 'What is it?'

'Read it, especially the chapter entitled "Death on the Beach". See if you think what it says could be true. I'm going to have a shower.'

The water was lukewarm, and she washed with some Wella shampoo she found on the shelf. She dried herself, put on her clean underwear, then went back into the bedroom, crossed to the french windows and looked out. Unlike her cell, this room faced away from the farmyard. The moon had risen over the hilly landscape, shimmering in the wetness of the leaves in the fields. *Cannabis sativa*. Since prehistoric times mankind had grown the plant, using it for rope, textiles, birdseed, a high-energy grain, a medicine and as a means of getting high. She turned back into the room as Nina closed the book, her head bowed.

'What do you think?' Annika asked. 'Could it be true?'

Nina tossed the book to the end of the bed, as if it had scorched her. 'No idea.'

'And you've never seen it before?'

'Mum didn't have a copy, I'm sure.'

'Even though she wrote it?'

'I went through all her possessions when she died. There was no book like this among them.'

Annika picked it up. 'If it's true, I can't imagine Astrid just left her copy sitting about on a bookshelf. Which means this must be Hannelore's.' She nodded to herself. 'That would explain how it got here. David found the book and brought it with him.' She leafed through it, and her eyes caught on the sentence 'And she would float and dance over Gudagården like the blessed child she was, conceived without sin with the approbation of the Lord.'

'How much do you really know about your mother's childhood?'

Nina stood up and paced restlessly around the room. 'What does anyone ever really know about their parents?'

'How about when they were grown-up? Astrid and Hannelore and your mother?'

Nina sat down again. 'Before I was born, Mum worked with Astrid on the Costa del Sol. I don't know what she did there.'

Annika went back to her bed. She put the book on the floor.

'I was three when Mum and I moved. I have no

memories of the Costa del Sol. We ended up in Tenerife, in an artists' collective where people made pots and painted sunsets and smoked grass. Mum called herself a poet . . .' Nina stopped and let out a little laugh. 'A poet, bloody hell . . .'

'Your brother and sister, they didn't go with you to Tenerife?' Annika asked.

'They stayed with Astrid in Marbella. They were both almost grown-up by then – Filip was twenty-two, Yvonne sixteen. Astrid paid for their education and they both became economists. I missed them.' Nina pulled her hair into a ponytail, securing it with a rubber band. 'I don't know why we moved. Maybe Mum wanted to get away from Astrid or Astrid kicked her out.'

'Why would Astrid have done that?'

Nina slumped slightly. 'Mum had problems with various dependencies,' she said. 'She never got over them. Once we moved to Södermanland she stuck to drink, and meths towards the end, but she used drugs of one sort or another through the whole of her adult life.'

'Did you ever meet Astrid?'

Nina thought for a moment. 'She came to visit us in Tenerife a few times. But Mum talked about her quite a bit, and about Hannelore, always when she was drunk. All I know about Veronica, Astrid, David, Torsten and Hannelore comes from Mum's drunken ramblings. She missed Astrid a lot.'

'Did you see much of Hannelore?'

Nina shook her head. 'Never.'

'How involved was Hannelore in Astrid's business dealings?'

'Not much. She's always been mentally unstable, but Torsten, her partner, acted as a kind of travelling salesman for the organization.'

'For their drugs racket,' Annika said. 'That's what it was, after all.'

They sat in silence for a while.

'I read your article in the paper today,' Nina said. 'About the jet-set Swedish woman who murdered Astrid and her family.'

Annika straightened. 'It was in the paper?'

'There was hardly anything else – it was on loads of pages. Who is she?'

So the email hadn't only arrived, it had fallen on fertile ground. 'Carita Halling Gonzales, a very good actress. She fooled everyone around her, possibly even herself. No one's that good at pretending. I've done a lot of thinking about her.' Annika shuddered.

Silence descended, until Nina said, 'I knew David had another family.'

Annika started. 'What? You've known about it all these years?'

'Yvonne told me, but I didn't believe her.' Nina was looking straight ahead. 'It was more than five years ago now. I knew she was infatuated with David – it had been a kind of obsession since they were little. I asked her to leave Julia alone.' She fingered her hair. 'That was when she told me that David had another family, a wife and three daughters. He could have several wives, four, according to the Koran, but Yvonne considered that she was his first wife, even though they weren't married. She was the one who'd got to him first. I thought she'd gone mad.' Nina pushed her hair off her face. 'So I broke off all contact. That was the last time I ever spoke to her.'

'And then,' Annika said, 'some small-time crooks tried to get their hands on the drug-money. Was it Filip who murdered those people on Sankt Paulsgatan? Or was it Yvonne?'

557

Nina stood up and went to the window. 'Does it matter? They're both dead.'

Annika looked at her stiff back, her straight shoulders, the ponytail that had dried to a perfectly straight whip. 'It wasn't your fault,' she said.

Nina raised both arms and pressed her palms to her forehead hard. 'Fucking bitch,' she said, in a low voice. 'She vanished into her hash-clouds, or the bottom of a bottle, and dumped it all on me.'

Annika waited, but Nina didn't go on. 'What?' she said. 'What did she dump on you?'

Nina's stiff back seemed to relax slightly. 'I grew up without my brother and sister, without any sense of belonging, but it was still up to me to make sure we all stuck together. She just grabbed me and left.'

'Maybe she wanted to spare you from a place in the sun.' Nina didn't answer.

Annika picked the book up from the floor. 'Do you know where Gudagården is?'

Nina swayed and grabbed the window-frame for support. 'I grew up there. Mum inherited it. We moved there when Gunnar and Helga died – that was why we left Tenerife. Mum was the only heir. They'd written a will saying they wanted everything to go to the church, but it hadn't been witnessed properly and was declared invalid.'

Annika waited in silence for her to go on.

'Mum hated the farm,' Nina said. 'I could never understand why she didn't sell it. It was always eating away at her from the inside.'

'Is there a lake nearby?'

'Spetebysjön is just below Gudagården. Or Solgården, as Mum renamed the farm. It's between Ekeby and Solvik, not far from Valla.'

'I know Valla,' Annika said. 'One of my school-friends lived there, on Häringevägen.'

'The farm's on the same side of the railway line, on the road down towards Björkvik.'

'Now I know where it is,' Annika said.

Nina looked out into the darkness. 'Just below the farm there's a lake with a little sandy beach next to a big oak,' she said tonelessly. 'It's huge. But Mum used to say it was dangerous there, that there were strange currents and quicksand.' She went over to the bed and picked up the book. 'What do you think?' she said. 'Could this be true? Was that why I was never allowed to swim there?'

Annika put her hand on Nina's arm. 'There's one way to find out,' she said.

A knock on the door made them jump. They looked quickly at each other.

'Come in,' Nina said.

The door opened and Suzette and Amira came into the bedroom.

'Hello,' Suzette said. 'Can we come in?'

'Sure,' Annika said.

The girls stopped just inside the door.

'Don't you want to sit down?' Annika said, gesturing towards the two armchairs.

They took one each. Nina adjusted her position on the bed.

'Did you want anything in particular?' Annika asked.

Amira nudged Suzette.

'Fatima says I can go home now,' Suzette said. 'I don't have to stay at the farm, because there's no danger any more. But I don't want to leave. I want to stay here, and Fatima says I can if I want.'

Annika looked at her seriously. 'Your mum back in Sweden has a right to know where you are.'

Suzette nodded. 'I know. That's why I want to tell them that they don't have to look for me now. I don't want to tell them exactly where I am, but I'd like to be able to send emails to Polly and call Mum . . .' She took a deep breath and her eyes filled with tears. 'I miss my mum,' she said, 'and I'd like to visit her, maybe next summer, when I'm grown-up. But I don't want to live with her in that flat. I just want her to know that I'm okay, and that I'll go back and visit . . .'

Annika remembered Polly's message on Facebook, about Lenita selling the flat and throwing Suzette's things away. 'Would you like me to say all this in the paper?' she asked.

The girl nodded.

'Have you really thought through what it would mean, staying here? Will you be able to go to school?'

Suzette shuffled in the chair, annoyed. 'Abbas is going to be the new foreman, taking over from Zine. I can go round with him and learn how to run the farm. It'll be like being an apprentice.'

Annika moved to the edge of the bed. 'Suzette,' she said, 'do you know what they grow on this farm?'

'Of course I do.'

'And you think it's okay to train to become a hash farmer?'

Amira flew up from her chair. 'My family's grown hemp on this land for two hundred years,' she said angrily. 'Why should we stop, just because the European Commission says we should? They can't make decisions about our lives.' The girl had clenched her fists.

'So you think it's a good life, growing dope?'

'I'm going to be an economist,' Amira said. 'My sister's going to be a lawyer, and we're going to help run the farm and Mum's business.'

'Do you think your dad would have wanted that?

You and Sabrina and Maryam working with this sort of thing?'

'Maryam has a different dad,' she said, 'a bad man from Sweden who violated Mum. But my dad killed him and married Mum, and saved our family's honour.'

Annika stared at the girl, thoughts racing through her head. 'A different dad? Was his name Torsten?'

'Dad did what was right for the family. He'd be really proud of me.'

Annika lowered her eyes. When she raised them again she turned to Suzette. 'We'll sit down together first thing in the morning, and work out exactly what we're going to say in the article. And then I want to take a picture of you with your horse, so we can show that you're fit and well.'

Suzette was smiling broadly.

Together the girls walked out of the room and closed the door behind them.

'So you got your article,' Nina said, and Annika couldn't tell if there was resignation or sarcasm in her voice.

'And everything goes on,' Annika said.

Epilogue
AFTER MIDSUMMER

The sky was grey as lead. The light that found its way through the banks of cloud was dull and filtered to the point where only a dubious sort of daylight remained.

Annika parked the newspaper's Volvo beside the road. She switched off the engine, got out and stretched her back. She looked both ways along the deserted country road. This ought to be the right place.

Between Ekeby and Solvik, not far from Valla. On the same side of the railway line, on the road down towards Björkvik.

She gazed at the traditional red-painted houses that lay scattered across the landscape, wondering which had once been known as Gudagården. She squinted in the thin light, trying to see the lake. There it was. It was actually visible from the road. Spetebysjön, between Stensjön and Långhalsen, one of the thousands of lakes and waterways in Södermanland, her low-lying home province with its oaks and fences and meadows.

She locked the car with a click of the remote, hung her bag on her shoulder and started to walk along a ditch towards the water.

The ground was soft and smelt of grass and cow-shit. The wet soaked into her trainers. She should have brought wellingtons.

She caught sight of the police forensics team and the cordon in the distance. The blue and white tape and the bright yellow tarpaulins were the only flashes of colour among all the grey-green. There were four officers, two digging and two checking the soil that was coming out.

Nina was standing some way from the cordon, wearing army-green rubber boots from Tretorn. A few curious onlookers from nearby farms had defied the grey weather to come and see what was going on.

'Have they found anything?' Annika asked.

Nina shook her head. She was staring implacably at the police officers who were digging soil and sand from the beach behind the oak tree. 'How did you manage to get them out here?' she asked.

'I said I'd received a tip-off,' Annika said, 'and that the caller wanted to stay anonymous. They can't do anything about that. They're not even allowed to ask me who it was because that would be a breach of the constitution.'

'I read your articles about Suzette.'

'The constitution's come in handy there as well. Her mother called me, in a complete state, demanding to know where she is.'

They stood in silence for a moment.

'Is everything okay otherwise?' Annika asked.

'I'm on temporary secondment as a duty officer for the summer.'

'Do you know if anyone's heard anything from Carita Halling Gonzales?'

'Not a sound.'

Annika took a step closer to her and lowered her voice. 'Has anyone reported Filip Andersson missing?'

Nina's shoulders stiffened. 'A young man called from Gibraltar. Apparently Filip was supposed to be taking over some sort of law firm.'

Henry Hollister, Annika thought.

'And his lawyer's called twice, something about his claim for damages. I told him exactly what had happened, that Filip had contacted me to ask if I could speed up his passport application, but that I wasn't able to help him. There's been no official report that he's disappeared.'

'And the others?'

'I don't know.'

Annika looked out across the lake. 'And Julia? How are she and Alexander?'

'Alexander's started back at nursery school. Apparently it's going very well. He plays with his old friends as though nothing ever happened.'

'What about his tantrums?'

'They don't happen as often now.'

They fell silent again.

In the end Annika cleared her throat. 'Have you said anything to Julia? About Fatima?'

'No,' Nina said. 'Moroccan marriages aren't registered automatically by the Swedish authorities. It's up to individuals to tell the tax office that they're married, and David never did. But of course he was married, which invalidates his marriage to Julia. Which in turn means that she wouldn't be counted as his next of kin.'

Annika tried to follow her train of thought.

'And that would mean she isn't entitled to his life insurance, which is all she's got to live on.'

'Precisely.'

Nina looked at her. 'Didn't the paper want to know where you'd been? When you met Suzette?'

Annika chuckled. 'They don't care where I've been. The only thing that interests them is where they can send me. They've just asked if I'd like to be the paper's Washington correspondent.'

567

Nina raised her eyebrows. 'Wow,' she said. 'Impressive.'

'Not really,' Annika said. 'It's mainly about getting me as far away from the newsroom as possible.'

'How's that going to work with the children?' Nina asked. 'Are you going to leave them in Sweden?'

Annika hunched her shoulders against the wind coming off the lake. 'Thomas might come as well,' she said. 'It's possible that the department will have a new policy proposal for him to—'

She was interrupted by cries and shouting from the beach. There was frenetic activity in the excavated pit. The officers were making calls on their mobiles and their radios were crackling.

The onlookers around them moved as one towards the cordon. Nina and Annika followed.

The two officers with the shovels had dug so deep that their heads were scarcely visible over the edge of the hole.

'Could three young girls really have dug down that far in one night?' Annika whispered.

'They were used to hard physical labour,' Nina said quietly. 'Sowing and harvesting and gathering hay . . .'

'Is it true, then?' a man called. 'Have you found a body down there?'

One of the police officers who had been checking the excavated soil came over to the onlookers. 'It looks like we've found human remains.'

'Who is it?' an old woman asked from a distance.

'We don't yet know what sex the body is, or how long it's been here. It'll be up to the forensics team and the pathologist to work that out.'

'Could it be my brother?' the woman cried. 'Could it be Sigfrid Englund?'

The police officer went to her. 'Was he reported missing?'

'He's been missing since 1953, when he was twenty-one years old. He was raised as a foster-child on a neighbouring farm.'

Annika began to head back towards the car.

Nina hurried after her. 'Aren't you going to write about this?'

'I'll leave that to the local paper,' Annika replied.

Acknowledgements

This is fiction. All events and characters depicted are entirely the creation of my possibly somewhat morbid imagination.

But, as in all my novels, the events, physical locations, and laws and regulations are often, but not always, grounded in reality. As a result, I have, as usual, conducted some research.

I would therefore like to thank the people I bothered with numerous hypothetical questions. Their titles below refer to the positions they held at the time of my investigation.

For information about the European drugs trade, and how narcotics are smuggled and distributed, I would like to thank Rolf M. Øyen, police attaché at the Norwegian Embassy in Madrid and also Nordic liaison officer for Malaga, as well as Detective Inspector Göran Karlsson and Detective Superintendent Jan Magnusson of the regional narcotics unit in Stockholm. I would also like to thank the drug-squad officers working undercover whose names I can't reveal here: I've thanked them in person.

Kent Madstedt, Chief District Prosecutor at the Financial Crime Authority in Stockholm, for explaining how money-laundering and financial crimes are carried out in Europe.

Joakim Caryll of the information department of Stockholm Police, for help with contacts.

571

Hampus Lilja, judge referee to the Supreme Court, for information about how decisions are reached regarding applications for a retrial.

Fredrik Berg from the Office of the Prosecutor General, and public relations officer for the Public Prosecution Authority, for help with the procedures and formulations used in decisions of the Prosecutor General.

Anders Sjöberg, Detective Inspector for Interpol in Stockholm, for information about the criteria for international alerts via Interpol, both for missing people and suspects.

Anna Block Mazoyer, counsellor at the Swedish Embassy in Rabat, Morocco, for information about registers covering people and property in Morocco.

I would like to thank Peter Rönnerfalk, chief medical officer at Stockholm County Council, for ongoing help with a whole range of things, but in this instance particularly for information about narcotic gases, naloxone and fatal doses of morphine.

Thomas Bodström, of course, chair of the Parliamentary Standing Committee on Justice, for proofreading and discussions on judicial and political matters.

Anna Rönnerfalk, psychiatric nurse, for help with the diagnosis and symptoms of patients suffering severe mental stress.

Niclas Salomonsson, my agent, and his staff at Salomonsson Agency in Stockholm.

Emma Buckley, my British editor, all the dedicated staff at Transworld Publishers and of course Neil Smith, who translated it all into English.

Tove Alsterdal, my editor, obviously, who has been involved the whole way through, from start to finish, as always. Thank you for being there.

And, always, Micke Aspberg, my love throughout all these years, for everything else.

Any mistakes or errors which have crept in are entirely my own.

LIFETIME

LIZA MARKLUND

The most famous police officer in Sweden is found murdered in his bed. His four-year-old son is missing. His wife is suspected of killing both of them. No one believes her when she says she is innocent.

No one except for news reporter Annika Bengtzon. Her personal life in turmoil, she turns all her energies to her work, investigating the life of the murdered man.

But if his wife is innocent, where is their son? And will the truth be uncovered in time to find him . . . before it's too late?

'An astonishing talent'
JEFFERY DEAVER

LAST WILL

LIZA MARKLUND

Knowing the truth can be deadly.

A frosty December night in Stockholm. Inside the City Hall, over a thousand guests attend the prestigious Nobel Prizewinners' dinner. With a lavish meal laid on to the backdrop of a full orchestra, this is one of the city's most glamorous events of the year. But things are different this year. Two shots are fired on the dance floor.

Crime reporter Annika Bengtzon is there, covering the event for the *Evening Post*. As the police realize she caught a glimpse of the suspect, she is far more interested in getting back to the newsroom.

But as more brutal murders follow, Annika finds herself in the middle of something far larger than she had anticipated. No longer just a reporter but also a vulnerable key witness, she begins to close up the gaps linking these crimes, just as the suspect starts closing the net in on Annika herself . . .

'Twists and turns you never see coming'
KARIN SLAUGHTER

VANISHED

LIZA MARKLUND

People can't just disappear . . . or can they?

At a derelict port in Stockholm, two brutally murdered men are found by a security guard. In the same area a young woman, Aida, is on the run from a deranged gunman.

Meanwhile, journalist Annika Bengtzon is approached by a woman wanting her story published in the *Evening Post*. She claims to have founded an organization to erase people's pasts – giving vulnerable individuals a completely new identity.

Annika helps Aida to get in touch with the foundation. But as she begins to investigate this woman's story, more bodies turn up and she finds herself getting dangerously close to the truth – that all is not as it seems . . .

'One of the most popular crime writers of our time'
PATRICIA CORNWELL

RED WOLF

LIZA MARKLUND

AN ACCIDENTAL DEATH

Reporter Annika Bengtzon is working on the story of
a devastating crime when she hears that a journalist
investigating the same incident has been killed.
It appears to be a hit-and-run accident.

A SERIES OF MURDERS

Several brutal killings follow – all linked by handwritten
letters sent to the victims' relatives. When Annika
unravels a connection with the story she's writing, she is
thrown on to the trail of a deadly psychopath.

THE HUNT IS ON

Caught in a frenzied spiral of secrets and violence,
Annika finds herself and her marriage at breaking
point. Will her refusal to stop pursuing
the truth eventually destroy her?

'An exceptionally well-crafted and suspenseful work'
DAILY MIRROR